Nora Roberts published her first novel using the pseudonym **J.D. Robb** in 1995, introducing to readers the tough as nails but emotionally damaged homicide cop **Eve Dallas** and billionaire Irish rogue **Roarke**.

With the **In Death** series, Robb has become one of the biggest thriller writers on earth, with each new novel reaching number one on bestseller charts the world over.

Become a fan on Facebook at **/norarobertsjdrobb**

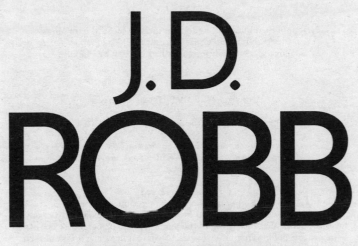

J. D. ROBB

VENDETTA IN DEATH

piatkus

PIATKUS

First published in the United States in 2019 by St Martin's Press
First published in Great Britain in 2019 by Piatkus
This paperback edition published in 2020 by Piatkus

1 3 5 7 9 10 8 6 4 2

A CIP catalogue record for this book
is available from the British Library.

ISBN 978-0-349-42205-3

Printed and bound in Great Britain by
Clays Ltd, Elcograf S.p.A.

Papers used by Piatkus are from well-managed forests
and other responsible sources.

Piatkus
An imprint of
Little, Brown Book Group
Carmelite House
50 Victoria Embankment
London EC4Y 0DZ

An Hachette UK Company
www.hachette.co.uk

www.littlebrown.co.uk

To the magickal Griffin,
the newest light and love in my life,
who came into the world, and spent
some time in my arms while I wrote this book

Sigh no more, ladies, sigh no more,
Men were deceivers ever.

WILLIAM SHAKESPEARE

Justice without force is powerless;
force without justice is tyrannical.

BLAISE PASCAL

1

He needed killing.

She'd researched, studied, planned the who, when, how, and why for more than a year, and had chosen Nigel B. McEnroy to be the first.

At forty-three, he had a wife of eleven years, two children — both girls, ages nine and six. He had, over the course of eighteen years, built his own executive headhunting business with two partners. As CEO of Perfect Placement, he oversaw recruitment both on- and off-planet.

Though he maintained his base in London, he traveled extensively. Perfect Placement kept offices in New York, East Washington, Tokyo, Madrid, Sydney, New LA, Dubai, Hong Kong, Vegas II, and most recently had established a center on the Olympus Resort.

He lived well, entertained lavishly, had earned a reputation for pinpointing the precise needs of a client and making what he thought of as a perfect marriage.

In business, Nigel B. McEnroy was scrupulous, exacting, ethical, and diligent.

None of that stopped him from being, in his private life, a liar, a cheat, an adulterer, and a serial rapist.

The man was unquestionably a pig, and it was time for the slaughter.

She looked forward to it, and felt she'd chosen her first very well.

He liked cheating with redheads, ones with large breasts, ones — most usually — lower on the food chain of power than himself. When he wasn't fishing in his own company pool, he enjoyed hunting in upscale clubs.

If that wasn't bad enough, considering his wife and two children, he usually tipped a drug into his chosen prey's drink, to ensure co-operation. Capitulation.

Worse, perhaps, he had at least once (she suspected more) roofied a potential candidate for a position, one he would pass over — for a *male* — just to add insult to injury.

Of course, the poor girl hadn't been able to prove a thing, could barely remember the assault, had been too afraid to accuse the son of a bitch.

But she'd heard enough from other victims, more than enough to begin her research, stalking, trailing, watching the pig in action. And twice had documented his rapist routine.

Finally she had everything in place, and now took a long last look at herself in the full-length mirror in her workshop.

Her hair long, wavy, bold red, her eyes dyed a deep, sharp green and carefully made-up. Her lips plumped and as red as her hair.

She'd worked for some time to give her nose the appearance of a slight uptilt, her chin the slightest point.

The temporary fake boobs looked and felt absolutely real – you got what you paid for. To finish it off, she'd padded her ass just a bit and used a very subtle self-tanner for a slight golden hue.

The dress she'd chosen, green like the eyes, slick as water, fit like skin. The heels, sparkling silver, gave her more height – especially with the narrow lifts.

Pig Nigel hit six-one, and with the shoes, she'd stand at five-eleven. A good fit.

She looked statuesque, bold, sexy.

With the wig, the body and face enhancements, why, her own mother wouldn't recognize her.

She gave one more turn in the triple, full-length mirror, fluffed the wig. 'Engage, Wilford.'

The droid, designed to simulate a white male in his sixties with a trim silver mustache to match the flow of hair, opened quiet blue eyes.

'Yes, madam?'

She'd programmed his voice to a plummy British accent, outfitted him in a black suit, crisp white shirt, black tie.

'Bring the car around,' she ordered. 'The town car. You'll drive me to a club called This Place, then park and wait for further orders.'

'As you wish, madam.'

'Take the elevator. I've unblocked it.'

While he followed her instructions, she checked the contents of her bag, then walked to the monitors.

Her grandmother – bless her – slept peacefully with the medical droid on watch. Dear, dear Grand would sleep through the night – helped along by the sleep soother she'd added to the glass of brandy sweet Grand drank every night.

'Be back soon.' She blew a kiss to the monitor, took the elevator to the main level of the glorious old house she adored nearly as much as Grand.

Always careful, she blocked the elevator again, walked with a satisfying *click* of heels to the opulent foyer, stepped out into the cool of the April night, secured the front doors.

She shivered a little, with cold, with anticipation, but Wilford stood holding the car door open.

She slipped inside, crossed her legs. April 11, 2061, she thought. The day that marked the rise of Lady Justice.

Nigel was on the prowl, and ready to celebrate a long, successful day of work. With his wife and daughters enjoying tropical breezes during spring break, he had a full week on his own – no need to make excuses about working late when he felt like a bit of strange.

He enjoyed This Place for its discretion (no cams), its VIP booths – screened off from the hoi polloi – its excellent martinis and music. And, oh yes, the variety of attractive women looking for a bit of strange themselves.

He'd reserved a VIP booth, of course, but during this first hour roamed the glittering silver floors, scanned the pumping lights of the dance floor, took the glides up and down the triple levels.

He thought of this part of the evening as the hunt, and enjoyed it immensely.

He'd scored very well the night before, thank you, with a twinset. Two strawberry blondes happy to share their attributes for a few hours in his New York pied-à-terre.

He imagined he could have tagged either — or both — back for a return engagement, but he wanted fresh. In any case, as always, he'd deleted their contacts.

He knew he looked his best, trim in black pants, a studded belt, a pale blue sweater that matched his eyes. He wore a sleek wrist unit that said wealthy to anyone with an eye for such things.

He could have paid for a top-level licensed companion — and had done so when time squeezed his choices. But he much preferred the hunt, and the score.

At the moment, he had his eye on a redhead with sinuous moves on the dance floor. A bit young for his usual pick, he admitted, and the hair — spiked and short — not as sophisticated.

But those moves.

Keeping her in sight, he began to circle the floor. He'd find an opening, and then—

Someone bumped him lightly from behind. He started to glance back, heard a throaty, '*Excusez-moi.*'

The voice, the faint French accent, that throaty purr had him turning completely.

He forgot the dancer with the sinuous moves.

'*Pas de quoi.*' He took the vision's hand, brought it to his lips, and was rewarded with a sultry smile.

He kept the hand – she didn't object. '*Êtes-vous ici seule?*'

'*Ah, oui,*' she said, with what he read as a clear invitation. '*Et vous?*'

He turned her hand over, brushed his lips lightly over the inside of her wrist. Spoke in English. 'I hope not anymore.'

'You're English. You speak French very well.'

'I hope you'll allow me to buy you a drink, and we can speak in any language you like.'

She trailed her free hand down that glorious fall of hair, angled her head. 'I would enjoy that.'

He thought: *Score*, as he led her away, through the crowd, around tables, past one of the many bars, and to his booth. 'I hope you don't mind. I prefer a bit of privacy.'

Beyond the curtain waited the plush semicircle of black, generous with silver-edged pillows. She sat, crossed those excellent legs, reclined just a little. Just enough.

'I like the booths,' she told him. 'The curtains where we can see out, but no one can see in. It's . . . titillating, yes?'

'Yes indeed.' He settled beside her, gauged his timing. Not too fast, he decided. This green-eyed wonder knew the ropes, would expect some sophistication. 'And what's your pleasure?'

'I have many.'

He went hard, but only chuckled. 'As have I. But to drink?'

'A vodka martini, very dry, two olives. I prefer Romanov Five.'

'As do I.'

'Ah, we have found our commonality.'

'The first of many.' He ordered from the comp menu, let his gaze travel over her, enjoyed the movement behind the filmy one-way curtain, the pulse of music. The titillation.

'I'm Nigel—'

She touched a finger to his lips. 'First names only, ça va? Some mystery for us. Solange.'

'Solange,' he repeated. 'And what brings you to New York?'

'If I told you, we would lose the mystery. Let me say then, perhaps this moment. I enjoy New York for its many pleasures, and its . . . ' She seemed to hunt for the word. 'Ah, yes, anonymity. And what do you enjoy, Nigel?'

'This moment.'

She laughed, tossed her hair. 'Then we should savor it, and the moments yet to come. Tonight I come here to . . . yes, divest – it is to divest the day and the things that must and needs be done. So to do what pleases instead. A night for me, yes?'

'Yes. This is also the same for me. Another commonality.'

'So . . . ' She opened her evening purse, took out a tiny compact. 'Tonight we are creatures of the moment. Together.'

He started to lean toward her, and the drink slot signaled, opened.

'We should toast the moment.'

As he turned to retrieve the martini glasses, she tossed her purse to the floor. He set the drinks on the table, bent to pick up her purse.

As he did, she spilled the contents of the vial in the compact into his drink.

'*Merci.*' She took the purse, slipped the compact back inside. She accepted the glass, tapped it lightly to his. 'To the moment,' she said.

'And the many pleasures.'

Her eyes glittered at him over the rim of her glass. 'And tell me one of the many pleasures you seek.'

'A beautiful woman who wants what I want.'

Watching him drink, she laid a hand on his thigh, trailed her fingers teasingly toward the bulge in his crotch. 'But how can you seek what you have found?' When he leaned toward her, she brought the hand up to his chest. '*Mais non.* We drink first, to this moment, the savoring, and the anticipation of pleasures to come. See them beyond the curtain, moving, touching, a ritual of mating, yes? And some may while some may not. And we, we could do what we like here, unseen.'

'Titillating,' he said, and felt oddly light-headed.

'Finish the drink and come with me. I have a place that is more so. A place of many pleasures.'

Eager, he downed the rest, took the hand she offered when she rose. 'My flat's close,' he began.

'I have a place,' she repeated.

He thought it was like moving through a silver-edged fog, and never saw her tap her wrist unit to signal the droid, barely heard the music as she led him down to the first level, out into the night.

She nudged him into a car, and inside he groped for her breasts as his mouth sought hers.

He thought she said, 'Straight home, Wilford,' in a different voice, but he was sinking, sinking into her, into pleasures.

Into the dark.

He woke with his head banging, his throat burning dry. When he tried to move, the muscles of his arms screamed. He blinked his aching eyes open, winced against the light.

He saw a large room, counters, monitors, screens, a massive workstation. None of it made sense.

It took him nearly a full minute to come around enough to realize he was naked, his hands cuffed over his head to a chain that hung from the ceiling. His feet barely made it to the floor.

Kidnapped? Drugged? He twisted against the restraints, but it hurt.

No, no, the club. He'd gone to the club. The Frenchwoman. Solange. He remembered, but it blurred, and when he fought to think it through, his head screamed.

No windows, he thought as fear popped cold sweat over his skin. He saw stairs leading up and, if he craned his throbbing head enough, a door at the top.

He tried to call for help; his voice came out in a croak.

Pleasures – he remembered that. They'd talked of pleasures, and she . . .

He sensed movement behind him, felt a terrible, shocking pain. His cry started as a croak, broke into a scream.

And she stepped into view.

Not the Frenchwoman.

Who was this woman, this creature smiling at him who wore a silver mask, with dark hair edged with silver spilling around her face, with her body curving in black?

She wore silver boots and a kind of – good God – breastplate in black leather with the letters *LJ* emblazoned on it in silver, like the boots.

'Who are you? What do you want?'

'I want my many moments of pleasure.'

He felt a thin thread of relief weave through the fear. 'Solange? Don't—'

'Do I look like Solange?' Snarling, she tapped the electric prod a bare inch above his penis, had him convulsing with pain as the burn seared across, spiked down. 'I'm Lady Justice, you adulterous prick. And Nigel B. McEnroy, this is your time of reckoning.'

'Stop, stop, don't. I can pay. Whatever you want, I can pay.'

'Oh, believe me, you will. For your wife.' She slapped the prod over his belly. 'For your daughters.' His chest. 'For every woman you've raped.' His buttocks.

His screams bounced off the walls. 'No, no, no. I haven't raped anyone. You've made a terrible mistake.'

10

'Have I? Have I, Nigel?' She gave him a little lick of shock across the balls, and imagined only dogs could have heard the high pitch of his scream from that one.

Each time she said a name – one of his victims – she shocked him again.

He gibbered, went limp, but she was patient. After snapping a vial under his nose to revive him, she started again.

He begged – oh, how he begged – he cursed her, he wept and screamed and pissed himself.

And oh, oh, oh, those moments of pleasure.

'Why, why are you doing this?'

'For all the women you've betrayed, humiliated, abused. Confess, confess, Nigel, to your crimes.'

'I never hurt anyone!'

She slapped the electric rod hard over his buttocks. When he could speak again, he sobbed out the words. 'I love my wife, I love my wife, but I need more. I'm sorry. It was only sex. Please, please.'

'You drugged women.'

'I didn't— Yes, yes!' He shrieked it to hold off the pain. 'Not always, but I'm sorry. I'm sorry.'

'You used your position to intimidate, to pressure women who wanted work to have sex.'

'No— Yes – yes! I have needs. Please.'

'Your needs?' She picked up a sap, slapped it across his face. Shattered his cheekbone. 'Your needs were more important than their free will, than their wishes, their needs? Than your vows to your wife?'

'No, no. I'm sorry. I'm so sorry. I – I need help. I'll get help. I'll confess. I'll go to prison. I'll do whatever you say.'

'Say my name.'

'I don't know who you are. Please.'

'I *told* you!' She shocked him again, knew by the way he convulsed that she was nearing the end. 'I'm Lady Justice. Say my name!'

'Lady Justice,' he mumbled, barely conscious.

'And justice will be served.'

She had the bucket and the blade ready, brought them over. She set the bucket between his legs.

'What's that for? What are you doing? I confessed. I'm sorry. Oh my God, oh God, please, no!'

'It's all right, Nigel.' She smiled into his watering, horrified eyes. 'I'm going to take care of your needs. For the last time.'

She kept him alive as long as she could, and when it was done, when he hung limp and silent, she let out a long sigh.

'So. Justice is served.'

As dawn broke over the city, Lieutenant Eve Dallas stood over the naked, mutilated body. The early breeze frisked through her choppy cap of hair, flapped at her long leather coat as she read the bold, computer-generated print on the sign tacked securely where the victim's genitals had been.

He broke his vows of marriage,
and woman he disparaged.

His life he built on wealth and power,
to lure the helpless to his tower.
He raped for fun,
and now he's done.
LADY JUSTICE

Eve shifted her field kit, turned to the uniformed officer, the first on scene. 'What do you know?'

The beetle-browed, mixed-race female snapped to. 'The nine-one-one came in at oh-four-thirty-eight. A limo dropped off a female, one Tisha Feinstein, on the corner of West Eighty-eighth and Columbus. Feinstein states that after attending her bachelorette party with fourteen friends, she wanted to walk, catch some air. Catching said air, she walked the three blocks uptown to Ninety-first, saw the body laid out across the sidewalk here. She ran into the building – this is her residence, Lieutenant – woke her fiancé, one Clipper Vance. He came out, saw the body, called it in.

'My partner and I responded, arrived on scene at oh-four-forty, secured the scene, called for a pair of beat droids to help with that. Officer Rigby is inside with the wits.'

'All right, Officer, stand by.'

After sealing up, she crouched by the body, opened her field kit. Then, pressing the victim's thumb to her Identi-pad, she read out for the record:

'Victim is identified as Nigel B. McEnroy, Caucasian, age forty-three, British citizen. His several listed residences include an apartment at 145 West Ninety-first, New York

City. That would be the same building as Tisha Feinstein, who discovered the body.'

Eve scanned the face. 'Hardly a surprise she didn't recognize him if she'd known him. Severe bruising and burn marks, most likely electrical, on the face, the body, ligature marks, deep, both wrists, indicate the victim was bound during torture and struggled during same.'

She took out microgoggles, took a closer look at the cuts and bruises on the wrists. 'From the angle, I'd say his arms were bound over his head, carried the weight of his body. ME to confirm. The genitals have been severed.'

She bent close, lifted the bottom edge of the sign for a clearer angle. 'No visible hesitation marks, looks almost surgical. Possible medical knowledge or experience?'

She took out her gauges. 'TOD oh-three-twelve. COD, possible blood loss from castration, possible cardiac incident from electric shocks. Maybe a combo.'

She sat back on her heels. 'So he was bound, tortured, killed elsewhere – need some privacy for that – placed here. Not dumped so much as arranged, basically on his own doorstep. And with this handy, poetic note.

'Lady Justice. Somebody was really pissed at you, Nigel.'

She took small pliers, a couple of evidence bags from her kit. As she pulled out the first tack, she heard the familiar clomp of her partner's pink cowboy boots trotting up the sidewalk.

Peabody badged the beat droids, moved through the barricades. She took a look at the body, said, 'Harsh.'

'It's all that.'

Eve remembered a time, not so long before, when Peabody would have taken that look and gone green. A couple years as a murder cop brought out the sterner stuff.

'When I get this love note detached – there. Peabody, call the morgue team, the sweepers. Let's get him bagged and tagged before people in this nice, quiet neighborhood start walking their dogs or taking a morning jog. Officer, help me turn him to finish the on-site.'

She found scores of burns, many that had seeped open during the torture, on the back, the buttocks, the hamstrings, the calves.

'Had to take some time,' she murmured. 'Couldn't do all this without taking time. And what do you suppose Lady Justice did with the cock and balls?'

Rising, Eve turned to her partner. Peabody wore her pink coat with a thin blue scarf with – jeez! – pink flowers scattered over it. She had her dark hair in a bouncy little tail.

'Wits inside. Hold the scene, Officer. What's Feinstein's apartment?'

'Six-oh-three, sir.'

With Peabody she started toward the entrance of a nicely rehabbed brownstone of about fifteen floors of dignity. No night man on the door, Eve noted, but good, solid security.

She badged her way through the beat droid on the door.

The lobby continued the dignity with navy and cream tiles for the floor, navy walls with cream trim, a discreet security desk – currently unmanned – a couple of curved padded benches, and fresh, springy-looking flowers in tall, slim vases.

Eve called for an elevator while she filled in Peabody.

'Wit's coming home from a girl party, sees McEnroy on the sidewalk, runs in, gets Vance, her fiancé. He goes out, verifies, calls it in. Nine-one-one logged at four-thirty-eight, first on scene arrived in two minutes. Vic's also a resident of this building – or has a residence here. He's a Brit, owns, with partners, some sort of international, interplanetary headhunter firm. Married, two offspring.'

'Wife,' Peabody said.

'Yeah.' She stepped into the elevator. 'We'll see if she's in residence after we talk to the wits.'

'Didn't keep his marriage vows,' Peabody said. 'If she did it, she left a really big clue with that note.'

'Yeah, well, people do the weird when they're pissed, and Lady Justice was seriously pissed. But ... unless the wife's a moron, she's going to have a damn good alibi.'

Eve stepped off, started down the quiet corridor on long legs. She noted security cams. 'Let's get the security feed for the vic's floor, for the elevators, the lobby, the exterior.'

She rang the bell at 603, flashed her badge for the uniform – young, male, fresh of face – who answered the door. 'I've got this, Officer Rigby. Contact the building security or supervisor. We want the feed for the cams on the victim's floor, the elevators, the lobby, and the exterior.'

'For what period of time, sir?'

'Forty-eight hours if they have it. Then start the knock-on-doors.'

'Yes, sir.'

She let him go, gave the couple huddled together on a long, shimmery green gel sofa a quick study.

The female – late twenties – had long, curly, coppery hair. Eyes nearly the same color showed signs of weeping and shock in a face pale and scrubbed clean of the enhancements she'd surely have worn for the night out.

She wore simple gray cotton pants, a long-sleeved shirt, and house skids as she clung to the buff, mixed-race male of about the same age.

He cast soulful brown eyes at Eve. 'I hope this won't take long. Tish needs to sleep.'

'I'm afraid to close my eyes. I know I'll see ...' She pressed her face into Vance's broad shoulder.

'I know this is difficult, Ms Feinstein, and we'll keep this as brief as possible. I'm Lieutenant Dallas, this is Detective Peabody. We're Homicide.'

'I guess I know. My friend Lydia's brother's a cop in Queens. I almost called him. We sort of dated when we were in high school, but ...'

'Why don't you just tell us what happened? Start with where you were tonight.'

'We were all over,' Feinstein began.

'I'm sorry,' Vance interrupted. 'Please sit down. Do you want coffee or anything?'

'That'd be great.' And would give him something to do, Eve thought. 'Black for me, coffee regular for my partner.'

'How about some more tea, cutes?'

Feinstein smiled. 'Thanks, Clip. I don't know what I'd do without you.'

'Never have to find out. Just take me a minute.'

He rose, moved quietly from the room. Feinstein curled up defensively.

'So, your evening?'

'We were all over. It was my stag party. We're getting married next Friday. The limo picked me up about nine. There were fourteen of us, and we club-hopped, you know? Clip's deal is tomorrow night. So anyway, we finished up with the all-male revue at Spinner's downtown. I know it sounds like—'

'A fun time with girlfriends,' Peabody finished with a smile.

'It was.' Feinstein's eyes filled. 'It really was. Some of us have been friends since forever, and I'm the first of our group to get married. So we did it big, and we drank a lot and laughed a lot, and the limo started dropping us off. I was the last one, and I had him drop me on the corner. I just wanted some air, to walk a little. I felt so happy, so silly, so *good*. I didn't want it to end. Then . . .'

She broke off when Vance came back with mugs on a tray.

'Clip.'

'It's okay, come on now, cutes. It's okay.'

He set the tray down, put an arm around her. Eve took

the mug of black coffee from the tray. From the smell, she knew she'd had worse. She'd had better, God knows, but she'd had worse.

'If I'd just had Shelly — that was the driver — drop me out front, she'd have seen it first. It's terrible, but I wish she had. He was just lying there. For a second I thought it was just some awful joke, but then I saw . . . I think I screamed. I don't know for sure, but I ran, and I could hardly use my swipe and code to get in I was shaking so bad, and I came right up to Clip.'

'I thought there'd been an accident. She could hardly tell me. Then I thought, well, she's pretty lit, she imagined it, but she was so upset.' He kept that protective arm around her as he spoke, his fingers stroking up and down her arm. 'I threw on some clothes, went out. And I saw she didn't imagine it. I called nine-one-one, and the police came.'

'Did you recognize the victim?'

'No.' Vance looked at Feinstein, who shook her head.

'I didn't really look,' Feinstein added. 'I know he was right under the streetlight, but I didn't really look at his face. He was all, I don't know, burned. I saw the sign, the note, and that right below it, he'd—'

'So did I,' Vance added when she broke off. 'Someone castrated him.'

'Could I ask how long you've lived in this building?'

'Two and a half months.' Feinstein managed a ghost of a smile as she took Vance's hand. 'We wanted to have our own place before the wedding. Our first place together.'

2

'Vic's top floor,' Eve told Peabody as they walked back to the elevator. 'Unlikely those two knew him or his wife. A couple of months in the building, eight floors away, twenty-odd years younger.'

'And this is only one of the vic's residences,' Peabody added. 'So he's not always here.'

'He was here long enough to get dead. Let's see if his family's in the building.'

They rode up.

'The killer's female, or wants us to think so,' Peabody said. 'If the message left has validity, possibly someone he cheated with or raped. But ... he was a trim guy, but you'd still need muscle to get him in and out of a vehicle – had to have one – and spread him out on the sidewalk. Maybe she – if it's a she – had a partner.'

'Definitely possible. The angle of the ligature marks on the wrists indicates he was restrained with his hands and arms held over his head – taking at least some of his weight. You could haul him up that way with muscle or with a pulley. Lower him onto some sort of dolly, wheel him up a ramp into a vehicle, wheel him out. It's a lot, but somebody gave all of it some thought. They sure as hell knew where he lived in New York, when he'd be here. And I didn't find any defensive wounds.'

The top floor held more generous units, for a total of six. The McEnroy apartment had the northeast corner with a wide, double-door entrance.

A cam, palm plate, swipe, solid locks.

Eve pushed the buzzer.

The McEnroys are currently not receiving visitors. Please leave your name, your reason for this visit, and your contact information. Thank you.

Eve held up her badge. 'Dallas, Lieutenant Eve, Peabody, Detective Delia, on police business. We need to speak with anyone now in residence.'

One moment while your identification is verified.

Eve waited out the scan, held another minute before she heard the locks disengage.

A house droid opened the left-side door. He stood – like the building – dignified in a dark suit. The sturdy body style told Eve he could likely double as a bodyguard. He spoke in a, well, dignified Brit accent while he looked over Eve and Peabody with eerily steady blue eyes.

'I'm sorry, Lieutenant, Detective, but Mr McEnroy has not yet returned from an engagement. Ms McEnroy and the children are out of town on holiday and not expected back for five more days. Is there anything I can help you with at this time?'

'Yeah, you can give us Ms McEnroy's location and her contact information.'

'Again, I apologize, but that information is private.'

'Not anymore. Mr McEnroy won't be returning from his engagement, as he's on his way to the morgue.'

She watched those steady eyes flicker. Processing the unexpected.

'This is very unfortunate.'

'You could say. We're coming in.'

'Yes, please do.'

He stepped back, closed the door behind them.

The wide foyer opened into a generous living space. She could see hints of the Hudson through the tall windows, showing silver in the morning light.

The living area boasted a recessed viewing screen above a long, slim fireplace, upscale furniture in quiet tones of blues and greens, some framed cityscapes, a scatter of fancily framed family photos, and no clutter whatsoever.

'What time did Mr McEnroy leave the premises?'

'At nine-eighteen last evening.'

'Where was he going?'

'I don't have that information.'

'Was he alone?'

'Yes.'

'What was he wearing?'

Again she saw the flicker as the droid searched memory banks.

'Black Vincenti trousers, a Box Club light blue sweater, silk and cashmere blend, a black leather Leonardo jacket, black leather Baldwin loafers, and matching belt.'

The specificity of detail reminded her there were times droids came in very handy.

'When did the rest of the family leave New York?'

'Two days ago, at eight A.M. The Urban Ride Car Service picked up Ms McEnroy, the children, and their tutor to take them to the shuttle. From there they traveled to Tahiti, and are in residence at the South Seas Resort and Spa, in beach villa Paradise, for their holiday.'

Yeah, she thought, very handy. 'Has Mr McEnroy entertained any guests in their absence?'

'I don't have that information. I am habitually disengaged when Mr McEnroy departs, and reengaged when he wishes my assistance.'

'You've got a door cam. I need the feed.'

'Of course. The security hub is just off the kitchen.'

'Take it, Peabody. Contact info for Ms McEnroy.'

This time, without hesitation, the droid reeled off a number.

'What time is it in Tahiti?'

He blinked. 'It is currently twelve-thirty-three A.M. in Tahiti.'

'That's just stupid,' Eve muttered.

'I don't understand.'

'Me, either. I'm having Crime Scene come up, go through this unit, and EDD will take all electronics in. Are there other droids in residence, or any housekeeping staff, human or otherwise?'

'There are small tool droids for cleaning floors and other tasks. There is a tutor for the children, but as I relayed, she is also on holiday with Ms McEnroy at this time. Mr McEnroy's administrative assistant and other business staff in this location are often called to the residence but, by and large, Mr McEnroy works daily, when in New York, from his base in the Midtown Roarke Tower building.'

'Huh. I'll let you know if I have more questions. What have you got, Peabody?' she asked when her partner came back.

'He left when the droid says, wearing what the droid says. No one came to the door until we did. He overwrote the previous seventy-two, but just a standard from what I can tell. EDD can get under that.'

'Tag McNab, and get sweepers up here.'

Eve made her way to the master bedroom. More soft, tasteful colors, more tasteful art. Though the bed's headboard spread like a peacock fan, the fabric covering it followed that soft and tasteful tone with a quiet peach one a few shades lighter than the fluffy duvet, which itself was shades lighter than the pillow shams, the stylishly arranged throw.

But the kicker was an all-directional vid camera on tripod placed in the center of the room.

She checked it, found it cued up for voice command, and currently no vids in its storage.

She went back out, called the droid. 'Up here.'

'Of course.'

He climbed the stairs, followed her back into the bedroom. She gestured to the camera. 'Is that usually here?'

'No. I have not seen that instrument before.'

'Here, or at all?'

'At all, Lieutenant.'

'Okay. You can go back down, stand by.'

She checked the drawers in the polished pewter bedside tables, found e-readers in both that she tagged for EDD, condoms in the one closest to the windows, a nail buffer and hand lotion in the one closest to the attached bath.

No sex toys or enhancements.

Interesting.

Curious, she turned down the duvet, ran a hand over the sheets, bent down, sniffed. Crisp and fresh and smelling very faintly of lavender.

She walked back out to the droid. 'Master bedroom sheets. When were they put on fresh?'

'Yesterday morning. Ten A.M.'

'Did Mr McEnroy request the change, or is that the usual?'

'When Mr McEnroy is alone in residence, the sheets are changed daily.'

'And when the family is in residence?'

'Twice weekly.'

'Where are the sheets you took off yesterday morning?'

'With the laundry service.'

'Too bad. Peabody, we'll start in the master.'

'McNab's on his way. Sweepers should be up in twenty. Well,' Peabody added as they stepped into the master and she saw the camera.

'Yeah, all-directional vid cam, set to voice activation, in the bedroom. Sheets changed twice a week when the wife's with him, daily when she's not.'

Peabody curled her lip. 'He taps his side pieces in the bed he shares with his wife, and records the action?'

'That'd be my take. And I'm betting he's got toys stashed somewhere. Start in his closet. I need to talk to his wife.'

She contacted the resort first, confirmed Geena McEnroy, her daughters, and a Frances Early were currently guests, their check-in date, checkout date.

Then she used the contact the droid had given her, prepared to notify next of kin.

Geena answered on the third beep with blocked video and a sleepy voice. 'Yes, hello?'

'Geena McEnroy?'

'Yes, speaking.'

'This is Lieutenant Eve Dallas with the New York Police and Security Department.'

'What? Oh my goodness!' The voice leaped alert, the video flashed on to reveal a pretty, sleep-rumpled woman with tousled brown hair, alarmed blue eyes. 'Was there a break-in?'

'No, ma'am. Mrs McEnroy, I regret to inform you your husband is dead. His body was found earlier this morning. I'm very sorry for your loss.'

'What? What? What are you talking about? That's not possible. I spoke to Nigel just this afternoon – here. I-I-It would have been evening there. You've made a mistake.'

'I'm sorry, Mrs McEnroy, there's no mistake. Your husband was killed early this morning, approximately three A.M., and has been officially identified.'

'But you see, that's not possible. You said there hadn't been a break-in. Nigel would have been home, in bed, at that hour.'

'According to your house droid's statement and your apartment security feed, your husband left your West Ninety-first Street apartment shortly after nine last evening. His body was found' – no need for the harsh details now, Eve thought – 'a short time ago. Again, I'm sorry for your loss.'

'But . . . ' Confusion, the edge of annoyance, simple disbelief began to melt into shock and shock to grief. 'What happened? What happened to Nigel? An accident?'

'No, Mrs McEnroy. Your husband was murdered.'

'Murdered? Murdered? That's insane!' Her voice pitched up, then she seemed to catch herself. She pressed a hand to her mouth. 'How? Who? Why?'

'Ms McEnroy, it might be best for you to return to New York. We've just begun our investigation. Is there anyone I can contact for you at this time?'

'I— No – I— Wait.'

The video blurred as Geena obviously ran from the bedroom with the 'link in hand. Eve saw pieces of a living area – bold, tropical colors, a hint of moonlight through glass, long, narrow feet with toes painted pastel pink.

'Francie!' The harsh whisper shook. Tears, Eve calculated, were coming. 'Oh God, Francie, I need you.'

'I'm up, I'm up!' A light flashed on. 'Are you sick, honey?'

To Eve's best guess, Geena thrust the 'link at the woman in bed, sat, and burst into tears.

The screen filled with the outraged face of a mixed-race woman of about fifty, hazel eyes firing out of a dusky face. 'Who is this?'

'This is Lieutenant Eve Dallas with the New York City—'

'Oh, bullshit! I've read the book, I've seen the vid. Dallas is . . .' Those hazel eyes blinked before she rubbed them clear. 'Oh dear God. What happened? Who's dead?'

She shifted as she spoke, showing a sturdy body in a pink – not pastel – sleep shirt with a unicorn prancing over it. 'Here now, Geena, here now. I'm going to get you some water. I'm going to take care of this, all right? What happened?' she demanded again, obviously on the move.

'Nigel McEnroy is dead. He was killed early this morning.'

'Ah God. How— No, don't bother with that.'

From what Eve could see, the woman dumped ice and fizzy water in a glass in some sort of kitchen. 'She needs me. The girls need me, so we'll wait on that. They loved him. I'll take care of things here. We'll be on our way back to New York as soon as possible. Did it happen in the apartment?'

'No.'

'All right. We'll go there, as soon as I can arrange it.'

'Your name, ma'am.'

'Francie – Frances,' she corrected. 'Frances Early. I teach the girls. I need to see to Geena.'

'Please contact me when you arrive in New York.'

'Geena will. She'll have steadied up by then, for the girls. I have to see to her now.'

When the woman clicked off, Eve shifted modes, did a quick run on Frances Early.

'The tutor,' Eve began as she walked into what was a his-and-hers dressing room rather than a closet. 'Frances Early, one marriage, one divorce, no children. Age fifty-six, educator, twenty-two years in the public school arena, New York, born and raised. Seven years with the McEnroys as tutor to first the older daughter, then both. Travels with the family when they travel. Lives here or with her sister when they're in New York, has rooms in their London home, and is given accommodations in their other residences. One bump – assault charge brought by her ex, then dropped. She seems solid.'

'I'm not finding anything in here except really nice clothes, his and hers, and excellent products in the makeup and grooming area. But there is a safe.'

Eve eyed it, calculated she could open it – she'd been taught by the expert thief (former) who happened to be her husband. 'It's going to be jewelry,' she decided. 'She'd likely have the codes, so he wouldn't stash anything in there he didn't want her to see. Shared space.'

'Keep at it. I'll hit his home office.'

Wandering through, she paused at a bedroom obviously shared by the two daughters. All pink and white and frilly, it said girlie girls. One section held a pair of facing desks, another toys and games.

She identified the third bedroom as the tutor's. The bright floral spread indicated a fondness for color – added to when a glance in the closet showed a wardrobe in bright, cheerful hues.

One wall held a big frame, with various kid art on display, and on a table under the window sat a trio of photos – the girls, the tutor with the family.

She'd called the wife by her first name – called her honey when concerned. Kid art, photos. Part of the family, Eve concluded. And people who lived as part of a family knew things.

She'd want to talk to Frances Early.

She moved on, found what she figured served as the kids' classroom/playroom, a kind of gathering room, formal dining, and McEnroy's office.

No office or separate space for his wife, she noted, but McEnroy's work space hit upscale in every note. The view, the desk, the chair, the sofa, the art, the data and communication system.

Top-of-the-line, she mused, as would behoove a man of his position and wealth.

She found his memo book, passcoded; his work comp, passcoded; communications, passcoded.

A careful man, even in his own home.

Desk drawers locked and coded.

Even the closet required a swipe and code.

She started there.

Opening her field kit, she took out a tool – one Roarke had given her – and got to work.

She heard the sweepers come into the unit, heard Peabody talking to them. Ignored it.

She could do this, and she'd be damned if McEnroy put this kind of security on an office holding freaking memo cubes and work discs.

Ten minutes later, frustrated, she nearly gave in and just kicked the damn door down. But then she'd have to report herself.

She heard McNab's cheery, 'Hey, She–Body!' And doubled her efforts.

She'd also be damned if she'd work this long, then pass the stupid task to the EDD geek, have him show her up.

She set her teeth as she heard his airboot prance coming her way.

'Hey, LT.'

'Start on the electronics,' she ordered. 'Open what you can here, do a quick pass, tag and transport. Shit, shit, shit! Open the hell up! Take what you can't open back to EDD.'

'On it. Hey, that's a mag code reader. Is that a TTS-5?'

'How the hell do I know? Stop breathing on me.'

'Looks like you're through everything but—'

She made a sound deep in her throat even a rabid dog would have backed away from. McNab just leaned closer.

When the pad blinked green, he tapped a fist to her shoulder. 'Nice.'

'Fucking A,' she said, and used the master to swipe through the rest.

She figured McNab could have done it in half the time she'd taken, and Roarke? He probably could have slid through by his damn Irish charm.

But she'd done it.

She opened the door, saw the memo cubes, the discs, the other organized office supply paraphernalia – and a case she judged would hold the camera in the bedroom.

And a locked cabinet. 'Jesus Christ. Is he storing the crown freaking jewels?'

'Just a key lock this time,' McNab noted. 'We can pry it.'

'No property damage.' From the field kit she took lock picks – again courtesy of Roarke. She had a better hand with key locks than e-locks, and had the cabinet open in under five.

When she opened the door, McNab let out a low whistle. 'Wowzer. Kink City.'

'I knew it.'

'Dude could practically open his own sex shop.' McNab slipped his hands into two of the many pockets on his plutonium-infused purple baggies.

She couldn't disagree as she scanned the padded cuffs, the

vibrators, the oils and lotions, the cock rings, nipple clamps, ticklers, silk cords, blindfolds, the supply of condoms, of Stay Up, feathers, gels.

She gestured at a bottle clearly marked ROHYPNOL, another marked RABBIT, and a small one labeled WHORE.

'Son of a bitch. He's got travel vials. Go clubbing, take a vial, pick your target. Get her back here, do what you want. Lady Justice's poem wasn't wrong.'

'Poem?'

'We'll get to it. Electronics, McNab.'

'On it.' He stepped back, a skinny guy with a pretty face, a long tail of blond hair, an earlobe weighed down by silver hoops. 'The toys, you know, that's one thing. No harm, no foul if everybody's having fun. But the chemicals, that's fucked-up.'

'And now so's he.'

And whatever he'd done, whatever he'd been, now he was hers.

She went out, spoke to the head sweeper, rounded up Peabody.

'Let's take his New York admin. That's the best chance of getting his habits, his schedule, his friends, and his side pieces if he had repeats.'

'Lance Po,' Peabody read from her PPC as they started out. 'Thirty-eight, mixed-race male, married five years to Westley Schupp, worked the New York base for just under eleven years, the last four as the vic's admin. The apartment was so classy,' Peabody added as they rode down.

'Yeah, that's how it looked. Nice, quiet, upper-class class. He had photos of his wife and kids on his desk ten feet from a locked cabinet full of sex toys and bottles of roofies, Rabbit, Whore. Not so goddamn classy.'

'So he didn't just cheat on his wife in her own damn bed. He used rape drugs.'

'Hard to believe he had them – and not all the bottles were full – and didn't use them. Let's see if the admin knows where he was heading last night, and who – if anyone – he headed out to meet.'

They went outside, where life in New York hit full churn. Ad blimps blasting, traffic snarling, pedestrians surging. No body lay over the sidewalk now, and no sign remained that it had.

Inside the building was a different story. She had uniforms knocking on doors, sweepers spreading over a family home, an EDD geek who'd dig through what that family had documented, what they'd talked about on their 'links, what they'd keyboarded, what photos they'd saved on any device.

Death unearthed secrets.

When Eve slid behind the wheel, Peabody gave her the admin's address. 'It's going to be a hard trip home for his wife and kids,' she commented.

'Yeah. Did she know?' Eve wondered. 'Maybe, maybe she didn't know about what he kept locked in a cabinet, but how could she not know about the cheating? A guy doesn't have that kind of sex supply – out of the bedroom he shares with his spouse – and not cheat as a matter of habit. How could she not know?'

'Some women just believe, and some guys are really good at covering.'

Eve shook her head. 'Nobody's that good.'

She punched out, muscled her way into the snarling traffic.

Po and his husband lived in a Midtown unit over a Greek restaurant. A reasonable walk to work, if Po was inclined, Eve calculated. She buzzed in at the street-level door, and in seconds got a cheerful 'Hey, yo!' through the intercom.

'Lieutenant Dallas, Detective Peabody, NYPSD. We need to speak to Mr Po.'

'Yeah, right, and Roarke's up here having a bagel. Is that you, Carrie?'

'Lieutenant Dallas. Am I speaking to Lance Po?'

'Well, yeah. Come on, seriously?'

'Seriously. We need to come up.'

Eve heard some cross talk, a laugh. 'Says she's Eve Dallas. It's gotta be Carrie.'

But the buzzer sounded, the locks clicked open.

The tiny hallway held a skinny elevator Eve wouldn't have trusted if Po had lived a mile up, and an equally skinny set of stairs.

As they climbed up, she heard the door open above. 'You sounded pretty kick-ass, Carrie, but—'

The man in the doorway broke off.

He hit about five-eight of trim, slim, mixed-race Asian. He looked younger than his thirty-eight years in a natty metallic-blue suit, a red-and-blue-dotted tie, and with raven black hair in short, curly dreads tipped in gold.

His eyes, nearly as gold as the tips, popped wide.

'Holy shit! Holy shit, Wes! It's fucking Eve Dallas.'

'Get real, Lance.' The second man, with a muscular, shaved head, black skin covered in faded jeans and a long-sleeved red T-shirt, stepped out. He blinked, laid a hand on Po's shoulder, said, 'Well, son of a bitch.'

Then he blinked again, and his dark eyes filled with worry. 'Jesus, somebody's dead.'

'Oh God. God. Is somebody dead?'

'Can we come in?'

'My mom. My mom—'

'It's not about your mother, Mr Po, or any family member. We're here about your boss.'

'Sylvia?' He reached up, grabbed his partner's hand.

'No, Nigel McEnroy.'

'Mr McEnroy's *dead*?'

'We'd like to come inside.'

'I'm sorry, I'm sorry.' He stepped back. 'Yes, please. I was – we were – just thrown off. We're big fans, of both of you. Not just the book and vid, though totally mag there. But we've been following you since you and Roarke – big fans there, too – and it's your work, and the fashion, and the no-prisoners interviews when they get you on camera. We're just—'

'You're babbling, honey.' Schupp nudged Po aside, reached for Eve's hand, then Peabody's. 'Please, sit down. We don't have your coffee, but—'

'We're fine.'

The living space, though small, struck Eve as a lot more friendly and comfortable than the McEnroys'. A high-backed navy sofa ranged along one wall, topped with a long, interesting pencil sketch of the city. It faced a couple of easy chairs in bold, multicolored stripes. A bench padded with fake leather added more seating, and a jog to the left opened into a smart-looking little kitchen and eating area.

'I'm going to tag in, get a sub. I teach art and coach football,' Schupp explained. 'High school. How about I make you some tea, Lance?'

'That'd be great. I'm just … It wasn't an accident. Like I said, we're fans, so I know you're with Homicide. Was it a mugging?'

He gestured to a chair as he spoke, so Eve took one, Peabody the other, while Po lowered to the sofa.

'No. You were Mr McEnroy's admin?'

'Yeah. Yes. He travels a lot, and when he's not in New York, which is about half the year, really, Sylvia Brant runs things. I mean, Mr McEnroy and his partners run everything, but Sylvia's like captain of the ship when he's not here. Should I tell her?'

'We'll take care of that. Do you know Mr McEnroy's schedule?'

'Sure. Absolutely. A ten o'clock this morning with the leading candidate for the VP of marketing position at Grange United, New York office. Eleven with—'

'How about yesterday's?'

'Right, sorry.'

Po rattled off names, times, purposes like a computer while Schupp brought him a pretty cup of tea. The cup, the floral smell, made Eve think of Mira.

She imagined she'd be talking this case through with the department's top profiler and shrink before too long.

'So, no dinner meetings, no evening appointments?'

'No, he finished at the office just before six. His wife and kids are on spring break, in Tahiti. Oh Jesus, Wes, those sweet little girls.'

Schupp took Po's free hand, gave it a squeeze. 'Can you tell us what happened?'

'Mr McEnroy was killed early this morning. The evidence so far indicates he left his residence just after nine P.M. He was killed at another location before his body was dumped outside his residence.'

She gauged her witness. 'There are also indications the murderer was female, or purports to represent females Mr McEnroy may have . . . misused.'

Po exchanged a look with his partner.

'You don't seem surprised by that,' Eve commented. 'Tell us why.'

3

'You always said,' Po murmured.

'Call 'em like I see 'em. He had a vibe – a player, a hard type of player,' Schupp told Eve. 'I only met him a few times, but he had a vibe. Tell them, Lance.'

'Well, it's just feelings or observations mostly. Except I know damn well he hit on a couple of the lower-level staff. One of them complained to HR, and boom, she was gone. Word was he paid her off. And Sylvia – he was always respectful of her, but . . . see, she's older and she'd kick his ass if he tried anything. Anyway, she reamed him over it, threatened to file a complaint. They really went at it – about a year ago. He was pretty steamed – I could see it – but he stopped fishing in the company pool, if you get me.'

'I get you. Why didn't Sylvia file a complaint?'

'I think, mostly, because of his wife and kids. She would have if he didn't straighten up. But . . . '

'You're not being disloyal, Mr Po,' Peabody put in. 'His behavior and habits very likely led to his death. His family needs to know who caused that death, and what you tell us helps us.'

'I didn't like him,' Po said abruptly. 'But I loved the work, and Sylvia, and the others I work with. And he wasn't here half the time, anyway. He treated me well, I don't mean to say otherwise.'

'You were an asset, honey. You're the best admin going.'

'A little prejudiced.' Po managed a smile. 'I am good at my job, and I like the job. He, Mr McEnroy, just didn't strike as a good husband. He loved the girls, that was clear and real. I think in his way he loved his wife. But he had that vibe, like Wes said. And, well, plenty of mornings when he came in – and his family wasn't in New York – he had that I-got-laid look on him. He didn't trouble to hide it.'

'Did anyone make threats?'

'You mean, like to hurt him? No. Unless it was on his private line or email. I see everything else. Honestly, I don't think he felt threatened. He always looked . . . smug, satisfied. The only time I saw him steamed was that time with Sylvia. I swear she'd never hurt anybody. She'd have roasted him professionally, but he laid off because, I think, he knew she would.'

'Would you know any of the venues he might have frequented after work?'

'Maybe.' He shifted, clearly uncomfortable. 'It's part of my job to keep things organized – when he's in New York and when he's not. Some clubs have little trinkets or amenities, especially when you spring for a privacy or VIP booth. He had swag from a few in a drawer in his desk.'

'We'd like the names, if you remember.'

'Lola's Lair, Seekers, This Place, Fernando's. Those were the usual as far as I know. There could be more, and he didn't keep the souvies.'

'That's very helpful.'

'I don't know what I should do.' Po lifted his hands, then used them to grip his elbows. 'Should I go to work?'

'We'll be taking all Mr McEnroy's electronics in for analysis.'

'I think he keeps – kept – a 'link, a second, private one, locked in his top left-hand desk drawer. I didn't have access, but I did see him speaking on another 'link several times in his office. And, ah, he kept some clothes there, too. I would sometimes be asked to have the ones he'd worn the day before sent to the cleaners. So I'd know he'd changed at work, after hours.'

'Would you know if he brought women there?'

'I really don't think so. There's security, and the cleaning service. I would, occasionally, send an invoice for a hotel room to our accountants. They would pop up now and again, when Mrs McEnroy was with him in New York.

'I knew what he was.' Po stared into his tea. 'But he was the boss.'

'Mr Po, why don't we give you a ride into work? It's our next stop.'

41

He looked at Eve, then at Schupp. 'Is that what I should do? Should I go in?'

'Actually, Mr Po,' Peabody said, 'you could help us out if you went in, showed us the office.'

The relief of being given direction, a task, streamed over his face. 'Okay, then I'll do that.'

'I'm going with you.' Schupp gave Eve a steady look. 'I not only know the people Lance works with, a lot of them are friends. I can help.'

Since she'd found him as steady as the look, she nodded. 'That's fine. Are you ready now?'

'Yeah, sure. I guess.' Po walked over, picked up the satchel by the door, put it on cross-body. 'Thanks, Wes.'

'No problem.'

Once they were down and in the car, Schupp let out a sigh. 'I know I shouldn't say this, under the circumstances, but it's pretty damn frosty riding with Dallas and Peabody.'

'In the DLE.' Po managed a wan smile. 'Even if I feel a little sick – not boot-it-up sick, but—'

'It's okay.' Peabody shifted to smile back at him. 'You've had a shock, it's natural. And since you are riding in the DLE, you should probably hold on.'

Even as she said it, Eve punched out into traffic, swung around a lumbering crosstown maxibus, and zipped through the light at the corner seconds before it went red.

Several pedestrians already trying to surge across the intersection aimed vicious looks.

'Whee,' Schupp said under his breath, and took Po's hand.

Eve skinned between a couple of Rapid Cabs, whizzed past a bike messenger with an obvious death wish, and barreled into the underground parking of the steel tower of Roarke's headquarters.

The security scanner beeped her through, droned out the parking level and space under reserve for the DLE.

She pulled into the slot minutes after she'd pulled away from the curb.

Po said, 'Wow,' and actually let out a quick laugh. 'Better than the vid.'

'Welcome to my world,' Peabody told him.

'Um. We're on the twenty-second floor. I can swipe us right up.'

So could she, Eve thought, but nodded. 'Good enough. We'll need to see Mr McEnroy's office, and speak to Ms Brant. I also need the names of the two women you mentioned. The ones you know were harassed by Mr McEnroy.'

'Oh man. I guess I knew that, but it feels ... I didn't know Jasmine – that's Jasmine Quirk – very well. She wasn't here very long. She quit about three weeks after she started. And Leah Lester didn't last a lot longer, maybe three months. She didn't go quietly, and that's how Sylvia got wind of what was going on. Allegedly, I guess. Leah and Jasmine left about the same time.'

He swiped into the elevator. 'I don't really know where they are now, but Sylvia might.'

'Okay.'

The ride up was smooth, as one expected of a Roarke

property, and since she added her own swipe to Po's, they went express.

The doors opened into the small, tasteful lobby of Perfect Placement.

Rich brown chairs in the waiting area contrasted richly with pale gold walls. The company logo arched on the wall behind reception where a man and woman, both in black, manned the echoing curved counter.

'Good morning, Lance.' The female offered a smile as she tapped her earpiece. 'Hey, Westley, nice to see you.'

'Ah, is Sylvia in?'

'Isn't she always?' The woman's smile faltered as she skimmed her gaze over Eve and Peabody. 'Is something wrong?'

'We need to speak with her,' Eve said.

'We'll go straight back, okay?'

Without waiting, Po turned toward the glass doors. They whispered open even as the receptionist said, 'I'll let her know.'

Cubes first, Eve noted, with worker bees already at it, and the smell of street coffee and economy pastries rising through the air.

Around a corner to a handful of offices, some open, some closed. Another corner, bigger offices, snazzier views, the sound of keyboarding, of 'link calls.

Po paused outside of one of the snazzies.

An athletically built woman with strong shoulders sat behind a desk working a keyboard with a blur of fingers. She didn't look up from the work.

'Hold there a minute, Lance. I need to get this sent asap.'

'Sylvia—'

'Ten seconds,' she muttered, fingers still flying. She paused, her bird-bright black eyes skimming the screen. 'Send,' she ordered, then sat back, glanced up. 'Hi, Wes. Now, what's all this?'

Eve held up her badge. 'I'm going to close the door.'

Sylvia sat straight again. 'That sounds ominous. Could I have a closer look at your identification?'

Obliging, Eve stepped closer, offered the badge. Sylvia, her short, dark hair artfully streaked with silver, studied it. 'Holy crap. Somebody killed Nigel.'

'That's quite a guess, Ms Brant.'

'I have two murder cops in my office, along with Nigel's admin and Lance's husband. I don't think you're here to pass the time of day. And in fact, I tried to tag Nigel five minutes ago, and got nothing, not even v-mail. Sit down, Lance.'

She rose as she spoke, went to him, gave him a one-armed hug as she pointed him toward a chair. 'You look pale. Everybody sit down. Give me a second to process.'

'You're processing pretty well,' Eve commented.

'It's what I do. What happened? When? Why? Though the why's not hard for me to process – unless it was an accident or a mugging.'

'Tell me why,' Eve suggested.

'Nigel, a man with a lovely, intelligent wife and two beautiful children, a successful business that afforded him the opportunity to live well, travel well, couldn't keep his

45

dick in his pants. If a husband, boyfriend, brother, father didn't eventually bash his head in, one of the women he used and abused would – and so I told him not fully a year ago.'

'And you, Ms Brant? Did he use and abuse you?'

Sylvia let out a barking laugh. 'Take a closer look.' She spread her arms – strong and muscled like the rest of her. 'I'm sixty-three, tough, not curvy. I'm a handsome woman, some might say. Sexy, young, naive – no one would say.'

'I think you're beautiful,' Schupp told her, and made her smile.

'And didn't I tell Lance to snap you up for good reason? No, Lieutenant, Nigel wasn't interested in me in that way. Plus, I'm far too valuable to the company. He hunted the younger, curvier, and often the powerless. Not quite a year ago when it became clear he'd been bobbing in the office pool, I threatened him with lawsuits, my resignation, and a conversation with his wife, someone I like quite a lot.'

'You didn't follow through.'

She showed the first sign of tension by rubbing two fingers between her eyebrows. 'No, I didn't, because he stopped hunting in this particular forest, agreed to pay the two women I'd learned of a generous private settlement. He could have fired me – it wouldn't have been easy, as he had no cause – but I'm valuable to the bottom line here, and I'd have made one hell of a stink. He knew it.'

She paused, sighed, rose. 'I'm breaking into the VIP coffee. I need it, and I expect so do we all.'

She walked to an alcove, programmed an AutoChef.

'Before I answer the questions I expect, I'm giving you full disclosure. I respected Nigel's business sense, tremendously. He was a driving part in building a damn good company, with skill, determination, creativity, foresight. I admired that part of him, and the part who had a seer's sense of placing the right person in the right position.'

She passed around coffee, brought over a tray of creamers and sugar substitutes. 'He was an excellent father from what I could tell, and his children adored him – clearly and genuinely. Geena, his wife ... It's hard for me to believe a woman as generous and intelligent as Geena didn't know what he was doing, but then I didn't know until a year ago, and I'm no idiot. I believe she genuinely loves – loved – him. I admire a man who can generate that kind of love.

'As for the rest of him, I found him despicable. Both women who finally came to me claimed he pressured them, used his position, and one of them believed he'd given her something, roofied her. He denied all this, of course, when I went at him, but he was lying. I could see it. And he agreed to the terms I gave him.'

'I appreciate your candor. Can you give me your whereabouts last night, particularly between the hours of nine P.M. and four A.M.?'

'Oh, but, Lieutenant, you can't—'

'Shh.' Sylvia shook a finger at Po. 'She needs to know. I left here shortly after Nigel, met my husband, our older son, and his fiancée for dinner at Opa. We had seven o'clock reservations. I think we left about ten. Ray and I took a cab home. I'd say we were both in bed and asleep before midnight, and I left this morning about six-forty-five to hit the gym, and was in the office by eight-forty.

'We do have security on our building,' she added. 'You would see Ray and me get in last night, and you'd see me leave this morning. I found Nigel despicable in many ways,' she said again, 'but my heart breaks for his children. They've lost their father, and however I felt, those kids need their daddy.'

'All right. Would Jasmine Quirk and Leah Lester be the women who reported the harassment to you, and accepted the settlement?' Dallas asked.

'They would, yes.'

'I'm sorry, Sylvia, I—'

'Don't be a boob, Lance, this is a murder investigation. You tell the truth, you say what you know. I demanded he pay each of them a hundred thousand, USD, provide each of them with solid references, and have no other contact with them. If he balked on any of it, I'd follow through. Both women agreed to those terms as well, or it would've been a different matter. They just wanted out.'

'A hundred thousand seems a small payment for rape,' Eve commented.

Sylvia's lips flattened. 'And I agree. They couldn't prove it, either of them. They couldn't even be absolutely sure of it, either of them. Jasmine, in particular, felt she'd participated, felt she'd done something wrong, and wanted to forget it. She relocated to Chicago, where she had some family. Leah

48

was angry, understandably, but refused to give me any solid details. She's still in New York as far as I know, working in international finance. It may be I should have gone to the partners, or even the police, but all I had was the word of two women who both wanted to move on.'

She pinched the bridge of her nose. 'I thought I did what was best for them at the time. I don't know. I just don't know.'

'Do you know who'll inherit his percentage of the company?'

'I . . . His wife and daughters, I imagine. I honestly don't know. Geena and the girls are away. God, what a mess.'

'Do you know of any other women he harassed?'

'Once I knew about Leah and Jasmine, I suspected there had been more, but no. No one else came to me or filed a complaint. And, believe me, since then I've kept my eyes and ears open. I feel certain Nigel knew I'd take action if he played among the office staff again.'

'All right, Ms Brant. We're going to need to go through his office, and we'll need to have any and all of his electronics taken in to EDD.'

'God, the client files. So much confidential data.' She squeezed her eyes shut. 'I'm going to clear you through, save us all time, but I'm going to ask you to cover all our asses and get a warrant. I have to inform the partners.'

'We'll also need to speak with them.'

'Of course. I can, if you like, arrange a 'link or holo-conference. Neither partner is in New York. However I felt about him, Lieutenant, Nigel was my employer, he had a family I'm very fond of, and I'll see that everyone in his office gives you every cooperation. His family will need closure. They won't have it until you find who took him from them.'

'I'll let you know about the conference. I appreciate your time and cooperation, Ms Brant. I'm going to have Mr Po take us to Mr McEnroy's office. EDD will arrange for the transport of the electronics. I'll secure the warrant.'

They left her to walk down the corridor to the impressive double doors of McEnroy's office.

It made two of Brant's, with Po's adjoining office a kind of afterthought. It boasted a full en suite, an entertainment nook, with an AutoChef, a friggie, a bar. And a snazzier yet view of the city.

'I don't have the passcode to his private files, or the locked drawer,' Po began.

'We'll take care of it.'

'I can get you into the company files, emails, and so on. I have those codes, if it helps.'

'It does. Peabody, tag Reo for the warrant, then EDD.'

'On that.'

'If you need me to explain any of the data . . . '

'Getting us in's enough for now. We're going to need your office electronics, too.'

'Oh boy. I could open them if you want.'

'Appreciate it. Once you open things up, why don't you take a break? If we need you, we'll let you know.'

'He's better busy,' Schupp commented.

'Yeah, I am. Wes knows me. I could maybe help Sylvia, keep busy and out of your way.'

'Go ahead. You've been a big help, Mr Po, both you and Mr Schupp.'

'It doesn't really seem real,' Po murmured, as he efficiently opened the office comp, a memo book, a calendar. 'Not all the way real. I guess it will.'

As he moved off to do the same in his office, Eve eyed the locked drawer. Then pulled out her signaling 'link to read a text.

> Come up and see me. I can give you some data on
> your victim.

Of course he could, Eve thought. Roarke would know she'd entered the building almost as soon as she had – and would by now have gathered up whatever data there was to gather up on his dead tenant.

It would be worth a stop.

> Got a few things yet to do down here – including
> picking a lock. We'll come up after.

> Need a hand with the lock?

Maybe, she thought, but answered: Don't insult me.

As it was now a matter of pride, she settled down, got to work.

'Warrant's in the works,' Peabody told her. 'McNab's heading over. He reports McEnroy didn't return to the apartment until around midnight – that's night before last. And he didn't return alone.'

Eve glanced up from the lock. 'A woman?'

'A duet. Two redheads, and McNab says they both looked seriously wasted. Drunk or high or both. They left looking pretty much the same about oh four hundred.'

'Didn't waste any time once the wife left, did he?'

Unsurprised, Eve went back to the very stubborn lock.

'The guy was a dick who thought with his dick. Anyway, EDD's sending a transport for what's tagged from the residence, then from here.'

'Bitch.'

'Huh?'

'Not you. The lock. I thought I had it. He's got a second layer on it.'

Curious, Peabody moved over to watch. 'A second layer on a desk drawer? Must be some goodies inside.'

'I've already deduced.' And she already felt the first trickles of sweat forming at the base of her spine. 'Go take a look at Po's stuff instead of breathing down my neck.'

'Sure, but McNab's on his way, and he could . . . '

The low growl had Peabody moving quickly to the next office.

Eve felt more sweat pop out on the back of her neck – which only pissed her off. She could open a damn drawer. She *would* open the damn drawer.

Kept shit here, she calculated as she struggled, because his wife would never fiddle around in his office. Because his admin was as trustworthy as they came. Because he was the boss and assumed — very likely correctly — no one would dare try to compromise anything he'd locked away.

Now being dead, all bets were off.

'Son of a bitching bitch.'

'That bad, is it now?'

She looked up, and there he was.

She should've figured.

Roarke stood in the doorway, tall and lean in the ruler-of-the-business-world suit — the darkest of charcoals without being black — a shirt so sharp it could have sliced bread in a palest of pale gray hue, with a craftily knotted tie that added thin hits of burgundy to a medium gray field.

His black hair swept thick and silky around a face that might have been formed with angel kisses — with a few taps of devil to add to the appeal. And those impossibly blue eyes smiled, just for her.

The whisper of Ireland in his voice just capped the package.

She shot a finger at him, said, 'No,' very decisively.

So he leaned on the jamb, a man at his ease, waited.

Having him show up — and knowing how easily he could show her up with a lock — had her doubling down. Maybe some of that sweat slid down the back of her spine, but she finally opened the stupid lock.

'Done.'

'And good for you, Lieutenant.'

'He had two layers on it.'

'Is that a fact?' Brows lifted, he wandered in. 'And what is it the head of headhunting kept so secret?'

'Police business.'

He only smiled, then bent down to brush those perfectly carved lips over the top of her head.

'That police business might include my data if you want it. The media hasn't yet released any salient information on his death, but as you're here, it's murder.'

'It's murder, and it's nasty.' She took two 'links, a memo book, and a few discs out of the drawer. 'Close the door, ace.'

He walked back, did so, and paused in the adjoining doorway. 'Good morning, Peabody.'

'Hey, Roarke!'

He moved back to Eve, leaned a hip on the desk. 'Caro will send you a copy of the data,' he began, speaking of his own efficient and trustworthy admin. 'In the meantime, I can tell you McEnroy and his company have had their New York headquarters here for about six years. They're in the first year of their second five-year lease, and have routinely paid the rent and fees in a timely manner. They have opted for the building cleaning service – nightly – as well as our IT services and maintenance. They brought in their own decorators, but employ our live plant care service and often use our floral company, bakery, and other craft services.'

'Did you know him?'

'I did not, though one hears what one hears.'

'What does one hear?'

'He enjoyed golf, tennis, boating, and sex. His wife wasn't always his partner in any of those hobbies. He preferred high-end clubs for all his sports. Give me an hour, I can tell you where he ordered his suits, his shoes, where he bought jewelry, and so on.'

Roarke glanced around the office. 'He wasn't as discreet as his office decor might indicate.'

'So cheating on his wife wasn't a secret?'

'He had a reputation. He also had one for being almost preternaturally good at matching clients, so the less savory business was often overlooked. His wife's business more than a client's, after all.'

'Looks like somebody disagreed with that.'

'And is that what killed him?'

'Early evidence indicates. Somebody who disagreed left his body, naked, mutilated, castrated, essentially on his doorstep early this morning.'

'Well then,' Roarke said mildly. 'That would be a very severe sort of disagreement.'

'Bet your fine ass. Whoever that was took some time letting McEnroy know she – most likely she – disapproved of his hobbies. Which, early evidence indicates, included drugging targeted females, some of whom worked for him.'

'Ah, well then.' Rising, Roarke studied the view. '"Less savory" doesn't quite come up to it, does it now? Do you suspect his wife?'

'Unlikely, at least not directly.' You had to look at the

spouse, Eve thought. Always. 'She and their two kids were in Tahiti. I confirmed that before I notified her. She's heading back. Whoever did it — and there's the possibility the wife was complicit — left a poem, and signed it Lady Justice.'

'A poem. And a poetic signature.' He turned back to her. 'Intriguing.'

'You could call it that.' She'd already determined the 'links and memo books were passcoded. And he was right there.

'Seal up.' She pulled a can out of her field kit. 'And open these, will you?'

He studied the can with resignation. 'I hate this bloody stuff, but anything to serve.'

He had the 'links and book cleared in a very short and annoying amount of time. Eve checked the book first.

'He's got the wife's schedule, each daughter's schedule in here. Travel, music lessons, blah blah, even playdates. What is it with making dates to play? Why don't kids just, you know, play?'

'I couldn't say. But from the looks, he was either a very involved father, a conscientious husband — in this area — or having the schedules so outlined helped him find his windows for his own version of playdates.'

She'd thought exactly the same. 'It can be both. His schedule, too — family stuff, work stuff. And those a lot less savory playdates. Right? See here, he's got dates and times, names of clubs — or bars, or venues of some kind. Here in

New York, in London, Paris, Chicago, New LA, and so on. All carefully documented.'

With a hand on her shoulder, Roarke leaned down. 'Mixing them up – it seems he didn't want to repeat locations, not too closely on his calendar. But from the number of locations and dates, this was a man with a serious addiction.'

'First names of women – just first names – and some dates with two, even three. So he liked to keep track there, too. Jesus, he's got notations in here when he used drugs on them, what kind, where he took them after. If and when he paid them off.'

'Perhaps Lady Justice had a point,' Roarke suggested.

'Murder doesn't have a point, and it's not justice.' Eve closed the book. 'McNab's heading in to take care of the electronics, and I'm getting full cooperation around here.'

'And so I'm no longer useful.'

Since the door was closed, and Peabody occupied, she rose, pressed her lips to his. 'You're always useful, but I've got places to go, people to grill. I'll look for Caro's data, it'll add.'

'Then, unless I prove useful elsewhere, I'll see you tonight.' He glanced at the disc. 'Are you thinking he might have memorialized some of his rapes? As rape is what they were.'

'I'm thinking that wouldn't surprise me, since he had a cam set up in his bedroom. All-directional vid cam, on a tripod, already cued for voice activation. So I'll take the discs in, view them at Central. Appreciate the assist.'

'You'd have opened the rest. Take care of my cop,' he added, then called out a goodbye to Peabody as he left.

Yeah, she'd have opened the rest. But, she admitted, she'd probably still be at it.

4

As Roarke walked out, Peabody walked in.

'A quick look,' she began, 'nothing to see. The kind of business stuff, scheduling, contacts, and all that you expect to see on an admin's e's. He keeps his personal schedule, contacts, separate. It's all flagged for EDD.'

'Good enough. The vic kept his personal separated, you could say. His personal schedule includes regular visits to a group of clubs, and his memos include first names of women, dates, what drugs were used, where he took them after he dosed them.'

Peabody's puppy-dog eyes hardened like marbles. 'Jesus, what a slime sack.'

'Yeah, but he's our slime sack now. We'll talk to the staff here, see if we get more buzz. And let's arrange to have conversations with the two targets from here we know of. Let's see if Quirk had any travel to New York in the last few days. We'll also check the partners' travel.'

By the time they'd finished at the offices, Eve believed

Brant had it right. The threats had pushed McEnroy out of the company pool.

As they rode down to the garage, Eve calculated. 'We get another woman who admitted – or claimed – McEnroy acted inappropriately toward her around about a year ago. To her recollection. But then backed off completely.'

'Sylvia Brant's ultimatum.'

'It fits. And she didn't report it, as he stopped. Or she says he stopped. Let's run her, Peabody, and keep her on the list for now. Then we need to take a good look at another pool. Clients.'

'Yeah. Oh, you want this position? I'm going to personally review your qualifications. Slime sack,' Peabody repeated as they stepped out of the elevator, started toward the car.

Eve checked her wrist unit as she slid behind the wheel. 'We'll split up interviews with the partners, but first, we'll have that conversation with Leah Lester. Plug in her work address.'

Peabody programmed the in-dash. 'I did a quick run on Allie Parker already – the no reporting since he stopped. No criminal, no change in finances that shows on the speedy first-level. She came on at PP right out of college, is midway through her second year as an administrative associate. The timing works, doesn't it? She's new, McEnroy rolls into the office, sees the fresh meat, gives it a little squeeze. Before he can do more, or before the meat really decides how to react, Brant comes down on him, and he decides to shop elsewhere.'

'Agreed, and there wasn't an Allie in McEnroy's book. But she stays on the list. Next run, for everybody on the list, any payments to the clubs McEnroy favored. That's where his killer picked him up, so she – or he if that's a blind – likely stalked him first.'

Peabody made notes as they went. 'I get, sort of, why the ones he went after in his own firm settled for the money and walked away, but . . . What would you do if a boss or superior tried the grab-ass on you?'

'First year on the job a detective – second grade – tried to corner me in the locker room – shoved me back against the lockers, grabbed my tit with one hand, my crotch with the other. I'd just started in Homicide under Feeney, and we'd been out on a long one. It's about two hundred hours, and he comes in while I'm changing. Big guy, asshole, figured he'd initiate the rook his way.'

'Jesus, Dallas! Did you report him to Feeney?'

'Didn't have to. While I was busting the asshole's nose, bruising his balls, Feeney heard the commotion and came in. Detective Fuckface starts going off on how I came at him, lost my shit, and he was filing charges. While he's spouting off, I'm thinking how I've been in Homicide a handful of weeks, I'm the rook, and this guy has a gold shield, so I'm screwed. Why would anybody believe me – he's bleeding, I'm not. And while I'm thinking that, while the asshole is spouting off, Feeney gives him a shot in the gut that drops him.'

'Holy shit.'

Odd, Eve realized, it wasn't an incident she thought about, but now she could see it all again, clear as glass. 'I'm about half-dressed, my support tank's ripped at the strap, so Feeney turns to me – puts his boot on the asshole's chest, and turns to me. He looks right in my face, just my face, and asks me to say what happened, so I did. Then he tells me to put on my shirt, wait in his office. So I did, and almost lost my shit then.'

Yeah, she thought, clear as glass.

'I wanted Homicide like I never wanted anything, and I didn't know if I was going to get written up, dismissed, or if my lieutenant was going to shrug it all off as a done deal, tell me to do the same, just let it go.'

She glanced over at Peabody. 'And I'd have to swallow it, because I needed the badge more than my pride.'

'I get that,' Peabody murmured. 'I really get that.'

'Then Feeney comes in, and he digs this really crap bottle of whiskey out of his file cabinet, pours some in a couple of coffee mugs, tells me to sit. And how he needs me to file a formal report, and how I have to speak about the incident to Mira. Man, last thing I wanted, but he's not hearing that. He'll keep it quiet, he tells me, because he knows otherwise some can blow back on me, but I have to follow through, and he'll have my back. And he tells me Detective Fuckface will be taking early retirement. Nobody, he says, nobody puts hands on one of his. Then he tells me to drink up, to suck it up, because it won't be the last time I have to bust some fucker's balls.'

'I love Feeney.' Peabody blinked damp eyes. 'I totally do.'

'Yeah.' She spotted the shining downtown tower that housed Leah Lester's employer, Universal Financial. 'The fact is,' she said as she started hunting for parking, 'if he hadn't stood up for me, I'd have swallowed down what I had to swallow to stay on the job, to stay in Homicide. I could kick the fucker's balls, but without Feeney's backing, I couldn't have done much else. He showed me what made a real cop, and what made a real boss, that night. I guess, come down to it, what made a real man.'

She hit vertical so fast Peabody yipped like a Pomeranian, then zipped across the lane, shimmied down into a spot.

'Score.'

'A little heads-up next time,' Peabody managed. Then she stepped out on the sidewalk, lifted her face, sighed. 'It's really starting to feel like spring. I'm going to stop by a flower stall on the way home and buy a whole bunch of daffodils. Hey, I should buy some for the bullpen!'

'Do that, prepare to eat them.'

They had to walk down to the corner, cross the street, but Peabody nearly bounced in her pink boots. 'I bet they taste like spring.'

'You could find out.'

They crossed with the surge of pedestrians who may or may not have been happy it felt, sort of, like spring. Most seemed in too big a hurry to notice.

The big shiny building had glass entrance doors – blast-proof – a sprawling tiled lobby, and heavy security. To keep it simple, Eve pulled out her badge, held it up for one of the three guards. 'What's the floor, Peabody?'

'Sixty-second floor, Universal Financial.'

'You can stow your weapons here.'

'No,' Eve said, again keeping it simple. 'Scan the badges, clear us through. We're on NYPSD business.'

He didn't like it, curled thin lips, but scanned and verified. 'If you insist on keeping your weapons, you're required to have an escort.'

'I'll take them up, Jim.' The female guard stepped out of the security booth, gestured across the lobby to a bank of elevators. 'Jim's a little bit of a jerk,' she said when they were out of earshot. 'It's nothing personal.'

'Okay.'

The guard swiped her card at an elevator, then stepped in with Eve and Peabody before holding up a hand at the next person trying to get on. 'Sorry, please wait for the next available car.'

Once the doors shut, she swiped her card again. 'Going express,' she explained. 'Otherwise it could take twenty minutes to get up to sixty-two this time of day.'

'Appreciate it.'

'Hey, we're all just trying to keep people safe, right? Anyway, I know somebody who's a cop. Well, we just met, really, but she's a cop in your division, Lieutenant. Dana Shelby.'

'Officer Shelby's a good cop.'

'Maybe you could tell her Londa said hi. Sixty-two,' she

announced and stepped off when the doors opened. 'Just let me clear this with Universal's security.'

She walked to the counter, had a word with one of the people manning it. More people sat in the cushy gray-and-black waiting area busily working their handhelds. Still more breezed in and out of various doors in their power suits.

The entire area smelled of privilege in the wisps of expensive perfumes and real leather.

In under a minute, a square-jawed man with a shaved head and a black suit stepped out of a side door, gave Eve and Peabody a quick glance before walking to Londa.

'Got it from here. Appreciate it, Londa.'

'No prob, Nick.' Londa sent Eve and Peabody a little salute before she headed back to the elevator and the guard crossed to them.

'Nick Forret, head of security for Universal. How can I help you?'

'We need to speak with Leah Lester.'

With a nod, he turned to the counter. 'Is Ms Lester in her office?'

'I'll check, Mr Forret. Yes, sir. Her office 'link is engaged, with a do not disturb.'

'Then don't disturb her,' Forret said mildly. He gestured to another door. 'I'll take you back to Ms Lester's office. Do you expect any difficulties, Lieutenant?'

'No. Ms Lester may have information that could assist us in an investigation.'

They didn't go far, though Eve noted Lester had moved

up beyond cube status to the next level. Her office door was shut with the red DND light blinking. Ignoring it, Forret issued one sharp knock, opened it.

The woman at the desk jabbed a finger in the air out of range of the 'link even as she continued a conversation in the calmest of tones. 'Absolutely, Mr Henry, that is fully understood. I'd be more than happy to discuss all of this with you tomorrow, as planned.'

Eve let the conversation roll as she looked around the office. Smaller than hers at Central, but it did have a bigger window. No frills, no fuss – she respected that.

'I look forward to meeting you, sir, and very much appreciate the chance to show you what we can offer you as a member of the Universal Financial family.'

The minute she signed off, her polite, professional expression went to snarl. 'Damn it! Did you see the DND? I've been working on getting this face-to-face with Abner Henry for weeks.'

'Lieutenant Dallas, Detective Peabody.' And with that Forret stepped out, shut the door.

To add to it, Eve held up her badge. 'NYPSD, Ms Lester. We need a few minutes of your time.'

'Cops?' The irritation shifted to puzzlement, then jumped straight to panic as she surged up. 'My parents? My brother? What—'

'It has nothing to do with your family.'

'Frankie.' Now she pressed a hand to her heart, sank into the chair again. 'Oh God.'

'Or Frankie,' Eve added. 'We're here about Nigel McEnroy.'

Color flew back in her face — a good face, Eve noted, more than pretty, with refined features, lips carefully dyed a quiet coral. Her eyes changed, too, the clear, pale blue of them going glacier cold.

'I've got nothing to do with McEnroy or his company, and nothing to say, either. I left his company's employ more than a year ago. Now if you'll excuse me   '

'Nigel McEnroy is dead.'

Something flickered in those eyes, then she sat back, blew out a breath, lifted a hand to skim it through her carefully styled mane of gold-streaked red hair. 'Dead? As in . . . God. How do I feel?' she murmured. 'I don't know how I feel. Not sorry,' she decided. 'It's not a crime to not be sorry.'

Hit the core straight off, Eve decided. 'Can you give us your whereabouts from nine P.M. last night until four this morning?'

'Why . . . Jesus, was he murdered? He was murdered, and you're looking at me.' She shut her eyes a moment, then picked up a little red ball from her desk, started squeezing it. 'Things follow you no matter what you do. Someone killed him, that's what followed him. And that follows me.'

'Your whereabouts?'

'I . . . I was with Frankie from about eight until about midnight. We just started dating. We met for dinner at Roscoe's, then we caught some music at the Blue Note. He walked me home — that's his thing, he always takes me home — and I got in about midnight. I went to bed — alone.

That's my thing, but I'm about to try to change that. I left for work this morning about eight.'

She put the ball down, rose, turned to her window. 'He's dead, and I'm not sorry. He was a terrible excuse for a human being. You must know that, or know why I think that, or you wouldn't be here. I should be scared, I guess. Should I be scared that you're here?' She turned back. 'I'm not. I'm just pissed off that this brings it all back when I've managed to push it out.'

She sat again. 'I guess you've talked to Sylvia. To Ms Brant.'

'We're aware of Mr McEnroy's alleged behavior with you and other female employees.'

'Alleged.' For an instant her eyes went dead. Then they fired with icy rage. 'Of course alleged. We took the money and walked away, Jasmine and I. So it'll always be alleged. And even if we hadn't? How can you prove what you don't clearly remember?'

Eve understood that all too well, and the helplessness that came with it. But pushed it aside to do the job. 'You told Ms Brant that Mr McEnroy sexually assaulted and harassed you.'

'Raped me. I know it. I *know* it, but I can't prove it. Sylvia believed me – us – me and Jasmine, and she made it stop. We took the money. You can call it a payoff, or compensation, or a bribe, I don't give a shit. What it was? Something to help us get through until we could find our feet again, sleep at night again, get another decent job. It was making him pay.'

Eve didn't mind the angry venting. The anger told her a great deal.

'Are you in touch with Ms Quirk?'

'She moved to Chicago. She couldn't stay here, and she has family there. We keep in touch, not as much as we did. We went to the same support group for a while. She convinced me to go. Maybe it helped. Misery loves company.'

'I walked away,' she said again, and sat. 'Even knowing the money it cost him meant nothing to him.'

'Did Ms Brant urge you to take the money and walk?'

'No. She was willing to go to the wall. We weren't.'

'Why?'

'He had vids. We didn't tell Sylvia — we just . . . We weren't ready to talk about that part. He had vids, of both of us — not together,' she said quickly 'Jasmine told me about hers after I told her about mine.'

Peabody spoke, soft, gentle. 'Can you talk about it now?'

'Yeah. I got through that wall. I woke up that night in his house, in his bed. I don't remember how I got there. I don't really remember any of it. But I knew I'd never have gone with him like that. I'd already made that clear, even told him I'd report him. Then I'm naked in his bed? When I woke up, sick, confused, humiliated, he already had the vid cued up. And there I was, in that room, having sex with him.'

She had to look away — not to fight tears, Eve noted. To pull back the rage.

'I didn't just look willing, but eager. He told me if I tried to say I hadn't been willing and eager, he'd ruin me. He had

69

the lawyers, the money, the vid. I'd never get a decent job in the field again – anywhere. Then he told me to get dressed and get out. His wife was coming home that afternoon.

'Tell me I should've gone to the police,' she snapped even as, at last, her eyes filled. 'When he had that vid.'

'Ms Lester.' Peabody spoke in what Eve thought of as her heart voice. 'We're not here to tell you what you should've done. He had all the power, and not just in that moment.'

'He broke me, and I did nothing.'

'That's not true,' Peabody corrected. 'You went to your supervisor.'

'Not right away. I thought I could just bury it, you know, pretend it didn't happen. Especially when he went back to London, and I didn't have to see him. But I walked into the bathroom, and Jasmine was in there. She was sick. I didn't even know her very well, but she was sick, so I said something about could I get her some water, or help her get home or whatever. She just blurted it all out. She said she had to quit, had to leave, she'd had sex with McEnroy and couldn't even remember. And she's puking and blaming herself, and I realized he'd done the same thing to her somehow. I told her, and I guess I used her, because she was so sick and shaky she let me take over. That's when we went to Sylvia.'

'It seems to me you helped each other. That's not using. It's supporting.'

'Maybe. What I know is I've tried to put it behind me, and I was getting there. Now the bastard's dead and I'm a suspect. I should probably get a lawyer.'

'Do you want a lawyer?' Eve asked her.

She sent Eve a look of unbearable weariness. 'Then I'd have to go through all of it again, tell someone else.'

'We're going to need Frankie's full name and contact info. We need to verify your statement on your whereabouts last night. We can tell him we're simply checking off boxes on some routine matter.'

'He knows about McEnroy. I haven't felt ready to have sex – and boy, I used to like sex – since that morning. I wanted to have sex with Frankie, but ... not ready. So I told him why. He's waited. He's Frank Carvindito. He's an editor for Vanguard Publishing. And he's pretty goddamn terrific.'

'Okay. Can you tell us the last thing you remember before you woke up in McEnroy's bedroom?'

'Oh yeah. I've been over it a million times. He called me into his office, and the son of a bitch apologized. He said he realized he'd been inappropriate, that he'd misread signals, how I was already a valued member of the team. He laid it on, and I accepted it. I loved the work there, so I accepted it. And the coffee he offered me when he started to talk about work. I have a vague memory of walking out with him. I think most everyone was gone by then. I remember feeling off, like I'd been drinking, but good drinking, you know? Loose. Then I was in the back of a car with him, and his hands were on me, but I didn't mind. He gave me a drink, and then ... nothing. I just don't remember after that. Some flashes – like dream blips – but nothing clear.'

'All right.' Eve got to her feet. 'We appreciate your time and cooperation.'

'That's it?'

'For now it is. We'll verify what you've told us. As long as it jibes, as long as you didn't kill him, you've got nothing to worry about.'

Her lips twisted into a mockery of a smile. 'Well, there's good news.'

Eve paused, waited until Leah's eyes met hers. 'I'm a cop, and I'm telling you this. What he did to you was rape. He drugged you, raped you, then blackmailed you. He's to blame, every level, every step. You're not. And you stood up when you realized he'd done the same to someone else.'

'I . . . ' She had to stop, had to swallow. 'Thanks. I mean it. Now, you're going to go around all this with Jasmine, even though she's in Chicago. Take it easy with her, will you? She's always going to be a little tender because a part of her is always going to at least half believe she caused it. And to add insult, he passed her over for a promotion right after. Just another little sting, right?'

'We'll keep that in mind.' Eve walked to the door, stopped. 'Are you still in the support group?'

'Me? Not really. Once Frankie and I got serious – once I realized I actually could have good feelings for a man – I sort of let it slide. Jasmine's got one in Chicago. I think she's a lifer.'

'Does it have a name? The group?'

'Women For Women. I thought it would be as stupid as it sounds, but it actually helped. I might just hit the next meeting.' She smiled a little. 'Just a quick booster maybe.'

They left her staring into space and squeezing the red ball.

'She struck me as telling it straight,' Peabody said as they rode down.

'Yeah, but we verify. I'm going to dump you at Central on my way to the morgue.'

'I love when that happens.'

'You verify Lester's statement with the boyfriend. You contact Jasmine Quirk, run her through it, verify her statement. Set up a meet with the vic's spouse, get any updates from EDD on the electronics. Write up the report, copy to me, Whitney, Mira. Get what we need for a search and seize on all the vic's residences and offices.'

'Worldwide.'

'That's affirmative. See what you can find on this support group.'

'The support group?'

'Remember Mr Mira's cousin? A conspiracy of female vics turned revenge killers. It's not impossible we have something similar here, so let's take a look at the group. Contact the vic's transpo service, a driver, from Po's files. No way he risked a cab getting Lester from the office to his residence, so if he headed out to a club last night to hunt, he probably didn't take public transpo.'

'I'm starting to think the morgue and a dead, mutilated body's easier.'

'Make lieutenant, then you can call the shots.' Eve whipped to the corner. 'Out.'

'At least this way I can grab a street dog before I go in.' Peabody climbed out, beelined for the cart as Eve bullied her way back into traffic.

She ran through questions in her head along the drive.

Could one person, working alone, have lured McEnroy, incapacitated him, transported him to an as yet unknown location, tortured, mutilated, and killed him, then transported the body back to the dump site?

Not impossible, but it seemed more likely a partnership of some sort.

Alternately, had McEnroy left his residence to go to that as yet unknown location voluntarily, most probably expecting sex? And there the killer incapacitated him, and the rest, before transporting the body to the dump site? If so, a stronger case for working alone, but still . . .

Even as she walked down the white tunnel of the morgue, she ran other scenarios. The one point that stuck in any and all: The murder, the method, the victim had all been meticulously planned.

When she swung through the double doors of the chief medical examiner's theater, she found Morris sitting on a stool at one of his counters, munching on soy chips as he studied a comp screen.

He still wore the clear protective cape over a stylish suit of steely blue with a sharp-collared shirt of the same exact tone. He'd chosen a tie the color of warm apricots, twined his long black braid with a cord to mirror it.

He swiveled on the stool, smiled. 'A fine day it is for the living. Where's our Peabody?'

'Central. Verifying and so on.' She walked to the steel slab where McEnroy still lay spread open by Morris's Y-cut. 'Bad end for him.'

'Bad, long, painful.'

'Did you get tox back yet?'

'Just now.' Rising, Morris walked first to his cold box, took out a couple tubes of Pepsi. He tossed one to Eve, cracked his own.

'Thanks.'

'We're here to serve. The unfortunate Mr McEnroy had traces of Rohypnol mixed with a very dry martini. More traces of a drug, street name Black Out. Both of those chemicals, or the results of them, would have worn off before the torture began.'

'Roofied him – that's the lure – then knocked him out in order to get him where he/she/they wanted him. The roofie? The killer would consider that justice. It was one of his favored tools in what's looking like serial rape.'

'Ah, so a bad end for a bad man. From the ligature marks on his wrists – you see here?'

'Yeah, clear enough.'

'He was hung by the wrists, arms above the head, as you deduced on-site. His weight caused the restraints to dig into his flesh, and also put considerable strain on his rotator cuffs, arms, shoulders. There are, as you also noted, no defensive wounds. He would have been incapable of attempting to defend himself. The facial injuries, some from a weighted sap, some from an electric prod. Much the same with the torso, the back, the legs. Some wounds, the prod straight on, like a jab, others a lash, like a whip. All would have been excruciating. The prod had to be on high voltage to cause burns this severe.'

As a matter of routine, Morris picked up two pairs of microgoggles. 'The torture, given the extent of the wounds, went on for between three and four hours. He would have lost consciousness off and on. There were traces of Alert on and in his nostrils.'

'No fun torturing an unconscious man.'

'No indeed. He was still alive when his genitals were – quite efficiently – severed with a sharp blade.'

'Medical training? A scalpel?'

'Medical training's possible, or someone who spent some time practicing. A sure hand, in any case. But the blade used wouldn't have been a scalpel. You're more likely to be looking for a knife with a slight rise in the center of the blade. See here.'

He put on the goggles, leaned over the body, so Eve did the same.

'Not a hesitation mark,' he pointed out, 'not a stop and start again, but the slight deviation in the blade, cutting across the root of the penis.' He swiped a hand to demonstrate.

'Hold it up, lop it off.'

'In plain words, yes. A killing blade, but also, I think, ornamental. Perhaps ceremonial.'

'Ceremonial would fit. Same method on his balls. Not going to leave him anything.'

'Punishment for the rapist. You're thinking one of his victims or someone attached to one.'

'It leans that way. So far. Did you read the poem?'

'I did. Lady Justice. Well, hell has no fury, after all.'

'If there is a hell, he's burning in it now, so he probably figures there's plenty of fury.'

She took off the goggles, laid them aside. 'Opinion. Could a woman have done this, alone?'

He sipped Pepsi contemplatively. 'He's not a big man, tall but slim. A woman strong and determined enough, I'd say yes, it's possible.'

'Hanging him up by the wrists. Could've used a pulley system.'

'Yes, and a dolly and ramps to move him in and out of a vehicle. Quite a lot of physical labor, but . . . hell's fury.'

'Yeah.' But she pointed to the mutilated genitals. 'Seems to me hell's fury isn't usually so precise. Thanks for the tube.'

'Anytime at all. Enjoy the sunshine while you can.'

'Yeah, I'll do that,' she said as she left.

Morris looked down at the body. 'Well, Nigel, what do you say we close you up now?'

5

When Eve walked into her bullpen, Jenkinson's tie du jour scorched her corneas. His way to celebrate almost spring, apparently, equaled a forest of Peabody's daffodils – these infused with sulfuric acid – over a field of Venusian green grass.

She winced, turned away to save herself.

'Peabody, my office.'

In her office, with nuclear yellow still blooming across her vision, she hit the AutoChef.

At last, real coffee.

'Report's written and sent,' Peabody told her, adding a puppy dog look toward the AC.

'Don't beg, get coffee.'

'Thanks! I spoke with Jasmine Quirk – and was writing up that addition. No travel shows on the run for her, and I corroborated she attended a work meeting until six central time last night. Also corroborated she and her roommate, a family friend, then attended a birthday party, for her brother, from eight to eleven CT. After which she and her roommate took the L back to their apartment.'

Peabody sighed in some coffee.

'She didn't give any buzz, and though she was visibly more shaken than Lester, she gave me her version of her experience with McEnroy. It follows pattern, except since his wife was in New York at the time of the rape, she woke up, alone, in a room in the Blake Hotel. He'd left her a vid disc. Sex disc.'

'Well, he was a charmer.'

'Oh yeah. Lester's alibi holds, and EDD is making progress. I checked with McEnroy's usual transpo service. He didn't use them last night.'

'Then he's got a secondary he uses when he's hunting. He'd use the personal 'link to order it. Have McNab look.'

'Will do. Ms McEnroy's due back in about an hour. I contacted her, or mostly the tutor. She's – the widow – willing to talk to us as soon as possible, but won't leave the children and doesn't want them exposed to the conversation. She asks that we come to her this evening after nine when the children are in bed.'

'All right. I'll handle that.' With, she thought, her expert consultant, civilian. 'I need to set up the board and book. You can get the discs and memo book from McEnroy's desk drawer out of Evidence. Start cross-checking those first names with staff and clients. And we'll split interviewing the partners.'

'I'll get on it.'

As Eve sat to pull up Peabody's report, the sweepers' and Morris's preliminaries, she shot off a text to Roarke.

Need to interview vic's widow after 2100 – at her
request. Could use a slick rich guy. Interested?

She scanned the reports, pulled up her own notes, added more, and started her murder book. When she rose to set up her board, her 'link signaled a return text.

Meet me at half-seven at Nally's Pub, West 84
between Columbus and Amsterdam. A slick rich
guy will buy you dinner first.

Nally's Pub, she thought. Well, at least it didn't sound fancy.

She answered: Solid.

She finished the board, started to program more coffee for study and thinking time. Peabody clomped back in with an evidence box.

'Points for McNab,' she said. 'He found a contact tagged multiple times on the desk drawer personal. Tagged last at seventeen-twelve yesterday. Two-minute conversation with one Oliver Printz re limo pickup at McEnroy's residence at eleven-fifteen.

'And points for me,' Peabody added as she put the box on Eve's desk, then swiped a check mark in the air. 'Because I recognized Printz as McEnroy's usual driver through Urban Ride.'

'So Printz worked off the books.' She'd print out his ID shot, add it to her board. 'We need to talk to him. Have him brought in. Use the potential witness to a crime deal, but get him in.'

She unsealed the box. 'And shut the door.'

'You're going to review the discs.'

'I'm going to look at a sample, yeah, so shut the door.'

With a nod, Peabody backed out, shut the door.

Eve slid one of the discs into her unit, ordered play.

The McEnroy bedroom flashed on-screen, the bed neatly turned down. She heard voices, a man's, a woman's.

'No, in here,' it said as McEnroy came on-screen. The woman – redhead, late twenties – wrapped around him, rubbed against him.

'Anywhere. Everywhere.'

He took her wrists, turned her more toward the camera. 'What do you want, Jessica?'

'You. I want you.'

'More than anything?'

'Yes, yes! Nigel, please. I can't wait.'

'More than the position at Broadmoore?'

'More than anything.'

'Show me. Strip for me.'

She wore a simple black dress jazzed up with a thick silver belt, silver needle-thin heels. Her body quivered, her hands shook as she stripped down to bra and panties.

'Hold there.'

He stepped out of camera range while she shuddered, ran those shaking hands over her own body, begged him to touch her.

He came into range holding two glasses of wine. 'A drink.'

'I don't need wine, just you. Oh God, Nigel, please.'

'Drink.'

Dosed it with more, Eve thought as the redhead obeyed.

'That's enough for now.' He set her glass aside. 'On your knees, Jessica. Me first. You want to pleasure me, don't you?'

She dropped down, dragged his pants down. And while she fellated him, he sipped his wine.

She watched for thirty minutes, through to him taking her to the bed while she all but wept with need. Where he asked — oh so polite — if she was adventurous, if he could tie her to the bedposts. She agreed to everything he asked, begged for more.

Then she skipped to the end where he stood in a robe, obviously freshly showered, and she sprawled, pale and heavy-eyed, on the bed.

'Get dressed and go.'

'What? I don't feel very well. I feel . . . '

'I'm done with you. You can catch a cab at the corner or walk to the subway.'

'I don't know where I am.' She looked around, a woman still caught in a dream. But she got up, swaying, stumbling, put on her clothes. 'At the corner.'

'That's right.' He took her arm. 'You'll take the elevator straight down to the garage — you understand.'

'Garage.'

'Walk out, turn left, walk to the corner for a cab. You'll do very well at Broadmoore, Jessica. You have talent.'

'Broadmoore.'

The vid stopped. After a few seconds, another started. Same bedroom, same setup. Another redhead.

Eve stopped the play.

So he had a type.

Rising, she started to program coffee, then changed to water, cold.

She opened her door again, as it would take hours to review the discs.

Checking the memo book she found three Jessicas, a Jessie, and a Jess.

She brought up PP's files, ran a search on Broadmoore and Jessica.

It turned out Broadmoore, a company specializing in high-end kitchen and bathroom designs and furnishings, with its headquarters on the Upper East Side, had hired Jessica Alden the previous fall, through PP, as a marketing executive.

She was finishing an initial run on Alden when Peabody came back. 'Printz is coming in.'

'Good. He has a type. He likes redheads.'

'Quirk's a brunette.'

'She wasn't in her ID shot from a year ago. Red. I've got a Jessica Alden, redhead, on disc. He takes his time, makes sure they get plenty of camera time. He likes them to beg, and when he's done, he basically kicks them out. He gave her two doses, as far as I could tell, once he had her in the bedroom, just to keep her going. Bring her in.'

'All right. Listen . . . I can book a conference room, take some of the discs for review.'

'Do that. Note the name if he uses one, any company or business he might mention, cross-check it to nail it down. Otherwise we'll use face recognition. Zip through,' Eve added. 'There's no point in watching what he does unless it shifts pattern. We don't need evidence against him – he's dead. We just need to ID his victims. Get started.'

She gestured to the box. 'He's got multiples on each disc. We'll break off when Printz gets here. Then Alden. If this holds, we're going to be talking to a lot of rape victims as murder suspects, so get ready for that.'

She'd go through a couple more, Eve decided, closed the door again, went back to coffee. Zipping through as she'd advised Peabody, she identified two more, had one marked for facial recognition.

She shut it down at the knock on her door.

Detective Trueheart, fresh of face, stood outside. 'Sorry, Lieutenant, but an Oliver Printz is here to see you.'

'Good. Can you put him in an interview room, let Peabody know? I need another minute.'

'Sure. Ah, should I close the door?'

'No, that's all right.'

She replaced the discs, tagged the one she'd completed, resealed the box, initialed it. Then she put together a file before walking out to the bullpen.

'He's in Interview B, Lieutenant. Peabody's on her way.'

'Thanks, Detective.'

Eve detoured to the bathroom, let herself breathe while she splashed cool water on her face. Then stood another moment until the faint nausea faded off.

She met Peabody outside the Interview door. 'He's not a suspect,' Eve began, 'but may be complicit in McEnroy's ugly hobby. If so, we're going to nail him for it. But what we get out of him, absolutely, is where he took McEnroy last night.'

'Can I go hard? Watching that disc . . .'

'Take the lead.'

'Really?'

'Jesus, Peabody, it's an interview, not an ice-cream cone for being a good girl. Take the fricking lead.' She shoved the file at her partner, opened the door.

'Mr Printz.' Peabody started off with a sober nod. 'Thank you for coming in so quickly.'

'Don't know what it's about. Can't remember seeing anything like a crime.'

Peabody nodded again, took a seat.

He had a good look for a limo driver, Eve thought. Clean-cut, well-dressed, mid-forties. He kept his hands folded on the table, and his quiet face impassive.

'I'm Detective Peabody and this is Lieutenant Dallas. We're going to record this interview.'

'Inter— Record?'

'Yes.' Peabody pushed on, clipped, all business. 'Record on. Dallas, Lieutenant Eve, and Peabody, Detective Delia, in Interview with Printz, Oliver. Are you aware of the death of one of your regular clients?'

'What?' That impassive face registered shock. 'Who?'

'You don't watch or listen to media reports, Mr Printz?'

'I do, of course. But I've been running clients all day. Or lord, was it Ms Kinder? She's been looking awfully frail lately.'

'No. Nigel McEnroy.'

Now he went sheet white. 'Mr McEnroy died?'

'Was murdered in the early hours of the morning,' Peabody corrected in that same clipped tone. 'That would be sometime after you, off the books, picked him up at his residence.'

'I – I— Oh my God.'

'Can you account for your whereabouts between nine P.M. and four A.M., Mr Printz?'

'I – I—' He held up a hand as if to stop traffic. 'Did it happen in the club? He texted me that he didn't need me. He usually . . . '

'Usually what?' Peabody demanded, and now her voice lashed. 'If you even contemplate considering to think about lying, I'm tossing you in a cage with charges of accessory, before and after, to multiple rapes.'

'To what?' His eyes bulged in shock. 'To *rape*! This is crazy.'

'Whereabouts, Printz, or I'm reading you your rights, and we're going to get real serious real fast.'

'I picked Mr McEnroy up at nine-fifteen, or very close to that, at his building, his residence. I took him to This Place – that's the name of the club. I took him there, dropped him off, and I went home. He said he'd tag me when he was ready, but he texted he didn't need me. I was home with my wife, my two kids. I was home the rest of the night. I never raped anyone in my life! I'm a family man. I have a daughter.'

'Then you just stood by when McEnroy drugged and raped women?'

'I don't know what you're talking about.' He lifted a shaking hand to loosen the knot of his tie. 'I swear to God, I don't know what you're talking about.'

'How many times did you pick up Mr McEnroy and a woman at a club, deliver them to his residence or the Blake Hotel?'

'I couldn't tell you.' Printz took a couple of wheezing breaths. 'Often. Often, but he didn't rape them. I wouldn't have stood for it! They were maybe a little drunk, but that's not my business. He was cheating on his wife, and I don't approve, but that's not my business.'

'Is cheating your employer your business?'

He flushed, even cringed a little. 'It's not right, working off the books. Plenty of us do it, but that doesn't make it right. Mr McEnroy's a good customer, a good tipper, and . . . he was persuasive. My girl's going to college in two years, and the tuition . . . '

Face hard, Peabody brushed the excuses off like gnats. 'How much did he pay you to look the other way when he assaulted women?'

'I'd never do that. Never! He'd bring a woman out, different women, different clubs. But they were willing. He didn't make them get in the car, make them get out and go with him. Usually they were, well, all over him.'

Peabody kept cold eyes on his face. 'Did you subsequently drive the willing women home or to another location after McEnroy had finished with them?'

'No. Never. Look, when he went to a club, he gave me five hundred a night. It's a lot of money for a couple quick runs. But ten times that wouldn't have been enough for me to look the other way if he'd been hurting anybody. Any of the women he brought into my car, you could ask. They'd get in. I'd keep the privacy screen up, because that's what he wanted. But they'd get in on their own, and get out where he took them on their own.'

Eve finally spoke. 'Did you pick him up or take him to anywhere other than a club where he had a woman other than his wife with him?'

'Sure, sure, at a restaurant or at his office. But those would be on the books, and it's the same deal. She'd get in and out on her own. I never, I swear on my life, I never saw him force anyone. He was always so polite.'

'And she was always a little drunk?'

'I . . . I guess you could say. Driving people's my job. A lot of them might be a little drunk, or even a lot. It's my job to take them where they want to go safely. I've been driving professionally for twelve years. You can look at my record. Not one complaint. Mr McEnroy asked me to do this, and keep it between us. It was wrong, and I could lose my job over it, but that's all I did.'

Eve sat back, glanced at Peabody. 'Okay, Mr Printz, I bet you keep decent personal records. You're going to dig into those and show us the times, the dates and locations when you drove McEnroy off the books.'

'I can do that. Yes, I can do that.'

When they let the very cooperative and deeply shaken Printz go, Eve cocked a brow at Peabody.

'I believe him. Down the line,' Peabody added. 'He saw what probably other people saw. A man and a woman, a little drunk, a lot loose after some clubbing, heading off to have a bunch of sex.'

'Printz made the mistake a lot of people do. Sure, it's breaking the rules, but who does it hurt? And I can use the money. But he's no killer, he's no rape apologist, either. And otherwise?'

Peabody looked blank. 'Otherwise?'

'Why didn't McEnroy tag Printz for the pickup from the club, as arranged? As was his pattern?'

'Oh, okay. So the killer persuaded him to walk, maybe? Or the killer had the transportation.'

'It's going to be the second – more people see you walking, and why let more people see you? Pattern, Peabody, why does McEnroy break it, why does he give up the control of his own car and driver when all of this is about him having the controls?'

'Maybe he knew the killer, trusted the killer. The text to Printz came in just before midnight, so McEnroy was, probably, already incapacitated, and the killer sent the text. So . . .'

'This was planned, carefully. She — because the killer's going to be female — had to get McEnroy to her chosen location, with her in control. How did McEnroy get women into his transpo, and to his locations?'

'He drugged them. She drugged him at the club. Turned the tables, used his own methods.'

'Roofied him,' Eve agreed. 'Added more in the transpo — Morris got tox back. We'll check out This Place after we talk to Jessica Alden. We might hit some luck, get a description of his killer.'

'We're in some luck now,' Peabody said as she checked her communicator. 'Alden just got here.'

'We'll keep the room. Go ahead and bring her in.'

'I'm getting a fizzy.' Peabody rose. 'You want a cold one?'

'Pepsi works. Offer Alden whatever she wants. We'll start friendly.'

Eve tucked the fresh printouts gleaned from Printz in the file, cross-checked her notes on the time stamp of the vid she'd watched. Alden coordinated with a nine-thirty pickup at La Cuisine, a restaurant on the Upper West, the previous September.

Take the candidate — for job placement, for rape — to dinner, slip a little something in her drink, walk her out to the limo, slip her a little more on the drive home. Into the lobby, the penthouse elevator, up to the bedroom, where the camera's already set up.

She sat back, caught a glimpse of herself in the two-way glass.

Maybe she looked a little pale, she admitted, but she'd been at this since before dawn. And she'd forgotten to grab anything for lunch. No, she'd worried she wouldn't be able to stomach anything, she corrected.

She'd fix that, she promised herself. She wasn't going to fall into the comparison trap. She wouldn't let old wounds start throbbing again, old memories cloud her judgment or objectivity.

She had a job to do.

When the door opened, she had the file open as if reviewing the contents. She closed it when Peabody shut the door behind Alden.

The curvy redhead wore a good suit in pale blue, ankle-breakers covered with a floral pattern, and an expression of mild annoyance.

'Lieutenant, Ms Alden.'

Without waiting, Jessica sat down, tapped the tube of sparkling water on the table. 'Coming down here's put a hitch in my day. I heard the news about Nigel McEnroy, and it's shocking. But you can't be talking to everyone who ever worked through Perfect Placement.'

Maybe not so friendly then, Eve thought, and cracked the tube Peabody handed her. 'Not everyone, no. Just those we believe may have reason to want McEnroy dead.'

'Why in God's name would I want him dead? I barely knew the man. I was headhunted by PP, but I worked primarily with Sylvia Brant. I don't think I met with McEnroy more than three or four times.'

Eve went with the faintest of smirks. 'You did a lot more than meet with him last September eighteenth.'

'What?'

'Dinner at La Cuisine ring any bells?'

That drew Jessica's eyebrows together. Beneath them her eyes, a gold-flecked brown, went momentarily blank. 'What? Oh, yes.' The mild annoyance returned. 'Of course, last September. I was one of the two candidates up for the position I now hold at Broadmoore. He – McEnroy – he was in New York to weigh in on the placement, and we had a business dinner. A business dinner,' she repeated, and rubbed her left hand up and down her right arm.

'And after the business dinner you went with him to his home.'

'I certainly did not!' Hot color flashed into her cheeks. 'Are you actually implying I slept my way to my position? That's not only a lie, but an insulting one. I've worked hard to reach this point in my career, and I don't sleep around, or use sex for advancement. Add to it, he's married, has kids. And I was in a serious relationship.'

'What did you do after the business dinner?'

'I . . . I walked to the corner.' She cracked her own tube with a quick snap. 'I walked to the corner, got a cab, went home. I haven't seen or spoken to Nigel McEnroy since that night. Since . . . I went home.'

'What's the last thing you remember before you walked to the corner? Look at me,' Eve demanded. 'The last thing.'

'I . . . I wasn't feeling well. Nerves, that's all. The job was a big upgrade for me, so I was nervous. It was months ago.' She snapped it out like she'd snapped the tube. 'Why would I remember every detail?'

'You remember nothing,' Eve corrected, but gentled her tone. 'You don't remember, not clearly, even leaving the restaurant. You don't remember getting in the limo McEnroy had waiting.'

'I didn't.' But a tremor shivered into her voice. 'It would be unprofessional. I took a cab home.'

'After.' Even more gently now. 'Because he told you to. Jessica, you were one of many.'

I know what it's like, Eve thought, to block it out, all of it out to survive. I know what it's like when it floods back, when the walls break down, and it all lands in your chest like an avalanche.

'I don't know what you're talking about.'

Eve leaned to Peabody, murmured in her ear, 'Get Mira if she's available, or whoever she recommends as a rape counselor.'

Peabody rose, moved quickly.

'He drugged you.' Eve said it fast, fast was best. 'You did nothing unprofessional, nothing wrong. You did nothing because he drugged you, just as he did other women.'

'You're trying to say he ... he gave me a roofie, raped me? No, no, no, I'd remember!' Jessica insisted with the fierceness of desperation. 'I would remember. I'd have sued his ass off. I'd have gone to the police. I—'

Eve got up, walked around the table to sit next to her. 'He

drugged you, so none of it's clear, and what bits and pieces worked through, you blocked out.'

'You're saying he recommended me for my position because he raped me?'

'No, no I'm not. You were going to get the position, on your qualifications. One had nothing to do with the other. The bits and pieces, you told yourself they were anxiety, or weird dreams.'

'There's a room, and the birds – they fly out of the chairs, fly around the room screaming. Someone's inside me, and I can't stop it. I don't want to stop it, but I'm screaming, too.' She gripped Eve's hand. 'When I heard he was dead, when I heard the report this morning, I . . . I felt, just for a second, I felt satisfaction. It was horrible. But I don't remember. You can't be sure.'

Eve thought about the vid. Not now, she decided. 'We've talked to other women. He did this to other women. He had a pattern, Jessica. Did you talk to anyone about that night? How you didn't feel well, how you took a cab home?'

'No, not even Chad. I was ashamed because I thought I must've gotten ill at dinner, maybe behaved oddly. I couldn't remember, and I thought it must've been something I ate, or nerves. I told Chad it went great, but I didn't want to talk about it and jinx it. I lied, the first lie I told him.'

She squeezed her eyes shut, tightly shut.

'I told him others after. We were going to move in together. We were looking for a bigger place so we could move in together. But after that night I couldn't stand for him to touch me. I didn't want to hear his voice, or smell his smell. I couldn't stand being touched so I pushed him away. We lost it, what we had.'

She wept as she spoke now, silent tears streaming as she choked out the words. 'I got the job, and I told him I had to focus on my career. He said I broke his heart. What do I do now?'

'Start healing.' Eve glanced over as Peabody came back.

'Mira,' Peabody said simply, and Eve nodded.

'We have someone who'll help you.'

'I can take you.' Peabody offered Jessica her hand. 'You can come with me.'

'I need to say it out loud.' After dragging in a few breaths, Jessica swiped the tears from her face. 'I was raped. Nigel McEnroy raped me. Now I feel sick.'

'We'll stop by the ladies' room on the way. Here, let me take your water.'

With a compassion and efficiency Eve admired, Peabody slipped an arm around Jessica's waist, led her from the room.

Because she felt a little sick herself, Eve rose. She wanted her office, door closed, ten minutes with her head on her desk to just breathe through it.

As she passed through the bullpen, Santiago popped up from his desk. 'Hey, boss, Carmichael and I've got one we need to walk through with you.' He hesitated as he studied her face. 'You okay?'

'Fine. Come on back.'

'We can do it later.'

'It's fine now. Let's go, I've got my own to walk through.'

She went to her office, got more coffee, and did her job.

6

This Place didn't officially open its doors until eight – and anyone who arrived before nine earned a wheeze status – but Eve arranged an interview with key staff on-site.

'Even if I could get past the door,' Peabody commented, 'I couldn't afford the cover price in a club like this, much less a drink.'

'Lucky you don't have to shell out either then.' Eve held her badge to the security scanner.

Locks disengaged; the door swept open.

The man who did the sweeping hit six-four with a scarecrow build inside New York black. His hair – shaved on the left side to show off a scalp tattoo of a bleeding heart – fell ruler straight to his right shoulder in pure white.

He had eyes like green lasers, a silver incisor, and nails painted as black as his skin suit.

'Ladies.' His voice was like the pipe of a flute. 'Welcome to This Place.'

'Lieutenant,' Eve said. 'Detective.'

'And still welcome.'

He stepped back, gestured them in. 'I'm Maxim Snow, your host and the manager. I've assembled those I believe may be of most help to you.'

A whole bunch of cooperation, Eve thought, for a place Roarke didn't own.

She'd checked.

'We appreciate it.'

'Not at all. Mr McEnroy was a sporadic regular, and a valued guest, so whatever we can do to assist you in apprehending whoever committed this heinous crime, we're here to do.'

He gestured them forward. Under full lights the floor sparkled. Whatever drinks or bodily fluids had spilled on it during the night's revelry, not a sign remained.

Tables and booths gleamed, privacy shields swept back to reveal slick gel circles.

The air smelled just as spotless.

'You run a clean place, Mr Snow.'

'In every way we know how. Of course, This Place really shines at night. May I take your coats?'

'We're good,' Eve told him.

He led them to a table where the assembled staff sat.

'May we offer you refreshments? A coffee, a latte, some sparkling water?'

'We're good,' Eve said again before Peabody could accept.

'Well then, let me make introductions. Lieutenant Dallas, Detective Peabody with the NYPSD. We have Tee DeCarlo, head server, Edmund Mi, who works the door,

Lippy Lace and Win Gregor, bartenders on the level where Mr McEnroy engaged a privacy booth last evening. Please have a seat.'

They made an odd if diverse group. Snow, the gangly urban scarecrow. DeCarlo, with her frizzy ball of blond hair popped over a scowling face and a small, compact body in ragged sweats. Beside her Mi, with skin the color of gold dust, wore a snug black tank over tattooed, linebacker shoulders. The two bartenders sat together: Lace, young, pretty, black, wore her hair pulled back in an explosively curly tail, and a running tank and shorts showed off good muscles; Gregor, even prettier, played up the pretty by smudging up his eyes to enhance already long lashes.

'We appreciate you coming in,' Eve began, and DeCarlo let out a snort.

'Now, Tee.' Snow patted her hand with obvious affection. 'Be nice.'

'Don't like cops.' Her voice, in opposition to his flute, sounded like a foghorn with allergies. 'Gotta come into work on my time off 'cause cops say so. Don't like cops.'

'Tee, a man's dead.'

'People die every day, don't they? Get themselves killed every day, too, or else these two wouldn't have a job.'

Couldn't argue the point, Eve decided.

'Why don't we get on with doing our job so you can get back to your time off?' she suggested. 'You knew Nigel McEnroy?'

'Didn't say knew, did I? He don't look twice at ones like

99

me. He'd give somebody like Lippy a good look, but he liked the white ones. Redheaded white girls.'

'You saw him with women, redheads?'

'Not my job to see unless somebody wants service, but I ain't blind, am I? He'd come in, always had a VIP booth reserved in advance, and he always used the auto-order. Tipped decent, I'll say that, if he had cause to use a live server. He'd come in, troll the place, maybe send a drink over to one he had his eye on, or chat 'em up. Sooner or later, he'd take one back to his booth, and sooner or later, she'd leave with him.'

'Did you see the one who left with him last night?'

'Redhead.' DeCarlo shrugged. 'Like always. Didn't bother to leave any cash in the booth, either, even though we've got to clear it.'

'You saw him leave?'

'I caught a glimpse. We've got waiting lists for the VIP booths, so we need to turn 'em quick.'

'Who was in charge – McEnroy or the woman? You're not blind,' Eve reminded her. 'You've got a sense. You were keeping an eye, because once he gets a woman in the booth, they wouldn't stay too long. A drink, maybe two, then he'd leave, isn't that right?'

'Maybe. Maybe it seemed like she was leading him rather than the other way around like usual. But he was alive and kicking when he left, so what happened after isn't any of mine.'

'Can you describe her?'

'A redhead, big tits.'

'Tall, short, white, mixed?'

'Didn't pay any mind. Why should I?'

'What time did they leave? When did you turn the booth?'

'Jeez, how am I supposed to remember?'

'I can look that up,' Snow said, 'if you'll excuse me a moment.'

'Go ahead. You worked the door,' Eve said to Mi.

'Yes, ma'am.'

'Lieutenant. When did McEnroy get here?'

'He gets an auto-pass – he's on the list. I can't tell you exactly, but it was early. Maybe after nine, but before ten, for certain.'

'Did you see him leave with the woman?'

'I'm going to say, like Tee, I caught a glimpse. I looked twice because his car hadn't pulled up. It's routine, his car pulls up and he comes out, but his car didn't pull up, and he and the redhead walked out to where another pulled up.'

'What kind of car?'

'Wasn't a limo. I'm going to say a town car, but I didn't pay much attention. I was busy, and you just don't pay as much attention to people leaving as you do the ones who want in.'

'Can you describe her?'

'I'm going to say good-looking, a lot of red hair, and well, yeah, she had a body on her. We let in her type because it's good for business. And, hell, she slipped me two bills.

I think she was maybe French. She said, you know, *merci* when I passed her through.'

'Had you ever seen her before last night?'

'I don't think so, but it's real hard to say.'

'Would you work with a police artist?'

'I guess, but the thing is I see an awful lot of frosty women on any given night. I only remember because of the French thing and the two bills. I took them, but I was going to let her in anyway.'

A mistake? Eve wondered. Or deliberate?

'What time did she get here?'

'I'm going to say around ten-thirty, but I'm not real sure. I know they left before midnight because Blick spells me for my break at midnight and he was about due. I'm going to say when I caught that glimpse of her leaving with him, I thought how she didn't stay long for two bills, but I guessed she got what she was after.'

Mi shrugged those wide shoulders, then stopped, drew his brows together in thought. 'Oh, and now that I'm thinking about it, I thought how Mr McEnroy was maybe a little drunk.'

'Why?'

'Well, if I see him leave – not always, but if I do – he's got his arm around the woman he leaves with and she looks to have had a few, you know? This time it struck me as the other way.'

Eve decided the man on the door noticed more than he realized. 'I'm going to set you up with a police artist.

Peabody, find Snow and see about the security cam on the door between, let's say, twenty-one-thirty and midnight.'

Even as Peabody started to rise, Snow came back.

'I have that information for you. Mr McEnroy cleared his tab at eleven-fifty-three. He ordered a martini at the bar – your station, Lippy – at nine-twenty-nine, a sparkling water with lime at ten-fifteen, then two more martinis from the auto in the booth at eleven-twenty-six.'

'Thanks. If you'd show Detective Peabody the door security feed and make a copy for us, we'd appreciate it.'

'Of course. If you'd come with me, Detective. Are you sure I can't get you something? Coffee?'

'Well, I wouldn't mind a no-fat latte.'

Eve ignored them, studied Lace. 'Did McEnroy ever hit on you?'

'Not really, no. A little flirt, sure, but nothing real. It's like Tee said. He liked white girls – redheads, built redheads.'

'He always went to Lip at the bar when we were on together, even if she had a line going. Sorry, interrupting,' Gregor said.

'It's all right. So you interacted with him more than Mr Gregor.'

'I'd have to say. And if he went to one of the other bars, he'd go to the female. We talked about it, you know, just joking like. I didn't see him with anybody last night. I really didn't see him at all after he came up to the bar for his two drink orders – the martini, then the water. But ... I guess you could say that's his usual routine. Come, and like Tee said, too, sort of troll, walk around, get a drink. Then I'd see him order through the auto later – two drinks, sometimes three, then he'd cash out. I honestly don't remember serving a Frenchwoman last night.'

'How about you?' Eve said to Gregor.

'Nope. I chatted up these two blondes from Sweden, and a couple from Tokyo, but no single French ladies, not last night.'

'He'd occasionally buy a woman a drink, at the bar?'

'Sure. Now and then. He tips good, so you remember, even though he doesn't come in like every week. Sometimes weeks and weeks go by, then he shows. But you remember.'

'And when he'd buy a woman a drink at the bar, did you ever notice a change in her behavior?'

'I'm not sure what you mean.'

'Did she appear intoxicated after he bought her a drink, or more inclined to go with him?'

'Wait a minute, wait a minute.' DeCarlo slapped a hand on the table. 'You're trying to say he slipped something into the drink?'

'I'm not trying to say it, I am saying it.'

'No. Jesus!' Lace grabbed Gregor's hand. 'No, I never saw him do that. Ever. Win, Jesus!'

'You don't look so shocked, Mr Gregor.'

Shaking his head at Eve, he blew out a breath. 'I never saw it, but ... You know, the guy looked good, dressed good, but he wasn't like a vid star, right? I used to wonder how the hell he scored every single time he came in. He'd pick one out, move in, and later Tee or one of the servers, somebody, would mention maybe how he walked out with another one. I never thought ... but now.'

'You can't just say something like that about somebody,' DeCarlo objected. 'That's what cops do, they say shit about people.'

'We have statements from multiple women McEnroy drugged and raped. This was one of his hunting areas.'

DeCarlo's angry scowl crumpled. 'We're supposed to watch out for anything like that. We're supposed to make sure nobody tries to pull any shit with anybody.'

'He was good at it,' Eve told her. 'Kept the dose light here, or whatever club or venue he picked. Just enough.'

'I didn't see it,' DeCarlo murmured. 'I never figured him for ... He had that accent, that way. All charm, you know? I figured him for a player, sure, but not for this. Snow!' She pushed away from the table when the manager came back with Peabody. 'She's saying that son of a bitch roofied women right under my goddamn nose.'

'What?' He put a long, thin hand on DeCarlo's shoulder as he shot those laser eyes at Eve. 'Do you have evidence of this?'

'We do, yes, but we're not saying Ms DeCarlo or any of your staff was or is complicit. At this time we believe Mr McEnroy perpetrated these acts alone.'

'Win, be a friend and get Tee a soother from my office. Sit now.' He eased DeCarlo back into the chair. 'This isn't your fault.'

'I didn't see it. I got eyes, goddamn it. I know what to look for. I didn't see it.'

'He used the privacy booth,' Eve explained. 'He was good at it, and he was careful. He frequented a number of clubs, restaurants, following the same pattern. As far as we know, no one saw it. What they saw, if they noticed, was a woman, maybe a little drunk, leaving of her own volition with a man.'

'I can look back now, look back knowing, and see it,' DeCarlo muttered. 'The son of a fucking bitch.'

'Me, too.' Mi lifted his shoulders. 'When you know, you can see it. And when you know, you can see . . . last night, it was the other way around.'

'You mean she slipped him something?' DeCarlo's scowl came back. 'Good for her then. Goddamn it.'

'The individual who slipped him something followed up by murdering him,' Eve pointed out. 'And it's our job, my partner's and mine, to find her and see that she faces justice.'

DeCarlo let out another snort. 'There's why I don't like cops.'

When they walked back outside, Eve glanced up at the door cam. 'Can we use the feed?'

'We've got her at the door, but she's not stupid,' Peabody replied. 'We don't get a look, not a good one, of her face. A lot of hair, the killer body. We're going to be able to peg height and weight, and – I assume – Yancy will have something to work with between the feed and working with the door guy.'

'Set it up, and get me the best image of her, copy to my units. We're going to hit a couple more clubs, see if we can shake something, and the restaurant where he dosed Alden.'

She checked the time. 'Then you're off. If EDD has any more, shoot it to me.'

Once she cut Peabody loose, Eve hunted up parking near the pub Roarke had chosen. She settled on a second level, jogged down to the street to join the throng of pedestrians on the half-block walk.

She found the pub had a trio of skinny tables outside – and that Roarke had reserved one. A little cool yet for it, she thought, but the table heater took care of that. As she was early, she ordered black coffee and settled down to review her notes, write fresh ones.

'Still hard at work.' Roarke slipped in across from her.

'A lot of leads means a lot to tie together. Why don't you own This Place?'

'Happens I do.'

'No, not this place, the club called This Place.'

He smiled at her. 'Would you like to?'

'Not especially. It just struck me it's got some of your style and class. I hit two others you do own – also classy.'

He smiled at her, but she saw the way he studied her face. 'It's just been a long one,' she said.

'And more to come. We'll have a pint and some food.'

'I'm good with coffee.'

'Which is what you've downed, no doubt, most of the

day. A half pint for you, which won't hurt you a bit. I'll suggest you follow it with the fish and chips, which is exceptional here.'

A beer might smooth out some of the edges, she thought. And fish and chips never hurt. 'Okay, that'll work.'

While he ordered, she put away her notes. And when he simply took her hand, the wall she'd held in place all day crumbled.

'It was like his hobby, that's how I see it. I know it was a sickness. Nobody takes so many risks – personally, professionally – needs so much control over women, gains such satisfaction out of using them the way he used them without a sickness. But he treated it like . . . like a hobby, a serious one. The way some people treat, I don't know, golf, or crafting, or whatever. I'd bet my ass if he was alive, if I'd caught him, had him in the box, that's just how it would come out he saw it.'

'It's your job, Lieutenant, to know that, understand that, as much as it's your job to find his killer.' Those eyes, those incredibly blue eyes, looked straight into her. Saw everything. 'Empathizing with the women he used doesn't change any of that.'

'Empathizing isn't objectivity.'

'And bollocks to that. If feeling, relating, understanding isn't part of the job, well then, why aren't droids investigating?'

She frowned over that while the server brought out the beer. 'It's a line though, and some cases make it harder not to tip over on one side or the other.'

'You have excellent balance.'

'It pisses me off. He got away with it for years, using his power, his money to use, abuse, and humiliate to get his rocks off. And it pisses me off that someone decided to be judge, jury, and executioner. It pisses me off that some have the mind-set that taking a life is some sort of act of heroism. She – because it's going to be a woman or women – tortured and killed him and called it justice.'

However weary she might have been, her eyes went hard, went cop flat. 'And it's not, goddamn it. He's out of it now, isn't he? He suffered for a few hours, and now he's out of it, when real justice would have put him in a cage, taken away that power, that money, his freedom for years.'

He listened, nodded, sipped his beer. 'There was a time, not so long ago, before I met a cop such as you, I'd have tipped on her side of the line.'

'I know it.' She muttered it, scowled at her own beer.

'And the fact that I now lean more toward yours can still surprise me, but there you have it. And I see, too, because I know my cop, what else is in that heart and mind of yours, and you need to put that part of it away, as you're nothing like the one you're hunting.'

She started to object, then to dissemble, then just shrugged and drank some beer.

But he knew his cop, his wife, his woman, and pressed.

'You were a terrorized child who took a life to save her own. You suffered for it more and for longer than you'd ask of another.'

'I know what it's like to make that choice.'

Because the flash of fury that spiked inside him wasn't what she needed, he smothered it, and spoke in practical tones.

'And more bollocks to that, as it wasn't a choice planned or calculated, or even on impulse. It was live or die in the moment. Pity the child you were, Eve, and stand for her as you would for any victim.'

'I know it was self-defense. I know you're right.'

'And if you didn't still have these moments of inner conflict, you wouldn't be the cop or the woman you are. I'm madly in love with the woman you are, even though she's a cop.'

She started to smile, then sighed. 'Shit, shit. Couple walking this way – he's mid-forties, beige jacket, about five-ten, a hundred and sixty. Tell them to wait here while I get his wallet back.'

With that, she vaulted over the low wall to the sidewalk, zipped through the throng of pedestrians, and jogged toward the street thief making good time toward the corner.

She tapped his shoulder. 'Bad luck,' she said when his head swiveled toward her. As he shifted to sprint, she simply stuck out her foot, tripped him. He went down in a sprawl, coat flapping.

'Bad luck,' she repeated, whipped his arms behind his back, slapped on restraints. 'It was a pretty decent bump and grab, too.'

He cried, 'Help! Help!' so Eve just rolled her eyes, took

out her badge. Pedestrians veed around them like a fork in a river.

Since he flopped and squirmed – and would likely try to bolt even with the restraints – she just put a boot on his ass, called for uniforms.

By the time she wound it up, Roarke had the couple seated at the table with Irish coffees. 'Lieutenant, this is Mark and Jeannie Horchow from Toledo. They're in New York to celebrate their fifteenth anniversary.'

'Okay,' Eve began. 'Mr Horchow—'

'I never felt a thing! I don't know how he got my wallet.'

'He'd consider that his job. I'm afraid you'll need to go into the Fifteenth Precinct to retrieve your belongings, as he had several other stolen articles in his possession. An officer will transport you, and walk you through the process.'

'Oh my!' Jeannie, all bubbly blond hair and wide eyes, goggled up at Eve.

'I'm sorry for the inconvenience.'

'No, no! We wouldn't have even known, would we, Mark? We were just walking, and . . . We can't thank you enough. So kind!'

She glanced over as the black-and-white pulled to the curb. 'We're going to ride in a police car. Wait until we tell the kids.'

Mark laughed a little, rose, offered Roarke his hand. 'We appreciate it, very much. Thank you, Lieutenant.' He offered his hand to Eve. 'We really enjoyed *The Icove Agenda*. Who knew we'd end up being rescued by Dallas and Roarke?'

'Wait until we tell the kids,' Jeannie said again.

Eve waited until she watched them get in the cruiser, then since it was quicker, vaulted over the barricade again. Even as she sat, the server set another half pint in front of her.

'The other went warm,' Roarke told her. 'And you'd barely touched it.'

'Okay.' She touched it now, drank. Then she smiled. 'I feel better.'

He smiled right back. 'Thought you would.'

7

Body fueled, emotions settled, Eve rode up to the McEnroy penthouse with Roarke.

'And how do you want to handle the widow?' he asked her.

'I need to get a sense of her, and the tutor. From Peabody's take the tutor's going to be looking out for her as much as the kids. She's been with the family for years. She comes off clean, but unless they're both idiots, they had to know, at a minimum, Nigel McEnroy cheated routinely.'

'Some spouses turn a blind eye for any number of reasons.'

'Some do.' Eve turned her very sharp eye on Roarke. 'Me, I'd've strapped him naked to the bed, tied his dick in a knot *after* I'd slathered it with honey for the fire ants I'd have in a jar, which I'd dump out right on his knotted dick.

'But that's just me,' she added as the elevator opened.

'It is very much you.'

'Then I'd fly off to wherever it is they do the tango, and do that.'

'Argentina comes to mind.'

'Okay, there. Blind eyes are for wimps, idiots, or don't-give-a-damn-anyways.'

'None of which you are.'

'You, either.'

'Agreed. I might take a page from your book on whomever my adored wife might cheat with. Then I'd buy up every coffee bean in the known universe, and burn them, as well as the plants they grow on.'

'That's sick,' she said with feeling. 'Sick and inhumane.'

'Ah well, that's just me.' He took her hand, kissed her knuckles before pressing the buzzer on the McEnroy penthouse.

'Maybe it's a weird thing to say after that, but I'm glad we're us.'

The McEnroys are unavailable. Please respect the family's privacy at this difficult time.

Eve held up her badge after the comp message. 'Dallas, Lieutenant Eve, with civilian consultant Roarke. We have an appointment.'

One moment.

She waited for the scan, the verification. In short order the door opened. She recognized Frances Early from her ID shot. Mid-fifties, sturdy and attractive, mixed race. Tired hazel eyes assessed Eve before she stepped back.

114

'Lieutenant, sir, Ms McEnroy is still up with the children. If you'd come in and wait until she's able to come down.'

She caught the faint whiff of sweepers' dust though the living area had been ruthlessly cleaned to remove any other trace of the police.

'I've let Ms McEnroy know you're here. The children are understandably distraught, and she'll stay with them until they fall asleep. May I offer you anything while you wait?'

'We're fine. To save time, to ensure we don't keep either you or Ms McEnroy any longer than necessary, we can start by talking to you.'

'To ... I see. Of course. Please, sit down. I hope you understand I'm a bit distraught myself.'

'Understood. You were close, you and Mr McEnroy?'

Francie sat, ran a hand over a chin-length cup of deep brown hair. Her nails, Eve noted, glinted with bright pink polish that seemed at odds with her conservative white shirt and black pants.

'I've been with the McEnroys for eight years. I tutor the girls, help tend to them, travel with them and Geena – Ms McEnroy.'

'And you were close with Mr McEnroy?' Eve repeated.

Francie spread her hands. 'We're family here.'

Which didn't answer the question, but told Eve what she wanted to know.

'Mr McEnroy stayed in New York while you, his wife, and children went to Tahiti on vacation. Is that usual?'

115

'Due to his work, and his business travel, Mr McEnroy often joined the rest of the family at some point during a holiday. Or traveled alone. I came on as tutor so that the girls – though Breen was a bit young for schooling when I started – could continue their education while traveling. Most usually between New York and London, but we often accompanied Mr McEnroy on other extended trips.'

'Or didn't,' Eve put in. 'Meaning Mr McEnroy was often without his family here in New York, or in London, or Paris, or wherever his work schedule took him.'

'Of course.' Francie folded her hands with their pretty pink nails, set them on her knee. 'It was the nature of his business. As a result, the girls are excellent travelers. I want to add Mr McEnroy was devoted to his daughters. He often juggled his very demanding schedule to be with them, or bring them with him for birthdays, Christmas, and so on. He was a loving, involved father.'

'Was he a loving, involved spouse?'

Francie shifted, took a moment, then looked straight into Eve's eyes. 'I would prefer you discuss any marital business with Ms McEnroy.'

'I'm asking you – and you've stated you're family – your opinion on the nature of the McEnroys' marriage.'

'I won't gossip about my employers, or my family.'

'This is a murder investigation, not gossip. You were aware McEnroy had numerous and habitual sexual ... encounters outside his marriage.'

Francie's face went blank, but the knuckles of her folded

hands whitened. 'You're pushing me to say ugly things about a man who provided me with family when I had none.'

'I'm asking you to tell me the truth about a man who was murdered to assist in the investigation. To help find who killed your employer, who robbed a woman you're clearly fond of of her spouse, and the children in your charge of their father.'

Tears blurred Francie's hazel eyes. 'Their private life should be private.'

'It stopped being private when he was tortured and killed by an individual who accused him of multiple rapes.'

Her hand flew to her mouth. 'That's a vicious thing to accuse anyone of, and he's unable to defend himself from such a vicious thing.'

'I've confirmed the rapes, Ms Early Multiple. He kept records.'

'Oh God, oh my God.' She rose, hands pressed to her face as she walked to the wide window, back again, glanced toward the stairs. 'You're saying to me I've worked for, lived with, spent my holidays with a man who ...'

'You knew he cheated. I imagine his wife confided in you even if you didn't see the signs yourself.'

'There's a wide, wide difference. I don't have to approve of adultery, but can say and mean it's not my business. It's between husband and wife, and for them to deal with. Or not. But rape isn't ... They could be lying.'

She whirled back. 'Lying to try to extort money.'

'He kept records,' Eve repeated. 'He had a routine, and

he had a type. We also confiscated date rape drugs he kept in a locked cabinet in his office.'

She folded her hands again, and those knuckles stayed bone white. 'You're saying ... oh, if you're lying to me, I'll have your badge. You're saying Nigel drugged and raped women. It will destroy her, Geena. She's already shattered, but this ... Can you not tell her? She loved him, and she believed he'd stopped. Stopped cheating. She'd believed it before, but this time, she was so sure. She was so happy.'

'There's no way to keep this from her, and due to the multiple women involved, there's no way to keep it from coming out in the media.'

'Keep what from me?'

At the top of the stairs, Geena McEnroy stood with one hand gripping the polished rail, the other pressed to her heart. She wore a straight, simple black dress. Its mourning color accentuated her delicate beauty. Everything about her read fragile, from the quiet brown hair swept back in a knot, to the long neck, to the slender build. Her eyes, soft blue, were swollen from weeping; her lips, unpainted, trembled.

The only bright point came from her nails, glowing in hot red.

'The girls?' Francie asked.

'Sleeping. Finally sleeping.' Geena started down, hesitated, swayed.

Rising, Roarke moved to the stairs and up to take her arm. 'Let me help you.'

'Nothing seems real. It feels as if I might take a step and fall off the world.'

'I'm so very sorry,' he said as he led her to a chair. 'Shall I get you some water?'

'I— Francie?'

'Some tea.' Francie took a mini remote from her pocket. 'You've barely eaten all day.' Her tone turned matter-of-fact.

A smart move, Eve decided, as Geena looked as if she needed to be reminded to breathe in and out.

When the droid came in, Francie ordered tea. 'A pot, as I could use some myself. And perhaps our ... guests would like a cup.'

'You said ...' Geena looked around blankly, finally focused on Eve. 'I can't remember who you are.'

'Lieutenant Dallas, Ms McEnroy—'

'Oh yes, of course. The girls nagged and nagged to see the vid, the one about the clones, so I screened it. I thought it too violent and frightening for them. They're too young. I don't want them exposed to— But now. Oh God, now.'

'I'm sorry for your loss, Ms McEnroy, and I know this is a very difficult time, but we need to ask you some questions.'

'I don't understand any of it. How can I have answers when I don't understand? The girls ask and ask where their father went. Why can't he come back? Why did he have to die? Was he sick? Did he fall down? And I can't answer. What do I tell them?'

'That's for you to say.'

119

'But I don't know. You said someone ... but I don't understand why anyone would hurt him. Was it a robbery? Was it—'

'We don't believe robbery was a motive.' Deal with it, Eve thought as the droid wheeled in a tea cart. Stringing it out only prolonged pain.

'Your husband was killed in a location unknown at this time, then his body was transported back to this building and left outside. We've traced his movements on the night of his death. He left the building at approximately nine-eighteen P.M., took a limo to a club called This Place, where he had reserved a VIP booth. A privacy booth.'

'A – a business meeting.' Geena's voice wavered as she spoke, and her eyes pleaded for Eve to agree.

'No, not a business meeting. We've confirmed Mr McEnroy frequented This Place and other venues for the purpose of acquiring women for sexual activities.'

'That's not true.' Flushes of color, high and bright, rode her cheekbones. 'I won't have you slander my husband, the father of my children. I won't have it.'

Blind eye, Eve thought. Deliberately, desperately blind.

'We've confirmed, with evidence and with firsthand accounts, what he did, where he did it, and in many cases already with whom. You were aware of his proclivities, Ms McEnroy. Attempting to protect your husband now also protects his killer. It's my job, my duty, my purpose to find his killer and bring that individual to justice.'

'Do you think I care about your duty?' Her voice pitched

high as the color on her cheeks. 'You'd destroy a man's reputation for your duty? Destroy his family?'

'Your husband hunted women for sport,' Eve snapped out. 'He used them like toys. He drugged them, and in many cases brought them to your bed, recording the sex for his private library – and to humiliate them, to prevent them from taking action against him. Were you unaware of this?'

'You're lying!' She hissed it out, a venomous snake with terrified eyes. 'You're a liar.'

'Geena.' Roarke spoke softly even as Francie rushed over to sit on the arm of Geena's chair, wrap an arm around her. 'This is a terrible time for you, and these are horrendous shocks, one after another. Someone killed your husband out of a twisted sense of justice that is in reality revenge. The lieutenant's purpose *is* justice. She'll stand for your husband, work to find the person who took him from you and your children.'

'She's saying terrible things about him.'

'You loved him very much. That only made it more difficult for you, more painful when he was unfaithful. You understood, through all that, he loved you and your children.'

'He did! He did!' Weeping now, she buried her face against Francie. 'He wasn't perfect. None of us is perfect. He had a weakness, but he fought it. For me, for the girls, he fought it. And he stopped. He swore to me he stopped.'

'You have some tea.' Gently, Francie drew away, picked up the cup to press it on Geena. 'Dry your eyes now and have some tea.'

121

'He was so attractive, you see. Women were drawn to him,' Geena claimed as she obeyed and dabbed her face with a tissue. 'And with his weakness he sometimes . . . He faltered. It shamed him, and he struggled. But in the last year, he renewed his vows to me, and kept them. He swore it. And he never used drugs, he never touched illegals. He'd have no need to use them on a woman. He was magnetic.'

Eve let that slide for the moment. 'Did you speak with anyone about this aspect of your marriage? The difficulties you had when your husband faltered?'

'No one. Francie,' she corrected, reaching for Francie's hand, gripping it. 'She's family, and more of a mother to me than my own.'

'Anyone else? A friend, a therapist, a doctor?'

'It was no one's business but ours. It is no one's business but ours. If you try to say he did these things, used illegals on women, brought them into my home, I'll sue you for slander. Do you hear me? I'll go to your superior and have you fired.'

Eve let the fury, and the fear behind it, roll off her. Duty, she thought, couldn't always be kind and patient.

Could rarely be either.

'Would you like to see one of the vids? He liked red-heads, curvy ones. He kept date rape illegals locked in his office. Did he ever use them on you, with or without your consent?'

Shock came first, stripping even a hint of color out of Geena's face. But her eyes went hard. 'How dare you?'

'That's not an answer.'

'He did not. My husband loved me. Why are you trying to destroy what I have left of him?'

'Someone knew his habits, his routines, and used that knowledge to lure him to his death. If you told no one, someone else did or one of the women he used sought and found her revenge. If you lie to me, or hide information that relates to the investigation, you're obstructing that investigation. If you knew of and/or participated in his use of illegals for sexual compliance and deny same, you're obstructing.'

'I say you're a liar, a woman so blinded by ambition she would smear a good man, a family man, a father, to further those ambitions.' Fury forced color back into her face as she surged to her feet. 'I want you out of my home, and I'll see to it you're removed from this investigation if not removed from the NYPSD over this vicious vendetta you're waging against my husband.'

'Geena,' Francie began, but Geena shook her head.

'Get them out. Get them out,' she repeated, and rushed to the stairs, all but sprinted up them.

'I'm very sorry.' Francie twisted her hands together. 'She's not herself. Understandably. I'll talk to her, but I can assure you she knew none of this. He was so attentive, so loving to her and the girls.'

'But you knew.'

'Not about the illegals. I swear it. She's like a daughter to me, and those girls are my grandchildren in all but blood. If I'd known, I'd have told her. I'd have found a way. I allowed myself to believe he'd turned a corner and was faithful, but there were signs I ignored because Geena and the girls were happy.'

Francie paused, pressed her fingers to her eyes, then dropped them. 'I can tell you this, with no hesitation or doubt. She was telling you the truth as she knows it. She believed him, absolutely, and she would have told no one but me about the other women. She needed her illusions, Lieutenant, so she believed him.'

Francie rose. 'I'll talk to her. I'll do what I can.'

'One more question. Did you speak to anyone else about Mr McEnroy?'

'Whatever Geena shared with me stayed between her and me. He broke her trust time after time in the past. I wouldn't, couldn't. I never would.'

'Thanks for your time.'

'She'll want to see him,' Francie added as she walked them to the door. 'If not tomorrow, then soon. She'll need to see him.'

'I'll arrange it.'

Eve stepped out, started for the elevator. 'Don't tell me I was hard on her.'

'Well now, you were hard on her, but you had to know, didn't you?'

She jabbed the call button. 'Know what?'

'If she knew what he was about, if she had any part in it, overtly or by her silence. If knowing, she finally had enough and helped arrange his murder. Or simply cried on shoulders who might do it for her.'

Saying nothing, Eve strode onto the elevator, jammed her hands in her pockets.

'And now you know,' Roarke finished, and called for the garage level. 'So you can stop being hard on yourself for doing your job.'

Eve shot him a look. 'You gave her strokes and pats.'

'I felt sorry for her, true enough – as did you. But it wasn't my job to go hard. It seemed clear enough she's one who needs someone to lean on likely in the best of times, so certainly in the worst of them. She has the tutor, her surrogate mother, but it seemed to me she'd respond to a man. Was I wrong in that?'

'No.' Eve hissed out a breath. 'You're a hundred percent right, which is why you're the emperor of the business universe. You read people fast and accurate. You stay with someone who cheats on you, time after time, out of love – to a point. Love might be there, sure, but you really stay out of need, out of insecurity, out of not knowing what the hell else to do. She rings all the bells to me.'

'You don't suspect her of having a part in his death after this.'

'If you don't eyeball the spouse and eyeball hard, you're stupid. But she's about as low on the list as it gets. She didn't know about the drugs. I'm betting some part of her knew he was still cheating, but she buried that. But not the drugs. She was shocked, and an instant later, even though she went off, she knew it was true.'

'I think you're right on that.' Roarke led the way to the

car, slid behind the wheel. Then he turned to Eve. 'It's why she denied it so strongly. The truth makes it impossible for her to keep believing she loved and stayed with a good man. He was a rapist, an opportunist, not just unfaithful. And he brought the women he victimized into her home, into her bed. How does she live with that, how does she keep his light shining for her daughters if she accepts the truth of it?'

Tired, tired to the bone, Eve let her head fall back against the seat. 'She can accept whatever she wants at this point.'

'She'll go after you,' he warned as he drove out of the garage. 'The foundation of her world demands it.'

'Maybe. I'll handle it.'

'I've no doubt.' He went quiet, letting her think until he approached the gates of home. 'We joke about what each would do if the other strayed – and I admit you usually outdo me in creativity there. But the fact is we never would. It's not only love that keeps us faithful. It's respect, for each other, for ourselves. That's a bond that holds.'

'I know it. Still, I can be even more creative if you ever tested it.'

'And I know that.'

He shot her a grin as he drove through the gates.

The house rose and spread, lights gleaming in the windows. Its turrets and towers speared under a glass-clear sky that opened the night to the April chill.

Home, she thought, no longer just the house he'd built, but home. Because they'd learned how to make it one together.

'I thought, when I first moved here, it couldn't last. You'd realize: Jesus, what was I thinking with her? Or you'd start bitching about the job, the hours, and I'd start bitching about the wife-of-the-business-emperor deal, and it would all just go south.'

She turned to him as he pulled up in front of the house, then leaned over, took his face in her hands. Kissed him. 'It's really nice to be wrong.'

'I had moments when I wondered if you'd walk away, unable to accept who I am, who I was, what I've done. It's very nice, yes, to be wrong.'

When they got out of the car, he met her, took her hand. 'But then again, I knew I had you at the cat.'

'At the cat?'

'You brought Galahad here, and that I took as a sign in my favor.'

'Maybe I just wanted to dump him on you.'

'No,' Roarke said simply, and walked inside with her.

She shrugged out of her coat, tossed it over the newel post as Roarke hung his own in the closet. Then she simply stood there in the wide, quiet foyer.

'Problem?'

'I'm just waiting to see if Summerset slithers into view.'

Roarke rolled his eyes, well used to her digs at his major-domo, and started up the stairs. 'I let him know we'd be late, and would have dinner out. The night's chilly enough for a fire. I expect you'll want to set up your board and book.'

'Yeah, and more, I need to review more of McEnroy's

vids. We need to ID the women, run them, interview them. I've had the London cops hit his offices and residence there. I've got copies of more vids coming.'

They made their way to her office, where he walked to the fire, ordered it on low. The cat, sprawled in her sleep chair, rolled his tubby body over, stretched. 'You haven't spoken with his partners as yet?'

'On for tomorrow.'

Since Galahad deigned to jump down, stroll over to wind through her legs, she bent to scratch him.

'If I were going to kill the guy, I might try to cover it by doing it in New York if I lived elsewhere. So I've got travel to check.'

'Why don't I see to that for you when you have it ready?' An equal opportunist, Galahad wandered to Roarke, ribboned there until he got a good stroke. 'I've a few things to deal with, so you can let me know if you want that help.'

'I will, thanks.'

When Roarke went into his adjoining office, Eve programmed a pot of coffee. She poured a large mug, began to set up her board.

Drinking coffee, adjusting her board, she glanced over to where Galahad lay, once again, sprawled in her sleep chair.

'You know, he had that right − big surprise. I wasn't dumping you on him. I was bringing both of us home. You just got used to it faster.'

Once she had her board and book finished, she sat to open the file from London. And found a very helpful detective inspector had written a detailed memo attachment. She'd identified the hotel McEnroy used, statements from staff at the clubs McEnroy had detailed in his memo book – the London version also locked in his office there.

She'd also confiscated the illegals and all electronics.

Same pattern.

Moreover, Detective Inspector Lavina Smythe had reviewed a full dozen of the vids and run face recognition on the women.

Eve now had a list of names to work with, in addition to a comprehensive report. Smythe ended the memo with:

While Nigel McEnroy's murder occurred in New York City, he is now posthumously under investigation for possession and use of illegals, for rape, extortion, and abduction, all of which took place in London. We will arrange interviews with all individuals related to said investigation, and subsequently copy you on these reports. We request any information you gather in the course of your investigation be shared.

'You got it, DI Smythe.' And in that spirit, Eve wrote her own memo, attached it to a report, shot it to London.

She printed out the ID shots Smythe sent her – all redheads – added them to her board under a section she headed as LONDON.

She walked over to Roarke's office, where he sat working

on his comp, making minute changes to some weird-ass schematic.

'I've got a dozen names from London, if you want them.'

He glanced over. 'That was very quick.'

'London did the work. There's a DI Smythe, and if I'm reading between the lines, she looks at it like I've got the DB, but she's got a lot of female vics – potentially suspects, but vics. And she's going to see they get justice. So we'll share salient data. I can hope I get the same level of co-operation from Paris and so on.'

'I'm nearly done here so—'

'How can you tell?'

He merely smiled. 'Do you really want to know?'

She looked at the wall screen, the lines, curves, tiny notes and numbers. 'Absolutely not.'

'Well then. Shoot me the data, and I'll check the travel.'

'Smythe would probably do it, but—'

'As it's the middle of the night in London, she can have the information when she gets up in the morning.'

'I'm not going to think about stupid time zones. I'll send you the ID shots.'

Back at her desk, she did that first, then poured more coffee before she cued up the next vid from McEnroy's office.

The hotel room this time, obviously prebooked, as he'd already set up the camera. Another redhead, no surprise there, but Eve judged this one at barely legal age, and giggling high. He called her Rowan when he put on music, ordered her to dance.

Eve paused the vid, ordered magnification on the woman's face.

'Computer, run facial recognition on female subject. Resume video.'

Acknowledged.

She ran through the dance, the striptease in case there was any useful dialogue. Noted down the run time when he added a dose from a vial to a glass of wine, offered it to her.

After she downed it, the giggling playfulness ended, turned to desperate moans, grappling. Eve switched to split screen when he shoved the woman on the bed, mounted her.

She studied the young, pretty face of Rowan Rosenburg, age twenty-one, calculated the rape had occurred only two weeks after her twenty-first birthday. A student at Juilliard, Eve noted, living in New York for the past two years and originally from Vermont.

Eve ran the vid through to the end, tuned back in when McEnroy told Rowan to get dressed – and run along now like a good girl. She looked used and confused, but wiggled back into the sparkly club dress. She nodded, eyes vague, when he told her where to walk – away from the hotel, Eve noted – to take the subway back to the club.

When she stumbled out, he picked up his 'link.

'Text to Geena. Hello, darling! I'm about to escape from this tedious meeting. I should be home within the hour.

Let's raid the kitchen, shall we, for a midnight snack. I'm famished! See you soon.'

He set the 'link aside, glanced – smirking – toward the camera.

'Camera off.'

She cued up the next.

By the time Roarke walked in, she'd reviewed six, identified the victims.

After a look at her face, he walked over to open the wine cabinet.

'I'm working.'

He said nothing, simply opened the bottle, poured two glasses.

'How many more do you have to view?'

'Too many.'

He set her wine on her command center. 'I have the data for you. Why don't I take some of the vids, run the face recognition and so forth.'

'I can't. It's not right.' She gave up, picked up the wine. 'It's not right to let a civilian view them, even you. These women, their privacy – well, that's pretty much shot to shit already. But it's not right.'

With a nod, he turned to her board. 'What can I do?'

'He humiliates them.' She took a long swallow of wine. 'It's not just his ugly sexual gratification that gets him off, it's humiliating them.'

'Of course it is. If it was just to get off, he could and would hire a professional. He could engage a licensed companion who fits his needs. But that would put her on an equal footing, as that's a kind of partnership.'

He turned back to her. 'What can I do?' he asked again.

'You could take the six I've ID'd, run them. Check travel, employment, if they live alone, have a spouse or cohab. You can take it down a level, see if any of them have medical – a physical issue, an emotional one – after the date of the attack. It's a goddamn attack.'

'It is, yes.'

'She worked with somebody,' Eve muttered. 'It's damn near impossible to believe a lone woman pulled this off. She got him in a vehicle – who was driving? Could she trust using full auto? She brought him back to his residence, got him out on the sidewalk. Doing that alone? I don't buy it. Who is she close to – another victim, a sister, a spouse, a father, a brother? Someone she trusts.'

'I'll keep that in mind when I look at them. Send them along.'

'Roarke.' She sighed, realized she didn't know what she wanted to say. 'I appreciate it.'

She set the wine aside, cued up the next vid.

While Eve worked, so did Lady Justice.

Once a cheater, she thought as she again checked her appearance. This time she'd chosen a short, spiky wig, a honey blond tipped with sapphire blue. Her eyes matched the tips, as did the skin suit that dipped down nearly to her navel. She'd taken the time – quite a bit of time – to tint her skin in a color called Mocha Riche. She wore an appliance that gave her an overbite and a product that plumped her lips before she dyed them Rebellious Red. Her boots had scalpel-thin heels and lifts.

Thaddeus, she thought, liked tall ones.

She had to stop a moment, sit a moment, as even thinking his name enraged her. After composing herself, she ordered her droid to bring the car around. Before she left, she checked her beloved Grand on the monitor.

Fast asleep, with the medical droid on alert.

It had been child's play to hack into Thaddeus Pettigrew's 'link. The only glitch had been a change in schedule. The whore he lived with had left a day early, so the cheater had booked another whore for tonight. Not tomorrow night as expected.

Still, easy enough to change her own plans, to cancel the paid whore and take her place.

Maybe her hands shook a little on the drive, but she wouldn't fail. Hadn't she already proven she could follow through?

She had the droid drop her out front. And Thaddeus, a creature of habit, would have disabled the security cams – in case his live-in whore decided to check on him.

Any nosy neighbors would see what she wanted them to see.

When he came to the door of the brownstone, her heart actively fluttered.

'Good evening, Thaddeus.' She made her voice a gravelly purr. 'I'm Angelique.'

She offered her hand, and when he took it, smiling – oh so charming – she pumped the drug into his palm from the mini syringe in hers.

'Please, come in.'

'I'd love to.' She watched his face go slack. 'But I have a car waiting. Come with me. I have such an amazing evening planned for us.'

'With you?' he said, biddable.

'Close the door, Thaddeus.'

He obeyed, walked to the car with her. Inside, as the droid drove back uptown, she handed Thaddeus the wine she'd already dosed. 'Drink up! It's your favorite red.'

'Thank you. I feel a bit strange.'

'The wine will help.' She tipped it up, toward his mouth.

When his eyes drooped, she couldn't help herself. She drew him to her, kissed his mouth, arched under his hand when he stroked her breast.

And cradled him when the drug took him under.

8

Roarke wanted to tell her she needed sleep, but he let her be. It might be better, he considered, if she simply wore herself out with this one. And perhaps her sleep, when it came, would be quiet.

He ran the names she sent him, studied them, wondered if any of them would prove a murderer.

Students, businesswomen, chefs, assistants, technicians.

Some married, some not. Some city residents, some not.

Rowan Rosenburg was the youngest at twenty-one, with Emilie Groman the oldest at thirty-six.

So far, he added.

Eve sent him four more, and when he completed those, he got up to check on her.

She sat at her command center, the cat in her lap, studying the board.

'Taking a break,' she told him. 'The last one I did? She started to come out of it when he was finished with her. She started to cry, so he dosed her again, just forced it down her throat. He got her dressed, kept telling her she'd had a lovely time, but the party was over and she needed to go home. Told her where to get a cab. I don't know how he got her out of the house, she was barely functioning, because he turned off the camera.'

'Cecily Freeman?'

'Yeah.'

'She works in IT, and from what I dug up, was recruited by Perfect Placement for a position in Windsor Hotels sixteen months ago. Shortly after she took the position she engaged a therapist. She's twenty-five. She's gay.'

'They're all just bodies to him, wills to be broken, objects to be used and humiliated. It's all I can stomach tonight.'

'Good. You need sleep.'

'Freeman,' she said as she dumped the cat and rose. 'She was coming out of it, went into therapy. She might remember more than most. And, remembering, want payback.'

'Possible.' Roarke steered her to the elevator. 'She's five-four, a hundred and fifteen pounds. She'd surely have needed help.' He kissed the top of her head. 'Why don't we split a soother?' he suggested as they stepped into the bedroom.

The cat sprinted in behind them, took a flying leap to land his pudgy body on the bed.

'I was thinking of a soother.' She turned to him, turned into him. 'But not that kind.'

He wrapped his arms around her. 'Darling Eve. You're so tired.'

'I passed tired awhile back. But I need to let myself feel, let myself know, what sex can be. What it's supposed to be when it matters. I need to show you.' She brushed her lips to his. 'And for you to show me.'

He kissed her temple, called for the lights to dim, the fire to light. In that soft glow he eased back, eyes on hers, to unhook her weapon harness.

They could soothe each other, he thought as he set the harness aside. Perhaps he needed that gift as much as she.

He'd taken off his suit coat, his tie in his office, so she unbuttoned his shirt as he unbuttoned hers. As the shirts slid to the floor, he circled her toward the bed.

He eased her down to sit, to take off her boots.

When she reached for him, brought him close, the cat let out an annoyed grunt before stalking to the side of the bed and leaping down.

It made her laugh, curl closer. Then their lips met.

Slow, soft, spinning out the moment, saturating the moment with tenderness as the kiss deepened.

As she gave herself to it, to him, she wondered how she'd ever gotten through all the hard, dark days before him. Having this, arms to hold her, a heart to beat against hers, shined a light so constant, so steady, she could always find her way out of the dark and the hard.

She laid her hand on his heart, thinking: This. This, this. Knowing he gave her that heart, every day, changed the world.

As they drowned each other in the kiss, she traced the shape of his face with her fingers, drew in his scent.

This, she thought again, mattered. This held. This shined.

And closed all the ugly in the world away.

While the fire crackled, the bed sighed, he drew off her support tank to trace his hands over the long lines of her, the subtle curves of her.

He traced his lips over the sharp line of her jaw, over the slight dent in her chin, down the strong line of her throat to where her pulse beat.

He knew where to touch, how to touch to make that pulse quicken, thicken. As it did, as her fingers skimmed through his hair, he whispered kisses over her breasts.

Half dreaming, she breathed out his name, let herself float on the tenderness he offered. Giving hers to him as her hands roamed.

They built desire in delicate layers, clouds of sensation to shimmer. When he shifted, when their eyes met, she rose to him. She cupped his face with her hands; he slid inside her.

Joy, so simple, so elemental, flowed through her like a river warmed in sunlight.

He lowered his mouth to hers; she linked her fingers with his. Lost in her, he murmured in Irish, words that streamed from his heart as they floated on the joy.

Even when they slipped under, they held strong.

And so he showed her, as she showed him.

Later, with her curled against him, the cat a furry lump at the small of her back, Roarke felt her drift.

'There now, *a ghrá*,' he murmured. 'Only quiet dreams tonight.'

*

As Eve drifted, Lady Justice waited for the next scream to die away. After all, she didn't want to rush.

She stood, booted feet spread, one hand on her hip, the other tick-tocking the electric prod. Behind her mask, her eyes gleamed.

'Not such a big man now, are you, Thaddeus?'

Trembling, blood trickling out of his mouth from where he'd bitten his tongue, he lifted his head.

'Why are you doing this? Why?'

'Why? Let's see.' Head angled, she tapped a finger to her cheek. 'Because I can. Because you *deserve* it!'

She slashed the prod across his abdomen, watched him convulse, watched his naked body jerk and sway. 'You've really worked on that six-pack, haven't you, Thaddeus? Gotta stay in shape to screw all your whores.'

Sweat and blood ran down his face, piss down his legs. 'Please stop. Please. I can pay you, anything you want. I have money. I have plenty of money. I can—'

'Do you?' Rage burned through her like a brushfire. 'Where did you get all that money, you cheating, lying, thieving son of a bitch?'

All but shrieking it, she slashed, slashed with the prod, until his screams no longer sounded human, until those screams broke into wild sobs.

She had to walk away to compose herself. This wasn't to be done out of anger, she reminded herself, not out of hot fury, but cold-blooded justice.

'Confess. Admit you're worthless. Admit you're a liar.

A cheat. Admit you cheated and stole from your wife, a woman who loved and trusted you. Admit you cheat now on the whore you took over your vows.'

She jerked his head up. 'Admit all that, and I'll stop. I'll let you go.'

'Anything.' His head lolled to the side, so she gave him a light, almost teasing flick with the prod.

'Say it. Confess!'

'I confess!'

'To what, Thaddeus? Say it, say it all.'

'I— Tell me what to say. Please, I'll do anything.'

'Say you're worthless.'

'I'm worthless.'

His head lolled again so she had to give him a good slash with the prod across his cheek. His scream tore the air like claws.

She didn't mind a bit.

'Say you're a cheat.'

'I'm a cheat.'

The words, barely audible, garbled, pleased her.

'A liar.'

'Yes, yes, a liar.' A fit of coughing had him gasping for air. 'Please, I need water. Please, have mercy.'

'A thief. Say it, say it!' She shouted the words like triumph. 'You're a thief. A cheating, lying thief who stole from his wife to live on her money with a whore.'

'I – I stole from my wife.'

'You cheated on her, lied to her, stole from her, tossed her aside like she was nothing. Say it all!'

141

He struggled and wept his way through it.

She walked away again as he hung limp, half-conscious. And brought back the bucket and the knife.

'Now say her name. The name of the woman you betrayed.'

'Darla,' he mumbled. He opened his swollen eyes. 'Please let me go. You said you'd let me go.'

'I did, didn't I? Say her name again. Loudly, clearly.'

'Darla.'

She smiled at him. 'Look at me now. Look right at me. Guess what, Thaddeus. I lied.'

She used the knife.

Eve's communicator jolted her out of sleep. As she groped for it, Roarke ordered the lights on at ten percent.

'Block video. Dallas.'

Dispatch, Dallas, Lieutenant Eve. The mutilated body of an adult male at 26 Vandam, probable connection to previous homicide. Officers on scene.

'Acknowledged. On my way. Contact Peabody, Detective Delia. Dallas, out.'

She leaped out of bed. 'Fuck, fuck, fuck.'

While the cat complained, she sprinted into the bathroom, into the shower. Thirty seconds later, she stepped out as Roarke handed her a mug of coffee, then stepped in.

'I'm going with you.'

'There's no need for—'

'I'm with you.'

Rather than argue, she hit the drying tube, gulping coffee as the warm air swirled.

Moving fast, she hurried to her closet, grabbed clothes at random. Since it was easiest, she went with black all the way.

By the time she strapped on her weapon harness, Roarke buckled his belt – and managed to look elegant in black jeans and a thin, steel gray sweater.

'I'll drive, and you can check who lives at 26 Vandam.'

She didn't argue there, either. As she strode out of the room, Galahad gave them a glare with his bicolored eyes, yawned, then rolled over and went back to sleep.

Eve started the search while she jogged downstairs, grabbed her coat on the fly.

'I've got a Thaddeus Pettigrew and a Marcella Horowitz – single-family residence. Male DOB means that's him if it's the resident. He owns the house.'

As Roarke had already remoted her vehicle from the garage, it slowed to a stop as they walked outside in the dark, the chill.

He got behind the wheel, ordered two black coffees from the in-dash AC. Eve downed more coffee while he punched it toward the gates. Rather than wait for them to open, he hit vertical.

'I'm checking to see if I can find a connection – personal, business – with McEnroy. If this does connect, one way or the other, she's killed two in two days. That's fast work. Fast work.'

'A mutilated male body left at his residence? Odds are.'

'Yeah, well. I've got a Pettigrew in McEnroy's London office, but that's a Mirium, and no connection to a Thaddeus that shows. This guy was a lawyer, a partner in Moses, Berkshire, Logan, and Pettigrew. Looks like he specialized in financials, estate law, like that. Divorced, no kids. Ex lives Upper East.'

She kept searching. 'Might not be Pettigrew.'

'Odds are,' Roarke said again.

'We wait and see. Vandam. Quiet neighborhood. Upper middle class. Pettigrew can afford the neighborhood, since he rakes in a good annual with the law firm. And since he came into a windfall . . . the same time he got the divorce. Settlement? Fifteen-point-six million isn't chump change.'

She let it ride. Better to walk into the crime scene without theories or leans.

When Roarke pulled up behind the cruiser, Eve noted the cops on scene had put up the barricades. Even as she got out, she spotted Peabody, with McNab in tow, hoofing up from the corner.

She held up her badge, ducked under the tape.

'My partner and an EDD detective.' She gestured as she studied the body. 'Report, Officer.'

'We got the nine-one-one at three-forty-three, Lieutenant, and arrived on scene at three-forty-five. My partner's walking the nine-one-one caller down the block to his place so he can put his dog in the house. He was walking his dog, found the body. We secured the scene and the wit, rang the bell on the house here, knocked. No response. The wit said he thinks it could be the guy who lives here, but he couldn't be a hundred percent. Wit's Preston DiSilva.'

'Peabody,' she said as her partner approached. 'Take the nine-one-one caller.'

'Officer Markey's got the wit, Detective,' the uniform said to Peabody. 'His pup was getting pretty agitated, so Markey escorted him back to 22 Vandam.'

'I've got it.' She looked down at the body, back at Eve. 'Two for two.'

No mistaking it, Eve thought, and took the field kit Roarke handed her. Crouching, she opted to ID the victim first. No surprise there, she mused.

'Victim is identified as Pettigrew, Thaddeus, of 26 Vandam. McNab, Roarke, take the house, clear it. Check the security feed. There are outside cams. He lived with a female. Horowitz, Marcella. If she's in there, keep her in there. Just let me know if she's in there and breathing.'

As they moved past her, Eve settled into it.

'The body shows multiple and severe burns, welts, lacerations, contusions. Wounds on the wrists indicate restraints. It appears both arms are dislocated at the shoulders. ME to confirm. Possible COD, blood loss from the amputation of genitalia.

'Escalation of violence demonstrated with this victim

from McEnroy though method appears to match. As with McEnroy, a sign is tacked to the body, a poem.'

> He had it all but wanted more,
> So he cheated whore by whore.
> He lived through lust and lies and greed,
> The quest for money, sex, and power his creed.
> At last judgment called his name,
> And he has no one else to blame.
> LADY JUSTICE

Eve took an evidence bag from the kit, untacked the sign, slid it into the bag, sealed it.

McNab hustled out of the house on his plaid airboots. 'House is clear, LT. Nobody's in there, but it looks like somebody was expecting some company in the master bedroom. Fire's going, bed's turned down, a bottle of wine, two glasses, and, ah, several sex toys lined up beside the bed.'

'You sealed?'

'Sure.'

'Help me turn him.'

McNab stepped up to assist. 'There's a house droid, but it's been shut down since about nineteen hundred. And the security cams were shut down about an hour later. Roarke's taking a look, but we can't get anything from twenty hundred on. Jesus,' he muttered as they turned the body facedown. 'Somebody was seriously pissed off.'

'She went at him harder than McEnroy. Sodomized him

with the prod. She didn't go that far with the first. No time off between hits, either. Major escalation.'

She picked up her kit, pushed to her feet. 'Wait for Peabody, would you? And go ahead and call in the wagon, the sweepers. I want a look at the house.'

'Security hub's main floor in the back, off the kitchen. Droid station's there, too.'

With a nod, Eve started for the house. Nice place, she thought, three-story brownstone, well maintained. And with top-of-the-line security.

No sign of forced entry.

And, she thought as she stepped in, no sign of struggle in the entranceway. A long, narrow hall – a delicate-looking table along the left wall with a slim vase of fresh flowers on it.

'Vic was a well-built man,' she said for the record. 'If a man his size and build had put up any sort of a fight in this space, there'd be signs.'

She continued back – rooms to the right and left. Fancy living space to the right with what she thought of as a lot of fluffy, female touches. Lots of pillows, more flowers, dust catchers. Big wall screen in the room on the left, a built-in bar, read a bit more masculine.

'No sign of struggle, no visible signs of robbery.'

A formal dining room, a kind of little sitting room that didn't look as if anyone routinely sat in it.

In the kitchen, white as a laboratory with a lot of gleaming silver, Roarke stood examining what she thought of as a Summerset droid. Silver hair, bony face, black suit.

Roarke glanced at her. 'Just checking to see if anyone tampered with it, and it doesn't appear so. I can reengage him if you like.'

'I'd like.'

Roarke reengaged manually. The dark eyes of the droid flickered to a simulation of life.

'Scan the badge,' she ordered it. 'This is a police investigation.'

'I require a warrant as well to allow you access to the home.'

'No, you don't. Not when Thaddeus Pettigrew is lying dead outside.'

'I see. This is unfortunate.'

'Yeah, I bet he'd agree. When did you last see or speak to Mr Pettigrew?'

'Mr Pettigrew shut down my services at nineteen-thirteen this evening.'

'Is that usual?'

'It is not unusual. Mr Pettigrew had a light supper from eighteen-twenty-five to eighteen-fifty-eight, and ordered me to shut down after I had cleared the kitchen and dining areas.'

'Was he alone?'

'Yes.'

'Where is Marcella Horowitz?'

'Ms Horowitz left at ten-eighteen this morning for a three-day visit, with her mother, sister, and a friend, to the Water's Edge Resort and Spa in Hilton Head.'

'This was planned?'

'Initially Ms Horowitz was to leave tomorrow, but they were able to secure the accommodations for an additional day.'

'I need her contact information.'

Eve took it. 'Who was Mr Pettigrew expecting tonight?'

'I am not aware of any appointments for this evening or tonight on his calendar.'

'Why are the security cams shut down?'

'I am not aware.'

Droids could be handy, Eve thought, and sometimes not the least damn bit.

'Did Mr Pettigrew entertain women when Ms Horowitz was out of town?'

'I am not aware.'

'Did you take a bottle of wine and glasses to the master bedroom before you shut down tonight?'

'I did not.'

Dead end, Eve decided. 'You can shut down.'

'I ran the feed back,' Roarke told her when the droid shut down. 'I have Pettigrew arriving home, alone, at seventeen-twenty. Prior to that, no activity in or out between the time a woman – I assume Horowitz – left at ten this morning. The droid walked out with her, with a suitcase. It came back minutes later without. Pettigrew left the house just before nine A.M. He and Ms Horowitz shared a quite steamy goodbye kiss in full view of the camera.'

'Okay. I'm going up to the bedroom. You could check the house 'link, see if he talked to anyone, invited anyone over.'

'I can do that from the bedroom.' Roarke walked up the back steps with her. 'He obviously expected someone for a sexual liaison, but from the looks of the bedroom, he died unsatisfied in that area. At least here.'

Eve walked into the master. Lots of pinks and blues, lots of fussy details. A kind of decorative, topless cage held what she assumed would make a mountain of pillows on the bed. The large bed with its slim, gilded posts had been tidily turned down. Just as an impressive variety of sex toys had been tidily arranged on the nightstand.

A gilded table in the sitting area held a bottle of white wine – open, but full – two glasses. The fire – a small circle in the blue wall – simmered low.

A man's black silk robe lay across the foot of the bed.

'Looks like he had the evening planned out,' she said. 'And here's what it looks like. Someone he expected – or someone he wasn't expecting but invited in – got him out again without incident. Maybe slipped him something right in the entranceway or up here before he had a chance to pour that wine. But more likely downstairs. Why cart him all the way down and out? Have to get him out, into a vehicle, get him where you can spend a few hours torturing him.'

'Nothing on the house 'link on that today,' Roarke told her. 'There's a confirmation on the car service pickup for Horowitz, and a conversation with her mother – I assume since she calls her Mom. She had the 'link on speaker while she dressed. It's just chat about spa treatments and so on. Very cheery.'

'Yeah. So whoever killed him knew he'd be alone. Someone he knew or who knew his schedule. Horowitz's schedule.'

She heard Peabody clomping up the stairs, turned.

'The wit comes off straight,' Peabody began. 'He and his wife – two kids – just got this puppy. Adorbs! Anyway, it was his turn to do the walk – house-training deal. He said he was almost walking in his sleep, then the puppy got really agitated, fighting the leash, barking, whining.'

'Smelled the body.'

'You gotta figure,' Peabody agreed. 'So he's about to pick up the pup, and he sees the body. Called it in, and stayed back on the sidewalk until the cops responded. He says he didn't know Pettigrew or Horowitz, or not much. To wave at or nod at if he walked by.

'Meanwhile,' she continued, 'Officer Markey picked up another wit on the knock-on-doors that said she's pretty sure she saw Pettigrew getting in a car with a woman about nine.'

'A redhead?'

'No. She says short hair, brown or maybe blond, tipped with a darker color. Blue or purple or maybe black.' Peabody gave a shrug, knowing, as Eve did, some wits didn't register or retain. 'It was dark, and she wasn't really looking.'

'But she saw Pettigrew and a female?'

'She's not sure – not a hundred percent – it was Pettigrew

because when she glanced out he was already half in the car, but the car – black, maybe dark blue, maybe dark gray – was right in front of his house.'

'We'll talk to her. Or you go talk to her now, see if you can work more out of her than Markey. I'll contact the cohab.'

'Can do.'

'He'll have a home office. Since you're here,' Eve said to Roarke, 'you can help go through it. Maybe he has secrets locked away like McEnroy.'

'I do enjoy looking for secrets.'

Eve sat, and for the second time in two days, woke a woman with very bad news.

'Um, what? Hello?'

'Marcella Horowitz?'

'Yeah, what? Who is this?'

'Ms Horowitz, this is Lieutenant Dallas, with the NYPSD. Can you give me your location?'

'Is this a joke? I'm in bed, whaddaya think? It's like, what, six in the freaking morning. Who is this, really? I'm going to report you to the management.'

'Ms Horowitz.' Eve held her badge up to the screen. Marcella had blocked the video on her end, but she'd see the ID perfectly. 'I regret to inform you Thaddeus Pettigrew is dead. I'm sorry for your loss.'

'That's a horrible thing to say. Unblock video.'

Eve watched a woman with masses of blond hair rip off a sleep mask, glower at her.

'Listen, you—'

'Ms Horowitz.' Eve held up her badge again. 'I'm in the residence you shared with Mr Pettigrew. I am the primary investigator in this matter. I've officially identified Mr Pettigrew's body. Again, I'm sorry for your loss.'

'I don't believe you!'

But she did, Eve thought, she could see it in the shocked eyes as the woman, dressed in a silky red sleep shirt, tossed covers aside, leaped out of bed. The image on-screen bounced as she sprinted out of the bedroom, calling for lights, calling for her mother.

'Good God, Marci!' A woman in pink pajamas shoved up in bed. 'What in the world—'

'She says she's the police. She says Thad's dead. Mom!'

'Give me that 'link! Who is this?'

'Ma'am, this is Lieutenant Dallas, NYPSD. I'm sorry to inform you Mr Pettigrew was killed in the early hours of this morning.'

'It's a lie, Mom!'

'Hush now, sweetheart. You go wake up your sister and Claudia. Go on now.'

Sobbing, Marcella ran out of range.

'How?'

'I'm sorry, I'm not able to give you that information at this time. Your name, please.'

'Bondita Rothchild.'

'Ms Rothchild, it would be best if you bring your daughter back to New York as soon as possible.'

'You said Thad was killed. You didn't say he died, but was killed. Was it an accident? Surely you can say that much.'

Steadier by a mile than her daughter, Eve thought. 'No, it wasn't an accident. I'm Homicide.'

'Oh dear God.' She looked away as raised voices, sobs rolled toward the room. 'Yes, we'll come back right away. I need to go, to calm her down.'

'Contact me, Lieutenant Eve Dallas out of Cop Central, when you've made the arrangements to travel back to New York.'

'Yes, yes. I have to go. Marci—'

She clicked off.

Replacing the 'link, Eve spent some time going through the closets, spent more of it opening the jewelry safes in each. Good practice, she decided, even if neither had been particularly complex safes, and when both turned out to be exactly what they were.

Safe holds for jewelry, wrist units, a little spare cash.

She made her way down to the home office, where Roarke sat at a muscular workstation.

No female touches here, she thought. Another bar – a small one – a too-small-for-a-nap sofa in port-wine leather. A muscular data and communication center to go with the muscular desk.

Wall screen, a couple of chairs, framed degrees and awards rather than art on the walls.

'I've something for you,' Roarke began.

'Secrets?'

'One I'm going to assume is so. He has semi-regular transactions with a company called Discretion. That's a licensed companion broker. Every month or two, he places an order, makes the payment. It may be the woman he lives with is aware, of course, but given the circumstances it's doubtful. More,' he continued before Eve could speak, 'he ordered an LC for last evening, made the payment. It shows a refund, less cancellation fee. He made the payment two days ago, canceled it yesterday afternoon.'

'Canceled it?'

'You'll want EDD to have a good look, a more thorough one, but I'd say, on a quick dive through? His account was hacked.'

'Now that makes sense. Makes sense,' she mumbled again as she wandered the room, as she put it into her head. 'She knows, if she's hacked his system, Horowitz is leaving town, and he has a paid side piece coming in. She waits, cancels it, and she comes instead. Why wouldn't he open the door when he's expecting a woman? When he's got the wine, the bed, the evening mapped out?'

She spun around. 'Can you pin the hacker's location?'

'Possibly. That would be the location where the hack was done, and would take a bit of work. Someone this good? Well, if it were me, I'd use an unregistered portable and hack it from a remote location. Still worth the look.'

'Yeah, yeah, we'll look.'

'There's a bit more, not a secret, but a bit of a surprise.' He waited until he had her full attention. 'The fifteen million and change from a couple years ago? He got that from me.'

She stopped dead, stared at him. 'What? Why didn't you say you knew him?'

'Because I don't – didn't.' With a shrug, he rose. 'I acquired, as I do, a small company a couple years ago. More absorbed it, and it was done through lawyers and brokers. It didn't ring with me until I dug into his files. Data Point, it was. A private concern that manufactures droids and other complex electronics.'

Irritation flickered over his face – the sort she recognized came from him not being a hundred percent on every detail.

'I'll need to check on it all,' he continued, 'but as best I recall, the lawyer repping Data Point contacted one of my lawyers as Data Point looked to sell out. We had a look, the company seemed solid enough, the price was right – even what you could call a bargain. Pushing through my memory, I'm thinking the reason for it was divorce by the principals, but I may be projecting on that. I'll check on it. But, bottom line, Roarke Industries acquired it, absorbed the company and its assets.'

Complication, she thought, and advantage. She'd take the advantage and deal with the complication later.

'Did you meet them – the DB or the ex?'

'I wouldn't have on an acquisition such as this. A small one, as I said.'

She narrowed her eyes. 'Fifteen million is small?'

'Twenty-two, actually. It appears the ex-wife got the seven, but the matter was done through lawyers and reps because yes, in the overall, it was a small addition. A solid one, but not a competitor or a major deal.'

'I want whatever you can get me on it. The poem mentioned greed. He got double what the ex got, and that could be part of the motive. Sex, greed, power. We've got sex with his use of LCs – and potentially Horowitz replacing the ex. We get greed with the money. That leaves power.'

She looked at her wrist unit. 'I'm going to talk to the ex. Wake her up most likely. People don't have their shields fully engaged if you get to wake them up. I need to grab Peabody and get to it. Do you need a lift?'

'I'll find my way well enough. I may go straight to the office, get those details, as I'm curious about it now.'

'Get me what you've got when you get it.'

He walked to her, gave her a tug in for a kiss. 'I'll do that. Get yourself and our Peabody something to eat from the AC in your car.'

Distracted, she glanced back at the workstation. 'I'm sending McNab up. He'll have the unit transported.' Then she frowned. 'You're not dressed for the office.'

'Happens I have a suit or two on hand there. You take care of my cop, and see that you feed her as well.'

'Yeah, yeah.' She started for the door, glanced back. 'This is good information. Maybe, before you go, you can scan for a safe – I got the jewelry ones in the bedroom already. But maybe they have another. Maybe there's more good information inside.'

'More fun for me.'

9

She nabbed Peabody coming in as she was going out.

'Tell me in the car.'

'Okay, where are we going?'

'To talk to the vic's ex. I've got some information. Tell me yours, I'll tell you mine.'

'Okay, can I have coffee, too?'

'Two coffees.' Roarke's words echoed in her ears. Annoying, she thought, but inescapable. 'And there's probably food. Like a pocket or something.'

Thrown off, Peabody blinked twice. 'You want food?'

'Just program something easy, and start talking.'

Thrilled by the prospect of food, happy to oblige, Peabody searched the menu while she updated.

'The wit's cooperative, but she barely caught a glance. She just happened to look out the window when she closed it – she'd had it open for the fresh air, and it was chilling down. So she saw the car, and thinks it was Pettigrew getting in, but barely saw him. She said the woman was – and this is all maybe – on the tall side, really built. She noticed that because she was wearing a really low-cut skin suit. And her hair was short and dark blond or brown with darker tips. Purple or black. Maybe.'

'She can work with Yancy.'

'She said she would, but that she really only closed the window, then turned around and walked out of the room. She's not sure about the car, either. Dark is the best she could do, and I worked her, Dallas. She's just not sure. She says not a compact, but not a limo. She wasn't even a hundred percent on the time because she was doing little chores, but she knows it was at least nine because her kid was in bed, and she's got a nine o'clock bedtime, and it was the kid's window. She closed the window, told the kid good night, and went out.'

You couldn't always ask for detail, Eve thought. You took what you got.

'We'll check if Yancy's got the sketch finished on the first murder, maybe it'll jog something if we show it to this wit.'

'Like I said, she's cooperative. It spooked her, having a murder basically across the street. What did you get?'

'I got the live-in was with her mother, sister, and a friend at a spa resort — and unless they're all in on it, she's going to be clear for this, because I'm not buying she plotted and planned this and McEnroy. But we'll look at her.'

Eve glanced down as Peabody programmed the in-dash AC. 'They're coming back to New York. We found he likes to hire LCs, every few weeks, and he had one on the books for tonight.'

'Bang, big one. Low-cut skin suit could be an LC,' Peabody added. 'Or somebody who wanted to look like one.'

'I'd say number two. Bigger bang, Roarke says it looks like Pettigrew's system's been hacked, and the LC was canceled a few hours before she was due.'

'Two bigs. It's an omelet pocket.' She handed the crusty little snack to Eve. 'Eggs, cheese, bacon.'

'Fine.' Grabbing it, Eve took a bite, thought: Okay, pretty good. 'Possibly McEnroy's widow and Pettigrew's live-in made a deal, did the deeds, one doing the other. We've seen that, but it doesn't feel like it.

'Who was driving the car?' Eve added and took another bite. 'Somebody was driving the car because it would be crazy to risk putting it on full auto. Somebody helped with the body, somebody has a quiet, private place to do the work.'

'Plus, hacking,' Peabody said around her own bite. 'Somebody knows how to hack. You hire that out, you've got one more person who knows. It adds more risks, right?'

'It's very personal.' Weaving through traffic, Eve gulped some coffee. 'It's very specific. Men who cheat. In McEnroy's case, add rape. With this one, hiring sex. Both bringing the sex into the home. Drugs and humiliation for women for McEnroy. Greed for Pettigrew. He got the lion's share of the money from the sale of a company during the divorce. They had to both own it – I'm getting the details from Roarke. He bought the damn thing.'

Peabody nearly choked on her pocket. 'What? He knew the vic?'

'No, but he'll get the details.'

'You got all the bigs,' Peabody complained.

'McEnroy and Pettigrew are going to connect some-where. We need to find where they cross. How does she pick her targets? How does she know going in they cheat? Because that's the deal,' Eve muttered. 'That's the link. Maybe she was one of McEnroy's vics, but with this? Not necessarily. I need that consult with Mira.'

'I'll set it up. Two for two, Dallas. You've got to figure she'll go for the hat trick.'

'She'll have him selected already,' Eve agreed. 'She'll know his weak spot, use it. He'll be married, divorced, or seriously involved.'

She could see it. She could see it, but it didn't help.

'He has to have someone to cheat on. Both of these were heterosexual,' Eve speculated. 'Does that matter to her? Would she look the same way at a same-sex relationship, or someone who cheats with the same sex? Question for Mira.'

'She has to be attractive,' Peabody put in, chowing down – yay! – as she tried to work it out. 'Or able to make herself attractive. McEnroy targeted really attractive women. Redheads – maybe she is one, and wore a wig for Pettigrew. Or she wore a wig both times. Like you said, she needs to have or have access to a private place, and the transportation. She has to trust at least one person enough to help her. Drive, transport the body. At least one person.'

'One of them has hacking skills good enough to impress Roarke.' Eve tapped her fingers on the wheel as she braked at a light. 'The poems. That's a sense of drama, right? And a need to demonstrate she's enforcing justice. They deserved it, and here's why.'

She hit the gas, pushed through traffic. 'It's personal. She knew them, or one of them. Or she knows one on her list and hasn't hit him yet. But there's a man who set her off, started her on her crusade. She was tuned in enough to Pettigrew to move fast – when he switched his LC to last night because Horowitz got off a day early. She was ready to go, she had it all in place.'

'Well, Jesus, she'll have the next in place unless she's done.'

'Not done.' Grim, Eve swung around a lumbering maxibus, punched it in front of a Rapid Cab. 'She'd have, I don't know, signed off or whatever you'd call it if this was it. And she's escalated. She's into it.'

She fought her way to the Upper East Side through traffic thick and jagged as a pile of bricks. And did her best to ignore the blasting cheer of ad blimps announcing *Spring Sales! Top New Fashion Trends!* until she slid into the wealth and privilege of Carnegie Hill. In the world of dog walkers, au pairs, and chauffeurs, she pulled up to the security station at a set of iron gates.

Through them, only a stone's throw from the sidewalk, the house rose and spread, white limestone, tall, narrow windows, frilly balconies, dignified columns.

'Wow. It's no Dallas Palace,' Peabody decided, 'but it's pretty mag. She must've done all right with the sale of the company.'

'It's her grandmother's. The ex lives with her grandmother.'

The Callahan household, the security comp announced, **is unavailable for visitors at this time.**

'Lieutenant Dallas, Detective Peabody, NYPSD. We need to speak with Darla Pettigrew regarding a police investigation.'

She held up her badge for scanning.

Ms Pettigrew is not available at this time.

'Make her available or I'll come back with a warrant and we'll have this visit at Cop Central. Scan the badge.'

A red light shot out, scanned.

Ms Pettigrew will be informed of your arrival, Dallas, Lieutenant Eve. Please drive cautiously through the gates.

They slid apart with the faintest hum.

Eve drove through, parked in front of the wide, columned front entrance.

'Who's the grandmother?' Peabody wondered as they got out of the car. 'This place is abso-swank.'

'Some actress. Eloise Callahan.'

Peabody stopped dead, probably to avoid tripping over her jaw when it dropped to her feet. 'Eloise Callahan! *The* Eloise Callahan?'

'The one who lives here.' Both clueless and disinterested, Eve walked to the arched double doors, rang the bell.

'Jesus, Dallas, Eloise Callahan isn't just some actress. She's like a legend.' Thrilled, Peabody had to press a hand to her heart. 'She won like a zillion Oscars and Tonys and Emmys and you name it. And she was a total activist, too. She used her clout to help spearhead the Professional Parents Act, the gun ban. My granny actually marched with her. Granny said people tried to talk her into running for president, but she—'

Peabody broke off as the door opened.

Female droid, Eve thought after a moment. Seriously exceptional droid designed to mimic mid-thirties. Slim, attractive, with dark hair, dark eyes.

'Lieutenant, Detective, please come in.'

They stepped into a wide foyer with soaring ceilings. A massive chandelier hung overhead, dripping with elongated crystals in the iciest of blues.

The gleaming antiques – long tables, fancy chairs – the art – soft, sweeping watercolors – made her think Roarke would approve.

'Ms Pettigrew will be down as soon as possible. May I take your coats?'

'No, thanks.'

'I'll take you to the main parlor to wait.'

Rooms spilled from the foyer through wide archways. The main parlor had enough seating to hold about fifty asses by Eve's estimation. More antiques, more soft colors, lots of fresh flowers.

A fire simmered low in a hearth flanked by slim, carved

columns. Above it, above the thick mantel of natural wood, hung a painting of a woman about a decade younger, Eve thought, than the droid's simulated age and a man maybe four or five years older.

They stood, both ridiculously beautiful, with him behind her, his arms wrapped around her waist and her hands over his. She wore white, bridal white, Eve realized, an unadorned sweep that skimmed to her ankles. Her hair, richly blond, tumbled down. She wore a crown of flowers. Her head tipped back toward his shoulder. His black suit contrasted sharply with the white gown.

Looking as ridiculously happy as they did beautiful, they smiled off into the distance.

'Will you join Ms Pettigrew for coffee?' the droid asked.

'Sure. Great.'

'Please sit. We'll be with you shortly.'

Peabody waited until the droid walked out before breathing, reverently: 'That's her. That's Eloise Callahan. Jeez, she was just seriously gorgeous, right? And that's Bradley Stone. Big love story. He was an actor, too, and they met on set, and fell big-time. They got married and had a couple of kids. I think they were together about twelve, fifteen years.'

It didn't interest Eve in the least unless it connected to the case. But in case it did ... 'Love story gone wrong?'

'Well, yeah, because he died. He was filming on location, somewhere down South, I think, and some guy, one of the extras, I think, got a real gun on the set and just blasted away. The story is there were some kids in the scene, and he – Bradley Stone – shoved one of them to safety and took the hits.'

'He was a hero.'

Eve turned toward the woman in the archway. 'My grandmother never married again. Darla Pettigrew,' she said as she walked in, offered her hand. 'I'm sorry to keep you waiting, but I wasn't dressed for the day.'

She was now, Eve thought, in black pants and a light gray sweater. She'd clipped her brown hair back from her face so it hung somewhat limply down her back. Though she'd slapped some makeup on, she still looked a little pale, a little tired.

'No problem. Lieutenant Dallas. My partner, Detective Peabody.'

'Yes, I know very well. My grandmother's going to be disappointed she missed you. *The Icove Agenda* was her favorite vid from last year. She'd hoped to attend the awards, but she hasn't been well. Please, sit and tell me what— Oh thank God.'

She let out a rusty little laugh as the droid came in with a tray.

'Coffee. Thank you, Ariel, just set it down. I know you both drink coffee, as I've seen the vid myself. More than once,' she added as she sat and began to pour the coffee, 'since I spend a lot of time with Grand. She contracted pneumonia over the winter, and it's been a long recovery. She's still weak and needs considerable rest.'

'I hope she's fully recovered soon,' Peabody put in. 'I

admire her work, on all fronts. In fact my own grandmother marched with her at the first Stand Up protest in East Washington. Well, I think it was still D.C. then.'

'Is that right? She'll be delighted to hear it.' Darla handed Eve black coffee, doctored Peabody's, then added a splash of cream to her own. 'Now. Ariel said you needed to speak to me about an investigation. I have to admit I'm nervous and curious. Am I in some sort of trouble?'

Rather than answer, Eve pushed straight in. 'You were married to Thaddeus Pettigrew.'

A quick flicker of what might have been pain, a tightening of the lips. 'Yes, I was. We divorced two years ago.'

'Amiably?'

'Not really. Is there truly such a thing as an amiable divorce? We were married eleven years, together for thirteen. Unlucky thirteen, I suppose.'

'He wanted to end the marriage?'

'Yes. It's an uncomfortable subject for me, Lieutenant, and a private one.' Her mouth, her eyes, her voice all tightened. 'I can't imagine why you'd ask me about it.'

'Mr Pettigrew's dead.'

'What?' Darla's face went blank, as if swiped clean of all expression. 'That can't— What?'

'He was killed in the early hours of this morning. Can you verify your whereabouts between nine last night and four A.M. this morning?'

'I— What?' The coffee cup shook so violently in her hand Peabody reached over to take it from her.

'If you could verify where you were between nine last night and four this morning.'

'Thaddeus.' She pressed both hands over her mouth, began to rock. 'Thaddeus. Are you sure? No, no, it's not possible. It must be a mistake.'

'It's not a mistake.'

'But how? No, no. How can he be dead?'

'He was murdered.'

Her hands dropped, gripped the edge of the chair seat. 'Oh my God. Oh my God. That woman. Was it that woman?'

'What woman?'

'The one he left me for, of course.' She started to push to her feet, swayed, sat again, pale as death. 'Marcella Horowitz.'

'Ms Horowitz was out of town, that's verified, at the time of his death. I'd like to verify your whereabouts, Ms Pettigrew.'

'You think I'd hurt him, kill him? I loved him.' Now she pressed a hand to her heart. 'Despite everything, I loved him. He's the love of my life.'

Eyes brimming, she looked up at the portrait. 'I'm like Grand that way. We love forever. How did it happen? How did this terrible thing happen to Thaddeus?'

With her eyes steady on that pale face, those shocked eyes, Eve pressed. 'Your whereabouts, Ms Pettigrew.'

'Here. I was here.' Darla fumbled a napkin off the coffee tray, dabbed at her streaming eyes. 'I rarely go out. I told you my grandmother isn't well. I'm her primary caregiver.'

'Was anyone with you?'

'Grand, of course. The day nurse left at five. She's very pleased with Grand's progress. We took a short walk yesterday afternoon, then the nurse helped her bathe.

'I can't think, I just can't think! Oh, Thaddeus.'

'And after the nurse left,' Eve prompted.

'We had dinner about six, I think. Grand was already tired — she tires so easily. It frustrates her, as she's always been so active. By around eight, I had her in bed, and we watched a vid. She drifted off watching it, but I sat with her, finished watching it. I went to my own room to read. I keep an intercom by the bed so I can hear her if she's restless or ill. I checked on her before I went to bed. I think by midnight. I woke about three, I think. I don't know why. I thought I heard her, but when I went in to check, she was fine. Sleeping. I went back to bed.

'I haven't been out of the house since we took the walk with Donnalou — the nurse. Thaddeus,' she murmured as those brimming eyes spilled over again. 'I just can't believe it. Did I wake because I sensed . . . That's crazy, I know it's crazy, but I woke and felt something was wrong. I thought it was Grand.

'Thaddeus.'

She pushed to her feet. 'I'm sorry, you have to excuse me a moment. I need a moment.' She rushed out of the room.

'Man. This hit her hard.'

'You think?' Eve said, cold and cynical. 'You're married for a chunk of your life to a guy who decides to ditch you for a younger skirt, and takes the bulk of the money from a company you co-own – and maybe, like the divorce, didn't want to sell. Are you going to still have stars in your eyes over him?'

'Well, probably not,' Peabody admitted. 'But some people do hang on to what was. And maybe hold on to hope they can get it back. Like if Roarke pulled something stupid like that, you wouldn't be able to just turn off how you feel about him.'

'Maybe not. But I'd have already peeled the skin from his body, fried it up, and fed it to the wolves.'

'Huh.' Peabody drank more coffee. 'Some people just get their hearts broken. Still . . . '

She trailed off as a panel in the wall opened, and a woman stepped out.

Eloise Callahan was no longer the vibrant young bride in the painting, but she wore her ninety-plus years well. Her hair, still blond – with, Eve assumed, plenty of assistance – waved around a face where beauty hadn't faded. It lived in the bones, in the eyes the same blue as the chandelier.

She looked frail, a little pale, but had obviously gone to some trouble to counteract that with expertly applied enhancers, with the silky flow of black pants and a rose-pink tunic.

Peabody surged to her feet, actually stammered. 'Oh-oh, Ms Callahan.'

'Detective Peabody.' Her voice, like the silk, came soft and smooth as she slowly crossed the room. 'What a treat! Ariel said we had visitors, and finally told me who. I am such a fan! Eve Dallas. Oh my.' She clasped Peabody's hand, then Eve's before she lowered herself into a chair.

'I want to thank you both for all you do for the city I love. I came here to lose myself after I lost my love.' She looked to the painting. 'Beautiful, weren't they? The city, its energy, kept me going, helped me push myself back into the world, back into the work Bradley and I both loved.'

'I . . . my granny marched with you,' Peabody blurted out.

'Oh? Did she? Who's your granny?'

'Josie McNamara.'

'No! Josie?' Eloise let out a bright laugh, clapped her hands together. 'Josie, really? How marvelous! I'll be damned. I remember Josie so, so well. What a spitfire. Tell me she's still with us.'

'Yes, ma'am, and still a spitfire.'

'Of course she is.' She laughed again, full and rich. 'Oh, what times we had. You tell Josie that El sends her the very best. God, what times we had,' she repeated. 'Changed the world some, too, by God! Is that black coffee?' she asked Eve.

'Yes.'

'Could I just . . . '

Bemused, Eve handed Eloise her cup.

'Darla's so strict about my caffeine intake these days. It's juice, meds, water, juice, meds, water.' After a roll of her lovely eyes, Eloise sipped the coffee, sighed in pleasure. 'That's what I'm talking about.' She took another sip, then handed the cup back. 'Our secret,' she said with those crystal eyes sparkling.

'Sure.'

'She takes such good care of me – too much of her time doing so. I've been under the weather recently, and I'm past the age where I just bounce back. Pissed me off, if you want to know the truth.' She sighed again. 'Now tell me, what brings New York's finest to my door today?'

Before Eve could respond, Eloise glanced toward the arch. Age, Eve concluded, hadn't hurt her hearing. At the sound of footsteps, Eloise grinned. 'Uh-oh, busted.'

Darla, composed again, stepped in. But grief lived in her swollen, red-rimmed eyes. Age also hadn't dimmed Eloise's vision.

'Darla!' When she pushed to her feet, wobbled a bit, Eve moved quickly to steady her. 'What's the matter? Sweetie, what happened?'

'Oh, Grand.' Composure cracked, and fresh tears spilled through the fissures. 'It's Thaddeus. He's dead. Thaddeus is dead.'

'Dead?' Eloise opened her arms as Darla rushed into them. 'Oh, my poor, sweet girl. Here now, you sit.' She steered Darla to a sofa so she could sit beside her, keep an arm around her. 'I'm so sorry, Darla. So sorry.'

She looked over at Eve as she soothed and stroked. 'Jesus, I'm slow this morning. You're Homicide. I should have known it was something like this, but I was so delighted to meet you both, I didn't take the next step.'

'You should rest,' Darla began. 'You shouldn't get upset.'

'I'm fine, just fine. You stop. We'll get you a soother.'

'No, no, I have to feel. I have to get through it. Oh, Grand, someone killed Thaddeus.'

'I know. I know. We'll get through it together. How did it happen?' Eloise asked Eve.

'We're investigating. I can tell you he left his residence in the company of an as yet unidentified female at approximately nine P.M. last night. His body was discovered at his residence several hours later.'

'At?' Eloise frowned as she hugged Darla to her side. 'Outside? You didn't say in, but at.'

Sharp mind, too, Eve concluded. 'That's correct.'

Eloise started to speak, then as Darla continued to struggle beside her, appeared to change her mind. 'He lived with a woman. But I'm sure you know that, know about Marcella. So the woman wasn't she?'

'Also correct, as Ms Horowitz was out of town at the time, and with several other women. We will, however, speak with her and confirm.'

'How can we help?'

'We need to verify Ms Pettigrew's whereabouts from nine P.M. to five A.M.'

Darla sobbed, struggled to compose herself. 'They think I hurt Thaddeus.'

'Oh, don't be silly. You're upset, but you're not stupid. They need to know to eliminate you from suspicion. You were married, sweetie, and – I'm sure they know, too – he tossed you aside for Marcella.'

Eloise cuddled Darla close.

'Darla was here.' She spoke firmly, eyes direct on Eve's. 'We were watching a vid. I'm afraid I fell asleep – I tire out much too easily. But we were settled in for the night. You checked on me,' she said to Darla. 'I don't know the precise time, and I admit I was half-asleep, but I remember you laying your hand on my forehead to check for fever. Which I haven't had in weeks.'

She squeezed Darla's hand. 'Darla moved here with me, at my request, during the divorce. Thaddeus, his betrayal, hurt her very deeply.'

'You helped me so much, Grand.' The picture of grief, Darla pressed her face into her grandmother's shoulder. 'You helped me get through it.'

'We've helped each other.' The sweetness in the tone vanished as Eloise looked back at Eve.

Here was a woman with fiber and spine.

'More, Darla had her own company, one she'd worked so hard to build, and he cheated her out of her fair share, insisted as part of the divorce they sell it.'

'If you'd built it, Ms Pettigrew, how did he force you to sell?'

Still holding Eloise, Darla wiped at her eyes. 'Because Grand's wrong,' she said with a sigh. 'Sometimes I can be stupid. I gifted him the majority. It was supposed to be for tax purposes, estate purposes. I believed that, and I believed him. And I simply didn't notice he used that majority to draw funds from the company until it was too late. I had to agree to the sale or the company would sink. And me with it. And, to be honest, I didn't have the spine to fight him. But I got through it, with Grand's help. She pushed me until I finally agreed to go to a support group, and they helped, too.'

Big buzz, Eve thought. 'What support group is that?'

'Women For Women. Going showed me I wasn't alone, and I hadn't been stupid as much as I'd simply loved and believed someone who'd betrayed me. I haven't been in months now because I did get through it. I did!'

'And you wouldn't leave me when I was ill.' Stroking, Eloise spoke gently. 'You should go back for a booster, sweetie. We all need our women to encircle us in hard times.'

'Maybe. Yes, maybe I will.'

'In this group,' Eve said, 'you shared the issues and details of your marriage, divorce?'

Darla cast her swollen, red-rimmed eyes down. 'Yeah, that's the point. To share. It's private – you agree to that going in, and that helps encourage you to share, to open. We all only use first names.'

'Did you attend any meetings with a Jasmine or a Leah?'

Darla's shoulders drew in. 'I – it's confidential. I don't feel right saying yes or no.'

'It may help with the investigation.'

'I don't see how—'

'It's not your job to see how,' Eloise put in, still gentle but firm. 'It's theirs, sweetie.'

Darla sighed. 'It still doesn't feel right, but yes. A Leah and a Jasmine were both in group, at least for a while. As I said, I haven't been in months, and I'm pretty sure both of them stopped coming even long before that. How could that help? How could that have anything to do with Thaddeus?'

'We'll find out. I want to thank you for your cooperation and your time.'

'Lieutenant,' Darla began as Eve and Peabody rose. 'I know we were no longer married, but . . . Will you tell me if you find a suspect? If you find who did this to Thaddeus?'

'We'll relay any information that's appropriate.'

'Thank you. I'll walk you out.'

'I'll do that.' Eloise also got to her feet. 'I need to move, remember? And I'm starving, Darla. Would you go back and see that breakfast gets going?'

'Absolutely! I'm so glad you're hungry. Grand's appetite hasn't been the best,' she explained. 'I hope you find the person who did this. I hope you find them soon.'

Darla went out, and Eloise slowly started forward.

'What did you want to say?' Eve asked her.

'You're very astute. Two things, actually,' she said as she led them into the foyer. 'First, I'm going to say I'm not sorry he's dead, but that's personal. I'm sorry for Darla because this upsets her, and she'll grieve. The other's a question. The way you said he'd gone with someone, then hours later his body . . . Left outside his house. I've spent far too much time watching the screen these last couple of weeks since I'm better but not all the way back. Was this, was Thaddeus like the man – I can't recall the name – left outside his apartment building?'

Word would be out soon enough. 'There are similarities.'

'Oh dear God. I'll keep her away from the news as much as I can. That will crush her. Find him.' She took both Peabody's and Eve's hand. 'Find who's doing this. I hope we'll see each other again, in happier times.'

10

'My granny's going to flip when I tell her I met Eloise Callahan.'

'Which is, of course, the main point of this exercise.'

'Just getting it out of the way,' Peabody said breezily as they got in the car. 'Darla Pettigrew's alibi's shaky, and she has motive.'

'Agreed.'

'On the other side, her grief seemed genuine. So did her devotion to her grandmother.'

'Also agreed.'

Considering, Peabody looked back at the house. 'It's hard to believe she'd leave her grandmother alone, potentially for a number of hours, while she's recovering from a long illness.'

As she pulled away, Eve glanced at the rearview mirror. 'Big house. I bet there are a lot of private, soundproofed rooms where you could torture a man to death while keeping tabs on Granny.'

Peabody's eyebrows rose. 'You like her for it?'

'She's on the list.'

'You really think she'd torture, mutilate, and kill McEnroy and her ex while her ninety-odd-year-old grandmother's sleeping in the same house?'

'That's exactly why it's damn good cover – because that's going to be the expected reaction. She's on the list,' Eve repeated. 'High on the list. Interesting she brought up the support group before we asked.'

'You think that's suspicious?' Baffled, Peabody shifted to study Eve's profile. She knew her partner, understood Eve felt a vibe she hadn't. 'I mean she was talking about how her grandmother helped her, and one of the ways was to nudge her into a support group.'

'Not suspicious necessarily, but convenient. Convenient for us, too. We've got the connection now. High probability one or more of the support group killed two men. Let's track down the woman who runs the group.'

'Already on it. They've got a web page,' Peabody said as she worked her PPC. 'No names or contact numbers – that anonymous deal, I guess. There's like, a mission statement.

'"Women For Women offers support without judgment for women from women. We stand for each other through divorce, infidelity, loss, harassment, rape, depression, recovery, and whatever difficulties you face as a woman.

'"Our group offers a unique understanding of the issues women face in their daily lives. If you need someone to listen, we're here."'

Peabody scrolled on. 'It says the group's led by a licensed

therapist who will provide recommendations for shelters, legal representation, rehabilitation facilities upon request. McNab showed me a few tricks,' she told Eve. 'Let me see if I can dig out the IP, a name, a location.'

'Meanwhile, plug in the meeting site. We'll try that.'

Peabody programmed the address, then rolled her shoulders, started punching keys.

Eve gave Peabody silence, and herself some thinking time as she headed back downtown.

Big house, she thought again. And there'd been a garage so probably a vehicle. Very private residence. Good potential.

Then again, the grandmother had seemed on the frail and shaky side, like a woman recovering from a bad illness. Wouldn't hurt to check that, just make sure the pneumonia thing wasn't a cover.

Low probability there. Which made it tough to see a devoted granddaughter leaving her frail and shaky grandmother alone for however long it took to lure the target, get the target back to the very private residence.

But . . . way overblown on the grief for a cheating ex.

Darla mentioned a day nurse, Eve thought. Maybe she'd hired a night nurse, someone who'd cover while she was busy elsewhere. Maybe off the books.

'Holy shit, check me!' Bouncing, Peabody pumped a fist in the air. 'I got it. IP's registered to Kendra Zula. Hold on, I can get the address. Hey, it's a couple blocks from the meeting site. We're already on our way.'

'Nice work.'

'Thanks. Want me to run her?'

'What do you think?'

'I think you want me to run her. Jeez, she's only twenty-one. A student at NYU. Parents cohabbed, no marriage. Father's living in Kenya, like Africa. No sibs. Mother lives at the same address. Natalia Zula.'

'Mother runs the group, daughter set up the page,' Eve surmised. 'Run the mother.'

'Natalia Zula, age forty-four, and yeah, a licensed therapist. Licensed since '56. She has a practice, specializes in women and kids. Looks like she runs the practice out of the same address.'

'Then it should be easy to find her.'

She found the address, a slim duplex on the edges of NoHo. Someone had painted the front entrance door a deep blue. On the small pad up the short steps from the sidewalk sat a boldly striped pot where something poked up green through the soil.

Good security, Eve noted as she rang the bell. A woman's voice – not a comp – answered, 'How can I help you?'

'Lieutenant Dallas and Detective Peabody, NYPSD. We need to speak with Natalia Zula.'

She must have come on the run, as the door swung open before Eve finished, and the woman who answered breathed fast. 'Kendra.'

'Is fine as far as we know. We're here about another matter.'

'Oh God.' She pressed a hand to her heart. 'My daughter,

181

Kendra, stayed over with a friend last night. I was afraid—
Sorry. Can I see your identification?'

Eve pulled out her badge, studied the woman as the
woman studied the badge.

Tall, well built, but that ebony skin would be hard to
disguise, and the unsub wasn't − according to the wits −
black. She had diamond-edged cheekbones, huge dark
eyes, and black hair that spilled to her shoulders in dozens
of thin braids.

She wore a simple, well-cut navy suit, sensible shoes, and
a crisp white shirt.

'Thank you. Please come in. Perhaps we should go into
my office.'

'Fine.'

She had the faintest accent, musical, precise, and led the
way down the hallway into a room with a small desk, a
couple of good-size chairs in soft gray, a sofa in navy. The
art on the walls depicted flowers in meadows, quiet forests,
winding rivers.

'Please sit. May I offer you tea?'

'We're good, thanks.'

Natalia sat behind the desk, folded her hands on its surface. 'How may I help?'

'You run a support group, Women For Women.'

'I do, but this is a confidential matter. Any who attend
are promised that confidence.'

'Two men have been murdered, Ms Zula. Your group
connects them.'

She sat back abruptly, as if punched. 'But no. We have no men in the group. It's only for women.'

'A woman killed them.'

'Ah.' She closed her eyes a moment. 'I can assure you, our group promotes support, understanding, steps toward peace, recovery, stability. We do not promote or sanction violence.'

'That may be, but there's a connection. Both men were involved with women who attended your group. The women attended your group because of experiences with these men.'

Worry clouded those dark eyes now. 'I see. But surely these men were connected in other ways to have been killed together.'

'Not together. Nigel McEnroy was murdered night before last.'

'I heard this. I don't know the name, but I heard of his murder.'

'You'll also hear Thaddeus Pettigrew was murdered, the same method, last night.'

'I— This is terrible, but I don't understand. You're saying these men didn't know each other?'

'Not that we can ascertain. Two women who worked in McEnroy's office have given either me or my partner statements attesting to the fact that he drugged and raped them. They both attended your group. Pettigrew's ex-wife, whom he left for another woman and, according to her statement, cheated her financially as well, attended your group.'

'But . . . ' She lifted a hand, pressed it to the base of her throat. 'You cannot believe these women somehow worked together to kill.'

She holds calm, steady, Eve thought, despite the growing concern on her face.

'Evidence indicates more than one person may be involved. And I believe there will be other men, other murders unless we identify and stop this person or these persons.'

'I don't know how to help you.'

'We need the names of women who've attended your group sessions over the last three years.'

'But I cannot.'

'We can and will get a warrant.'

'No, no, I mean to say I literally cannot. Above even the need to keep confidential, I have only first names – and many may not use their real name even then. I keep no records from the group. It is simply a place, a safe place, where these women can come when they feel the need, where they can say what they need to say and not be judged.'

'You have notes. How could you remember who comes, what they need, what's happened to them if you didn't keep notes?'

'I have notes, yes, with first names.' With those deep, liquid eyes trained on Eve, Natalia turned her hands palms up. 'Please understand I want to help, but if I gave them to you, how could any of the women trust me? If you get a warrant, I will have no choice but to obey the law.'

'All right. Peabody, see if Yancy's got the sketch from the McEnroy witness.'

'I'm sorry I can't give you what you want without this,' Natalia continued. 'I feel if another dies, I'm responsible, too. And yet, the ones who come to us are hurt or frightened, broken or despairing. A woman beaten who blames herself for the blows. A woman discarded who wonders why she wasn't enough. I was one of them once.'

'It would help if you give us your whereabouts between nine last night and five this morning.'

'I understand. I also connect.' And still calm, still steady, Natalia took a breath. 'Last night I was with a man. His name is Geo Fong. He's a good man, I think, but I've been wrong before. We've been seeing each other for several months, and I don't think I'm wrong. Last night, I made him dinner. He came at seven, and after dinner, we went upstairs and were together. My daughter, as I said, was at a friend's. He left only shortly before you arrived.'

'And the night before?'

'With my daughter. We had dinner out, went to the vids. Then we came home and talked until almost midnight. She believes she's in love. He seems a nice boy. I hope he is. She's my world, Lieutenant. I can swear to you, I would do nothing that would hurt her. And if her mother took a life, she would be deeply hurt. Lost.'

With the faintest smile, Natalia turned around a framed photo to show Eve and Peabody a pretty girl with her mother's eyes.

'My world,' she said again. 'Her father left when she was only a baby. I came to America with my parents – they are doctors. They hoped I would follow that path, but I fell in love, and then there was Kendra. It hurt my heart when he left, but I had her. I had my world. And then there was a man, one I thought a good man. I let him into our lives. I learned, when my beautiful girl was just fifteen, he had . . . touched her. She was afraid to tell me at first, and I was blind. But when she did, finally did, I took her to a doctor. I took her to the police.'

'What happened to the man?'

'He's in prison. And he will be for a long time more. He had pictures of my child he'd taken when she didn't know. When she was in the shower, or in bed. I was here, but I didn't see. He forced himself on my child, told her he would deny and I would believe, told her he would kill me. Told her many things. But he's in prison now, and my girl is well. She trusted me, and we trusted the police. If ever I had it inside me to kill, he would be dead.'

Peabody rose, held out her PPC. 'Do you recognize this woman?'

Natalia studied it, rose, took the PPC to the window to look at it in stronger light. 'I think she's very beautiful, but I don't think I know her. I don't think she comes to our group. I would say yes if I did. I wouldn't give you more, but I would not lie.'

'I believe you. We'll get the warrant. Have you shared your story in group?'

'Of course.' She lifted her ringless hands. 'How can I ask for trust if I don't trust? But he's in prison.'

And justice was met, Eve thought.

'If you'd give my partner Mr Fong's contact information, we'll verify.'

Natalia gave it, then rose. 'I hope you're wrong. I hope you find it's no one who's come into our circle.'

You can hope, Eve thought. But I'm not wrong.

She headed to the morgue next.

'Push for the warrant, Peabody,' she said as she drove. 'First names only don't give us much, but it's better than nothing. And I want to talk to whoever booked Pettigrew's LCs. Let's see if he had a type.'

'On that. Do you want me to contact Zula's alibi, see if it holds up?'

'Yeah, we'll get to it. It's going to.' When her 'link signaled, she answered through the in dash. 'Dallas.'

'This is Bondita Rothchild, Marcella's mother. We're en route to the city, and should be there within the hour.'

'All right, Ms Rothchild, we'll come to you.'

'I'm taking Marcella home with me. I don't want her in that house.' She rattled off an address in Cobble Hill, which meant a trip across the river into Brooklyn.

'We'll come to you,' Eve repeated. 'About ninety minutes.'

'I'll expect you to be respectful of Marcella's delicate emotional state,' Bondita added before she clicked off.

Once they'd parked, started down the tunnel, Peabody checked her own 'link. 'The warrant's in the works.'

'See who's loose in the bullpen. I'd rather a detective, but a uniform will do. Have them serve it, get the data.'

As they approached Morris's doors, her comm signaled. 'What now?' Then she read Commander Whitney on the readout, and had a pretty good idea what now. 'Dallas. Sir.'

'Lieutenant. You're needed in The Tower for a conversation with Chief Tibble.'

That proved a higher what now than she'd expected. 'Commander, I'm in the field, currently at the morgue about to speak to Dr Morris regarding Thaddeus Pettigrew, who all evidence indicates is the second victim in my current investigation. We also have an interview with Pettigrew's live-in scheduled in ninety minutes.'

'Report to The Tower at thirteen hundred hours.'

'Yes, sir.' She stuffed her comm back in her pocket. 'Geena McEnroy.'

'She went straight to the top,' Peabody commented. 'At least we've got some time to interview Horowitz.'

'He didn't send for you. You weren't there for my interview with her anyway.'

'Uh-uh.' Peabody put her stubborn face on. 'Partners. You have to risk an ass-frying, my ass is in the pan with yours.'

'I didn't need the visual of your ass bumped up against mine in some damn pan. Ass partners,' she muttered, and pushed through the doors when Peabody snorted out a laugh.

Morris had one of his favored bluesy numbers going and wore a suit in forest green. Cord, stone gray like his tie, wound through the braid he'd doubled up at the back of his head in a loop.

He currently had his hands in Pettigrew's open chest.

'Once more unto the breach, dear friends. This poor soul won't fight another battle.'

'He didn't get to fight the last one,' Eve pointed out.

'No, he didn't. No defensive wounds though he suffered more trauma than our previous guest. I have no argument with your on-scene conclusions, Dallas. He hung by the wrists, from above, and his weight, his struggle eventually dislocated both shoulders. An electric prod – the same dimensions as the one used on McEnroy – was used to beat, burn, sodomize. I estimate at least four hours between the first burn and the last.'

'She's . . . dedicated.'

'I'd say that's an accurate term for it. It takes a kind of dedication to torture another human being for hours. There's no sign of gagging, so he'd have screamed, likely have pleaded. COD would be severe blood loss from the amputation. He was, as was McEnroy, alive when she used the blade. The same blade, in my opinion, that was used on McEnroy.'

'Was he drugged?'

'As before I put a rush on the tox report. It's the same mix. In this case, the first dose was administered into the palm of his hand.'

'Okay, okay, that's how it's done.' Nodding, Eve circled the body. 'He comes to the door to let her in. She introduces herself, offers her hand. She's got the syringe palmed. He wouldn't even have time to react. She just leads him out to the waiting car, and she's got him.'

'He ingested the second dose.'

'Probably in the car.' She could see it. Yes, she could see it very clearly.

'Puts him out,' she continued. 'Whoever's driving helps her get him inside once they get where they're going, maybe helps her string him up.'

'Only one deviation I've found thus far,' Morris told her. 'Have a look at his toes.'

He offered her, then Peabody, microgoggles. Peabody eased back a step.

'That's okay. I can see fine from here.'

Eve adjusted hers, bent down with Morris. 'With McEnroy, there were scrapes and bruises on the balls and heels of his feet. He'd swing, you see, when the prod struck, or jerk. And his feet would beat on the floor or ground. But in this case—'

'Yeah, yeah, I get it. She elevated him a little higher. He barely had his toes on the floor surface, so he's digging in with them to stay up, to try to relieve the weight on his arms and shoulders. They're scraping over the floor when he swings. Anything under the toenails?'

'Funny you should ask.' Smiling, Morris straightened. 'Yes, I scraped substance from under them, sent it to the lab. It's not fiber, so not a rug or carpet, not fabric. I don't think it's wood. Stone or concrete perhaps.'

'Good, that's good. She didn't think of that, did she? Wanted him to hurt so she didn't think of that.'

'One can never overestimate a human being's capacity for

cruelty.' Morris drew off his goggles, met Eve's eyes. 'But this one runs wide and runs deep. I hope you're closer to her than she is to the next.'

'We think she's using a support group for women to pick her targets,' Peabody told him.

'That's cruel in itself, isn't it? To take that circle of compassion and outreach to inflict suffering. Ah well, we'll do what we do. I'll have the full report to you this afternoon.'

'Appreciate it.'

Eve dug credits out of her pocket as they walked out, then tossed them to Peabody. 'Cold caffeine.'

Peabody went for two tubes of Pepsi – hers Diet. 'You okay?' she asked when Eve rubbed the cold tube against her forehead.

'Yeah. Little headache.'

'I've got blockers.'

'No, it'll pass.'

'Are you worried about Tibble?'

'No. We did our job. If he has to give us a smack for it, we take the smack, then go out and keep doing our job.'

'You said "we".' Smug, Peabody bopped her shoulders. 'Ass partners.'

Back in the car, Eve sat for a moment, then cracked the tube. 'We're going to tell a second woman the guy she lived with liked to have some strange when she wasn't around. She may get her bitch on over that – and we'll be the ones that falls on.'

'It's hard to get bitchy about the bitch on when we had to

tell her the guy's dead, and now we're going to tell her he's dead because he went off with the strange.'

'Here's the thing.' Eve drank. 'He cheated – on his ex with the current. Why the current believes he wouldn't cheat on her is beyond me, but that's usually how it goes. But, thinking from the killer's perspective, there's no evidence this one drugged women, raped them, abused them. He hired them. We're going to talk to the booker, see if he went for the violent end of things with LCs, but there was no sign of that in the bedroom setup. The toys were toys. No illegals, just aids. You add the money in – him maneuvering the ex with the company she started. But even with that, he doesn't reach the level of McEnroy.'

'But she went at him harder.' Following, Peabody nodded. 'The other way around would make more sense.'

'Yeah. So that's not in play. It's not – from a twisted thinking – the punishment fits the crime. It's either escalation or she had more reason to want Pettigrew to suffer.'

'Taking us back to the ex.'

'To the ex, to someone else he screwed with, or to the current.' Eve pulled out. 'Let's go to Brooklyn.'

'Okay, warrant's in.' Peabody studied her 'link. 'Jenkinson and Reineke are on tap to handle it. And . . . hey, the offices for Discretion are on the way to Brooklyn. We'd have time to hit there before we talk to Horowitz.'

'Even better. Plug it in.'

As she did, Peabody frowned. 'They might want a warrant, too. Discretion, right?'

'We'll risk it. They have a dead customer,' Eve pointed out. 'One who got his johnson whacked off. Seems they'd want to prove one of their LCs didn't do it.'

'That's an angle. Do you think if sex was your job it'd get really boring, or more exciting because you were always mixing it up?'

'I think because it's not just sex that's the job, it's pretending attraction to somebody who put me on their credit card – or, lower level, picked me up on the street, and on the upper levels you actually have to have conversations with the john like you give a rat's ass what they think about anything – I'd rather work the night shift in some factory that tests cat food.'

'Like they have to taste it, the cat food? They don't do that, do they?'

'How the hell do I know? I don't work at a cat food factory. There!'

She spotted a curbside slot, hit vertical, did a one-eighty in midair, and dropped down.

'I woulda walked,' Peabody managed. 'I'd've been happy to walk blocks. Loose pants. And more no cardiac arrest.' Because her legs still trembled, she eased out carefully to stand on the sidewalk.

'It's starting to rain,' Eve pointed out.

'A walk in the rain's refreshing.'

'A walk in the rain's wet.' Pleased, Eve walked into the soaring downtown office building.

A small horde of business types moved at a quick pace in

the lobby. To elevators, from them, with briefcases, suits, earbuds, take-out fake coffee.

She walked straight to the security desk, held up her badge. 'Discretion.'

The short man with thin, graying hair gave them a once-over. 'Sign in please, with the name of the party you're here to see.'

'I'll know the party when I get there. What floor?'

'Twelfth floor, east bank.' He checked his log screen. 'Twelve hundred for the main office.'

Eve scrawled her name, waited for Peabody to do the same, then headed for the east bank.

They got on the elevator along with more business types. She tuned out the talk of marketing strategies, Jenny in accounting's birthday, brainstorming sessions, lunch meetings as the damn car stopped on every damn floor to let some off, let more on.

She grieved for the glides at Central.

Everything smelled like too much perfume, cologne, fake coffee, somebody's mid-morning muffin, somebody else's fear sweat.

On twelve she stepped out into a moment of blessed quiet.

Discretion's office, behind double-frosted glass doors, held more quiet yet, and the faint scent of . . . she didn't know what the hell, but it was good – and probably discreet.

The waiting area held deep scoop chairs, each with an individual screen. Maybe to preview choices of companions, she thought.

A single female – late twenties, silky blond hair, sharp green eyes, and a red suit that showed just a hint of black lace at the cleavage – sat at what looked like an antique desk or excellent replica.

She swiveled away from her comp screen, smiled. 'Good morning and welcome to Discretion. How can I assist you?'

Eve pulled out her badge. 'Manager.'

The smile faded. 'We're fully licensed and inspected.'

'Not my area, not my question. We need to speak to whoever runs the show, regarding a dead guy.'

'Wh – how – Please wait.'

She didn't call back from the desk, but popped up and rushed away on shoes so high Eve wondered she didn't suffer nosebleeds.

'You've got to give them classy,' Peabody decided. 'The colors, the furnishings – and those are real miniature orange trees over there. In blossom. What a great smell.'

Okay, Eve thought, so that was it.

Another woman came back – tall heels again, these with toes so pointed Eve imagined they could jab a hole in brick. A good two decades older than the desk girl, she had an air of what Peabody would have called class.

The dark suit with its short skirt showcased excellent legs; the fitted jacket, an excellent body. Her hair, a kind of caramel, coiled tidily at her nape. Her skin, a few shades lighter, all but glowed, and her eyes, sea green, showed only polite curiosity.

'I'm Araby Clarke. Why don't we speak in my office?'

195

'Okay.'

She gestured, led them to a wide doorway, into a long hall. 'I'm sorry, I didn't get your names, but I swear . . . have we met?'

'Don't think so. Lieutenant Dallas, Detective Peabody.'

'Oh, of course! No, we haven't met until now.' She gestured again into a spacious office. 'But I did see the vid, and admit I've followed you and Roarke, and you, Detective, whenever there's media. Please sit.'

The office suited her, deep cushioned chairs in dull gold, glass tables holding glass vases and exotic flowers. Art of beautiful men and women – oddly romantic rather than sexual. And a view of command through the window behind the long, glossy desk.

'You gave Kerry quite a jolt.' She sat, crossed her killer legs. 'She said someone was dead. Is it someone I know?'

'Thaddeus Pettigrew.'

That polite curiosity flashed away. Eve wouldn't say the woman jolted, but she registered distress. 'Oh no. Oh, I'm very sorry to hear this. He's been a client for years.'

'Years. As in?'

'I'll have to check, but I believe at least a decade.'

So, not a new habit, Eve thought. 'I'm going to need you to check on that, and several other things.'

Araby sat back. 'You put me in an interesting position. Under most circumstances we would refuse to answer any questions regarding a client. Even with a warrant, I would contact my legal department and do what could be done to void that.'

'He was murdered, Ms Clarke.'

'I realize that, or why would Dallas and Peabody be in my office? And that's precisely why I won't demand a warrant. I do want just a moment to talk to my legal people. I've owned Discretion for sixteen years, and we've never had anything like this happen. I want to make certain I do the right thing for everyone involved. If you'd just give me a minute.'

When she hurried out, Eve nodded. 'She'll give us what we ask for.'

'You sure?'

'Yeah, because she wants to. She liked him – at least the way you like a longtime, regular customer. We'll get what we came for.'

So Eve settled back to wait.

11

Eve shoved her way over the bridge to Brooklyn, weaving through, leapfrogging over the thick river of vehicles heading in the same direction. The river clogged when neck-craners slowed to study the delivery truck and sedan with crunched fenders along with the police cruiser dealing with the encounter in the breakdown lane.

Eve cursed them all for idiots, hit lights and sirens, pushed into vertical for a whooshing half a mile. During which Peabody clutched the chicken stick like a lifeline.

'Do they hope to see blood and bodies?' Eve ranted. 'Is it: Oh look, honey, an accident. Break out the freaking popcorn.'

Once they crossed the bridge, Eve eased back a bit to follow the computer prompts to the address in Cobble Hill – and Peabody flexed her aching fingers.

It proved to be a lively street with a scatter of restaurants, a few shops, a small park where a number of people walked dogs or watched kids risk broken bones on playground equipment.

Marcella's mother had the ground floor of a triple-decker with its own little patio off the side. It also boasted a narrow driveway currently occupied by a dark blue town car.

Eve pulled in behind it. 'That matches the basic description of the car the wit saw at Pettigrew's. Run the tags,' Eve told Peabody as they got out.

'It's registered to Bondita Rothchild.'

'Might be interesting.' Eve walked to the door, pushed the buzzer.

The woman who answered was tall, slim, and blond. Not Marcella, Eve thought, but by the family resemblance, related.

'Lieutenant Dallas and Detective Peabody.' Eve offered her badge.

'Yes, we're expecting you. I'm Rozelle, Marci's sister. This is just horrible. Marci's a wreck. Claudia — that's our friend who was with us — is back making her tea because Marci won't take a soother. I just . . . I'm sorry, I guess I'm a wreck, too. Come inside.'

The entrance opened into a generous living space where someone had turned on lights and lamps to combat the gloom from the insistent drizzle outside. They'd lowered the privacy shades as well.

Marcella sat on a sofa, a chocolate-brown throw over her lap, and cuddled close to her mother.

Bondita, spotting Eve and Peabody, wrapped a protective arm around her daughter. They all looked exhausted.

Another blonde, this one tall and curvy in black skin

pants and a flowy white shirt, hurried from the back with a tray.

'Our friend, Claudia Johannsen. These are the police, Claudia. Go ahead and take Marci her tea.

'You drink this now, Marce.' She used the firm tone of a veteran schoolteacher, a determined mother, or a sturdy nurse. 'We're all here for you. You drink some tea, too, Bondi. And you come sit down and have yours, Roz. Officers, can I make you some tea?'

'Lieutenant, Detective,' Eve corrected. 'No, thanks. Ms Horowitz—'

'Since that's two of us here, why don't you go with first names,' Rozelle suggested. 'It's just easier.'

'All right. Marcella, we're very sorry for your loss. We understand this is a difficult time for you.'

'Difficult? Difficult?' Her voice pitched up three registers on the three syllables. 'Is that how you think it is for me? The man I love is dead!'

Okay, Eve thought, it's going to be one of those.

Before she could continue, Sympathetic Peabody shifted into gear. 'Marcella, we want to help. We're here to do everything we can to find out who did this to the man you love. As hard as it must be for you, we know you want us to find those answers, so we need your help. Thaddeus needs your help.'

'Thaddeus!' Marcella wailed it.

'Stop now.' Bondita hugged her, rocked her. 'Stop now, Marcella, or I'll have to make you take a soother.'

'Nothing could make me stop feeling. How could this happen? How could this happen to Thad?'

'It's our job to find out,' Eve told her. 'There are questions we need to ask you so we can go out and do that job.'

'You talk to the police now, Marce,' Claudia insisted. 'We're here with you.'

'I'm sorry, sit down, both of you.' Bondita waved a hand. 'My husband and I managed to raise a son and two daughters without ever having the police at the door. None of us are behaving well.'

'I want to know what happened to Thad.' Once again Marcella's voice rose up, pitch by pitch. 'I deserve to know!'

'Mr Pettigrew left the residence you share with him last night at approximately nine P.M.'

'He told me he was staying in,' Marcella interrupted.

'That may be, but he left the residence at that time in the company of an as yet unknown female.'

Her slumping shoulders shot back, stiffened. 'He did not!'

Eve just pushed on. 'He left with said unknown female, and with her, got into what is described as a dark town car.'

'But you said— Mom, didn't she say his – his – Thad was home when he . . . '

'His body was discovered by a neighbor out walking his dog early this morning, outside the house. His verified time of death was two-twenty this morning. The nine-one-one call from the neighbor logged in at three-forty-three.'

'Where was he all that time?' Marcella demanded. 'Did he come back home, then someone broke in, and killed him, and left him outside?'

'Mr Pettigrew wasn't killed inside the residence.'

'How do you *know*?'

'It's my job to know,' Eve snapped back. 'He opened the door to the female because he believed she was the licensed companion he had booked for the evening.'

'That's a lie! A lie, a terrible lie, and I won't listen.'

To Eve's bemusement, Marcella literally clamped her hands over her ears.

But when she started to lurch up, her mother held her in place. 'Sit still, Marcella. Be quiet. Can you prove that?'

'We've verified it, yes. He made the booking yesterday. It appears his system had been hacked, and the booking was canceled. This individual took the place of the LC he'd hired. Subsequently, she drugged him, led him out to the waiting car. He was taken to another location.'

'I don't believe you. I don't believe any of this. Thad would never, never do that. He would never cheat on me.'

Really? Eve thought. Unlike the way he cheated on his wife with you?

'You're stating you were unaware Mr Pettigrew regularly used the services of Discretion, a company that facilitates customers who wish to hire licensed companions.'

Marcella's eyes streamed like a toddler's after being told she couldn't have candy. 'He never did that.'

'He used their services for at least nine years.'

The tears dried up, and a mutinous expression replaced them. 'Maybe, maybe he did before we fell in love, but—'

'And has continued to use their services every few weeks up until his death.'

'You're trying to ruin everything for me.' She bunched her fists, actually shook them. 'Saying horrible things to ruin my life. I want you to go. Get out.'

'That's enough, Marcella. Claudia, would you take Marcella back to my bedroom? She needs to lie down.'

'Of course. Come on with me, Marce.'

'She's lying, Claudia.'

'Let's just go lie down. You have to rest. It's an awful day.' She tugged Marcella up, got a firm arm around her.

'You're a horrible person,' Marcella spat at Eve.

As Claudia pulled Marcella out, Bondita pressed her fingers to her eyes. Rozelle shifted over, stroked her mother's arm.

'I apologize, Lieutenant.'

'I've been called worse.'

'Not in my home.' She dropped her hands, took her daughter's. 'She believed she loved him, believed he loved her. She'd made him the center of her world. Learning this will be nearly as shattering for her as his death.'

'Were you aware he used LCs?'

'I was not. I'll admit I wondered if he'd stray, or simply tire of Marcella. She's young, and naive, and, well, demanding. But he seemed genuinely devoted to her. They seemed happy together. Are you saying this woman, the one who posed as an LC, killed Thaddeus?'

'Yes.'

'It makes no sense. I can't think of anyone who'd want to kill Thaddeus.'

'No,' Rozelle agreed. 'It doesn't make sense. We had this trip planned for weeks. And he surprised Marci with the extra day. He asked me to arrange it, a surprise because, apparently, she complained she wouldn't be able to get all the treatments she wanted in the two days. I couldn't get the extra day because they were fully booked – then there was a cancellation, so I grabbed it. She was so excited.'

'When did you book the extra day?'

'Just two days ago. It was really last minute, so Claudia had to scramble to work in the extra day. Thad even arranged for champagne and flowers in our suite.'

'You all had rooms in the same suite?'

'Yes, it's a two-level, their best. Marci treated – or, realistically, Thaddeus treated us to the suite.'

'I need to go up to my daughter.'

'Bondita, before you do, can you tell us the last time you used your car?'

'My car? What does that— Oh my God! You think ... We weren't even here!'

'It would just help to have that information.'

'Two days ago, for my volunteer work. And to run some last-minute errands before the trip.'

'Who else has access to your car?'

'My husband, of course. He has his own, but we have the codes to each other's. Before you ask, I know he was home because I spoke to him last night, just a check-in, around midnight. He had friends over for a poker party – something he likes to do if I go out of town. We spoke, not long, as they were on the last hand of the night. He had at least six people here, you can check.'

'Thank you. We will if we find it helpful. We appreciate your time.'

As they rose, Peabody spoke up. 'We could give you the names of some good grief counselors. It might help Marcella.'

'Yes. Rozelle, I want to go up to Marcella.'

'You go. I'll get the names. She wouldn't have had a clue,' Rozelle said quietly as her mother went out. 'Marci, I mean. If she had, she'd have told me, or Claudia. Maybe not Mom, not right away, but she'd have told me or Claudia.'

'Why not your mother?' Eve asked.

'Because she knew our parents didn't really approve, at least at first. Thaddeus won them over, for the most part. He really seemed completely devoted, made her so happy, indulged her. But he was older, divorced, and they'd hoped for something, someone different for her.'

Rozelle paused, pressed her fingers under her eyes.

'She'll get over this,' she said. 'She doesn't think she will, but she will. Once it gets through he'd cheated on her, she'll get over it, move on. She's young. But for now, a grief counselor would help.'

After Peabody gave the names, Rozelle showed them out. Eve studied the town car as she walked to her own.

'It's not going to fit. You'd have to figure, if the family — speaking of which, she mentioned a son, so let's find him — but if the family's covered, why use this car? People in the house, maybe going in and out, they'd notice if the car came and went. So it's not going to fit.'

Eve got behind the wheel, took a moment. She shook her head, pulled out of the drive. 'She's a girl.'

'Well,' Peabody said. 'Yeah.'

'No, not a woman, not a female. A girl. The youngest of the family, and they baby her. You can see it, the dynamics there. Maybe she loved Pettigrew, maybe at least she thought she did, but the older sister's got it right. She'll get over it, move on. She's not going to torture, mutilate, and kill two men because the one she lived with hired LCs. That takes purpose. She doesn't have one.'

'That came loud and clear,' Peabody agreed. 'And I'm going to say she struck me as the type who'd squeal if she saw blood. I can't see her slicing off a dick.'

'People take care of her. She doesn't take care of people — for good or ill. They also didn't talk about the big gorilla.'

'What big gorilla?'

'You know, the fact that she cheated with Pettigrew on his ex when she wasn't his ex. He cheated with her, but everybody was real careful not to mention it. Like the big gorilla in the room everybody pretends not to notice.'

'Oh, oh, elephant. It's the elephant in the room.'

'That's stupid. You can't ignore a freaking elephant who

wouldn't be able to fit in most rooms anyway. Plus, there'd be massive piles of elephant shit. Try not noticing that.'

'I think that's actually the point of the saying.'

'Which just makes it stupid. You could pretend to ignore a gorilla because some people bear a freaky resemblance thereto.'

Considering that, Peabody pursed her lips. 'I knew this guy at the Academy who sort of did.'

'There you go. In any case, they all avoided that area of discussion, and they'd all know. Just like they all know she'll go through the hysterics, then settle down and move on. But let's check on the brother anyway.'

Peabody worked it while Eve fought the traffic wars back over the bridge.

'He was at the poker party,' Peabody reported after a brief conversation on her 'link.

'Should've figured it.'

'He left about eleven because he had an early series of meetings today. And he's at a conference in Connecticut right now. He left this morning about seven. I did a run while I talked to him, Dallas. He comes off pretty squeaky clean. One marriage – eight years in. Two kids. He doesn't have a license to drive, doesn't own a vehicle.'

As Eve avoided contact with a compact that swerved into her lane, she snarled. 'A lot of people shouldn't have one.'

'Grew up in New York, moved to Hoboken after the first kid from the timing on his data.'

'It's not going to be him. They're not going to be

involved. Just not enough there for the level of violence. It's a vendetta.'

She pulled into the garage, thrilled to be finished, for now, with the hordes of people who shouldn't have a license to drive.

'I'm going to say it again. You don't have to do this thing with Tibble.'

'I'm going to say it again,' Peabody countered as they got out of the car. 'Your ass, my ass.' She made a fist, pumped it. 'Pan.'

Eve just shook her head.

They rode the elevator as far as Eve could stand it, squeezed out when a bunch of shiny new uniforms trooped on, herded by the grizzled vet she assumed had drawn the short straw for leading an orientation.

She hit the glides. 'Check in with EDD, see if McNab's made any progress.'

The more she had to present, Eve thought, the better.

'He's into it.' Peabody read the reply on the 'link screen. 'Hack confirmed, but it's multiple. So far he's got them going back for sixteen months. He hasn't been able to pinpoint. Can't ascertain as yet if it's one hacker or more.'

'Good enough for now. The killer cyber-stalked him.'

They switched back to an elevator for the rise to The Tower. Tibble's offices soared high above the streets, and the desks of the cops who worked them. But Eve had reason to know that distance, that height, didn't remove New York's Chief of Police and Security from those who served and protected.

But those who rose that high had more than law and order to oversee. They had to deal with politics, with optics, with media perception.

She acknowledged that reality, more or less accepted it, and often thought: Better them than me.

She paused outside Tibble's office where his admin manned a workstation with two screens, a D and C where several lights blinked insistently, a 'link humming incoming even as he talked on a headset.

'Hold, please.' He turned to Eve and Peabody. 'Just one moment, Lieutenant, Detective.' He tapped his headset. 'Sir, Lieutenant Dallas and Detective Peabody are here. Yes, sir.' He tapped again. 'You can go right in. He's ready for you.'

Eve opened the right side of the double doors.

The wall of glass showed the world of New York washed in the light drizzle of early spring rain.

The room itself, wide and deep, held a sitting area, a massive wall screen, a solid desk, high-backed visitors' chairs.

The two men in the room sat at their ease. Commander Whitney filled a visitor's chair with his wide shoulders. Gray threaded liberally through his dark hair, and the lines of command scored his face with a kind of stoic dignity.

Tibble, long and lean, took the desk with the drenched city at his back. He wore his hair close to the skull of a face as long and lean as his body. His eyes skimmed from Whitney to Eve to Peabody, and showed nothing.

She'd heard he was hell at the poker table.

'Lieutenant, Detective, have a seat.'

Though she preferred giving reports, or receiving a dressing-down, while on her feet, Eve followed orders.

'As you should be aware,' Tibble began, 'I rarely summon my officers to The Tower over a complaint. However, since this complainant has opted to reach out to me, personally, as well as the mayor, Commander Whitney and I agreed we should have a conversation.'

'Yes, sir.'

'You don't ask about the complaint or the complainant.'

'No, sir. The complainant would be Geena McEnroy, and her complaint would involve our investigation into her husband's murder. Or, more specifically, into the motive for his murder.'

'Which is?'

'Nigel McEnroy's confirmed sexual harassment of employees and clients – and more. His use of illegals to drug the women he targeted. His rape of multiple women, which he recorded and secreted said recordings in his offices here in New York and in London. Recordings I've viewed.'

Sober, direct, Tibble showed nothing in expression. 'These are very serious allegations made against an individual who can't dispute them or defend himself.'

'Yes, sir, they are. They are also fact. We have sworn statements from a number of women who were drugged, coerced, raped, and threatened. We have video and audio evidence, as McEnroy recorded his assaults. We have the illegals he used, the notebooks in which he listed his targets, corroborating witnesses from the venues in which he trolled those targets.'

Eyes unreadable, Tibble merely nodded. 'I see. Is there a reason why you didn't speak to Ms McEnroy about this preponderance of evidence?'

'But—' Peabody broke off, cleared her throat. 'Excuse me, sir.'

'You have something to add, Detective?'

'Sir, I read the lieutenant's report, and know she did, in fact, speak to Ms McEnroy about the evidence we'd gathered at that time. Basically, Chief Tibble, Ms McEnroy didn't want to hear it or believe it. She was understandably in a very upset state of mind.'

'One might be when one's spouse is tortured and murdered and left on one's doorstep.'

'Yes, sir.'

With the faintest of nods, Tibble looked back at Eve. 'Ms McEnroy states that you and the civilian consultant you took with you were both accusatory and aggressive toward her. Ah . . .' He swiveled his comp screen, tapped it. 'Badgering and belittling her,' he read, 'while smearing her husband's good name in order to blame him for his own murder.'

He tapped the screen again, folded his hands. 'She has threatened to bring suit against both of you and the department, unless you are both dismissed. She intends to appeal to the governor if you're not fired by the end of the day.'

'Respectfully, Chief Tibble,' Eve said, 'she can appeal to the deity of her choice, it won't change the facts. Her husband was a sexual predator, the fact of which she may or may not have been aware. Rather than badgering or belittling, Roarke – the civilian consultant – attempted to sympathize and comfort.'

Tibble raised a brow. 'I take it you did not attempt to sympathize and comfort.'

'He's better at it, sir. In order to investigate this matter, it was imperative to interview the spouse of the victim, to ascertain whether or not she was in any way involved or complicit in his death. If you don't look at the spouse—'

'You're an idiot,' Tibble finished. 'Do you believe the spouse in this case was involved or complicit?'

'I don't. I believe she turned a blind eye to his actions because she didn't want to believe him capable, didn't want to accept he continued to cheat on her. And now, faced with the raw truth, she lashes out.'

'Considering the facts regarding the victim's actions, behavior, crimes you've uncovered, do you feel capable of continuing to investigate his murder, without prejudice?'

'Sir. There's no question of that.'

'Good. Moving on. We now have a second victim. You believe they're connected.'

'By method, yes. In the killer's mind, yes. And there is a strong probability there's a connection to a support group for women who have been abused, raped, cheated on. Some of the women McEnroy raped and the ex-wife of Thaddeus Pettigrew, the second victim, all attended this support group.'

Interest flickered, for an instant, in Tibble's eyes. 'I take it McEnroy's widow didn't attend this group.'

'There's no evidence at this time to indicate that, no, sir.'

Tibble took pity on her, gestured for her to stand. 'Go ahead, since we're here, fill us in.'

Eve rose. 'We spoke with the woman who founded the group. We have no reason to believe she's involved. She requested a warrant for the names in her notes. They use first names only, but we have McEnroy's book, and may find some that cross.'

Pleased to be on her feet, and to talk it through, she continued. 'The second victim routinely hired, we believe without the knowledge or consent of the woman he lived with, LCs from a company called Discretion. The person in charge there confirmed Pettigrew has been a regular for several years – which would include his time with his ex-wife, and through his relationship with a Marcella Horowitz. Ms Horowitz was out of town with three other females at the time of Pettigrew's murder. Both Peabody and I believe her shock and upset at being informed and interviewed regarding his murder – and his predilection for LCs – was genuine.'

'She's young, Chief, Commander,' Peabody added. 'And while, like Ms McEnroy, she doesn't want to believe she was betrayed, we conclude she'll come around to it.'

'In addition, these murders took a cool head to plan. Both victims had their e's hacked. There's nothing in the widow's or in Horowitz's data that indicates they'd have the knowledge or skill, which both the civilian consultant and EDD confirm this sort of hacking entails.'

'And the poem left with the bodies?' Whitney spoke for the first time.

'A nice flourish' was Eve's opinion. 'And personal. A justification for the killings, and the torture. Pettigrew's ex-wife, Darla Pettigrew, started a company several years ago that manufactured and programmed droids. She may have the knowledge and skill.'

'If you don't look at exes,' Tibble began.

'You're still an idiot,' Whitney finished. 'You've spoken to her?'

'Yes, sir. Ah, I need to disclose, as the civilian consultant accompanied me this morning to Pettigrew's body, both he and McNab accessed the electronics. When doing so, Roarke discovered the company, Data Point, one sold during the divorce, had been acquired by Roarke Industries.'

'He knew the victim?' Tibble demanded.

'No, sir,' she replied. 'In fact, the transaction was done through lawyers and reps. It was, to Roarke's estimation, a small acquisition. However, Pettigrew had managed to acquire the controlling interest in the company, without his wife's full knowledge, and he forced the sale, took the lion's share.'

'Which was?'

She knew she was going to hate this part. 'Just over fifteen million.'

'And the ex-wife's take?'

'Just over seven.'

'So, an acquisition costing more than twenty-two million is ... small?'

It mortified, but Eve continued to speak briskly. 'Apparently it is in Roarke's world, yes, sir. I feel it was major in Darla Pettigrew's. Her company, and he not only cheated on her, left the marriage, he forced her to sell, and took the bulk.'

'A fine motive,' Whitney concluded. 'Opportunity?'

'She lives with her grandmother, who's recovering from an illness. Both claim she was there, though they both admit the grandmother fell asleep. However, Ms Callahan claims to remember Ms Pettigrew coming in to check on her during the night.'

'Eloise Callahan.' Peabody couldn't help herself.

Tibble actually blinked. 'Eloise Callahan? The actor? She's a legend.'

'I know, right? Sorry. Sorry, Chief, I know it isn't relevant.'

'It may be,' Eve corrected, 'as she's a legend for her acting. She came off very genuine, as did her granddaughter, but it's possible the granddaughter inherited some of that acting skill.'

Again, a flicker of interest as Tibble angled his head. 'You're looking at her.'

'Betrayed ex, big house – very private, and the killer needs private space – sick grandmother, or accomplice grandmother. A vehicle, a driver. We're looking at her.'

'All right.' Tibble nodded. 'Write it up. If you're going

to look hard at Eloise Callahan's granddaughter, you better have damn good vision. She's beloved, and through her activism she has political connections that make Geena McEnroy's threats to bring in the governor look like a toddler's tantrum.'

'Yes, sir. About those threats.'

'Consider them handled, Lieutenant.'

'Yes, sir, and that's appreciated. I want to say I don't have Roarke's or Peabody's ease with sympathy and comfort.'

'Not truc,' Peabody murmured.

'Quiet. While I don't have that ease, I would never belittle the obviously shocked and grieving widow of a murder victim.'

'To use your own words, Dallas, there's no question of that. Get to work.'

Once they stepped out, Peabody breathed out. 'He was never going to ream us.'

'You weren't even there, for Christ's sake. Why would he ream you?'

'Partners. Your ass—'

'Enough with the asses in the ass pan. No, he was never going to ream us or me or anybody over this. He called us in so he could tell the mayor and whoever else takes a poke he did. He spoke with us, has the facts, and while the department regrets Ms McEnroy's loss, while those involved in the investigation sympathize with her state of mind, we have to pursue the facts in order to find McEnroy's killer and bring that individual to justice.'

'That's good,' Peabody said as they got on the elevator.

'He knows how to work it, but he had to hear it from us, with Whitney in the room. It's how he covers – goddamn, I have to say it – everybody's ass.'

Even so, since she still held some tension in her shoulders, she rolled it out. 'Now let's go do the job.'

12

While Peabody wrote up the report, Eve updated her board and book. After checking the time, noting she had a decent gap before her consult with Mira, she propped her boots on the desk, studied the board.

There would be other women, she thought, women with stories to tell, ugliness and hurts to air. And maybe vendettas to wage.

If the killer fished in the pool of Women For Women for its justice-seeking, had that pool generated multiple killers or accessories? A kind of deadly pact?

Possible, possible, she decided, but . . .

Natalia Zula. She studied the therapist's ID shot, that of her pretty college-age daughter. They made it harder to buy the deadly pact theory. Zula knew the women, listened to their stories, gave them the time, space, place to air that ugliness, those hurts.

She'd been through them herself, had demanded and received justice the right way. Could a group of women form into a killing mob right under her nose?

Not nearly as plausible, but for now, she wouldn't discount it.

She wanted those names.

She swung her feet down, started to reach for her 'link to harass ADA Cher Reo about the warrant. Her unit signaled an incoming.

Another sketch came through with a short memo from Detective Yancy.

Can't give you much, as the wit didn't see much. A
glimpse in the dark. Wit was willing and cooperative,
but unable to give details.

'I'll say,' Eve agreed as she studied the sketch of a woman who ranged anywhere from twenty-five to fifty, may have been Caucasian or mixed race. No eye color, no defined features. The hair held the most details, the short, spiky style, the colors.

She split-screened Yancy's sketch from the wit at the club with the second sketch.

Resemblance? Maybe, maybe not. She pegged the first redhead as middle to late thirties, Caucasian, very attractive. The hair might have been a wig or dyed for the occasion, as the killer had known of McEnroy's penchant for redheads.

Hunted redheads, she thought, married a brunette. And what did that mean? Love, Eve supposed, but that love couldn't and hadn't outweighed his particular and prurient needs.

Second suspect, most likely a wig, or temp color job. In both cases, the hair made a statement – and was a detail that stuck in witnesses' minds.

The killer struck Eve as too smart to use her own style and color.

She added Darla Pettigrew's ID shot between the two sketches.

Again, maybe yes, maybe no on the resemblance.

Darla came in at thirty-eight – and looked it, if not a couple years older. Nondescript brown hair, medium length. Nondescript altogether, Eve mused, at least for the ID shot.

But she had those really good bones just like her grandmother. Eyes that might have sparkled if she bothered to smile, or didn't look tired. Wouldn't her actor grandmother know all the tricks with enhancements to play up the best features?

Then again, maybe Darla just wasn't interested in enhancements or painting up. And Eve had to admit she'd be the last person to criticize that stand.

Still . . .

Darla Pettigrew had motive, big motive to Eve's mind. She had access to privacy and a grandmother who likely wouldn't question her, and she had e-skills.

Eve checked for vehicles, found none registered in her name. Eloise had two, one all-terrain – white, one luxury sedan – silver. And neither fit the witness statements.

Didn't mean she didn't have access to another.

Because it just kept niggling at her, she contacted Leah Lester.

'Lieutenant Dallas, Ms Lester. I have a question about the support group.'

'Look, I told you everything I could. Why won't you let me just put this behind me?'

'When someone murdered Nigel McEnroy, they put it in front of you. Give me your impressions of a woman in the group named Darla.'

Leah's face closed in. 'And I told you the group was confidential and anonymous.'

'I've spoken to Darla, and I've spoken to Natalia. I'm asking for your impressions of this individual.'

'I was a lot more invested in myself, to be honest, than the others. I only went because it was important to Jasmine.'

'Do you remember Darla?'

'Maybe. Vaguely. At least I think so, but what I'm not going to do is put the finger on some poor woman who got screwed by a man.'

'Cuts both ways,' Eve tossed back. 'What you tell me may clear her. Her ex-husband was murdered last night.'

'Jesus Christ.' On a shudder, Leah pressed the heels of her hands to her eyes. 'Like McEnroy.'

'Yes. Now, impressions.'

'Vague, like I said. I stopped going, I told you that. I remember her as sort of broken – like a lot of us – but heartbroken, I guess. Her husband dumped her for a younger woman, and something about stealing the business she'd built. I guess I didn't feel all that sorry for her. She wasn't drugged and raped, just dumped.'

She let out a sigh.

'Like I said, I was more into my own problems. She looked like she had money, not like Un — not like one of the others whose ex smacked her around, until she got away with her kid.'

'How did she look like she had money?'

'I don't know. Her shoes. She had really good shoes, and she was still wearing a wedding set. If the diamond was real, it was worth something. I'm just saying she looked like money.'

Details mattered, Eve mused — even shoes. So she pressed. 'Do you remember if she seemed close to any of the women, developed a bond?'

'I don't know. I said I barely ... Wait, I did hear she gave one of the group some money. The one I said got smacked around. I don't know if it's true, just something somebody said.'

'Who? Who said it, who got the money? Two murders, Leah, don't make me bring you in.'

'Goddamn it. I don't remember who told me. It might have been Jasmine, it might have been one of the others. It was Una. If you're talking to Natalia, ask Natalia because Una wouldn't hurt a fly. She was a sweet woman trying to make a life for her kid after getting shafted. If Darla did give her some money to help, good for her. That's all I know.'

'I appreciate it.'

Eve clicked off, sat back, and wondered just how to track down a single parent named Una.

But right now, she needed to get to Mira.

She went out to the bullpen, stopped at Peabody's desk.

'I'm heading to Mira.'

'I was just about to let you know, I talked to the London partner. He finally tagged me back. He claims he didn't know anything about the harassment – or the drugging, the rapes. And seemed pretty grim about it. He did say he knew McEnroy – his word – strayed. That he had a thing, and always had for redheads, which to him – the partner – showed McEnroy loved his wife. He fell for her, a brunette, built a life, had a family. But he strayed from time to time.'

Peabody managed a simultaneous hiss and eye roll. 'It's "strayed" like, you know, he made a wrong turn walking to the bank. Anyway, the partner's coming into New York to try to handle things here, and he says he'll do whatever he can for the widow. He'll make himself available once he's in New York, for interview if you want to speak to him.'

'And the other partner?'

'Apparently scrambling to try to put out fires the murder, and the scandal attached, have lit. The company's taking a hit. Lawsuits threatened. I believe this guy with the grim.'

'Keep at it. It's not going to involve the company, unlikely the partners, but let's tie up all the threads.'

She rolled it around as she took the glides to Mira's level. No, not the company, not the partners, any more than it had to do with Pettigrew's law firm or partners.

It came down to the men themselves, sex, rape, greed.

She found Mira's dragon of an admin at her post. The

woman gave her own wrist unit a hard look but, as Eve hit the outer office exactly on time, couldn't work up a bitch.

'You're cleared to go in, Lieutenant.'

Mira, her sun-tipped mink-colored hair falling in a curly bob, stood by her AutoChef. Spring obviously inspired the trim lilac suit, the shoes of a few shades deeper with skinny heels so clear they looked like glass.

She'd added small purplish dangles to her ears, a trio of thin, braided chains around her neck, and as always, looked simply perfect.

She smiled at Eve, her soft blue eyes warming. 'I'm just making tea – and yes, I know, but I think you could use something calmer than coffee by this time of your day. You've been at it since before dawn.'

'She likes to kill early, after a long night.'

'Yes, I've read the reports.' Mira gestured to one of her blue scoop chairs as she brought over two delicate cups of floral-scented tea.

'Now.' She handed Eve one, sat, crossed her very fine legs. 'You say she, and I'm going to agree the killer is female, a justice seeker who believes she's enacted that justice by the violent murder of men who have misused other women.'

'The violence escalated with the second victim.'

'It often does, as we know. And executing – as I believe she sees it – two men in two nights is not only vindicating, but exciting.'

'Could she have had a more personal issue with Pettigrew?'

'It's certainly possible, but if she kills again, somewhat less likely. She killed him not first, but second. If there are more victims it's less likely, as the more personal would more likely be saved for the end. The crescendo, so to speak.'

'Maybe she doesn't have an end in mind. McEnroy was a kind of practice. Can I pull this off? Yeah, I can, so move on to the personal target.'

Interested, Mira sat back, lifted her eyebrows. 'Do you have a reason to believe that?'

'Pettigrew's ex-wife rings some bells for me.'

'What sort?'

'Her reaction to his murder? Way over the top. Divorced two years, right? And this is a guy who cheated on her, then dumped her for the younger skirt, and basically swindled her out of the company she'd built. For this guy she's a weeping wreck? I don't buy it.'

'Some love regardless of the insults and injuries.'

'Yeah, maybe so. But no.' The more she rolled it around, the more certain she felt. 'Just no on this one. I can't tell you exactly why, but just no. Add a shaky alibi, but one that's corroborated, sort of. She has considerable e-skills and Pettigrew's accounts were skillfully hacked. Big house, private house, plenty of room to do dirty deeds.'

'You believe she's your killer.'

'At this point, yeah. I have to look at all the angles, but, if she's not the killer, she's not altogether right. Just off somehow.'

'Keep me apprised there.'

'I will. Otherwise, the killer has the connection, one way or the other, with this support group. No way she just happened to target two men with women they'd . . . misused in that group.'

'So it may be more than one involved.'

'We've seen it before, but . . . I don't think the woman heading the group would have missed this sort of violent pact forming. And it feels like a single killer. It just feels as if it's one who enjoys putting on the mask. Being this lure for this target, this lure for the next. When she hits again, she'll present herself as his particular fantasy.'

'Lady Justice,' Mira added. 'Yet another persona. Singular as well. Add the poems. Poetry tends to be highly personal to the poet. Yet the sheer physicality, the logistics, make it difficult to say, with confidence, the killer acts alone.'

'Not alone. Someone's driving. It may be a partner, a hireling. It's certainly someone she trusts not to betray her, so I lean toward another female first. Men are the betrayers.'

'Yes. She's been betrayed or abused by a male. It may be a father or father figure if that betrayal was sexual.' Mira paused a moment, sipped tea as she studied Eve. 'Is that aspect giving you any difficulty?'

'I can handle it.'

'That wasn't the question.'

And until Mira had the answer to the question, Eve knew, she'd persist. So, get it out and done.

'I know what it's like to be raped, to be helpless, to have the rapist be my father. I know what it's like to kill, and

226

kill violently. If it brings that back, I can use it. I will use it. Finding who killed these men, whatever they did in life, is my job. I have to do the job, or even after all this time, Richard Troy wins.'

'If you have any trouble, I hope you'll come to me.'

'I'm here now. But I'm okay.'

And wanted to close that particular door.

'McEnroy was a predator,' Eve continued, 'and it would have satisfied me to take him down, to see him live out the rest of his life in a cage. Pettigrew? Weak, greedy, a liar, but there's no evidence he physically harmed anyone. Just cheated and cheated on his spouse, then continued to cheat on the woman he cheated with. Maybe a crappy human being, but not one who deserved what happened to him. I can stand for both of them.'

'All right. I'll tell you you're looking for a mature, goal-oriented killer. A female, at least thirty, probably some-what older. Controlled until she has her target subdued. Controlled enough to stalk, to research, to plan, to prepare, to lure him. Once she has him bound, unable to defend, that control is let off the leash. She has the endurance to physi-cally torture her victims for hours, the emotional distance to ignore their screams or pleas, as there's no sign they were silenced during the torture.'

'She'd want to hear them beg and scream.'

'I agree. Their punishment sustains her, their pain feeds her. The castration is the last stage, unmanning them, literally. And allowing them to hang, from the medical examiner's report, like meat, until they succumb to blood loss.'

'Why does she bring them back to their residence? She could dispose of the bodies altogether, or dump them – since she has to have transpo – miles away. But she risks, in both cases, bringing them back, leaving them outside, taking the time to leave them, and the poem, in plain sight.'

'She wants them found, and quickly. Doesn't it show their loved ones who they were? What they were? It shows the city, the world they were punished for their deeds. By her. I believe she'll be both pleased and upset that she's now being hunted by a pair of female cops. She'd appreciate your power – female power is essential to her psyche. And she'll be unhappy that, as women, you don't see she's doing what needs to be done when she would consider you colleagues.

'I suspect she has no man in her life now, nor does she wish to have that sort of connection. She may have female friends or companions, but men? Animals to be butchered, predators to be hunted. She believes in what she's doing, and so is only more dangerous.'

'She's not done.'

'No, I don't believe she is. If she has a job at this point, it's likely something she can do alone, or where she can flex her hours.'

Shifting, Mira uncrossed, recrossed her legs. 'As you noted in your report, she must have a place, a private area where she can carry out her torture, where she can take these men without being detected. I also agree with Morris.

She has some medical skill or has practiced the castration. The amputations were much too clean and precise for them to be done by a novice. Additionally, our ME's belief that a ceremonial-style blade was used says the castration – the unmanning, as you put it – is the main mission.'

With a slow nod, Eve thought it through. 'The hunt, the lure, even the torture, those are as much for her entertainment as punishment. The purpose, the point, is severing their manhood, removing that, taking that, so they die without it. Sexless.'

'Yes.' Mira smiled as if at a clever student. 'Exactly that.'

'She's able to project the persona, the image of what each of her victims wanted. That's part of the game, the entertainment,' Eve added. 'She's the attractive, available redhead McEnroy would invite into his privacy booth. Then the type of LC Pettigrew favors so he let her into his house. I think with Pettigrew it would have been quick. Hi, come on in. But with McEnroy there had to be some flirtation, some verbal foreplay. This wasn't a business transaction. She had to be what he was looking for. And even though it was quick, she had to be what Pettigrew expected.'

'She studies them, adapts.'

'Acts?' Eve leaned forward. 'I'm wondering if she has acting skills, experience, abilities. She has targets, and not just these two. They won't all be quick and done like Pettigrew. She has to entice, lure, meet specific expectations to put the men she selects into the situation where she can take them out.'

'That's certainly possible,' Mira agreed. 'But she believes in her mission, her goal. She prepares – that's the control. She becomes – that's part of the preparation. No doubt she practices. She has time, she has the space and the means. The wardrobe, for instance, the hair, whether wigs or styling, the transportation, the drugs. All that takes means. She's made an investment.'

Mira tilted her head. 'Does this, too, apply to Darla Pettigrew?'

'Yeah, the means, the acting skills – potentially. The shoes.'

'Shoes?'

'One of the other women told me she came off rich – expensive shoes. She's got the private home – a big one where she lives with her grandmother. The grandmother's recovering from an illness, and in addition you can see they're tight. That's the shaky corroboration on the shaky alibi.'

'And does Pettigrew have acting experience?'

'Not that shows, but the grandmother does. Big-deal actor. Eloise Callahan?'

'Really?' Shifting again, Mira blinked. 'Yes, a very big deal. She's brilliant, revered. And she's quite the activist, too.'

'She knows Peabody's grandmother, they did the activist thing together.'

Mira let out a light laugh. 'That shouldn't surprise me a bit. Callahan's also well known for her philanthropy. From what I know of her it's hard to picture her involved in torture murders.'

'She doesn't have to be involved, directly. It strikes me that the granddaughter may have picked up some tips over the years. Acting, makeup, wardrobe. Even, what's it – staging. The whole thing is full of drama, right down to the poems and the name she's given herself.'

'Yes, there's a flair for the theatrical. Is that how she struck you?'

'No. The opposite. Quiet, unassuming – even, I don't know, plain. But she overplayed the grief and shock. It just hit wrong. It looked, sounded, genuine, but it hit wrong. It's all I've got,' Eve admitted with a shrug. 'She hit me wrong.'

Sitting back again, Mira took a moment to process. 'Well, she would be in the age group I've profiled. She would have means, and motive, and the privacy. She attended the support group. You have ample reason to consider her a suspect.'

'Right now, she's prime. But I can't get a warrant on a hunch.' Eve rose, and as she set the cup aside found herself surprised she'd actually finished the tea. 'Thanks for the time.'

'Be careful. She's vicious,' Mira added. 'Once that part of her is unleashed, she's vicious.'

'Hey, me, too.'

As Eve headed back to Homicide, Darla ran a few errands. With the rain, both she and the day nurse agreed to cancel Grand's walk. But Darla enjoyed the rain, strolling in it as she stopped in the bakery for Grand's favorite cannolis, moved on to the market for some fresh fruit.

She'd used the excuse that she needed to get out, to walk, to keep busy to help settle herself over Thaddeus. Both Grand and the nurse, she thought as she examined bunches of the tart green grapes Grand liked, had been so understanding, so sympathetic.

God, she loved that.

She'd seen the hints of pity, too, for a woman discarded and betrayed who still loved, and could grieve for the man who'd hurt her.

She enjoyed the pity quite a lot.

But they'd never understand how true love and deep hate could live in the same heart.

Thaddeus hadn't known her. After all the years she'd shared her bed, her body, given him her trust and devotion, he hadn't seen her through the disguise.

He hadn't known until, in the last moments of his life, as the blood drained from him, she'd taken off the mask. He'd looked so puzzled, she remembered – fondly – staring at her as life poured out of him.

And he'd said her name, finally said her name, *Darla*, like a question. His last word had been her name.

And that, oh that, had been delicious.

'Excuse me.'

Darla came back to the moment as another woman nudged her impatiently.

'I need to get by.'

'Oh! I'm so sorry. My mind wandered.' With an apologetic smile, Darla shifted, chose some grapes, some berries.

When she finished in the market, she stepped back outside. Opened her umbrella, gave it a little twirl.

She felt lighter than air!

She hummed a bit as she walked, as she replayed her scene with the police. Perfect, just perfect, in her recollection. The shock, the grief, the struggle for composure.

So much fun! She hadn't known how much fun she'd have.

Maybe she'd worried, just for a moment, when she'd realized Grand had come down. But then that had turned out perfectly, too.

To have her sweet grandmother – and the acclaimed Eloise Callahan – vouch for her, essentially relate the same story, the same timeline.

And how smart had it been to run up to check on Grand when Thaddeus passed out. The police could hardly suspect her of killing anyone when she had her much-loved grandmother to tend to.

She had to admit it was fun to match wits with Eve Dallas. It felt as if they were characters – the leads – in a vid. Only she was directing it, too. And writing it. She'd designed the costumes (at least her own).

And she already had the next act written.

Walking home in the rain with her market bag, her bakery box, she smiled, even did a little dance inside her head.

All those years, she thought, all those years with Thaddeus, she'd been so devoted, so faithful.

So weak.

She'd created a company – herself! Used her brain, her skills, her energy to make it into something solid. Not earthshaking, but solid and respectable.

She'd done that.

And she'd let him take it from her, just as he'd taken her self-respect. At least she'd learned from the group that she wasn't alone. In fact, she wasn't nearly the worst case. So many women used, abused, betrayed.

They had a champion in her now. She'd given them Lady Justice.

She swiped into the house, put her umbrella in the stand, her jacket in the closet.

After carrying the marketing to the kitchen, she ordered the droid to make tea while she herself arranged the fruit, the pastries on pretty plates.

A treat for Grand.

She checked the time, deemed it perfect. Grand would have finished her physical therapy, and would be settled in the upstairs parlor.

She wheeled the cart into the elevator. Inside she arranged her face into what she thought of as a brave smile – keeping her eyes just a little sad.

When she wheeled the cart in, Eloise and the nurse sat already deep into a game of Scrabble.

'Cannolis.' Eloise rolled her eyes. 'There goes the waistline.'

'Not yours, Grand. I bet Donnalou worked you hard.'

'She's a slave driver.'

Donnalou, a tiny woman with a quick laugh, just shook her head. 'I can barely keep up with her these days. And she's already hit me with a seven-letter word on a triple.'

'Then you both deserve a treat.'

'Sit down with us, Darla.'

'No, you two go ahead.' Darla bent over to kiss Eloise's cheek. 'I've got a few things to do. Keeping busy's the best right now.'

'Don't push yourself too hard, Darla,' Donnalou advised. 'You look tired.'

'Don't worry. I might take a lie-down while you're here. We'll see. Now, Grand, don't you trounce Donnalou too hard.'

'No promises.'

Laughing, Darla got back in the elevator. And took it all the way down to her lair. Keeping an eye on the monitor and the Scrabble game, she checked to be certain the droid had thoroughly cleaned the floor, the restraints. And of course Lady Justice's uniform.

She double-checked her supply of drugs. More than enough for one more, she decided, but she might need to send a droid out to score. Especially since Grand, thank God truly on the mend, would need a slightly stronger dose of the sleeping draught to keep her safe and dreaming through the night.

She'd send the droid she'd named Jimmy – mid-twenties, tough face with a small scar on the right cheek. He could meet the dealer later that night, refresh her supplies.

She imagined her own doctor would prescribe something to help her sleep – given the circumstances. But she really didn't have time for that.

She needed to select the costume for the next scene.

13

When Eve walked back into the bullpen, Jenkinson's new obscenity of a tie greeted her. When he signaled her over to his desk, she scowled at it.

'Why, I ask sincerely, would a grown man, a cop, a veteran detective of the NYPSD wear an atomic-green tie with screaming yellow rubber duckies all over it?'

'They're not screaming, they're quacking. And it's what you call whimsy.'

'It's what I call felonious assault on the eyes. Did you get the notes and names from Natalia Zula?'

'Yeah, we got 'em – and her daughter was home.' Though he sat and Eve stood, he managed to look down his nose at her. 'She said my tie was mag. Just saying. You got the discs on your desk. And check it.'

He thumbed back toward Reineke, his usual partner. Obliging, Reineke hitched up his pants leg to reveal screaming yellow rubber duckies on atomic-green socks.

'Jesus, you're coordinating now?'

'Just the luck of the draw,' Reineke claimed. 'Anyhow,

Zula and her kid were both cooperative. Some shaken up at the idea one of the group might be killing people. The kid wants her mother to come in, give you a thumbnail shrink sketch on the members. Mom's conflicted.'

'She may have to get unconflicted.'

'They're tight,' Jenkinson put in. 'We got the feeling the daughter was going to work on the mom about it.'

'I'll take that for now. Thanks for the assist.'

She went to her office and plugged in the disc.

She scanned the names, the notes attached to each. Some of everything, Eve mused. Rape, abuse, emotional bullying, cheating partners, dumped by lovers, scammed, slapped, screwed over, beaten, belittled, badgered.

Some, by the notes, angry, some depressed, others guilt-ridden or ashamed. A lot of desperation and shattered egos.

Natalia had noted down if the woman mentioned children, her job, another relationship, a friend or family member, and whether those were supportive or combative.

She'd added whether or not the woman had reported the rape, abuse, or assault, if the woman had removed herself from the situation or remained in it.

Careful notes, Eve decided, and always nonjudgmental. Might pay to have her come in, give those thumbnails to Mira. Shrink to shrink.

Pausing, she took time to shoot a memo to Mira asking her if she agreed, and if so, would she contact Zula.

Then she read, with interest, the notes on Darla.

11/59: Husband left her for younger woman (had an affair with same during the marriage). Husband currently living with younger woman. Divorce entailed the sale of the company she'd built – his demand. Discovered he'd manipulated a majority share. Now living with grandmother.

Appears educated, bright, financially stable.

Appears emotionally shattered, feels worthless, unattractive, undesirable, foolish, bitter. Still in the grieving stage over death of marriage, broken trust, sexual betrayal.

Briefer notes illustrated progress or lack of same, mood, ability to connect with others in the group through the early part of 2060.

3/60: Appears stronger emotionally though cannot yet let go of her anger and sense of betrayal. I see a definite and encouraging bond with others in the group, a willingness to listen, sympathize. She no longer breaks down when she speaks of her own situation, but speaks with bitterness of her ex and the woman he left her for. Credits her grandmother for giving her support and strength.

Anger, bitterness, Eve thought. That she could buy. And that didn't jibe, to her mind, with the floods of grief.

5/60: More interactive, more easily offering support and sympathy to others. Stated, emotionally, the group, the other women have helped her find purpose again, find self again.

7/60: Am told confidentially by Una that Darla gifted her with several thousand dollars to assist Una in renting an apartment. Showing generosity and friendship, a willingness to offer a hand up.

12/60: Brought small gifts for the group for the holiday meeting. Seemed very upbeat – though expressed some concern re grandmother, who is feeling poorly. Left early.

And that was the last entry. Sitting back, Eve thought it through.

She could play it two ways. One, the group support, the healing time, and blah blah brought Darla out of her hole, helped her shake off the negative feelings, focus on the positive. Helped her bond with other women and lift herself back up to a productive life.

Or, as she put her shattered self back together, listening to the other women – the betrayals, abuse – she re-formed into something twisted. Began to see herself as a kind of champion – an avenger.

Finding her purpose.

'And nothing here, just nothing here to push that either way.'

She gathered her things, went back to the bullpen and Peabody's desk.

'Whatever it is shut it down, or bring it with you to work as we go.'

'Where are we going?'

'To light a fire under Dickhead at the lab. I want to know what Pettigrew had under his toenails.'

Peabody scrambled up, grabbed her coat. 'I've been crossing the names Jenkinson and Reineke got from Zula with McEnroy's list of victims and targets.'

'And?' Eve said as they walked.

'Some matches – it's just first names, so I expected to match some. I thought I'd reach out to Sylvia Brant at Perfect Placement, see if she'd give me full names on the matches. Go from there.'

'Good angle, do that.'

'Just me?'

'If there are more than ten, I'll take half, otherwise you push this angle.'

'You don't think it's going anywhere.'

'It could. Definitely could,' Eve countered as she suffered through the confines of a crowded elevator. 'We have two already crossed. On one hand, the odds would say it's a long shot for another. But offices have gossip trains, and somebody else might have gotten on, tried the group after the two we know of left.'

'Because they'd have mentioned another if they knew another.'

'Right. So it's worth looking.'

'What's your angle?'

'I want that substance, then I need to think. Some of the women in that group filed police reports. Not all, not even close, but some did. So I'm going to see what I can dig into there. First names, reported crime or offense, what other information comes out of Zula's notes. She lists their first attendance, so that gives a time frame. And I'll push Zula for more if I need to.'

'Do you want me on that?'

'I've got Mira on it, actually. You take your angle. Work it here, or take it home.'

'You're still looking at Darla Pettigrew,' Peabody commented as they – finally – pushed out into the garage.

'Just something there – and Zula's notes didn't make me think otherwise.' In the car, Eve paused a moment. 'First vic – a rapist, a vicious, ugly son of a bitch who drugged, raped, and threatened women. Second vic – cheated on his wife, then ends up with the woman he cheated on her with. He likes to bang LCs. He manipulated – and we can even say cheated – the ex out of a lot of money. But he doesn't reach the level of vicious and ugly that McEnroy does. So why is he next on her list? Why is his torture more violent?'

'Okay. You're going with it was personal because it was Darla.' Peabody considered as Eve drove out of the garage. 'But it could just be timing. He was next because she could get to him next. And the level of violence is characteristic escalation. Especially since there was no lull between.'

'Also true,' Eve admitted. 'All of it.'

'And it could be the level of the crime or sin or offense – however she looks at it – isn't the point. It's all the same to her.'

Eve frowned over that. 'That's good.' Though she hated to admit it. 'That could be true.' Still, she picked at it. 'And it may be the timing goes to, yeah, who she can get to – and who she felt closest to in the group. Who she felt deserved or needed her brand of justice most. That's something to add in there.'

'Maybe Natalia Zula would have some insight. Who she feels clicked, or made friends – maybe on the outside. Lester said some of them met for coffee or whatever.'

'Yeah. We'll look there, or have Mira work with Zula there. Two good angles in a row, Peabody.'

'Woot.' Then she sighed. 'I wish I didn't get this feeling like something was off with Darla Pettigrew, too. I don't know if I got it on my own or if I picked it up from you.'

'Right now, let's play the angles.'

When they walked into the lab, the white-coated lab nerds worked busily at their counters, at their stations, inside their glass-walled rooms. Eve headed straight for chief lab tech Dick Berenski – not so affectionately known as Dickhead.

He hunched at a computer, his thin black hair slicked back over his egg-shaped head. His spidery fingers crawled over keyboards, slid over touch screens as he rolled on his stool from tool to tool at his workstation.

He spotted Eve, gave her the gimlet eye. 'We're working

on it. Your DB isn't the only DB in the city. Plenty of live ones, too, need analysis.'

'How freaking hard is it to ID a substance sent to you hours ago — and flagged as priority?'

'Every other fricking substance comes in here's flagged.'

He had a point, she knew, but she also knew how he operated. He was chief because he was damn good — and he was Dickhead because he liked squeezing out a little extra.

'Box seat, Mets game — if I get the results in the next sixty seconds.'

'Who wants to go to a game solo?'

'Two seats. Clock's ticking.'

He smiled at her, and what she read in the smile just pissed her off. 'You already have the results, you little weasel.'

'Now, now.' Still smiling, he patted his hands in the air. 'I got 'em, and I was getting 'em refined when you came stalking in.'

He slid down the counter again, swiped another screen. 'What Morris sent over's scrapings of painted concrete.'

He tapped the screen again to bring up a bunch of figures and symbols only a nerd could translate. 'So we work out the type and grade of concrete, the color and brand of the paint. Top grade, all around.'

'What does that mean?'

He gave her the gimlet eye, and the smug smile. 'See, that's what I'm going to tell you now that we got it. Means he dug those toenails into high-dollar painted concrete, not your cheap or mid-priced stuff like you'd perhaps see in some recreation center – but more country club–like. Skirt around a pool, say, or somebody's finished–off fancy basement, a high–traffic lobby maybe. Perhaps an upscale apartment kitchen or john, like.'

'Okay.' Eve placed her bet on that fancy basement. Private. She'd add a bet for soundproofed. 'I need more.'

'I'm working on it!' And indeed those spidery fingers got busy. 'We're getting you a brand on the concrete. Yeah, yeah, see here – top grade. Six thousand psi, so you can eliminate big commercial buildings. You'd need a minimum of ten thousand psi there. So what you've got is most likely residential or a smaller building – like a duplex, a four-decker. Could be a pool skirt, garage floor, like that. It's, there it is, it's Mildock concrete. That's not going to narrow it too much.'

He might be an irritating son of a bitch, Eve thought, but he knew his job inside and out.

'Keep going.'

'I'm gonna say, he dug in to get through the epoxy – epoxy, not paint.' He swiped, tapped, swiped. 'Uh-huh, uh-huh. You've got nonslip additives here, so it's going to be a floor, not a wall. It's good stuff, like I said. Kreet-Seal brand. Their number EX-651, goes by Burnished Gold. Some waterproofing in there, so basement, kitchen, garage. Not likely around a pool, and not likely exterior. You'd want special epoxy for those heavy wet areas, and this isn't.'

'Mildock six thousand psi concrete with Kreet-Seal Burnished Gold epoxy – nonslip, light waterproofing.'

'That's it. It'll have dings and scratches on it.'

'Yeah.' Maybe he'd earned those box seats. 'Get me the written report.'

'You're freaking welcome,' he called after her, shook his head, muttered, 'Cops.'

Then checked his PPC for the next Mets home game.

'Do you want me to run this down?' Peabody asked Eve.

'I'll get going on it. You play those angles – and cross-check the names. It's easy enough from here to drop you back at Central or at home. Where do you want to work on this?'

'I'll take home, and the quiet. Plus, we're going down to Mavis's for dinner – if we're clear. I can bake something for dessert. Baking's good play-the-angles time for me.'

'Whatever works.'

'I can walk from here, no problem. Pick up a couple things on the way home. It's barely raining.'

'That works, too. If you hit anything, let me know.'

'Count on it. Hmm, spring shower. I think lemon meringue pie.'

As Eve got in the car, she wondered how anybody could think and bake at the same time. But apparently Peabody could manage it.

As she drove, she started a search on the in-dash on contractors who installed – she learned the term was *poured* – Mildock concrete floors.

She also learned there were a shitload of them who serviced the city.

She switched to the epoxy, got another shitload, narrowed it somewhat by filtering in the specific brand. From there she merged the two searches to see what companies both poured and painted.

She played with it in her head. Possible to do the whole job – pour the concrete, seal it up. Or possible to paint the seal on an existing floor.

Good news, she thought: They'd match the floor with the substance under the vic's nails when they found the location.

Bad news: Finding the location from the type of concrete and sealer used on some sort of floor was going to be more luck than skill.

With her mind spinning it, she was almost surprised to drive through the gates. Maybe working while driving was her baking and thinking.

Green stuff speared up along the drive, and more green hazed the trees. Maybe, just maybe, despite the chilly rain (because of it?) spring was pushing winter aside.

She parked, grabbed her stuff. She decided she'd take a break, hit the gym for a sweaty workout to thoroughly clear her head before she got back to work.

An insult for Summerset regarding stick-up-the-ass-replacement surgery at the ready, she walked in.

But rather than his looming in the foyer, she heard his voice from the parlor. And a quick belly laugh she knew well followed by quick, cheerful gibberish.

She tossed her coat on the newel post, left her file bag on the steps, then crossed over.

In a frilly pink sweater and blue pants with frills of pink lace on the hems, Bella sat on Summerset's bony lap. Her golden curls bounced in a pair of miniature ponytails secured with rainbow bands.

Mavis's nod to pink fountained around her head in hair as bright as candy. She wore the rainbow in a swirl of a dress that floated over the tops of her thigh-high pink boots.

Barely.

The three sat in front of a quiet fire looking absurdly and happily domestic.

Bella let out a squeal – the sort that, if she hadn't come to expect it, would've had Eve reaching for her weapon. Bella scrambled out of Summerset's lap and charged – in that stunning toddler speed – across the floor.

'Das! Das! Das!'

She flung herself at Eve's legs like a mini–defensive tackle. Galahad, who would normally stir himself to greet her by winding through her legs, just blinked his eyes and stayed on the arm of Mavis's chair.

Whatever Bella babbled with her seriously pretty face tipped up to Eve would remain a mystery. But Eve understood the meaning of the upstretched arms and had never been able to figure out how to refuse them.

She hauled the kid up, got the loving and sloppy kisses, then the long, sighing hug.

What the hell were you supposed to do?

Curious, Eve took a sniff. 'You smell like chocolate.'

Bella tossed back her head, gave her wild and happy laugh.

Babble, 'Someshit,' *babble babble,* 'cookies,' *babble,* 'yum!' *babble,* 'Das.'

'Got it.' Sort of.

She would have put the kid down, but Bella clung to her like a barnacle to a hull. So Eve just shifted her as she glanced at Mavis.

'How'd you know I was heading home?'

'I didn't. Bellamina and I came by to hang with Summerset.'

'Someshit,' Bella said, very fondly.

'So it's luck to the ult,' Mavis continued, 'you hitting the home fires early while we're hanging. Take off the load, join the hang.'

Work, Eve thought. Murderers to catch. But the kid was locked around her, and Mavis's smile shined like half a dozen suns. Trapped by joy, she carted Bella over. When she sat, Bella nuzzled in, jabbering.

Eve caught 'Ork,' 'Gahad,' something about Mommy, something about Daddy. Somewhere inside the chatter and embraces, Bella got a hand on Eve's sidearm.

'Uh-uh.' Though it was secured in its harness, Eve firmly removed the curious little hand.

'Toy!'

'No, it's not.'

'Bella toy!' Big blue eyes batted. 'Pease!'

'Forget it. It's not a toy. It's my weapon.'

Charm vanished. Big blue eyes hardened like steel. 'Want toy!'

In Eve's mind two little horns popped up through the golden curls. A forked tongue darted out between the rosy lips.

In the next chair, Mavis – no help at all – sipped something that smelled like tea.

'You think that's going to work?' It was pretty damn scary, Eve admitted privately. 'I kick ass for a living, kid.'

'Share!' Bella demanded.

'No. Think of something else.' Desperate to change the focus, Eve boosted up a hip, dug out one of her cards. 'Here. You get in trouble, tag me.'

Bella took the card, studied it with her lips pursed, her eyebrows drawn. Then she nodded, used her finger to jab the words.

'Bella Eve.'

'Right. Great.'

All charm again, she fluttered those eyelashes. 'Mine?'

'Yeah, all yours.'

'Ace on the distract, Dallas,' Mavis complimented as Bella cuddled against Eve and jabbered at the card. Then batting her own baby blues, turned to Summerset. 'Do you think you could take her back, maybe give her one more you-know-what before we take off?'

'Delighted. Bella, why don't we go to the kitchen and see what we might find?'

'Ooooh, Someshit cookies! Das! Mommy.'

She all but leaped to the floor, would have wound up Summerset's bony body like a snake up a tree if he hadn't bent down to pick her up.

She waved Eve's card like a flag, chattering away at Summerset as he nodded soberly and carried her off. 'Yes, of course we will.'

'No way he understood that.'

Mavis let out a happy little sigh. 'She said we need to share cookies with you and me, and get a treat for the cat. We're working hard on the whole sharing deal.'

'Yeah, you get it, but no way he could.'

'Oh, he's aces at it, like totally fluid in Bellamina. We try to get by every week or two for a quick hang. He's like her granddaddy.'

Since that stunned her speechless, Eve just stared.

'So, you know, we were at Jake's studio. We're going to cut a disc together, and that is mag to the ex, and he had to head off to meet Roarke, and I thought, hey, good time to see Someshit.'

'Roarke?'

'Yeah, and when his name dropped, Belle's all "Ork, Ork," so I tagged Summerset to see if we could do the pop-in. Didn't figure on catching you, but I'm taking it as a sign.'

'A sign of what?'

'That it's time to tell you what we weren't going to tell for a couple more weeks even though I've been busting and you have to be the first even though it weirds you out.'

Mavis popped up, did a dance in her thigh-high boots. Pointed at her belly. 'Encore!'

'What's that mean?'

With a roll of her eyes, Mavis mimed a mound over her belly. 'Encore! Knocked Up, The Return!'

'What? You're . . . again?'

'Again!' Mavis executed three pirouettes, then a booty shake. 'Sperm, egg, touchdown.' Then she mimed spiking the ball and what may have been a volcano erupting.

'I've been totally *dying* to tell you.' She dropped onto the arm of Eve's chair, grabbed her in a fierce hug. 'I've got two-plus months in – even had to pretend to drink wine at Nadine's bash 'cause we thought people would guess if I didn't. We were going to wait through the first tri, but here you are, and I can't, and now we can tell Peabody and McNab when they come over tonight, and I can tell Trina, and – oh, every-damn-body. You had to be first because total BFF, even though it weirds you.'

'It doesn't weird me.' At Mavis's snort, Eve had to concede. 'Okay, some. But you're happy. You look crazed, but I read it as happy.'

'Happy squared times a gazillion. Leonardo and I wanted to have kids close together – you know, so they could be buds – and we decided to start to hit it right after Bellamina turned one.'

She slid down, squeezed into the chair with Eve to cuddle much as Bella had. 'Do you remember how I got all whacked that time when I was pregnant with Belle, how I was afraid I'd just blow at being a mom, how I'd screw it all up? And you told me I'd be mag, I'd be a totally good mom?'

'You are.'

'I am. My moonpie and me, we're good at this. He's everything a daddy should be. I'm so lucky, Dallas. I'm so freaking blessed.' She turned her face into Eve's shoulder, weeping. 'And I'm so freaking hyped on hormones.'

'Okay.' Eve patted her back. 'Okay.'

With a sigh, Mavis settled in. 'I never thought I'd be here. Not here-here. Okay that, too, but you know, *here*. With someone so abso-mag like Leonardo, with a daughter who's sunshine and rainbows and everything good. With a life that's not just grabbing what you can grab when you can grab it and not worrying about what's next. Freaking blessed, Dallas.'

'You deserve it.'

'Getting arrested by you was the best thing that ever happened to me.'

'Glad I could help.'

With a watery laugh, Mavis shook her head. 'Serious, because it started me to here. Anyway, Leonardo and I want you and Roarke there, like with Bella.'

'There ...' Terror gripped her by the throat. 'Mavis, listen—'

'We'll talk about it, but now I need to fix my face back up. And probably puke. Yeah, pretty sure I need to boot.'

Mavis wiggled up, hurried out, and Eve sat just as she was.

In there, again, she thought. In the room where *it* happened. Again.

'Jesus Christ, what have I done to earn this torment?'

14

One thing a visit with a chatty toddler and a pregnant Mavis accomplished – it cleared Eve's mind every bit as thoroughly as a sweaty workout.

In fact she felt just a little breathless by the time she made it up to her office. Even though she got a cookie out of it.

She tossed her jacket over a chair, programmed a pot of coffee.

When she checked for incoming at her command center, she found Dickhead's report, and made a note to hit Roarke up for the tickets.

Another report from EDD told her Pettigrew hadn't kept a list like McEnroy. He simply kept a calendar on his office unit – under a passcoded personal file – marking dates, times when he booked a licensed companion.

More often than not, he also booked a hotel room for the encounter, but he had a scatter of those bookings at his home. According to EDD, the home visits coordinated with out-of-town dates on Horowitz's calendar on her home unit.

Older calendars indicated he used hotels exclusively

during his marriage. He didn't take chances with his ex, before she became his ex, Eve mused.

Because Horowitz was easier to fool?

Because he knew/feared Darla would be more wrathful?

More to lose with a wife, Eve thought as she updated her board and book. If Darla went for the divorce first, for instance, found a way to cut him out of the company, or just make his life hell.

Back at her command center, Eve put her boots up, sat back with coffee.

McEnroy – a criminal, a rapist, a predator, a man who if found out while alive would have spent a great deal of time in a cage.

Pettigrew – a crappy husband and partner. Greedy, an opportunist. But nothing she could see illegal in his actions. Nothing that would have landed him in a cage.

And still, to 'Lady Justice' they'd earned the same fate.

'Because they're all the same,' Eve murmured. 'Men, as a species, are a plague that needs to be eradicated. Start with your circle – the support group – eliminate them one by one. And after that, go on the hunt. It's in your blood now.

'Men are the enemy; destroying them the mission.'

'Well now, that's a warm welcome home.'

Eve glanced over as the cat rolled out of the sleep chair to trot over and greet Roarke.

'I'd keep you around,' she told him. 'You gotta get sex and coffee somewhere.'

'Such a comfort.' He strolled over to kiss her – and steal her coffee. 'I'm told you got home early – for you.'

'Wanted mind-clearing and thinking time. I got Mavis and the kid.'

'So I'm told as well. And how are they?'

'The kid's smart, scary, and pretty damn irresistible. Mavis is pregnant.'

'She . . . what now?'

'"Encore", she says. And if she were capable of doing handsprings, she'd have done them.' To demonstrate, Eve circled a finger in the air. 'It's on purpose – the knocked-up part. Telling me was because I showed up during what I found out is a routine visit with Summerset, and her seeing it as a sign to spill.'

'Well, that's lovely then. We'll send her flowers.'

'Don't get too happy about it. She expects us to do the encore, too.'

'What encore would that . . .' Quickly, visibly, he paled. 'You don't mean she wants us to be in there again when she—'

'Pushes another human being out of her? Yeah, she does.'

'I'm opening a bottle,' he said instantly. 'And I'm not discussing it or thinking of it. I still have images burned on my brain from the first that haunt me in the dead of the night.'

Desperately pleased to have company in her terror, Eve pointed at him. 'You, even you, won't be able to talk her out of it.'

'I could be out of town, even off-planet,' he said as he

walked over to choose a wine. 'I could very easily be off-planet for— When is she due?'

Eve frowned. 'I don't know. I didn't ask. I never know what to ask. She said she was pregnant at Nadine's bash, but didn't want to spring it on people then. And if I have to do this again, pal, so do you.'

'I'm not thinking about that part of it. We're having wine. Now talk to me about something less traumatic. Like murder.'

Because she felt entirely more comfortable talking about murder than childbirth, Eve took the wine he held out.

'Big break. Pettigrew dragged and dug his bare feet – toes, toenails – over the floor, and we've ID'd the substance. Which is why I need two box seats for the next Mets home game.'

'Dickhead.'

'Sometimes I want to get in his face and threaten and badger, other times I just want to get through it.'

'Understood. I'll take care of it. Let's sit a minute.' After he ordered the fire on low, Roarke drew her to the sitting area. 'What's the substance?'

'Painted concrete. I have the brand and – what's it – psi of the concrete – Mildock – the brand and color of the paint – or the epoxy. Additives therein indicate floor not wall paint, not enough waterproofing for an outdoor area, or around a pool. Most likely a garage or an interior space. Like a basement. I'm leaning basement. Private.'

Sipping wine, sitting with his wife? Roarke considered that a fine transition to his day. 'That is quite the break.'

'Yeah. Both the brands are popular, so it's going to be a bitch to try to narrow down, but once we have her, this'll cap it.'

She drank some wine, studied the board. 'Horowitz doesn't fit.'

'Pettigrew's live-in?'

'Yeah, even if I opened this up like it's a conspiracy – multiple women working together to off cheaters – she doesn't fit. Geena McEnroy fits better, but she doesn't fit smooth, either. She followed through,' Eve added. 'Tagged her way up the chain to Tibble and the mayor, threatened going to the governor.'

Roarke skimmed a hand over her hair. 'And?'

'Got called into The Tower.' She shrugged. 'Tibble's half a politician, because that's the job, but he's no dumb-ass. I ran it through for him and Whitney, including the fact you bought the company Pettigrew screwed his ex out of. Laid out the evidence and blah blah. He'll handle her.'

'No doubt. As to the company, I can give you a bit more on that now. Darla Pettigrew launched her company with backing from her grandmother, who, as it happens, is the completely amazing Eloise Callahan.'

'You know her?'

'Of. And I admire, very much, her work. You've seen some of her vids.'

He'd know better than she would, so Eve said, 'Probably.'

'I can promise we've watched a few together. But in any case the legendary Eloise backed her granddaughter financially. Darla had studied programming and AI engineering in college, worked for advanced degrees. Then married Pettigrew. Reading between the lines of the data I unearthed, she played lawyer's wife to the exclusion of her own ambitions for several years, but along the way something sparked her idea to start her own company with a focus on creating, programming, and manufacturing personalized domestic droids. Small scale, and with the eye toward quality and affordability.'

'Hers then. He didn't have the programming chops, right?'

'None at all, but he handled the legalities – and there he set himself up nicely. And,' Roarke added, 'craftily. The company had some success – enough for her to repay her grandmother, and build a reputation for reliability and customer service. A solid little company, as I said before.'

'Yours now.'

'It is, yes. A couple of years ago, Pettigrew's financial manager contacted our acquisitions department. Memos and reports from the time state the company would be on the block due to a divorce.'

'Would be?'

'Yes, we got a bit of a heads-up, an invitation to make an offer. My people did the due diligence, I cleared the offer, and after a quick and easy negotiation, we finalized within a couple of weeks. Simple and standard, no muss or fuss.'

'She didn't have a choice,' Eve replied.

'So it seems. It appeared, as I said, simple and standard on paper. She'd signed off, and he'd held the majority share.'

Eve rose, wandered to the board. 'Because he'd set it up that way, and she assumed he set it up fairly.'

'I'd agree with that. As I said, it was craftily done.'

'I bet. Plus, she was, most probably, focused on the work, the hiring, the getting it off the ground, and left the legal crap to him. Married a lawyer, after all.'

Roarke watched her circle, study. 'Hard to see it otherwise.'

'Impossible to, from where I'm standing. And it was hers, the idea – her education – her grandmother's backing, the work.'

She glanced back at him. 'And pride. She'd have been proud of it – proud she'd paid back her grandmother's investment, proud she'd built something.'

'Quite a nice something,' Roarke confirmed. 'A solid little company with potential to grow. She had reason to be proud of it, yes.'

'And he cheated her out of it. Cheated on her sexually.' Eve jabbed a finger at Darla's ID shot. 'I'm telling you that's the motive. It's not all of it, because this is one sick bitch, but that's the springboard, the break, the push.'

Roarke got up, went to the board, studied the photo. 'So you're convinced she's involved?'

'Not ready for convinced, but man, I'm leaning there, and hard.' She began to pace. 'Not Geena McEnroy. She's got two kids, and by every account – even people who actively disliked him – he was a good father. You heard the tutor – did she come off straight to you?'

'She did, yes. And like you, I believe she'd have known or would have had some inkling if the wife had a part in this.'

'Agreed. Horowitz. Young, a little stupid if you ask me, living the good life and happy there. If she'd found out about the LCs, I figure her to cry and rage and demand he stop – or run home to her mother. But help plan out two torture murders? No. Plus, with him dead, she's out. Not a spouse or a legal cohab. Just lived with him. She gets nothing.'

'All right.' Because he knew Eve, Roarke nodded. 'And what else?'

'Neither of them, not as far as evidence shows, had a direct connection with the support group. The killer's been in those meetings, been part of them, heard the stories. Darla.'

'You're convincing me.'

'It's not going to convince the PA or a judge to issue a search warrant for Eloise Callahan's residence.'

'You don't believe the grandmother's complicit, surely?'

'She's an actor, right? Legendary, everybody says. She didn't give me any buzz when we talked to her—'

'You talked to her.' Roarke held up a hand. 'You talked with Eloise Callahan?'

'Yeah, because, you know, murder investigation.' She had to smirk. 'Fanboy.'

'Being an admirer of her craft doesn't make me a fanboy. Maybe a bit,' he admitted with an easy smile. 'And I think this calls for a meal over which you can give me all the details.' He cupped her chin in his hand, his thumb grazing lightly over the shallow dent in it. 'I think steak. You look tired, Lieutenant. You haven't had much sleep in the last couple nights.'

'I could eat steak.'

He drew her in first, held her. 'When there's time, I think we'll watch Eloise in *Only Once*.'

'Do things blow up?'

Smiling, he kissed her temple. 'Not this time. It's a beautiful film. Staggeringly, sumptuously romantic. I think she'd have been in her twenties still. Gorgeous creature. Luminous.'

'Big fanboy.'

'Perhaps I am at that. You've seen her in *Rise Up* – and in that one quite a bit blows up. Urban War setting,' he began, but Eve pulled back, gestured.

'That was her? I remember that one. Sure that was her,' Eve realized as she studied the photo. 'She kicked ass.'

'She did. Steak,' he repeated. 'Top off the wine.'

Eve stood, studying the photo. She could see it now, though the woman had been easily three decades younger in the vid.

Did it apply that Callahan could project – hell, embody – every human emotion, make you believe she felt it?

When Roarke came out, she grabbed the bottle, his glass, took them to the table by the window. 'Do you figure that kind of talent is inherent or learned?'

'I suspect some of both, but you can't learn what isn't in you, can you?'

'Don't know. But I'm wondering if the skill can be passed on.'

Roarke set the plates down while Eve topped off the wine.

'Ah, as in could the granddaughter have her grandmother's talent? Interesting. Well, there have been dynasties, family members who share interest and skills in various areas, acting included. But from her educational choices, it seems the granddaughter's interest held in science and engineering, not the arts.'

'Yeah.' Still.

He'd chosen asparagus – a green thing she actually liked well enough – and tiny new potatoes with red skins roasted with butter and herbs. She added more butter to them anyway – she strongly believed you could never have too much butter – before she cut into the steak.

'Okay, so Eloise. She's been recovering from pneumonia, still looks on the pale and frail side, but she came down on her own when Darla was out of the room.' Now Eve rolled her eyes. 'She liked the damn vid, and wanted to meet us – me and Peabody.'

Roarke only smiled, and listened as she relayed the interview, her impressions.

'You liked her,' Roarke concluded.

'I guess I did.' Eve stabbed a bite of potato. 'Doesn't mean I won't take her down if she had any part in this.'

'You don't think she did. I know my cop,' he added. 'She's as far down on your list as she can get without dropping off.'

'Maybe, yeah. I'll say the affection between her and Darla

read real, even deep, and while she looks damn good for ninety-whatever, you can see she's getting over a serious illness. And she didn't like Pettigrew. She didn't roll over him – and I think she might have if the granddaughter hadn't been around. She still wears a wedding ring, and her husband died decades ago.'

'Bradley Stone,' Roarke remembered. 'Their love story's another thing of legend. If the legend's reality, she wouldn't think much of a man who cheated on and betrayed a grand-daughter she loves.'

Nodding, Eve waggled her fork. 'Which is why she's not all the way off the list. Maybe she's covering for Darla. She might not be absolutely sure what Darla's up to, but she covers for her. Like I said, the affection, devotion between them reads real. Would Darla leave her grandmother, still recovering from a serious illness, alone? Would she go out hunting and leave Eloise alone? Spend hours torturing her targets while Eloise slept upstairs?'

'Lady Justice,' Roarke reminded her. 'You and I know very well one can justify anything if they believe or want enough.'

'You're right.' She gestured with her wineglass. 'You're damn right. Still, what if Grand – she calls her Grand – wakes up while you're out, comes looking for you? How do you explain that? Oh, I just went out for a walk or what-ever – and left you alone.'

'But if Darla attended the support group, she'd have left Eloise alone.'

'Not really. Last time she went – last December – she talked about worrying her grandmother was coming down with something. They have a nurse come in during the day, but they both stated Darla's the main caregiver, and the one in charge in the evenings, through the night. Droids.'

Eve ate as she considered it. 'Crowded club, dim lights. Could she send a droid? Pettigrew couldn't have had more than a couple minutes with the LC, so would he have made her for a droid?'

'How long does it take you to make one?'

Eve huffed out a breath. 'I'm a cop. A really well-made droid could pass for a short time, especially in dim light. It lowers the risk, and it hits the irony meter hard re Pettigrew. Another droid to drive – or you have the one droid order autopilot at least until the target's compromised. A droid could easily lift an unconscious man, or a dead one.'

'Death by droid?'

'No, no, she needs to do that herself.' Needs the blood, Eve thought. Needs to hear them scream.

And ultimately, needs to cut away what makes them men.

'Sure, with her knowledge she'd be able to program droids for violence and block detection,' she considered. 'Probably. But she needs to confront, torture, kill. She's not going to be a passive observer to that. Lady Justice has to act.'

She stabbed some steak, then narrowed her eyes. 'Better – maybe better. How good is she at the programming, the creation? Maybe you've programmed a droid to watch over Grand while she sleeps. One who can send you a notification if you need to abort and get home, or get cleaned up – torture's messy – and get up to her. You can program a droid with medical skills, same as you do a beat droid, a domestic, a sex droid with whatever skills are needed.'

'Risky,' Roarke pointed out. 'If something happened to her, something went wrong while she was out of the house, how to explain it?'

'But nothing's gone wrong, has it? They've got a domestic droid,' Eve added. 'At least one that I saw. She piled on the shock and grief, Roarke. I mean piles and piles of it, and that just keeps hitting me wrong. It's off. Are you going to feel all that for a man who screwed you over? Still feel all that for two years?'

Studying Roarke, Eve considered.

And he sighed. 'I know that look.'

'I'd never get over you. If you screwed me over like that, it would crush me – I'd do my best to make you pay for it, but it would crush me.'

'No graphic example of making me pay?'

'They'd never find what was left of your body.' She smiled with it. 'But the point is, I wouldn't let people see it. If I grieved, if I still had feelings, they wouldn't see it. Or not like that.'

'Well, to be fair, not everyone is capable of controlling their reactions, their emotions.'

'Two years. I'm going to buy she's carried all this emotion for him around for two years when he stole what she built herself, when he tossed her aside for a younger – lots younger – woman with bigger tits? And at the same time, the group leader has notes on how Darla seemed to have turned a corner, how she seemed steadier and all that, but was still angry and bitter.'

Eve scooped up the last of the potatoes. 'Steadier,' she continued, 'maybe steadier because she'd worked out a plan, a solution. She bonded with the women in the group – that's in the notes. She brought in gifts for Christmas. She gave one of them money to help her get a safe place to stay. She found her ...'

She trailed off, searching, then grabbed the wine. 'Tribe. Sort of. Her tribe, and designated herself as their warrior, their avenger. Justice seeker.'

Pushing up, she went back to the board, circled, circled. Roarke stayed where he was, watching, enjoying watching her work.

'Maybe one or more of them joined in with her, but I don't think so. I don't see it – at least not yet. She's doing it for them. For herself, sure, but for them. For women who get screwed over, who get knocked around, forced, harassed. All of it. She's going to take care of the tribe first.'

'Not to toss a spanner in the works, but if she continues to kill men connected to women in the group, isn't she bringing the investigation to her own door?'

'Already has,' Eve agreed. 'Maybe she didn't expect us to connect the group this fast, but she's smart. She brings up the group herself. She can't know we already know about it, but she brings it up herself to throw suspicion away if we move in that direction, or someone else mentions it.'

'Of course. Why would she mention it if she used it to select her prey?'

When Eve glanced back at him, her eyes were flat and cool. All cop. 'She thinks she's got it all covered. And she's done a pretty good job of it. I've got no probable cause. None, zip. I just know.'

'How many in the group?' Roarke asked.

'It averages about fifteen.'

'When do they meet again?'

'Not soon enough. Not for another ten days. She's already got another lined up. It'll be soon, really soon. But who and where and why? She's the only one who knows.'

Shaking her head, she jammed her hands in her pockets. 'And I could be wrong, just wrong, and it's someone else in the group. Someone we haven't interviewed yet, who hasn't connected yet. So I need to put this aside, dig into what I've got. Painted concrete and a list of first names.'

'Isn't it likely some of the women bonded outside the group? Met outside the group for additional support? Forged friendships?'

'Yeah. Leah Lester indicated as much, but none of the three women we've interviewed knows full names – or admits to it.' She aimed a stare at Darla's ID shot again. 'Except ... Darla gave money to another member of the group. What did she do, just hand her a wad of cash? Unlikely.'

'Didn't you say the money was to help the other woman secure a safe place to live?'

'Yeah, yeah, let's just give that a push.'

She went back to her command center, found what she needed, tried Darla's 'link.

'Hello, yes, Lieutenant. Have you found who killed Thaddeus?'

'We're pursuing a line of investigation. You may be able to help.'

'Oh, of course. Anything. Just— I'm going to take this in the other room, Grand, and have Ariel make us that vid snack.'

Eve heard the murmur of a second voice, saw Darla give a quick smile. 'You know I will.' The screen wobbled a little as Darla moved from what Eve could see was a bedroom done in elegant rose and cream.

'I'm sorry, Lieutenant. I was just helping Grand settle in for the evening. We're actually going to watch *The Icove Agenda*. She wants to see it again now that she's met you. It's been a . . . ' Her voice shuddered, tears swirled. 'Just a horrible day. We both need some entertainment. What can I do to help you?'

'You made a monetary gift to another member of the support group last December.'

'Oh.' Distress rippled over her face. She ran a hand over the hair still drawn back in a tail. 'That's confidential.'

'Not anymore. I need the full name of the recipient.'

'Lieutenant, the entire framework of the group is built on

mutual trust. And I don't see that helping a – an acquaint-ance applies to this awful thing.'

'Two men connected to women in the group are dead. It applies. From what I've already learned, Una needed financial assistance to rent an apartment for herself and her young son.'

'He beat her!' Fury spiked, hot and fast. 'She was living in a shelter.'

'Did she go to the police?'

Darla shut her eyes, and when she opened them, sorrow lived in them. But Eve had seen that fury, that fire.

'No, at least not the last I heard. He said he'd kill the boy if she did. She'd gotten a restraining order months before, for all the good it did. She was terrified. I can't – I can't talk to you about her private business. It's not right.'

'Do you want your ex-husband's killer brought to justice?'

'I – of *course* I do!'

'Give me her name before someone else dies.'

'You put me in a terrible position.'

'Let's try this. Where did you transfer the money?'

As she pressed a hand to the side of her face, Darla's eyes watered up again. 'Oh God, how is that not just as bad? I wanted, I just wanted to do something good, something positive. I wanted to end a period of my life where I'd spent so much time wallowing in bitterness and self-pity into something positive.'

'And you did.'

Eve heard Eloise's voice, saw Darla turn her head, watched her tears spill over. 'Oh, Grand.'

'Tell Lieutenant Dallas what she needs to know, Darla. It's the right thing, and your friend will understand that. Do the right thing, sweetie.'

'Nothing feels right.' Darla closed her eyes again, drew a breath. 'She was trying to scrape together enough money for an apartment so she and her little boy could move out of the shelter. She'd gotten a job, but she just didn't have enough. I paid the security deposit and first and last month's rent, to give her a start, a chance. A place downtown. I honestly can't remember the address. I'd have to look up the transfer.'

'Her name. I'll find her.'

'It feels wrong,' Darla countered. 'Una Kagen. Her little boy's Sam. She'd never hurt anyone.'

'It's imperative we contact members of the group. Do you have any other names?'

Darla began to rub the spot between her eyebrows. 'I had coffee a few times after the meetings with Una and Rachel – they were close in age, both single mothers, and became friends. Una would know her full name. I think she's the one who helped Una find the apartment. It was in Rachel's building if I remember right.'

'Okay, that's helpful. Thank you.'

'Please, Lieutenant, these women have already been through so much.'

'And I'll do my best to prevent them from going through more. Thank you again.'

'She took back her maiden name,' Roarke said when Eve ended the transmission. 'She's Una Ruzaki since the

271

divorce finalized in February. Hold a moment,' he added, as he continued to work his PPC. 'There's a Rachel Fassley at the same address. One marriage, widowed, one son, age six.'

'You keep being handy.'

'My mission in life. Are we having a trip downtown?'

'It's always better to deal face-to-face. I'm going to say, first, you don't have to go with me. Second, a man might skew things. But third, it'd be good to have someone else's impressions, especially if I can get to both of them. And when you put on Charming Roarke, it usually skews to the positive.'

'It's easy, darling.' He swept a fingertip down her cheek. 'Charming's my default.'

'I wouldn't go that far. You drive,' she added as they started out. 'I want to look into the restraining order.'

When they got outside, she studied the vehicle he'd ordered out of the garage. Sleek, shiny, and cherry red, with doors that opened up in an arch rather than out.

'What is this?'

'New,' Roarke said easily and got behind the wheel.

Inside, the dash looked like the pilot's cabin of a luxury off-planet shuttle. 'How many vehicles do you need?'

He answered smooth as cream, 'I've yet to find out.'

When the engine gave a throaty roar, when they flew along the driveway, she wished she'd taken the wheel.

Next time.

She spent her time on her PPC. 'TRO against Arlo Kagen, age thirty-one, granted to Una Kagen. We've got a history of domestic disturbance reports spanning three years prior. Kagen did three months for misdemeanor assault – out in ninety days with probation, mandatory anger management. Bullshit. Guy's got a serious drinking issue – it's clear from what's on the reports. Tunes up the wife or goes on a rampage. She filed for divorce, got the TRO, and he went at her again. Charges dismissed there, as he claimed she went at him – and they both had injuries.'

'More bullshit.'

'Yeah, it is.' She switched to Rachel Fassley. 'Fassley's husband of three years was killed during a robbery attempt five years ago. It looks like he tried to intervene, got stabbed multiple times. I don't see anything . . . Hmm. Her employment history. Office manager until she had the kid, then professional mother status. Into the outside workforce last fall. Office manager – different office. Back to PM status after three months.'

'You assume something happened at the workplace.'

'Can't assume,' Eve said. 'But there's nothing else. No reports filed. None filed during the three-year marriage on the husband.'

Eve sat back, let it cook. 'I want to talk to both of them.'

15

Roarke opted for a lot near the apartment building on the Lower East Side. Considering the ride, Eve couldn't blame him for rejecting a street slot, even if they found one.

Plus, since the piss-trickle rain had finally stopped, it wasn't a bad night to walk a few blocks.

'I still have to try to run down the concrete, the epoxy,' Eve commented.

'You'll learn that Mildock's been in business more than a century, and the floor you're looking for may have been poured long, long ago.'

She'd thought of that herself, but still scowled. 'That's not helpful.'

'Alternately, it may be a newer pour, or a resurfacing before the color sealer. I'd push more on the epoxy, which would need refreshing every decade or so if the floor gets any real traffic.'

She blew out a breath. 'Odds of me hitting anything on either are slim to none. What it gives me is a match when we find the kill zone.'

He took her hand. 'I wager I could dig up blueprints of Eloise Callahan's home here in New York without too much trouble. Then you'd know if a basement area exists.'

'A garage does. I saw it. But I like basement better. Or there might be another outbuilding behind the main house.'

'I'll have a look when we get home again.'

They paused outside the building, both studying the layout, the security.

'I'd say the odds of the basement or subfloor of this building having a top-grade epoxy finish in Burnished Gold are too long to measure.'

Eve nodded. 'Decent, working-class, reasonable security, but nothing approaching top-of-the-line. Door cam, and it looks like it's in working order. We can take a look at the feed from the last couple nights, just to eliminate, but this isn't it. It's not going to be a multi-resident building. Not private enough.'

Eve glanced up. 'They're both on the fifth floor. Let's take Ruzaki first, and see if we can pull Fassley in. Hitting them together'll give me a sense of the dynamic.'

Ignoring the buzzer, she mastered into a small lobby that smelled lightly of pine cleaner and somebody's take-out Chinese. She eyed the pair of elevators suspiciously.

'Let's risk it.' Roarke called the car, tugged her inside. The elevator smelled exactly like the lobby.

When they exited on the fifth floor, she caught the pine, but not the Chinese.

'Right across from each other,' Eve noted, glancing from

one apartment door to the other. 'Ruzaki's got police locks and a door cam.'

'Violent ex-husband,' Roarke surmised. 'Still worried there, I'd say. Just the standards on Fassley's, so either she can't afford the extras, or she isn't worried about someone forcing his way in.'

'I'm betting on the second.' Eve pressed the buzzer on Ruzaki's door.

It only took a moment for the cautious voice to come through the intercom. 'Yes?'

'Lieutenant Dallas and civilian consultant, NYPSD.' She held up her badge. 'We'd like to speak with Una Ruzaki.'

'About what?'

'Ms Ruzaki?'

'Yes.'

'It would be easier if we came in to speak with you.'

'Would you hold your badge a little higher? I'm going to contact the police and verify it.'

'Sure. Contact Cop Central.'

While they waited, Eve heard the murmur of entertainment screens, occasional kid squeals. Then the locks opened.

'I'm sorry. It's better to be careful.'

'No problem.'

A quiet-looking brunette, Eve thought, mixed race, about five-three, on the thin side. She was dressed in what looked like plaid pajama pants, a white T-shirt, and bright red house skids.

'What's this about? Sorry, come in.'

The living area was decorated in quiet colors like the woman, except for an area sectioned off in a kind of playroom. That held brightly colored blocks and toys in a bin. Another section held a small table and chairs. The tablet, the glass of something fizzy indicated Una had been sitting there when they arrived.

'Your name's come up during the course of an investigation. We believe you might be able to provide additional information.'

Her fingers twisted together to match the nervous expression on her face. 'What kind of investigation?'

'I'm Homicide.'

'Oh. God. Wait.' She hustled down a short hallway, peeked in a room, then quietly closed the door. 'My son. He's only three. I don't want him to wake up and hear ... I don't know anything about a murder. Is it someone I know?'

When her lips pressed together, Eve read both hope and dread on her face.

'Do you know Nigel McEnroy or Thaddeus Pettigrew?'

'No, I ... wait, I heard about that killing uptown. The McEnroy person. I heard about that. I don't know ... I know someone named Pettigrew, but she's a woman.'

'Darla Pettigrew. Thaddeus Pettigrew was her ex-husband. You may have missed the reports that he was also murdered.'

'I – I'm sorry. I don't understand. I didn't know either of these men.'

'You knew women connected to them, women in your support group.'

She went very stiff. 'I go to a support group for women, it's confidential. It's anonymous. We only use first names.'

'I'm aware of that. I've spoken to Natalia Zula, who formed the group. I've spoken to three other members, ones connected to the victims.'

'But I'm not. I didn't know them.' Stress spiked through her voice. 'I don't know anything.'

'Would you like your drink, Ms Ruzaki?' Though Roarke spoke gently, quietly, she jerked. 'Let me get it for you.'

He walked over, got it off the table.

'You knew Darla's last name,' Eve pointed out.

'She did me a favor. She helped me.' Una took the glass from Roarke with hands that trembled.

'You seem nervous,' Eve commented.

'I have police in my house talking about murders. And my group, that's private. Yeah, I'm nervous.'

'Why don't you tell us where you were last night, and the night before, between nine P.M. and four A.M.'

'Oh my God, I'm a suspect. How can I be a suspect about murders of men I didn't even know?'

'It's a routine question. Can you answer it?'

'I was here.' Her eyes darted from Eve to Roarke, back again. Not in evasion, to Eve's gauge, but with the look of prey frozen before a predator's pounce. 'I was home. I have a three-year-old. I – I'd have been studying. After I put Sam to bed, about eight, I pick up around here, then I work or study. I'm taking courses, online business and management courses. Ah – ah, night before last we had an interactive lesson from nine to ten. I can show you! And I stayed on with a couple of the other students until about ten-thirty. Then I got ready for bed. I didn't go out at all. I have a baby.'

'And last night?'

'I studied until about ten. Then— Oh! Rachel came over. My friend. We had a glass of wine and talked until about eleven. Rachel, she watches Sam while I go to work.'

'That would be Rachel Fassley? Another member of the group?'

'It's private,' she said as tears filled her eyes.

'Una.' Roarke drew her attention with that same gentle tone. 'Would you be more comfortable if I asked Rachel to join us?'

'I don't want to drag her into this. I just—'

'We're going to talk to her anyway.' Eve spoke crisply, letting Roarke hit the soft spots. 'We can do it separately or together.'

'I— All right. Don't scare her. I can show you my work, show you I was online.'

'We'll get to that,' Eve said, and gave Roarke a nod. When he went out, she leaned into Una.

'When we came in, you thought – worried – we were here about something else.'

'I thought maybe it was something about my ex.'

'You had difficulties with him.'

'We're divorced. I have a restraining order. He has

visitation rights with Sam, but he never uses them, and I'm glad. I'll tell you about Arlo if I have to, but I can't tell you about what the others talked about in the group. It's private.'

'But Darla did talk about her ex-husband?'

'Please don't ask me. Please.'

'How about telling me the last time you saw or spoke with her?'

'Right before Christmas. She helped me get this apartment, she paid two months' rent and the security deposit. Nobody's ever done anything like that for me before. She's so kind.'

'But she hasn't been back to the group.'

'No. I keep hoping, because I want to thank her again.'

'You don't know how to contact her?'

'No. Even if I did, it would be rude. She knows where I live because she helped. If she wanted to talk to me, she could. We don't invade each other's privacy.'

She looked up as the door opened, and relief spilled out when a woman – trim, blond, in flannel pants and a sweat-shirt – came in.

'Oh, Rachel.'

'Easy does it, Una.' She had a sharp, native New Yorker voice and a no-nonsense attitude as she walked over, sat next to her friend. She gave Una a pat on the knee. 'Okay, what's all this about murder?' She took a glance at the device in her hand, set it on the table. 'My boy's across the hall sleeping. I've got a monitor on him in case.'

'We're investigating the murders of Nigel McEnroy and Thaddeus Pettigrew.'

'I heard there was a second one, but . . . Wait a minute. Pettigrew. That's not Darla's ex, is it?'

Una gripped Rachel's hand, nodded.

'Well, shit.'

'Two members of your group,' Eve continued, 'or former members, had a connection to the first victim.'

'Who?'

'Rachel, we can't—'

'Una, honey, two murders. Cops gotta do their job. My husband was killed. Best man I ever knew. The cops did their job, and the one who took him away from me and our son's in prison because they did.' She looked back at Eve. 'Who?'

'Jasmine Quirk, Leah Lester.'

'Jasmine, Leah.' Rachel shut her eyes. 'Let me think. Didn't they come as a set, Una? I mean one brought the other in, if I remember right. It's been awhile since they came around. I think one of them moved. They worked together, and the big boss raped them.'

'It's their story, Rachel.'

'And they've already told me,' Eve put in. 'You're not disclosing anything I don't know. Nigel McEnroy was the big boss.'

'Holy shit.' Rachel blew out a breath.

'Let's get where you were out of the way. Last night,' Eve said, 'and the night before. From nine P.M. to four A.M.'

'I'd have been going through the nightly battle of getting my boy in bed about nine, both nights. Once I won the war – I always win – I had my weekly marathon with my mom – she and my pop live in Florida now, so we blab on the 'link for an hour or so every week. Then I conked out watching some screen. Last night, same battle, same victory. Then I paid some bills, folded some laundry, and to reward myself, came over here with a bottle of wine, gabbed with Una for a while. I guess we broke up about eleven. We had work the next day.'

'Your data indicates you have professional mother status.'

'Yeah, I do, and I need it.' Direct in every way, Rachel pinned Eve with a hard look. 'You can be a jerk about it and report me, but once a week Una and I clean the public areas of the building. We get a break on the rent that way. It's under the table. I also get a little bit from Una for watching the adorable Sam. I don't report either.'

'It sounds as if you're an enterprising woman,' Roarke said, and earned a smile.

'I'm a widow with a growing boy. I have to be enterprising.'

'Why are you in the group?' Eve asked.

She heaved out a breath. 'Gotta go there. Okay. I managed a small office, and gave that up after we had Jonah. Chaz and I both wanted to give him a full-time parent for the first couple years, and Chaz made a lot more than I did. I was starting to think about maybe easing a toe back into the workforce, just part-time, when that hyped-up junkie son of a bitch killed my husband.'

Now Una moved closer, slid an arm around Rachel. 'So

I stuck with professional mother status until Jonah started school. Then I took a job managing another small office – a father-son deal. Travel brokers – brokered luxury resorts and houses worldwide. Good hours, decent pay and benefits. I could walk Jonah to school, then go another couple of blocks and be at work. I had a friend who picked him up with her kid, took him home after school. Everything close by, so I'd swing by and get him around five, and be able to put dinner together, spend the evening with my kid. It was perfect.'

'Until?'

'The dad portion's off for a few days, traveling to check out some new properties. The son portion locked the office. I didn't see him do that, didn't notice until he came at me. We were going to have some fun, that's what he said. Let's have some fun while he's shoving me against the wall, grabbing my tits, trying to pull my clothes off. I'm going to admit that at first I was so shocked I just kept asking him to stop and trying to stop his hands. Then I got pissed, really pissed, and I kneed him in the balls just like my pop taught me. First time I had to use the move, but it worked.'

'Good for you,' Roarke said.

'Yeah, well, I went a little nuts after, yelling at him, threatening to sue or go to the cops, and he just started laughing. He told me to go ahead, how nobody would believe me. His father owned the place, and his father would believe him, and I'd be out on my ass without a reference. Shit like that. The guy's rich, spoiled, good-looking, with a wife and a kid. He says how I'd be smart to just lie back and enjoy it because I'm fucked either way.

'And he was right, I could see it. I've got a kid to think about. So I grabbed my things and got out. Refiled for professional mother status. I didn't know how much it shook me until I caught myself making excuses for not going out, and when I had to, looking over my shoulder. And that started pissing me off.'

When Una offered her fizzy water, Rachel took it, drank, breathed out. 'Thanks. Anyway. When I saw this flyer for the group, I thought maybe that's something to do. At least I can talk about it. I couldn't afford to get my head shrunk, but this was free. And it helped, a hell of a lot. Some of the women, most of them, had it a hell of a lot worse than me, and more than that, they listened, they cared. Now I go for them, for the ones who need someone to listen, someone to care.

'Maybe one day I'll gear myself up to get another office job, but it's tough knowing I'll get asked why I left my last job so fast.'

Roarke pulled a case from his pocket, took out a card. 'Contact me when you're ready to look for that office job.'

Rachel glanced at it. Her eyes popped wide. 'Are you freaking kidding me?'

'Not in the least. I value strong women who know how to listen and care. I married one.'

Staring at the card, Rachel shook her head, slowly, side to side. 'This is a really strange night. Do you know who this is, Una?'

'He's a police consultant.'

'It's frigging Roarke.' At Una's blank look, Rachel shook her head and laughed. 'Una's a little insular, what with shaking off the asshole she married, working, raising a kid. I'll explain later,' she said to Una.

'You joined the group due to the asshole you shook off?' Eve said to Una.

'He used to hit me, knock me around, and make me have sex.'

'Say the word, Una.' Rachel patted her arm. 'Say it.'

'Rape.' Una breathed in and out. 'He hit me, and he raped me when he got drunk, when he felt like it. I was afraid to do anything about it for a long time. I was always afraid. I was more afraid after Sam because he said how he'd hurt Sam, or he'd take him and I'd never see him again. He even went to jail once for it, for a while, but it just made it worse. He always found us. Then, like Rachel, I heard about the group. I didn't say anything the first couple times – nobody makes you. Then I finally talked about it. Natalia helped me and Sam get into a shelter, a really safe place. I got a divorce. He didn't care so much after that. I don't know why.'

'She doesn't get child support,' Rachel said. 'He's supposed to, but he doesn't, and she doesn't report it.'

'He leaves us alone. That's enough. Rachel told me this apartment was going up, and I'd saved, but it wasn't enough. Then Darla helped. She said one day I'd help someone else. Maybe Arlo doesn't know where we are. Maybe he does, but doesn't care. But you're always afraid.'

'You talked about all of this in the group?'

'Sure.' Rachel shrugged. 'That's the point.'

'Did you name the man who assaulted you, or the business, did you use your ex-husband's name?'

'Probably. You start getting wound up. I probably said something that like asshole Tyler – James Tyler's the asshole. And I know Natalia counseled Una not to let Arlo make her live in fear. You, well, you need to put a name on that fear to beat it back, you know?'

'Yes. I need to speak to the other women in the group. I need full names.'

'I guess I know a couple, but I don't see ...' Rachel trailed off before her eyes popped wide again. 'Oh my God.'

'Rachel, we can't betray a confidence.'

'Jesus, Una, don't you see where she's going? Oh my God, you're saying you think someone in the group is doing this? Is killing guys who screwed with us? Killing them.'

She shifted until she faced Una, until she gripped her arm. 'That's making us a part of it, Una. Whoever's doing it, they're making us part of murder. We won't be part of that. Una, we've got kids. We're trying to be people they can be proud of, depend on. We can't be part of this.'

'Nobody in the group would do something like this,' Una insisted.

'Then give me names,' Eve said simply, 'and we'll clear it up.'

*

When they left, Eve had three more names, and a possible fourth, as the women disagreed whether one of the group was Sasha Collins or Cullins. They did agree however, she'd recently joined the group after an assault by an ex-boyfriend, and was somewhere in her late twenties or early thirties.

'And so are we off to another interview?' Roarke asked.

Eve, already busy searching for a Sasha Collins or Cullins, just shook her head. 'I'm going to set up interviews at Central tomorrow. Bring them in.'

She kept working as they stepped out of the elevator. 'I've got a Sasha Cullins who filed a police report on an assault six weeks ago. One Grant Flick, pled guilty – likely because he jumped her outside her apartment building in front of witnesses – is currently serving his time.'

She put her PPC away. She'd nail down the rest at home, have Peabody arrange the interviews.

'You're thinking,' Roarke began when they crossed the small lobby, stepped outside again, 'now that you have several names, the odds of identifying the entire group tip in your favor.'

'That's right. We got lucky with these two, because Fassley, particularly, is sociable, she's in the group now to reach out, to lend others support. So she gets closer to other members. She and Ruzaki are friends, neighbors, even coworkers. They talk, share. So, between them, we get more names.'

'And you'll find one who knows another, and so on.'

'That's the dream.' She glanced up at him as they walked. 'Would you really hire her? Fassley?'

'If she passes a background check, proves competent – as I expect she would on both counts. She has quality. I appreciate quality. And will you, Lieutenant, take a closer look at this James Tyler?'

'Unless he ends up in the morgue before I close this, yeah. If he went at her, he's gone at others. I can reach out to somebody in Special Victims, put him on the radar.'

'You're worried someone will end up in the morgue.'

Eve scanned the street, the sidewalk, the people strolling or stampeding along.

'It'd be crazy to risk going after another target tonight, but she could easily do the crazy. And no matter how hard I'm leaning toward Pettigrew right now, I don't have enough. Hell, I don't have anything. Not anything to justify a search warrant, not even enough to put a stakeout on her place.'

'Because anyone in the group would have, at the core, the same motivation.'

'So I have to find more.'

'Then you will,' he said when they reached the lot. When they got into the car, he glanced at her briefly. 'You know you must, so you are, looking beyond what your gut tells you. You're working to identify and interview everyone in the group.'

'That's just basic cop work.'

'That may be.' He wound the spiffy new car up the levels. 'But as you do it, you're eliminating. You crossed two off your list tonight. You know they weren't covering for each other,' he added.

'Not impossible, but not probable. Neither own vehicles, neither have licenses to drive and never have. Both have young children – and it'd be easy to check if either got somebody to watch the kids while they went out and murdered somebody. And they're both the wrong build. No place private or secure enough in that building to kill people. If they have access to a place that is, that brings yet somebody else into it.'

'And you think this is a solo act.'

'Feels like it. I don't think the killer signs the poems Lady Justice as a dodge. That's how she sees herself.'

'I agree. As someone enforcing justice, and a lady.'

Frowning, Eve shifted. 'I hadn't juggled in the second part. Sees herself as a lady. Not just female. Maybe. Maybe that's part of it, part of her. Something to think about. Me, it irritates the crap out of me when somebody calls me lady. But she embraces it.'

'Define *lady*,' he invited.

'Delicate female wuss.'

Laughing, he grabbed her hand, tugged it to his lips. 'And yet you are, and always will be, my lady.'

'That doesn't charge my batts. You define *lady* – outside the marriage rules.'

'In general terms then? A woman well-mannered and well-bred—'

'Leaves me out.'

He simply rolled over her. 'It can also mean a woman of rank, of course. Which would include you in the world of cops. And a woman generous and caring of nature.'

'One out of three for me then.'

'Darling Eve, no one would call you well-mannered or well-bred, but it's clearly two out of three. Regardless, your killer may see herself as any or all of those examples, or simply have enjoyed the ring, we'll say, of the title.'

He might find it insulting, but he thought like a cop. A good cop. Since he would find it insulting, Eve didn't mention it.

'Yeah, there's that. But you know Justice Warrior has a ring, Justice Seeker, and so on. Non-gender specific. She's proud of being, you know, a lady.'

'Ah, well there you have a fine point. It's back to Women For Women, isn't it then?'

'That's how I see it.' She studied the house as they rolled through the gates. 'What's a lady with a penis?'

'Possibly conflicted.'

'No, I mean a guy lady – the male version.'

'If I'm following, I suppose a lord.'

'Yeah, that could fit you.'

'I'd as soon not be a lady with a penis, if it's all the same.'

'Forget that part.'

'Happily.'

'Lords sort of rule their domain. It's a strong word, *lord.* Lady – I go back to wuss. But not in the killer's mind. It's something to be proud of.'

'You're circling back to Darla Pettigrew.'

Yes, she thought, but wondered how he saw it. 'Why do you figure that?'

'Well-mannered, well-bred. You could even add a kind

of rank as the granddaughter of a legendary star. Caring enough to help a fellow group member.'

Yeah, he thought like a cop.

'It depends, doesn't it, on if she sees herself that way.'

When he parked, she got out of the car, walked to the door with him. 'I'm going to nail down those names, get that going. Are you interested in poking into somebody's business?'

'My favorite game.'

'Both Eloise and Darla are licensed to drive. None of the vehicles registered to Eloise fit the description of the one seen at the club or the Pettigrew house. There's no vehicle currently registered in Darla's name – not her married name, not her birth name. But maybe she's got herself a couple of buried accounts, maybe a vehicle registered under another name that goes with them.'

She shrugged out of her coat, tossed it over the newel post. 'You up for that?'

'Delighted – with a caveat?'

'It that a sex euphemism?'

'Not in this case.' He took her hand as they walked upstairs. 'You've had a handful of hours of sleep the past two nights combined. You get your names confirmed, get Peabody started on the interviews. I look into this.'

'I don't see the caveat.'

'No coffee – and you're in bed, sleeping, inside two hours.'

'How am I supposed to work without coffee?'

He gave her a pat on the butt. 'Inner strength.'

*

291

While Eve worked and Roarke poked, Arlo Kagen sat on his usual barstool in his usual bar drinking his usual beer and a bump.

In fact his third beer and bump of the evening. The bar – a hole-in-the-wall called Nowhere – served cheap greasy food the booze helped slide down.

Arlo had already finished his mystery meat burger and limp soy fries while he bitched and belched at the Yankees versus Red Sox on the screen.

He didn't give half a rat's ass about baseball, considered it a pussy game, but the bartender refused to switch to Arena Ball.

He slurped up more beer, considered ordering some nachos, then noticed the woman come in.

Looked like a street-level whore to him, with the skirt up to her crotch, the fishnet stockings, the tight sweater with half her boobs – nice boobs – spilling out.

She had a lot of purple hair tumbling around to hide half her face – trying to hide the ugly pucker of a scar slashed down her right cheek.

Not much to write home about from the neck up, he thought. But she had it going on from the neck down. In Arlo's view a woman's face didn't much matter when sex was all they were really good for.

He could use a quick bang, if the price was right.

She slid on the stool beside his, ordered a beer in a squeaky voice.

Since she looked like she'd come cheap, and a cheap BJ

suited him better than a pussified ball game, he gave the bartender the sign.

'Put it on my tab.'

She looked at Arlo with grateful brown eyes from under the purple hair. 'Thanks, handsome.'

'No problem. Haven't seen you in here before.'

'New turf for me. Just taking a load off. Slow night.' She took a tiny sip of the beer set in front of her, gave him a little flirt. 'You come in here a lot?'

'Most nights.'

'I guess I'll come in more now that I know you hang here.' She took another tiny sip of beer. 'Maybe you wanna party?'

'Might. What's the rate?'

She gave him a smile, ducked her head, tapped a finger on the beer. 'You already made a down payment.' She took another sip as she reached over, pressed her hand to his crotch. 'You want more, why don't you finish your beer?'

She leaned in, leaned close. His gaze fixed on her breasts. He didn't see her pour the contents of a vial in his shot glass.

'Then we can go outside, work out the rate.'

A hell of a lot better than a ball game, he decided. He drained his beer, tossed back the bump. 'Let's go.'

They walked out together, his hand squeezing her ass – and her hand signaling the droid and car on the device in her little purse.

He started to stumble before they reached the corner. She just laughed, held him up, steered him to the waiting car.

'Let's go for a ride, big guy.'

'Give you a ride. Give you a helluva ride, bitch.'

He passed out before she gave him the second dose. Deciding better safe than sorry, she pinched his nose, tipped back his head, and poured the sedative down his throat.

Pleased, Darla settled back, conserving her energy for the main event.

16

The dreams came, sliding in like curling fingers of fog over a pool of exhaustion. In them she heard the screams of the tortured and tormented rising shrill behind a wide black door. Duty bound, she fought to open it, to break it down, to find the way through while the screams pounded in her head.

Behind her, above her, around her, a voice, calm and quiet as a spring breeze, spoke.

'They get what they deserve.'

'It's not for you to say.'

'Why not? Why do you get to decide?'

'I don't.' Pulling her weapon, Eve clicked it on full, blasted it at the door. 'The law does.'

'Who makes the law? Men.' The single word snarled. 'And you do their bidding.'

'Try that bullshit on somebody else.' Disgusted, Eve searched along the wall, stark white against the black door, for another opening.

Those screams, never ceasing, ripped at her.

'You defend them, even knowing what they are, you stand for them. I stand for the women they abused. I stand for their victims.'

She couldn't find a way in, couldn't find a way to stop the screaming.

'You stupid, self-righteous *bitch*! You've made them victims.' She pounded a fist on the wall, took a running leap to kick at the door. Black against white. White against black.

'I bring them justice. They suffer, then their suffering ends. Their victims suffer endlessly. You know! How can you defend them? How, when you know what they've done? When it was done to you?'

'Oh, shut the fuck up.'

She whirled around, furious to find herself in a small room, an empty room, only the white walls, the single black door. 'I'm going to find you. I'm going to stop you. I'm going to put you in a cage.'

'Why do you care about them?'

The voice, so reasonable, came from everywhere.

'You were betrayed, abused, beaten, raped, trapped, terrified, helpless. You know what we've endured as women. You know men use us. You know they thrive on it. But you would turn on me like this? You would seek to stop my justice? Why?'

No way in, Eve thought. No way out.

'Why? Because you're sick, sadistic. Because you pervert the justice I took an oath to uphold. Because, you twisted excuse for a female, I'm a cop. I'm goddamn fucking Eve

Dallas.' She yanked out her badge. 'Lieutenant, murder cop, NYPSD. And I will find you. I will open this bullshit door, and I'll find you.'

This time when she spun around, badge in hand, kicked the door, it burst open.

The screams snapped off. An insistent beeping replaced them.

Shot awake, she slapped out in the dark for her communicator.

'Shit, shit, shit. Block video. Dallas.'

Dispatch, Dallas, Lieutenant Eve. Report to 53 West 179th. Dead male possibly connected to current case. Officers on scene.

'Acknowledged. Contact Peabody, Detective Delia, request McNab, Detective Ian, accompany her. I'm on my way. Dallas out.'

Roarke brought her a mug of coffee. 'I'll be going along and you'll have two EDD men.'

'For what it's worth. Sorry.' She held up a hand as she got up. 'Didn't mean it like that. You're already dressed. What time is it?'

'Not quite half-five. If you'll trust me to get your clothes, you can grab your shower.'

'Fine. Good. Thanks.' She shoved at her hair as she strode toward the bath. 'That's Ruzaki's ex. That's Arlo Kagen's address. I checked it last night.'

So, Eve thought, she'd be waking up a pair of her detectives to go check on Ruzaki and Fassley, to question them.

For what that was worth, too.

When she came out, he'd laid what she needed on the bed. A thin sweater caught somewhere between gray and blue, dark gray trousers, boots of the exact same hue, a gray jacket with hints of that between color threaded through.

She looked at him, his dark suit, perfectly knotted tie. 'You're dressed to go take a meeting or something.'

'It can wait.'

'What was it about?'

'This? The villa hotel in Italy. It's near to done.'

'Oh.' She started to dress, watched him contemplate the choices on the AutoChef. Something, she imagined, they could eat on the go, because he wouldn't want her to go without.

Because he thought of her.

'I have to shut this down, shut her down.'

'You do, yes. And so,' he said, so matter-of-factly it swelled in her heart, 'you will.'

'I can't imagine now, just can't, why I used to fight, why I used to resent you helping, you being a part of what I do.'

He settled on pocket omelets. She could smell the bacon he'd programmed in them. 'Might be my criminal past.'

He said it as a joke, but she felt emotion squeeze her throat. 'Roarke.'

'Hmm?' He glanced back, saw her face. 'Now, what's this?'

'You make everything better, even when you don't.

That's not exactly what I mean, either. I said before I'd never get over you, but it's more than that. I've been trying so damn hard not to let what happened to me, what's part of me because it did, get into this case. I think I'm doing pretty well with that, but I couldn't be, I wouldn't be if you weren't with me on it.'

'*A ghrá.*' He crossed to her, touched her face. 'I'm with you on this, on all. Whether you like it or not.'

He made her laugh, a relief. 'I know it. Like now, for instance, when I don't want that damn egg thing, which I *know* has spinach in it, but you'll just keep at me until I eat it.'

So she snatched it up, took a bite. 'See?' she said around it. 'Spinach.'

'Ah, and how well we know each other.'

'Yeah, yeah. I have to shut this down,' she said as she dressed. 'Once I do, why don't we go check out that hotel thing?'

He paused as he poured more coffee. 'You want to go to Italy?'

Yeah, they knew each other, she thought. So well, she heard his surprise, felt it.

'Here's the thing. Okay, two things. After I shut this down, I need a couple days. I need to just clear it out, and Italy would work. Which is something I'd never have said a few years ago like, oh, sure, Italy would work. Second thing, I know you haven't been as hands-on with this project as maybe you'd like to be. So you could be that, I could clear it out. A couple of days.'

He held up four fingers.

And damn, her heart just swelled again.

'See, I knew you'd do that, which is why I figured on three, because you'd have to compromise. Three days, once I shut this down.'

'Three days it is.'

'Solid.' She grabbed her badge, 'link, comm, the rest of her pocket debris. 'I'm going to pull Baxter and Trueheart in to go talk to Ruzaki, make sure she and Fassley don't have fresh blood on them, and so on.'

'You don't believe that for a moment.'

'No, but you gotta cover the bases.'

Before she could walk out, he picked up the egg pocket, smiled. 'You do, don't you?'

She rolled her eyes, but ate it as they went downstairs. She contacted Baxter, set that in motion.

When she stepped outside, she realized spring had definitely broken winter's back. She felt the change in the air, a softness to it.

She got in the car – hers this time, not the slick one – waited while Roarke programmed the address.

'I had this dream.'

'Yes. I was about to bring you out of it when your comm signaled. You didn't seem upset so much as . . . pissed.'

'I was pissed.'

She told him about it as he drove.

'I get the dumb-ass subconscious symbolism. The whole black-and-white thing. I think in black-and-white.'

'Not at all,' he disagreed. 'Your scope of gray may be limited – from my view – but you have a scope. It's your killer who sees in black-and-white.'

'Huh. I guess I like that better. She also sees men, as a sex, as a species, as just evil. I felt that before, but it feels more right now. She may have started with a list, from the support group, but she'd never stop there. She's a serial killer now,' Eve stated. 'And she wants to rack up as many as she can.'

'One who wants to be seen as a hero,' Roarke added. 'And that's something you obviously believe matters or you wouldn't have dreamed of it.'

'I do think it matters. How she sees herself, and how she wants others to see her.'

Not yet dawn, too early for ad blimps or the smoking carts, for the angry snarls and snags of traffic, New York seemed almost peaceful.

'I forgot to ask you. Mavis said you were meeting with Jake on something yesterday.'

'I was, yes. He's volunteered to teach now and again at An Didean. To teach music, songwriting – and so would his bandmates.'

'That's . . . That's seriously good of him, them.'

'It is. But then, he's a good man and one who appears to be geared toward giving back. I took him up on the offer right quick.'

Roarke pulled up behind the barricades where early-rising gawkers gathered. It was never too early, Eve thought, or too late to take some time to view someone else's tragedy.

She hooked on her badge, turned on her recorder, and ignored the crowd as she strode through the barricade.

Eve spotted the officers on scene, moved to them.

'Officers.'

'Keller and Andrew, Lieutenant.'

'We're here with Brigg Cohen,' Keller put in, tapping the burly, balding man between them. 'Brigg used to be on the job. He called it in.'

'Cashed in my twenty ten years ago,' Cohen told her. 'Had this beat before these greenies moved in. Lived right here.' He gestured to the building behind them. 'Sixteen years.'

'Why don't you run it through for me?'

'I work night security, eight to four for Lisbon Corp. Clocked out, had some breakfast at my usual place, walked home. The DB's laid out just like you see him. That would be four-fifty-eight.'

He may have cashed out, but he still reported like a cop. Advantage us, Eve thought.

'I still pay attention to what's what,' he continued, 'so I see he's gone like the two other DBs I heard about. Naked, beat to shit, missing his works. Got that message on him. Nobody reported, like, a poem, but I figure you held that back. I know the greenies here had to be close by, probably scratching their butts, so I called it in, stood by until they meandered along.'

Andrew rolled her eyes; Keller just grinned.

Eve spotted Peabody and McNab trotting up. She signaled for McNab to stand with Roarke, gestured Peabody forward.

'DB's pretty beat up,' Cohen continued. 'But from the build and what I can see of his face, I'd say it's the asshole lives down the hall from me. Name's Kagen, Arlo Kagen. He's got a sheet, not surprising, as he's a mean drunk.'

'When's the last time you saw Kagen?' Eve asked him.

'Tonight, when I was heading to work. That'd be about nineteen hundred, seeing as I grab a bite on the way. He was heading out about the same time. Likely to go get his drunk on. He generally gets it on at Nowhere, a dive bar just a couple blocks from here.'

'Have you noticed anyone in or around the building who doesn't belong? Somebody who set off your buzzer?'

He shook his head. 'I sleep till fourteen hundred most days, maybe walk around in good weather. We got the tat parlor, the hair place, a couple cheap eats, and get some of the street levels off the stroll who patronize 'em. I head out for work pretty much the same time every day, so I'm not here all that much, and when I am, I'm sleeping.'

'Okay, appreciate the help.'

'Don't much like finding a DB at my door. Hope you close this down sooner than later. I'm gonna go get some rack time. You know where I am.'

Eve waited until Cohen went in the building. 'Any chance he touched the body, compromised the scene?'

'Not one in a million,' Keller told her. 'Brigg likes to rag on us, but he's solid.'

'He's a grizzled old fart,' Andrew put in, but with

affection. 'And he's got a rep as a good cop for a reason. We caught a break with him finding the DB.'

'All right then. You can start knocking on doors.'

'We're off shift at six hundred. Okay to put in the OT?'

Eve nodded at Keller. 'Check with your LT. I'd like you on this. Peabody, let's ID the body, just to cross that off. McNab, and Roarke if you're still in this, you can start on the e's once we do. The building's got a door cam. Let's find out if it actually works.'

She took her field kit from Roarke, walked to the body, crouched down to verify the ID.

Peabody hunkered beside her. 'I didn't think she'd hit again so fast. She'd go for another, yeah, but not three days in a row.'

'She's goal oriented. And she's on a streak. You don't mess with a streak. Victim is identified as Kagen, Arlo, age thirty-one, of this address. As with the two other victims, his body shows severe burns, bruising. His left arm's broken, most probably from a severe blow. Dig into it, Peabody. See if he was left-handed. Severe facial bruising – broken nose, some broken and missing teeth. His genitals have been severed and removed.'

She put on microgoggles, leaned in. 'Looks like the same weapon or same type, the same method. ME to confirm. TOD three-fifty-six. COD most probably blood loss from amputation. ME to confirm.'

Eve pulled out an evidence bag, slid the poem into it, sealed it, read through it.

He used his fists against his wife,
So with cruelty and violence he lived his life.
Though she gave him a child to cherish,
He stroked her fears until all hope perished.
This death he earned by my decree,
Now mother and son are finally free.
LADY JUSTICE

'She can't stop,' Eve mumbled. 'The world she's created and her place in it are too important to her.'

And that world was black-and-white.

'Vic was left-handed,' Peabody told her. 'That's why she broke his left arm. He probably led with his left when he beat his wife. It makes it specific. More specific,' she corrected. 'And you know what? This isn't just the third in a row. It's the third in a row who hurt or cheated on a spouse. All of them were married. Pettigrew and Kagen were divorced, but they committed their crimes – what she's using – while married.'

Eve sat back on her heels. 'You're right about that. She's going after the men who are or were married first. We can narrow down the next potential by factoring that in. That's good, Peabody.'

'Let's roll him— Wait,' she added as she heard a voice – firm and impatient – call her name. 'Crap. McNab! You and McNab roll him, finish with the body. Contact the sweepers, the morgue. I'll deal with this.'

'Good luck with that,' Peabody said under her breath

as Eve walked to the barricades and the camera-ready and chin-jutted Nadine Furst.

The crime beat reporter might have ranked as friend – and a good one – but that didn't make her less of a pain in the ass at the moment.

Glancing past her, Eve noted she'd brought the rock star with her. Looking casually scruffy, a streak of royal blue through his jet-black hair, Jake stood with Roarke. The two of them chatted as if they held freaking martinis at some high-class bar.

'I tagged you a half a dozen times yesterday,' Nadine began.

'I was busy.'

Nadine narrowed feline-green eyes. 'You're never too busy when you can use me, and my research team, on an investigation.'

'I was really busy, and you don't want to shove into my face right now.'

'Oh, don't I?'

'No, you fucking don't.' Eve gestured her through the barricades, then gripped her arm – hard – pulled her away from the body toward the corner of the building.

Watching them, Jake rocked back on the heels of his scarred boots. 'Think it'll come to blows?'

'Odd, I always wonder the same.'

'Nadine's pretty steamed. So's your cop from the looks of it. You come to many of these . . . events?'

'Too many. Your first?'

'Yeah. Pulled an all-nighter at the studio. Thought: Hey,

I'll head over to Nadine's, wake her up. She's already up, dressed, and here I am.'

A tall man, he easily looked over the heads of people still pressing at the barricade. 'I don't get it. I gotta say, I don't get why anybody wants a line of work where they deal with something like what's lying out there. But both our women do. Can't figure it.'

'The one who put him there thinks she stands for justice. She doesn't, but, in their different ways, our women do.'

While they talked, their women bumped heads in a pitched battle.

'I want a one-on-one, right here. Now.'

'You can't have one,' Eve tossed back. 'And you don't even have a camera with you.'

'I can have a camera here in ten frigging minutes.'

'Nadine, did you happen to notice the dead guy back there?'

'I noticed the dead guy. The third of his specific type of dead guy. I set an alert to signal me when you landed another naked, castrated dead guy. You're giving the media the runaround when the public—'

'Don't throw the right-to-know bullshit on me now. Three in three days. Do you think we've been sitting around playing goddamn mah-jongg or something?'

'I think you don't even know what mah-jongg is, and you could have returned a tag from someone you know you can trust.'

'I didn't have time!' Eve threw up her hands, paced in a

307

circle. 'I don't have time now to stand here and argue with you. I didn't have time to give you some damn sound bites. You need to back off.'

'I'm doing my job just like you're doing yours,' Nadine shot back. 'You know damn well I can get the information you feed me on the air, I get it out, and it might help. Just like you know I'll hold anything you tell me to hold.'

'It's not that. It's not fucking that. It's not about you, not about the you-and-me deal. Sometimes it's just about the work. About the bodies piling up. About not having enough left over to deal with anything else.'

Nadine paused, held up a finger. Paced in her own circle. 'Okay, all right. Here's what I'm going to do. I'm going to go get coffee – for everybody. Then I'm coming back, with a camera. If you can't give me a one-on-one or a statement, I'll take one from Peabody or McNab. With three bodies in three days, you need media support to get public support, whether you admit it or not.'

She did know it. Didn't like it, but knew it. 'I don't know when I or the detectives involved will be available.'

'I'll wait.'

She would, Eve thought. And since neither of them was wrong, she eased back herself.

'I'm not drinking any fake coffee. I have high standards. Where are you going to get real coffee?'

'I have my ways. And besides being an Oscar-winning screenwriter—'

'Yeah, that's going to get old.'

'Never.' The annoyance, frustration shifted to a smug smirk. 'Plus a bestselling author and Emmy-winning newscaster, I have a goddamn rock star with me. We can get real.'

'No real, no camera time. That's a deal breaker.'

'We'll get real.'

'Meanwhile, off my crime scene. And tell Roarke to come through.'

She turned on her heel, walked back to Peabody and McNab.

'McNab, you and Roarke can move into the building. Check the door cam feed, start on the vic's apartment.'

She stopped, frowned. 'What's that?'

Peabody held up the evidence bag. 'A hair, a black hair — not the vic's, he's medium brown. It was stuck to the dried blood on the back of his shoulder. We got a hair, Dallas.'

'Good work, good catch. They get sloppy,' she murmured, and felt a turn in the investigation as a physical twist in her gut. 'They almost always get sloppy.'

'The wagon's on the way,' McNab told her. 'Sweepers, too.'

He shot a wave to Roarke, pointed toward the building. Eve glanced around to see them walk off — Roarke in his king-of-the-business-world suit, McNab in his mint-green baggies and shiny electric-blue jacket, toward the dead man's apartment building.

'Let's flag the hair priority for Harvo.'

'Already did. I can get one of the sweepers to get it to her first thing. It's probably wig hair, but even then, the queen of hair and fiber will ID it.'

'Yeah. Pull one of the support uniforms to sit on the body until the wagon gets here. We need to hit the apartment. When we're done here, you're doing a one-on-one with Nadine.'

'Me? She'll want you, and—'

'She's not getting me, not for the camera. I'm going to give her a little more on the side. She'll hold it, and maybe dig in enough to find something we've missed.'

'Okay. Jeez, I wish I'd done something with my face.'

'Your face is your face,' Eve said as they walked. 'Live with it.'

'You can live with it and make it a little better. So, really weird time to say it, but it's great about Mavis, Leonardo, and a baby coming, right? We celebrated our asses off when she told us. Leonardo's walking about six inches above the ground.'

'They're good at it, all of it. The couple thing, the family thing, the parent thing.'

They moved into the building. The claustrophobic lobby wasn't nearly as clean as the vic's ex's, and smelled more like old piss than pine. Still, it had reasonable security, so she had hope for the door cam feed.

She ignored the elevator. The vic had lived on the third floor.

'We got lucky with the nine-one-one caller,' she told Peabody as they climbed. 'Used to be on the job, works a security night shift. Made sure the scene stayed secure until we had cops on-site.'

'I know Keller and Andrew a little, and they're solid.'

'Struck me the same,' Eve agreed.

'I feel like our luck's turned.'

'Yeah. So did Kagen's – the wrong way. I talked to Kagen's ex last night. Might have been talking to her when he got taken. Fuck it.' She wanted to scrub her hands over her face, to yank at her own hair. Barely resisted. 'I hauled Baxter and Trueheart out of bed to check on her – and her neighbor, who's also in the group.'

'Rachel Fassley. I read your report. We've got names, Dallas. Luck *is* turning.'

'Not soon enough,' Eve said as she mastered into Kagen's apartment.

Peabody took one look at the space – efficiency-style room with an unmade pullout with questionable bedding, the scatter of dirty clothes, the empty beer bottles, the pile of unwashed dishes. Sighed.

'Just your average pigsty. Why do average male pigsties smell like old beer farts and grungy socks?'

'Because both have a home there. Suck it up, Peabody. We do what we have to do. Then we're going to wake up whoever runs a local bar where the wit – who lives down the hall – says Kagen liked to drink the beer he farted out in here.'

'Great. Just a mag way to start the day.' Peabody mimed rolling up her sleeves. 'At least it's a small apartment.'

It didn't make the job more pleasant, but they'd finished the search by the time McNab and Roarke came to the door.

'Got the feed.' McNab held up a disc. 'We have the vic exiting just after nineteen hundred. Alone, and wearing a brown jacket, brown pants, tennis shoes. Another male exited at the same time, walked in the opposite direction.'

'That's our wit,' Eve told him. 'Former cop, lives down the hall. He's clear. No house 'link on premises, no pocket 'link. You've got that bargain-basement comp to work with. No hidey-holes, no happy clues, no illegals.'

'No sense of hygiene from the look and aroma,' Roarke added. 'The range of the door cam doesn't reach to where his body was left.'

'And the killer would've known that. She's not stupid. She does her research. Flag the comp for transport, McNab, for what it's worth. Peabody, go down and give Nadine her camera time. She's bringing coffee.'

McNab's face lit. 'What kind of coffee?'

'You'll get yours, Detective. Flag the comp, and when it's in EDD, dig in.' She looked at Roarke. 'You should go home – or wherever you planned to be. We're done here for now.'

'I could use some coffee.'

'You'll get yours, too.'

She walked out with him.

'You're asking yourself if you could have saved him,' Roarke said as they started down the steps. 'You couldn't have. He'd left before you had his ex-wife's name, before you knew he existed.'

'No, we couldn't have saved him. It doesn't make it any easier, but we couldn't have saved him.'

She walked over to where Nadine and Jake waited, took the black coffee Nadine held out.

'Doughnuts, too. Jake insisted.'

'You're all right, Jake,' Eve decided as she took a cream-filled.

'Anybody who starts the day like you did earned a doughnut.'

Eve glanced at Peabody, shook her head as she watched her partner carefully applying lip dye. 'What's that we say, Detective Face?'

'About what— Oh. Yeah.' Peabody smiled a little. 'Our day begins when yours ends.'

'Jesus.' Jake just shook his head. 'Cops.'

While Peabody did the one-on-one, Eve stepped aside to check in with Baxter.

'Is that a doughnut?' Baxter demanded when he came on-screen. 'Where'd you get it? Are there more?'

'Yes. The rock star. No. Status.'

'Well, shit, now I want a doughnut. When we got here, Ms Ruzaki was up and getting breakfast into her kid. Cute kid,' he added. 'Both of them still in pajamas. Ms Fassley, also up and trying to drag her kid out of bed to get breakfast in him. He's a pistol. Trueheart checked the security feed. No sign either woman left the premises at any time after you and Roarke exited.'

Baxter glanced toward a door where Eve clearly heard the sound of kids whooping it up. 'He's in there with them now – in Ruzaki's place. She's shaken up, and it doesn't read grief and sorrow, just shock. And some nerves about being a suspect.'

Now he leaned back against the wall beside the door. 'Both women agreed to show us their 'links, let us look through their comps for any communication. We can do that, it's pretty straightforward, and save EDD the trouble.'

'Do that, clean it up. I'm not looking at either of them, but we fill the holes.'

'Want my take?'

'It's why you're there.'

'These two are too busy raising kids and making rent to cook up a plot to kill three guys.'

'Yeah, that's my take. But fill the holes.'

'Are you sure there aren't more doughnuts?' he asked.

She cut him off.

When she glanced over to where Peabody still talked to Nadine, she frowned, and Roarke strolled to her. 'They're wrapping it up. She did well.'

'Great. Do you need transpo?'

'Actually, I'm catching a ride with Jake. I'm going to give him a quick tour of An Didean before I go to work and he goes to bed. Nadine's going in to work as well.'

'She'll be watching for it.'

'Sorry?'

Eve wanted to say Darla, but said, 'The killer. She'll be watching for the media, the reports, the reactions. She wants some credit, some attention. She always did. That's why she wrote the poems. Peabody!' she shouted when she saw the camera lower. 'With me. Now! Gotta go. No.' She jabbed a finger in his chest before he could lean in for a kiss. 'No mushy stuff on a crime scene.'

He simply caught her finger, then arched eyebrows when Nadine and Jake exchanged a pretty serious goodbye kiss.

'She's not a cop.'

'Well, if kissing my wife is off-limits, see that you take good care of my cop.' Then he tugged her finger to his lips, made her roll her eyes. 'She won't outsmart you, Lieutenant. Not for long.'

When he walked away, she looked back, watched the morgue team load the body bag in the wagon. Not for long just wasn't good enough.

She opted to walk the handful of blocks to the bar, spare herself the frustration of finding a place to park.

'It's going to be a beautiful day.' Peabody lifted her face to the breeze.

Eve jammed her hands into her pockets. 'Tell that to the dead guy.'

'Well, he'd be dead even if it was going to be a crappy day.'

'That's a point.'

'So, pretty day, and it's supposed to stick awhile. I talked Mavis into going with me, bringing Belle, to the community garden over the weekend if we're clear. Lots of things we can help plant this early in the season.'

Baffled, Eve turned her head and stared. 'Mavis is going to plant stuff? In the ground?'

'It's fun to dig in the dirt, and good luck when a pregnant woman plants.'

Eve couldn't figure where the fun was in dirt, but it took all kinds. 'Hasn't she already been planted?'

'Hah! Good one.' All but bouncing down the sidewalk, Peabody gave Eve a cheerful elbow poke. 'It's good to get out in the fresh air, plant living things. Plus, Bella learns how to make flowers, vegetables grow, how to take care of them.'

'Trying to make a Free-Ager out of her?'

'All Free-Agers are gardeners, but not all garden-ers are Free-Agers. Anyway ... We're meeting the owner? The bar?'

'No, the bartender-slash-manager. The owners are a couple of guys in Newark who, according to them and the bartender, haven't been in the place for weeks. We'll get more out of the guy who worked the bar last night.'

When they reached it, Eve studied the exterior.

A long, long way from McEnroy's watering grounds, Nowhere suited its name. It hunched between an empty storefront advertising it was for sale or lease, and a pawn shop with its steel doors locked down.

Its single window, dingy with grime, framed a swirl of neon – currently dark – reading NOWHERE. While security included triple police locks and a sign with a toothy dog claiming that Bulldog Alarm system guarded the building, it didn't include a door cam.

She didn't have to see the interior to recognize a drinking establishment where the patrons came to down the cheap until they had enough of a buzz to stumble out and face their crap-filled lives.

A dim excuse for a light came on inside. She saw movement, then heard the locks snap open.

The man who stood in the door had a lot of snarled ink-black hair with brassy streaks falling past his shoulders. The shoulders were wide, the arms bearing sleeve tats and biceps that bulged.

Dark circles dogged bleary brown eyes. Even his sneer looked tired.

'You the frigging cops?'

'Lieutenant Dallas, Detective Peabody. You the frigging bartender?'

'Yeah. Shit.' He jerked a thumb in aggrieved invitation. 'We got the licenses posted, right there.'

She noted them, and further noted she hadn't been wrong about the establishment. A dump of a dive, she concluded, for cheap and serious drinking, fellowship not required.

'We're not here about your license, Mr Tiller.'

'Whatever you're here about better be good enough to roust me out of bed at this hour.'

'Murder good enough for you?'

'Ah, fuck.' He walked away, flipped up the pass-through to go behind the bar. He pulled a bottle from under the bar along with a shot glass. Poured the shot, downed it. 'What's it to me?'

Eve stepped up to the bar, brought Kagen's ID shot up on her PPC. 'Do you know this man?'

317

'He dead?'

'He is.'

'Yeah, I know him. A regular. Regular asshole.'

'When did you last see or speak to him?'

Tiller jabbed a finger at a stool. 'He was sitting there last night, bitching about the ball game on-screen. Doesn't like baseball, and too fucking bad. I do, and I run the bar.'

'Was he alone?'

'Come in alone, like always.' Tiller pulled out another bottle, a tall glass. Eve didn't know what he poured, but it smelled like seaweed. He spiked it with another shot.

'What time did he come in?'

'Hell, I don't know. Ordered a beer, a bump, some grub. His usual. Had another, bitching about the game. I said how he could take off if he didn't like it. Not like he tips worth a shit anyhow. But he orders another round. I got some regulars watching the game, so I tell him to zip it or I'll boot him.'

'I bet he zipped it,' Peabody said, trying some flattery.

Tiller shrugged, downed half of the spiked seaweed. 'I booted him before, he knows I'll do it again.'

'Did he talk with anyone else, interact, leave with anyone?'

'Yeah. Some street snatch walks in, takes a stool, orders a brew. He plays big shot, has me put it on his tab. He runs a weekly, pays up or he don't get served.'

'What did she look like?' Eve demanded.

'Like a street snatch.'

Eve knew his type. Hard-ass, didn't like cops, and hoped to shrug them off.

Not going to happen.

'Tiller, would you rather have this conversation in the box at Central?'

'You can get off my case,' he tossed back. 'What the fuck do I know? I work the bar, I hold this crap joint together for a shitty paycheck, shittier tips, and the shithole apartment upstairs. Might not even have that much longer, as the dick-wads who own the place and don't put a goddamn dime into it start talking about selling it off. Bad frigging investment. I do my job, you get it? And my job isn't to pay attention to some pross. I got her a beer, that's it.'

'Try again. How old was she?'

'Fucking A.' He wasn't happy, Eve judged, but he knew when he hit up against another hard-ass – and one with a badge. 'Old enough to drink. Probably old enough to have a kid old enough to drink.'

'Give me a range.'

'Shit. Maybe forty. She looked used up.'

'Race?'

'Who gives a shit?'

'I do.'

'White probably. I keep the lights down, okay? It's not like we get high-class in here.'

'Hair color.'

'Fuck me!' He drained the rest of the seaweed, then frowned as if the taste had jogged something. 'Purple.'

'You're sure?' Eve pressed, thinking of the black hair. 'Light or dark?'

'Shit, purple-purple, what I know? Like those smelly flowers on the big bushes.'

'Lilacs?' Peabody suggested, and he half toasted her with his empty seaweed glass.

'Yeah, that stuff. Covered half her face now that I think about it. But you could see a scar down her cheek. She wasn't nothing to get wood over, you ask me, but that don't matter to Kagen, the asshole.'

'He left with her?'

'Yeah. She left a damn near full beer and takes him off for a bang or BJ. Not my business.'

'What time did she come in? What time did they leave?'

'Jesus!' Muscles and tats rippled when he threw up his hands. 'I don't the fuck know. You can drag my sorry ass to Central, and I still won't know. I had customers, okay? The cheap-ass owners won't even pay for a server. I'm on my own, every frigging night, six to two.'

'Did you have the Yankee–Red Sox game on the bar screen?'

He gave Eve his tired sneer. 'Shit yeah, what else?'

'What inning was it when she came in?'

He opened his mouth, closed it again. Narrowed his eyes. 'Bottom of the fifth. One out, runner on second. Jeraldo takes a ball, then knocks a nice blooper to right field. Runners on the corners. And what does that asshole Murchini do? He hits into a double play, retires the side with two on. She walked in about when Murchini came to the plate.'

'Okay. What inning did they leave?'

'Huh. Wait a minute.' Replaying the ball game tweaked his interest, just enough. 'I'm getting her beer and the Sox go three up, three down. So bottom of the sixth. Cecil fouls back the first pitch, low and outside for ball one, he takes the next pitch, misses the corner, ball two, then he hits one to the hole. Sox shortstop's all over it, but Cecil beats the throw to first.'

He nodded to himself. 'Yeah, bottom of the sixth, they walk out with Unger coming up to bat, Duran's on deck. Sox catcher goes to the mound to settle the pitcher down. They walk out.'

'Unger's a monster,' Eve said conversationally. 'What's he batting, .330?'

'Yeah, that's right. A guy who can walk out with a man on, no outs, Unger coming to the plate, the score tied two to two, that's an asshole.'

'Can't argue that. Would you say Kagen was drunk?'

A little less annoyed, Tiller shrugged. 'He don't ever leave here sober. Not my problem.'

'Have you seen the woman before?'

'Not in here. Outside, one street snatch is the same as the next, you ask me.'

Eve nodded to Peabody, who pulled the two sketches on her PPC, offered it to Tiller. 'Did she look like either of these women?'

'Nowhere near classy like that one, nowhere near sexy like that one. Look, you ask me, no way that used-up pross offed Kagen anyway. Not unless she had somebody do it, and what for? It's not like he had anything worth taking.'

'Did she take the stool beside him? Were there other seats, empty booths, chairs?'

'Yeah, she sat next to him. Sure there were empties. Not like we pack 'em in here, especially on weeknights.'

'Do you think they knew each other?' Peabody asked.

'Don't know, but I haven't seen her in here before. We get prossies come in now and then, trolling. He'd bite now and again, if they came cheap. He's a cheap bastard, but paying for it's the only way he'd get it, you ask me.

'Look, you gonna let me get some sleep anytime this frigging century?'

'Yeah. We appreciate your cheerful and selfless coopera- tion.' Knowing the futility, Eve still left a card on the bar. 'If you see her again, or remember anything else, contact me.'

'Right.'

She imagined he tossed the card before the door closed behind her.

'You don't want to have Yancy work with him?' Peabody asked.

'He wouldn't cooperate, and we can't make him. Plus, he didn't really see her.'

'But, the scar,' Peabody began.

'He saw the scar because she wanted him to see the scar. He remembers that, the hair color, the fact she came off as a used-up street LC because that's what she wanted people to see.'

With the long coat sweeping behind her, Eve shot her hands into her trouser pockets. 'He gave us plenty. She knew Kagen used street level, liked them cheap. She knew he'd be drinking in there, and by that time would already have a couple in him. All she has to do is offer him a bang or BJ at a bargain price, and he's going to go with her. All she has to do is distract him for a couple seconds, spike his drink, and he'd go with her.'

'Have a car waiting,' Peabody continued. 'Not in front, around the corner, down the block. Of the three, this one was probably the easiest. Not necessarily the quickest, but the easiest. Dim, grungy bar, target's already at least half-hammered.'

'You're right on that, all the way right.'

The police work continued at the crime scene, but the gawkers had lost interest.

Peabody climbed into the car. 'That was smart, using the ball game to jog his memory. He was a pissy wit to begin with, but using the ball game changed the angle. How does anybody remember all that?' she continued as Eve pulled away. 'I mean the inning and who's where, even balls and strikes and all that.'

Eve glanced over. 'Because, for Christ's sake, it's baseball.'

'I like baseball okay,' Peabody said. 'But I don't—'

Eve shot up a hand. 'Baseball is not to be *liked okay*. Revere it, or do not speak of it.'

'Well, okay, I can revere the players look frosty in those cute uniforms.'

'You make me sad, Peabody. You make me very sad.'
When Peabody started to speak, Eve shot up her hand again.
'Don't say anything else to make me sad enough I'm com-
pelled to punch you.'

'We could talk about murder. That won't make you sad
enough to punch me.'

'Wise choice.'

'It's not talking about you-know-what to ask what time
the bartender hit with the you-know-what with the things
that happen on the segments discussed.'

'Since I was working when said game happened, I can't
say, as such things vary according to the specific game, players, calls, and so on. Look it up.'

'Look up the . . . can I use the actual words, or will you
feel compelled to punch me?'

'You get a pass. Look up last night's Yankees game, run
a replay on the bottom of the fifth.'

'I can do that.' Peabody got to work, then cringed. 'Please
don't punch me, but I'm not sure I completely followed who
was where in the game when he said she came in.'

'Murchini's coming to the plate. There're runners on first
and third.'

'Okay, got it, wait . . . Oh, he *is* frosty. Time's
eight-fifty-three.'

'A little earlier this time. Check the bottom of the
next inning.'

'Okay, okay.'

'The Yankees have a man on first, with Unger coming up

to bat. You're going to have a time-out as the Sox's catcher talks to his pitcher.'

'Got it, got it. Gee, this Unger guy is seriously built. We've got nine-seventeen.'

'Didn't waste time, did she?' Eve mused. 'Got him out pretty quick.'

'Dallas, given the TOD, she spent nearly seven hours with Kagen.'

'Maybe she wanted more time. Maybe she overdosed him some since he'd already had so much alcohol in him. Maybe she had other things to do in there.'

She pulled into the garage at Central, into her slot.

'Darla Pettigrew,' Peabody said as they got out. 'If we look at her, and I know that's where you're leaning, so if we look at her? One of the maybes is she had to take some time out to do something for or with her grandmother. I mean she started earlier, so what if she had to come back, spend some time with Eloise, either to establish an alibi or because Eloise needed something? I just don't think the relationship there's faked, on either side.'

'I don't, either. And that's good, Peabody,' she added as they got in the elevator. 'That's good. It costs her some time, time she makes up on the other end. TOD's three-fifty-six, wit finds the DB, calls it in at four-fifty-eight.'

'If she's staked out the target's building – and she had to at some point, right? – she'd probably know when the wit got home, knew her window. I mean, why take chances?'

'She knew her window,' Eve agreed. 'I bet she cut it close,

but she knew her window. He's dead about four, and she has to get him loaded up, transported up to 179th, laid out before Cohen walks home, arriving right about five. Yeah, she cut it close.'

'It works for me.' Used to it, Peabody barely sighed when Eve shoved off the elevator for the glides. 'I see how it plays, so it works for me. But I don't see, right now, how we prove it.'

'We're going to write it up, send a memo to Mira to update any applicable profile. We're going to interview the other women identified as part of the support group. We're going to see if the DB told Morris anything new, then we're going to nag the shit out of Harvo on the hair.'

'So, another day in paradise.'

'We're going to run down that hair, Peabody. And we're going to pay another visit to the legend and her granddaughter.'

'Really?'

'Yeah. One step at a time.'

She headed straight to her office, coffee, her board, and her book.

It infuriated her to add the third victim.

'Okay, bitch,' she said aloud, 'you got your hat trick, but I'll be damned if you notch a fourth.'

At her desk, she wrote her report, then outlined a profile of her top suspect for Mira's review.

Subject is intelligent, organized, possesses IT and AI engineering skills. She is a member of the Women For

Women support group and, thus far, acquainted with the female connected to each victim. She is mature, has access to funds, currently resides in a large, private residence – in fact, currently controls said residence and staff.

Subject is the granddaughter of a legendary actor, a globally known and admired celebrity and activist, primarily for women's rights and status. Subject's grandparents had a long-term marriage, by all accounts a near storybook-style love affair until the grandfather's death. Grandmother still wears wedding ring. A wedding portrait hangs in the main parlor.

Theory: Subject expected and desired a relationship and marriage like her grandparents'. Expected and desired a spouse devoted to her as her grandfather appeared to have been to her grandmother. Subject also desired making a mark of her own by creating her own business through her personal skill set.

Subject's spouse failed to meet expectations by engaging LCs, having an affair – younger woman – manipulating the terms of the business to profit, then, with divorce, forcing the sale thereof. Spouse compounds the betrayal by purchasing a home with the profit, living there with the younger woman.

While I believe these betrayals would have incited subject to violence of some sort, at some point, the true break came with the support group. There, subject met, interacted, came to sympathize and relate with women who had suffered not only betrayal, but violence, sexual assault, rape. Crimes that had gone unpunished – and, at least in the case of the three victims, behavior that had continued.

Like her grandmother – her ideal – she found her cause, not one where she'd march or make speeches, but would take what she sees as real and necessary action. She would become justice. Again, in a way of emulating her grandmother, she takes on roles – complete with costumes, personalities – to lure the men, through sex or the promise of sex.

Drugging them not only serves the purpose of incapacitating, rendering them unable to defend, fight, overpower her, but makes them weak, takes their power. Stripping them naked humiliates. Torturing not only gives her control over their pain, but feeds her need to cause their suffering. Castration, obviously, unmans them. It robs them of the weapon they used on women. They die helpless, suffering, and sexless.

She leaves them outside their home to show their betrayal of the home, potentially. To leave them outside – never to have a home again – in public. A last humiliation.

The poem states their crime – in black-and-white. But it's the name she chooses – Lady Justice – that tells me this is another role, and one for which she wants attention, appreciation, and glory.

The profile of the killer, the profile of Darla Pettigrew mesh for me. Can you confirm or debunk?

Eve read it over, nodded. It helped to write it down, just lay it all out. Maybe Mira would pick it apart, but damn it, it played out. It worked. It fit.

As she sent it off, Peabody came to her door. 'First one's here. Jacie Pepperdine. Where do you want to interview her?'

Eve had already thought that one through. 'Get a box.'

Peabody lifted her eyebrows. 'Okay then.' She pulled out her 'link, did a check. 'A's open.'

'Book it, take her in. I'll be a minute.'

'Got it. I take it we treat her like a suspect.'

'Follow your gut.'

Rising, Eve put together a file. Following her gut, she prepared to go hard if needed. She walked to her skinny window first, took a minute to look out, look down.

Plenty of women out there – and some men, too – who'd experienced what the members of the support group had experienced. And worse, because there was always worse.

She could sympathize, and Christ knew she could relate. But murder sure as hell didn't balance the scales. Maybe the law didn't always get it right, but as long as she was on the side of it, she'd damn well try.

She picked up the file, walked out. She assumed Jenkinson and his tie, Reineke and his socks had caught one, as they didn't man their desks.

Santiago sat at his, scowling under his cowboy hat as he worked his comp. The hat meant he'd lost another bet with Carmichael – who looked pretty pleased with herself while she worked her own.

Baxter had his feet — and his fashionable shoes — on his desk as he held a conversation on his 'link while his young partner diligently wrote up a report. Uniforms buzzed in their cubes.

She scanned the cops under her command, then looked up at the sign posted over the break room door.

NO MATTER YOUR RACE, CREED,
SEXUAL ORIENTATION, OR POLITICAL
AFFILIATION, WE PROTECT AND SERVE,*
BECAUSE YOU COULD GET DEAD.
*EVEN IF YOU WERE AN ASSHOLE.

That's right, she thought, that's fucking-A right. And every cop under her command would follow that goddamn perfect son of a bitching motto.

And that's what she was doing right now.

She walked out, and into Interview A.

She noted both Peabody and Pepperdine had fizzies, and half wished she'd fought a Pepsi out of Vending.

Jacie Pepperdine, age twenty-seven, appeared to be a stunning example of a few generations of race mixing. She had Asian tilted eyes in ferocious green, skin the color of gold-dusted caramel, madly curling hair in jet-black she'd accented with caramel streaks, a long, narrow nose, a long, full-lipped mouth.

'Ms Pepperdine, this is my partner, Lieutenant Dallas.'

'Okay. Look, if we could just get to whatever this is, I have someplace to be by noon.'

She had a voice like velvet, which, Eve thought, explained why she made part of her living singing in joints – the other half waitressing in them.

'Sure. We appreciate you coming in. You belong to a support group called Women For Women.'

Jacie's mildly curious expression went to stone. 'That's a private, anonymous group. You have no right to poke in.'

'Maybe you noticed you're in Homicide,' Eve said easily. 'We're conducting an investigation into three connected murders. Those murders also connect with the support group.'

'That's ridiculous.'

'Do you pay any attention to the media?'

'I work. When I'm not working, I'm going to auditions. When I'm not working or going to auditions, I sleep.'

'Nigel McEnroy, the first victim, drugged and raped multiple women, including two who belonged to your group.'

'You want me to feel sorry a rapist is dead? Why didn't you arrest the bastard?'

'Maybe if one of *his* victims had reported him, we would have. The second victim, Thaddeus Pettigrew, was the ex-husband of one of your members. He left his wife for the woman – younger woman – he cheated on her with, and through some legal manipulation, forced her to sell the business she'd founded – with himself reaping most of the profits.'

Eve paused, watching Jacie's face. 'You know that story. You know that woman.'

In a gesture combining self-protection with defiance,

Jacie sat back, crossed her arms. 'I'm not discussing anything, and I mean anything, said in our group.'

'The third victim,' Eve continued, 'Arlo Kagen, also the ex-husband of one of your members, physically and sexually assaulted his wife, threatened to harm their young son. Another story you know.'

'Same answer.'

'Okay. What's your story?'

'I don't know you. I don't have to tell you my personal, private business. If that's all—'

'Sit,' Eve snapped when Jacie rose. 'We'll start with your whereabouts on the three nights in question. Monday, Tuesday, and last night. Say, between the hours of nine P.M. and four A.M.'

'Monday night, singing in front of a crap crowd – but a crowd at Last Call – from nine to one. I'd have gotten there by eight-thirty, left by one-thirty. I went home – alone – went to bed. That's the same last night. Tuesday, I served fancy drinks and fancy snacks to the fancy customers of Bistro East. Eight to two – that's closing. Today, I've got an audition to sing in another craphole, but it's closer to my apartment. You want the rest of my schedule? It runs pretty much the same, seven fricking nights a week.'

'That's a hard workload,' Peabody commented. 'Do you still go to the group?'

'Twice a month. I leave there and go to work. Not a lot of time in there to kill rapists, cheaters, and wife beaters. More, I don't care about rapists, cheaters, and wife beaters.'

'Somebody did.' Eve opened the file, went hard. 'Somebody cared enough to do this.'

Under that gorgeous skin, Jacie paled as Eve laid out the crime scene photos. 'Cared enough to torture three human beings, whatever their crimes and sins, for hours. To mutilate them, to kill them. What was the crime against you, Jacie, what was the sin? Is this how you want the man who hurt you to end? Do you want to share responsibility for that?'

'Please put those away. Please, can I have some water?' She nudged aside her fizzy. 'Just some water.'

'Sure. I'll get it.'

'Get me a Pepsi, will you?' Eve asked as Peabody rose. She put the photos back into the file. 'Give me his name. Start there. The name of the man.'

'I don't like to talk about it. I started going to WFW last fall, months after it happened. I didn't think I could talk about it, but ... Natalia – I guess you've talked to Natalia – she's so calming, so ... it's a fancy word but it fits, so empathetic. And the other women, it's like having sisters there for you, mothers, friends. It's helped me so much. I can't believe anyone in the group did what you're saying. Did what's in that file. I can't.'

'Give me his name. Start there, Jacie, because it's not going to help you if he ends up in this file. It's not going to help you if he's dead.'

'Cooke, Ryder Cooke. At about ten o'clock on August eighth of last year, he raped me, and he ruined my life.'

17

As Peabody came back in, Eve considered the best approach.

'Jacie, we can ask you questions, or if it's easier, you can just tell us what happened.'

'Nothing's easier.' Jacie took slow, small sips of water. 'I wanted to put it behind me, but he made sure I couldn't. I have to face it every damn day.'

Peabody started to speak, but Eve shook her head.

They waited.

'I'm a singer. I have a voice, a good voice, and I was willing to do the work, make the effort to improve. For as long as I can remember, I wanted to sing. I didn't have to be a star, you know? Just sing, make my living, use my gift. I was doing okay, then I got it into my head to come to New York, to push myself. I got some good gigs, too, some really solid gigs. Good reviews, some attention. And a shot at a recording contract. It was like a dream, more than I'd let myself want, but here it was.'

She took another sip, set the water aside.

'A scout from Delray heard me, told me to send an

audition disc. I spent a good chunk of my savings booking a studio, good musicians. If I had a shot, I was going to do it right. And it worked, or I thought it did.

'Ryder Cooke is Delray. He's the star-maker. So when Ryder Cooke asks you to his place to discuss your future, to talk about a contract, you go. I went. We had drinks. I was not drunk,' she added with considerable passion. Her eyes went very bright, not with tears, not now, but with that passion, and with memory.

'I'm not stupid enough to get drunk at the most important meeting of my life. But I had some wine. We talked, and he painted this picture of what I could have, what I could be that meant everything. Then he said there was something I needed to see upstairs.'

She squeezed her eyes shut. 'Was it stupid? I still don't know. He never made a move, never said anything that made me uncomfortable, so I went. I didn't even get a bad feeling when I went into the bedroom with him. Then he grabbed me. He's a pretty big guy, and I wasn't expecting . . . Doesn't matter. He had me pinned to the bed. I'm telling him no, get off. He says just lie back and enjoy it, baby. Just like that. Lie back and enjoy it, baby.'

She had to suck in air. Let it out again.

'I tried to get him off, to get out, but he was stronger, and he just . . . After, when I'm crying, and he still has me pinned, he tells me to deal with it. This is how it works. Be a good girl and he'll sign me, he'll make me. Tell anybody, make a stink about it, I'll be finished. Nobody'll believe me, and I'll be lucky to earn the price of a sandwich singing on street corners.

'When he rolled off, I ran out. He hadn't even bothered to pull my clothes off, just my panties, right? I ran out. I don't know why I didn't go to the cops.'

Tears spilled now, and she swiped at them with finger-tips, impatient. 'I was ashamed and shocked and afraid. I did everything wrong that night, okay? I admit I did everything wrong.'

She had to pause another moment, sip more water.

Eve waited her out, signaled Peabody to do the same.

'I went home and I showered. I took shower after shower, scrubbing him off me. And I cried half the night. Useless, useless. Then I started to get mad, and that was better. I went straight into Delray in the morning, and I told any-body who'd listen what happened. And just like he said, nobody believed me. Or if they did, they weren't going to go up against Cooke.

'I didn't get the contract, big surprise.' Bitter now, hard and brittle as ice. 'I got fired from the decent gigs I had. I couldn't get another gig in a good venue. He spread the word I was a troublemaker, a drunk, that I used, stole – the works. So now I take whatever gig I can get to make the rent.'

Eve gave it another beat to be sure Jacie had finished.

'Jacie, do you want to file charges?'

'With what?' It all but exploded out of her. 'It's my word against his, so I've got nothing.'

336

Peabody reached over, laid a hand over Jacie's. 'Do you think you were the only one?'

'I— Probably not. No, not the only one, but that doesn't make me less of a nobody. He's the star-maker. Who's going to believe me?'

'We do,' Eve said simply.

Her breath hitched, tore, and the tears rolled down again. 'If I try to go after him for it now, after all this time, I will be singing on street corners.'

'No, you won't. But we'll leave that for now. You told this story, identified the man who raped you, in your support group.'

'That's the whole point of the group.'

'Did anyone speak to you more about it, outside of the group?'

'Yeah, some of us went for coffee and bitch sessions after. I did that sometimes.'

'I need names, full names if you have them. We need to talk to them the way we're talking to you.'

'It doesn't feel right.'

'We've already talked to Jasmine Quirk, Leah Lester, Darla Pettigrew, Una Ruzaki, Rachel Fassley. And Natalia. We have interviews scheduled with Mae Ming, Sasha Cullins, and Bree Macgowan.'

Jacie pressed her lips together. 'I don't know a Jasmine or Leah from group.'

'Jasmine moved away, and Leah hasn't been for a while,' Peabody told her. 'Do you know the other women the

337

lieutenant mentioned? Were they part of your coffee sessions?'

'It's not always the same people. I can't always go after the meeting. But I've had coffee with everyone you mentioned. Honestly, the only other one I know like that is Sherri Brinkman. Another one dumped by an ex for a younger, but not before he gave her an STD, and pretty much hosed her in the divorce because he's the one with all the money and the lawyers. She's like sixty, and maybe hits five-two, a hundred and ten. There's no way she could do what's in that folder.'

'Okay. Can you give me an idea how long she's been in the group?'

'She was part of it before I started going in October.'

'Jacie, when we talk to her, when we talk to the others,' Peabody said gently, 'we're not the enemy. We need to find who's responsible for these murders, but that doesn't make us the enemy.'

When Jacie shrugged, stared down at the table, Eve leaned back. 'Do you know Mavis Freestone?'

Jacie looked up with a smirk. 'Oh sure, me and Mavis, we're tight. We have lunch every week. Jesus.'

Eve pulled out one of her cards. 'Peabody, do you have something to write with?'

Peabody dug out a pencil, handed it over.

'Still got that audition recording?'

'I've got my copy, sure.'

'Give me an hour, then tag Mavis at this number. Tell her

as much or as little as you want, but tell her Dallas said she should listen to your audition recording.'

Jacie took the card, stared at it. 'Are you bullshitting me?'

'What would be the point? It happens that Mavis and I actually are tight. What happens next there is up to you.'

Now tears shimmered, but didn't roll. She stared at Eve with incredulity, and with just the faintest light of hope.

'Why? Why would you do this?'

'Because we're not the enemy. Now, whether or not you opt, at any time, to file charges against Ryder Cooke, we will investigate him. You wouldn't have been the only one. I'm going to do whatever I can to keep him out of this folder, and whatever I can to put him in a cage. That's it.'

'I – I need to think about it.'

'All right. My number's on the other side of the card. Thanks for coming in.'

After Jacie, visibly dazed, left, Peabody blinked damp eyes. 'That was a totally frigid thing to do, Dallas. Mega frigid.'

'Didn't cost me anything. Run Sherri Brinkman before you contact her, ask her to come in.'

'Sure.' Peabody got up, started for the door. 'Mostly what we do is go after bad guys. It's nice when we can do something positive.'

'Going after bad guys is plenty positive in my book.'

'You know what I'm saying.'

Yeah, Eve thought when Peabody went out. I do.

She contacted Mavis, got a perky message:

Hey! Abso-truly wish I could chat, but I'm in the
studio. Lay a message on me. Cha!

'It's Dallas. Expect a tag from a Jacie Pepperdine.
Do me a solid, okay, and arrange to listen to her audi-
tion recording. If it doesn't blow, pass it to Roarke.
Appreciate it.'

She toggled to tag Nadine.

'Ready for that one-on-one?'

'You got it with Peabody. This is semi-connected, and
I'm tossing you a big, stinking fish.'

'Mmm, my favorite kind. Does the fish have a name?'

'Ryder Cooke.'

Nadine angled her head, narrowed her eyes. 'Don't tell
me you've got him on a slab.'

'No, and I hope to avoid that. You're going to want to
start digging, Nadine. I've got a woman who won't, as yet,
file a formal complaint, but she's very credible on my scale.
She says he raped her, and the way it went down tells me
she's not the first or the last.'

'Give me her name.'

'Can't do it. Same as you wouldn't do it, Nadine. When
and if she wants to go public, you'll have it.'

'Can you give me a timeline?'

'Last August. Dig.'

'You can count on it. Thanks for the tip.'

'Just use it.'

Next, she contacted SVU, laid it out.

340

'We'll get you, you son of a bitch,' she grumbled. 'One way or the other.'

Back in her office, she added the interview details to her book, ran Ryder Cooke.

Mixed-race male of forty-eight, worth several tidy billion. Producer and president at Delray. He had twenty-six years with the company, his own shuttle, homes in New York, New LA, East Hampton, Jamaica. Two ex-wives, a rep, from what she read when skimming entertainment media, for being a major player.

And going by that segment of the media, Cooke was currently in New LA producing a recording and vids with some band named Growl.

Which kept him safe, for now.

She ran Sherri Brinkman to get the ex-husband's name, but switched to a run on him.

Linus Brinkman, Caucasian male, age sixty-seven, one marriage, one divorce, two offspring. Currently cohabbing with LaDale Gerald, age twenty-five. (Which brought her in at five years younger than his own daughter.)

Residence in New York, second home on Grand Cayman, and a recently purchased flat in Paris.

Cofounder and CEO of Lodestar Corporation, a company used for promoting events – concerts, major fundraisers and auctions, sports both live and online.

His listed net worth hit nine figures.

Toggling back out of curiosity, she noted his ex-wife barely made six. While her employment data listed her as a

VP of marketing with Lodestar for twenty-six years – with two breaks for professional mother status – it now listed her as an administrative assistant, marketing in a smaller firm, for a fraction of the pay.

'Yeah, he screwed you over, didn't he, Sherri?'

She tagged Lodestar, went through a frustrating runaround to glean only that Mr Brinkman was out of town and unavailable.

She rose, paced the confines of her office, kicked her desk.

Tagged Roarke.

'Good afternoon, Lieutenant.'

'Is it? Already? Shit. Do you know Linus Brinkman of Lodestar?'

'More or less – more less. We've met.'

'How about you put on your expert consultant, civilian, hat, contact his office, and find out where he is and when he's due back? His assistant has assistants and nobody will tell me.'

'I'll do that if you make time to eat some sort of lunch.'

'Well for . . . fine. Just tag me back or text if you get the info. Thanks.'

She wasn't hungry, she thought, but the rest of her day equaled packed. She didn't want to make time to eat something, and doubted she'd be able to anyway.

But she could fix it. He had said 'some sort' of lunch. She figured a candy bar fit that criteria.

She locked her door, dug the remote out of her desk to turn off the blue dye trap she'd laid for the infamous Candy

Thief. After climbing on the desk, she carefully eased up the ceiling tile.

And stared at the empty space.

'Come on!' She dragged a mini light out of her pocket, shined it inside.

Nothing.

'Son of a fucking sneaky bitch!'

Not a sign of the dye – and there should've been. So the Candy Thief used a remote, too. Probably a scanner first, which warned of the trap.

She jumped down, scowled up at the tile. Then jammed her hands in her pockets.

She had to admit – hated to, but had to – it was pretty damn impressive.

She unlocked her door, stalked out to the bullpen. Jenkinson and his tie were back – and dear God, this one sported rainbows obviously generated in a nuclear reactor. So were Reineke and his socks, but she thanked the patron saint of vision she couldn't currently see them.

Santiago and his hat had rolled over to Carmichael's desk, where they held an intense conversation. Eve figured it involved an active case or another stupid bet.

Since Baxter and Trueheart were missing, she assumed they'd caught one.

Peabody looked busy with a report.

'This isn't over,' Eve announced. Activity stopped, heads turned. 'Believe me, it's not over.'

After stalking back to her office, she gave the ceiling tile

343

another scowl. She'd think of something else. Oh yeah, she would.

Her 'link signaled a text.

Brinkman is in Nevada – Vegas – completing some business. He's arriving in a company shuttle at Startack Transpo Station, private dock, at half-three. Where he will be met by his regular driver and car service. Is expected to check in to the office, but go straight home. He has a black-tie event this evening, and has bookings for a massage, with his stylist, in his home beginning at half-four.

You're welcome. Eat.

'Okay, okay, that's good.' Now she scowled at her AC, then turned back as she heard the brisk clicks of heels heading for her office.

It didn't surprise her to see Mira, or to see her looking pretty as spring in a suit of soft blue.

'I didn't mean for you to have to squeeze this into your day,' Eve began.

'Not such a squeeze. I'm heading out for a lunch meeting – with Natalia Zula – so I have a few minutes first. And I wanted to ask you if you're bucking for my job.'

'What?'

With a smile, Mira came the rest of the way in, took a scan of the board. 'Your profile of Darla Pettigrew is very astute. Your correlation to her relationship with her grandmother, what her own ambitions, emotional development, expectation may have been, may be through that relationship, strikes as accurate.'

Mira eased a hip on the corner of Eve's desk. 'Your summation there, and theory, lean heavily on your belief she's killed. How confident are you that's the case?'

'I've run probability scans that—'

'No, not what a probability scan calculates. How confident are you?'

'Ninety-five percent. I'd say a hundred, but there's always a chance I'm wrong, and I have to factor that in.'

As she spoke, Eve turned to her board, hooked her thumbs in her belt loops, studied Darla's photo.

'I have to factor in that she buzzed for me right off. Straight off, and I can't shake it. So because I've looked at her from the start, that could influence the rest.'

'I'd love a chance to speak with her, evaluate her myself.'

'I want her in the box.' Eve turned back. 'I need a reason to get her there. I'm working on that.'

'Then I'll leave you to it.' Mira straightened. 'So far, her violence has focused on men, and specifically men who have wronged women in her support group. But that violence would, unquestionably, spread to anyone who attempts to stop her from enacting her form of justice. So while, for the moment, she sees you as a kind of colleague, that will change.'

'Yeah. I figure to give that one a little push later today.'

'Then be careful.'

'One question,' Eve said as Mira started out. 'Is a bag of soy chips some sort of lunch?'

'No,' Mira said, and kept going.

'Damn it.'

Eve considered pizza, and also the consequences if the scent escaped into the bullpen. Chaos, rioting. Besides, she just wasn't hungry enough to waste a good slice.

She tried soup – noted she had several kinds. Roarke was a sneaky son of a bitch, too. She opted for a cup of minestrone – and a bag of soy chips.

Peabody came in as she was downing it. 'The next ...' Peabody sniffed the air. 'That's not Vending soup. That's real soup.'

'So?'

'Well, it's just ... Smells really good.'

Eve turned, programmed another cup. 'Here, and shut up about it.'

'Man, thanks. Mae Ming's here, and I shot you the basic details from the Brinkman run.'

'Take Ming. I'll take the morgue, and swing by the lab for Harvo.'

'Good deal for me.'

'Depending on timing, you take the other two we have coming in. Then tag Brinkman, get her in here. If you get more names, get them in here.'

'You can count on it.'

Eve grabbed her coat, dropped the bag of chips in her pocket. 'I am. Don't touch my AC.'

She walked out to the bullpen, scanned her cops, scanned the board, and noted Baxter and Trueheart had indeed caught one. In fact two, as they'd caught a murder/suicide.

She glanced toward Trueheart, who sat grim-faced at his desk working on a report. He'd lost a lot of the green, she thought, but part of what made him a good cop was his ability to feel the weight of the job.

She could see a lot of weight on his face at the moment.

She had a serial killer on her hands, Eve thought, but she had men who needed a boss.

She walked to his desk. 'Detective.'

'Sir.'

'Where's your partner?'

'He's in the break room, getting some coffee. We just got in from—'

'Yeah, I see the board.'

'It looks like a domestic dispute. They were in the middle of a contentious divorce and custody deal. Two kids, eight and ten. He went to her place. No forced entry, so it looks like she let him in. He stabbed her multiple times, then slit his own throat.'

'The kids?'

'In school, that's a blessing. A neighbor heard her screaming, couldn't get in because he'd bolted the door. Neighbor called it in, but it was too late. She had a sister. The kids are with the sister.'

'Trueheart, sometimes there's nothing for us to do but

write it up. There's nobody to hunt down, bring in, put in a cage. We can only write it up and close it.'

'I know it, Lieutenant. Baxter said the same.' He let out a breath. 'I'm writing it up.'

All they could do, she thought again as she headed out. Dealing with the times that was all you could do was part of the job. And you hoped it pushed you to do everything you could when you could.

She let New York roll over her as she drove to the morgue. Nowhere near peaceful now as its noise, hurry, color, anger, amusement rolled. You couldn't live and work in a city with all of that, with the intensity of all of that, and not hit times when you could only write it up. And times, she needed to believe more times, you could and would do everything.

So she walked that white tunnel for the third day running determined. Committed. And seriously pissed off.

Morris walked out of the double doors before she reached them.

'Dallas. You just caught me on the way to lunch.'

She pulled the chips out of her pocket. 'Trade you for a quick summary.'

'I do have a fondness for chips.' He stepped back in; she followed.

And saw three bodies on three slabs.

'Murder-suicide,' Morris said when he saw her study the other bodies.

'Yeah, I know. Baxter and Trueheart. The husband's way of settling a divorce and custody dispute.'

348

'She fought. I can tell you, even before my full exam, she fought. She didn't go down easy.' He patted Eve's arm, stepped over to Kagen.

'On the other hand, he didn't fight. Couldn't, as he was drunk, then drugged. My summation includes the belief that the initial stimulant to bring him around failed. He was too far under. It's the same barbiturate, the same stimulant as the other two victims. It's simply in this case, the victim had consumed nearly three pints of beer and three shots of rye whiskey prior to the addition of the barbiturate.'

'It's why she didn't do as much damage as she did with the second victim. Maybe. The broken arm, that's symbolic, as he's left-handed, beat his wife.'

'Yes, dominant left. He also had a very good start on cirrhosis of the liver, and other health issues. His first wounds, and the last? Only three to four hours between. You're quite right, she didn't have or didn't spend as much time with him.'

'No point torturing him until he's conscious. And I think she may have had to break off. Then she had to get him back before one of the residents came home from night shift work. Used to be on the job, so he was helpful.'

'A stroke of luck.'

'So was the hair Peabody found that I'm hoping Harvo's nailed down for us. He tell you anything else?'

'The scarring on his knuckles indicates he used his fists regularly over the years. The damage to his body tells me he drank to excess just as regularly, had a poor diet, sketchy dental hygiene. Not helpful.'

'You have to know the vic to know the killer. She knew all of this. He was likely the easiest mark of the three, and still she made mistakes. Gave him too much of the drug, had to rush her kill so she didn't check the body well enough to make sure she didn't leave anything.

'She's getting sloppy,' Eve concluded, 'and also taking bigger risks. She sat right at the bar with this one, long enough to order a drink, have a conversation, with the bartender right there. So . . .'

She tossed him the chips. 'Thanks.'

Eve thought it through on her way to the lab. Definitely sloppy to overdose him. She had to know him for a heavy drinker. Then again, big guy, and she didn't want to risk him having any fight left in him.

Sloppier yet to leave the hair.

Not the lavender wig. So she got rid of the disguise before she went to work on him.

She had to bank on Harvo matching the DNA.

When she reached the lab, Eve angled for Harvo's glass-walled domain. The queen of hair and fiber sat on her stool at a leg of her work counter. She wore what could be termed a lab coat providing your definition thereof stretched wide, as her version was a bunch of inexplicable symbols scrolled over a field of bright spring green.

Her own hair, drawn back in a little bouncy tail, matched the field. A tiny glittery stud − green ranked as the day's color − winked on the side of her nose.

She had tunes going, bouncy like her tail of hair, as

350

her fingers – tipped in more green – danced over her screen.

She glanced over as Eve stepped in, shot out a smile. She snapped her fingers three times. The music shut off.

'Hey, Dallas. Hanging tough? Just finished your deal. Take off a load,' she invited with a gesture to another stool.

'I'm good, thanks. A little pressed.'

'Yeah, yeah, I know how that rides. So your hair had your vic's blood and skin tissue all over it. And see, like, some started to scab over, so he was still breathing when she lost it on him – and it stuck in the blood. Just his blood and tissue, btw.'

'Could you get DNA?'

'Old hair, Dallas. Old, dead hair, no root. What you sent me came from human hair, yeah, but old. It came from an enhancement.'

No DNA, she thought. Not as big a turn in luck as she'd hoped.

'A wig?'

'Possibly extensions or lifters, but I say wig at a solid eighty-five percent. And no cheapie deal. Human hair, almost all non–color treated, so whoever sold or donated it had true black hair.'

'Almost all?'

Harvo swiveled, brought up a magnification of the hair on-screen. 'Just a touch – tiny – of silver there. And that's color added – hard to tell how much because this strand broke off. It's not root to tip, but a partial.'

Eve didn't bother to ask how she'd know all that. No need to question the queen.

'And that's a pro color – Numex brand, Lightning Strike. So I'm seeing what's most likely some drama streaks,' Harvo told her, 'because most people aren't going to add silver to a wig except for that.'

'Because most people remove the gray – or silver.'

All cheer, Harvo tapped a finger in the air. 'Exactamundo. Now, maybe somebody wanted to add age in – like for a costume or whatever. In any case, there'll be some silver streaked or dashed like through the wig. The hair? I'm saying Asian. It's good, thick, healthy. That costs. And it's been well-maintained. Professionally maintained, with professional-grade products. Specifically, Allure Hair Enhancement Conditioner.'

'You got a brand on that, too?'

'Dallas.' Harvo spread her hands. 'Who you talking to?'

'You got a brand,' Dallas repeated, this time as a statement. She wanted to ask if Harvo was sure about the wig, but didn't. She did know who she was talking to.

'She posed as a street level. Purple hair. The bartender said purple, like lilacs, not black. He was two feet away. Even in dim light, he couldn't mistake the color. Why does she change wigs? Why does she wear a wig when she's torturing them?'

'Above my pay grade on that. Could just be she likes different looks for different, you know, tasks.'

'Costumes?' Eve turned a circle, paced. 'Just like you said.

Is it all costumes? Part of the role? Wouldn't she want them to see her when she's got them in her control? When they're helpless? Wouldn't she—'

She stopped, turned back. 'They do. Son of a bitch. They do see her, as she sees herself. Lady fucking Justice.'

'Well, Lady fucking Justice wore a top-of-the-line, human hair, professionally maintained wig when she offed this guy. That I can tell you.'

'Yeah. Yeah, she did. Thanks, Harvo.'

'Here to serve.'

Eve stopped at the doorway. 'What's all that?' she asked, circling a finger toward Harvo's lab coat.

'On the coat? Dallas, that's the periodic table. Better life, and better death, through chemistry, right?'

'Hard to argue. See you around.'

18

Eve walked back into Homicide, saw Peabody's empty desk.

'Peabody?' she asked Baxter.

'In Interview.'

No point in pushing in on that, she decided. 'I may need a stakeout team tonight. Looking at maybe nineteen to twenty-three hundred. You and Trueheart volunteered.'

'Yeah, we're selfless that way. Is this the Lady Justice case?'

'She's on a streak, and I can't see her breaking it. One potential target's out of town, but the other's got a fancy deal later tonight. She may try to scoop him up from there.'

'Have tux, will travel.'

'You're not going to the fancy deal. You're going to sit on a big, fancy house. I need to know if and when my prime suspect leaves. Any vehicle, but so far she's used a dark town car. You see that vehicle or a white all-terrain, a silver sedan leave the residence, you tag me, and you follow.'

'Hear that, kid?' Baxter said to Trueheart. 'It's time for stakeout snacks.'

'If she hasn't gone after him by twenty-three hundred, she's taking a pass. But . . . stick an hour after that.' She rattled off the address, strode to her office.

Programmed coffee, pulled out her 'link.

'Lieutenant, aren't we chatty today?'

'Not chat. And shouldn't you be buying up some third-world country and crowning yourself king instead of answering your 'link?'

'I did that this morning.' Roarke smiled. 'And just finished a lunch meeting where I approved the plans for my palace. What can I do for you?'

'What's the black-tie deal Brinkman's going to tonight?'

'Ah, it's the annual Spring Gala hosted by Our Planet and benefitting various environmental causes.'

'Great. Can you get us in?'

He said nothing for a moment. 'Since I assume you haven't just been injected with a drug that causes you to want to socialize, and in a formal setting, I further assume this would be work.'

'Both assumptions are accurate. I figure she might try for Brinkman there. She likes the risk, likes to dress up in costume – and that's what these deals are, essentially. Just an excuse to put on the fancy. Peabody's interviewing a couple of other women, so we might come up with other viable targets, but right now Brinkman's high on the list. I want the option of being there to shadow him, and if I get lucky, take her down.'

'Watching you take down a suspect is one of my top forms

355

of entertainment. Especially when you're in formal dress. It just adds that touch of piquant.'

'I don't know what that means, but fine. Can you get us in?'

'As it's held in the grand ballroom of my Palace – hotel in this case – I certainly can. Shall I arrange for Trina to come in, see to your hair and so on?'

Eve breathed in and out her nose. 'That was mean.'

'I know, but also entertaining. I'll see you at home then.'

'Yeah. Do not tag Trina,' she added, and clicked off.

With her coffee in hand, she put her boots on the desk, studied the board.

'What part would you play on this one? A server? That's what I'd do. Easy to spike a drink if you're the one serving it. All you'd need to do is guide him away. And doing it in front of all those people, that audience? Yeah, you'd love that. Big step up from a shithole bar.'

Eve drank coffee, considered.

She could go as a guest. That would work, too. One of many of the rich and fancy.

'But how do you keep the grandmother unaware?' she wondered. 'Or am I wrong there? Is she part of it? Either way, either way, we have to have another conversation. I need another look at the two of you before tonight.'

Eve stayed as she was when she heard Peabody's boots clomp toward her office.

She looked pale, Eve noted. Pale and tired.

'Please,' Peabody said. 'I need coffee.'

'Go.'

At the AutoChef Peabody let out a long breath. 'I've got another name – another of the women. I'll contact her after this. And I've got another name – or two in this case – of potential targets.'

'Sit down.' Because her partner looked beaten down, Eve gave up her chair, pointed to it. 'And sum it up.'

'First, Ming's got an alibi for the first two nights. Visiting her family in Maine. I'll check it out, but it's going to hold. She got back yesterday afternoon. She has a roommate, another female, and they were both home until around eight, when the roommate went out. She says she went to bed about eleven – tired – and didn't hear the roommate come in. But saw her this morning about seven-thirty, and the roomie said she got in about one. Big date. It's sketchy, but it's not her, Dallas.'

'Check anyway. The targets?'

'Gregory Sullivan and Devin Noonan. They're all grad students at NYU. There was a party right before the Thanksgiving break, a lot of drinking, some illegals – she didn't hedge there or deny she'd had her share of both. She went into the bedroom to get her coat, ready to head home. They both came in behind her, locked the door. She says Sullivan's the one who forced her onto the bed, but Noonan helped hold her down while Sullivan dragged off her pants. It's loud, nobody hears her calling for help. They took turns with her.'

'Did she tell anyone?'

'No.' Peabody scrubbed a hand over her face. 'They told her she'd asked for it, the way she'd rubbed up against Sullivan when they danced. Everybody saw how she did, how she asked for it, then they left her there. She pulled on her pants, went home, got sick. The roomie had already left to go back home for the break, so she was alone. She'd seen flyers for the group on campus, and decided to go when she kept having nightmares. She started going early December.'

'Was Pettigrew there when she told the story, named her rapists?'

'Yeah. She said she started crying, couldn't finish at first, and Pettigrew came over to her, held her.'

'Will she file charges?'

'I didn't think so, but after we talked, she said she wanted to. She wants to talk to her mother first. She wants to tell her mother what happened. She told her roommate after she started going to the group, but she hasn't been able to tell her mother. I think she'll come back, Dallas, and file.'

'Good. Why don't you run the targets? I'll take the next woman.'

'No, I'm good.' To prove it, Peabody downed the rest of the coffee. 'I'm good. I just needed a break. I can interview the next one.'

'When you need to stop, you stop.'

'Not yet.' Peabody rose. 'Bad as it is, it feels positive, letting them talk it out, showing I believe them. I'll go write it up, check the alibis before the next comes in.'

'Peabody. You're doing good work.'

'I'll feel like I am when we close this – and closing it includes helping put assholes like this Sullivan and Noonan in cages.'

And that's what they'd do, Eve thought.

She ran the two names, found Sullivan had several alcohol-and illegals-flavored bumps. And a few weeks in a classy rehab center. His limited employment history stayed confined to a few weeks a year in the family business. He played lacrosse and tennis while he studied business and finance and floated on his trust fund.

She knew the type.

Noonan mirrored him closely – though he played golf and tennis, and put in some time working a couple months a year at the country club in Connecticut both families belonged to.

She gathered what she had, and this time instead of contacting Special Victims, she went in person, spent time discussing strategy with a couple detectives she knew and the lieutenant in charge.

And considered it time well spent. Positive.

With Peabody back in Interview when Eve returned, she read her partner's report, added her own notes from the trip to SVU and her runs.

Noting Peabody hadn't had time to check the alibi, she reviewed the information and began to process it herself.

While Eve talked to the roommate, Linus Brinkman disembarked from his private shuttle. He'd enjoyed a Caesar salad, a bowl of smoked tomato soup, and two glasses of pinot noir on the flight.

That, in addition to a very successful trip, put him in the finest of moods.

He clouded a bit when he saw the chauffeur holding a sign with his name.

'I'm Brinkman. Where is Viktor?'

'I'm sorry, sir, he took ill shortly ago. I'm here to see you're not inconvenienced. Please, let me take your bag.'

Brinkman handed it over, but his frown deepened. 'They sent a droid? You're a good one, but you're a droid.'

'Yes, sir. I was immediately available and dispatched to ensure you weren't required to wait for another replacement. I am, of course, fully programmed and licensed as a chauffeur. Your car is just out here.'

'All right, all right. I don't have time to waste.'

'Exactly so.' The droid rolled the bag toward the car, opened the rear passenger door.

Brinkman saw the woman as he started to climb in. 'And who would you be?'

'I'm Selina, sir. The company sent you a companion to compensate for the trouble.' She offered a hand, injected the drug into Brinkman's palm.

'Not another droid, are you?' he demanded, already slurring his words.

'Not at all.' She offered him a glass of wine. 'Flesh and blood, just like you.'

He was out cold before the car pulled away from the center.

'Stop by the salon, Wilford, then we'll go to the market.'

'Yes, Ms Pettigrew.'

'Afterward, you'll take him in the usual way. Chain him up.'

'Of course, Ms Pettigrew.'

'I gave him enough to keep him out for a few hours, so when you're done, you can shut down.'

'As you wish.'

Yes, she thought. Just as she wished.

Between interviews, Eve had Peabody relay the results, give her the names, information. She did the runs, checked alibis herself – and found the loan officer who coerced or attempted to coerce female applicants to provide him with blow jobs for loan approval a strong candidate.

Maybe he'd – finally – lost his job and done six months in a cage, but she doubted that would be enough for Lady Justice.

When a hollow-eyed Peabody came in, Eve rose. 'Run this one for me on the way.'

'Where?'

'We're going to pay Darla Pettigrew another visit. A follow-up, we'll call it,' Eve said as she grabbed her coat. 'I'm going to spring you after, but I want the sympathetic element there.'

'I'm so frigging full of sympathy it's giving me heartburn. I've got brothers, Dallas.' They stopped at Peabody's desk for her jacket. 'I've got an amazing dad, uncles, cousins. I've got McNab. Roarke, Leonardo, Charles, the guys in the bullpen. I know men aren't all pigs and users. But, Jesus, these men? I don't have bad enough words.'

'They're going to pay. Not with their lives, but they're going to pay.'

'I think it's hearing it, one after another, all in a kind of horrible lump that's hit me, you know? We see worse, we know worse, but this is one after another.'

'They'll pay,' Eve said again, and forced herself to stay in the elevator all the way down to the garage. 'When we're done with Darla, go home.'

'I can stick,' Peabody told her. 'I can see it through.'

'There's not much to see through, and there might be later tonight. I've got Baxter and Trueheart to sit on the Callahan residence. If she heads out tonight, I'll pull you in.'

'What are you doing after Darla?'

'I'm going to have a talk with Linus Brinkman. I don't need you on that. No sympathy factor required. I've dumped names on SVU, and I've got Nadine sniffing out what can be sniffed on Ryder Cooke. I have a feeling he's going to get a surprise when he comes back to New York.'

'This is making me feel better,' Peabody decided when they crossed the garage to the car. 'This last one? She goes to stay with her sister after her ex-boyfriend puts her in the hospital. And he's in the wind, so they can't find him. Then her sister's little dog is poisoned. A little dog, Dallas. And the sister's car gets its tires slashed, the windshield busted. Has a rock thrown through the living room window, shit like that.'

She settled into the car. 'Meanwhile she says she's seen him – in the subway or on the street – but the cops haven't found him. She's scared to stay with her sister, but she's got no place else to go.'

'We'll find him. We'll get him. Do a run on him now.' Keep busy, Eve thought. 'Reach out to the investigating officers, get the file.'

Peabody took out her PPC to get started.

'Two other assault charges – and both dropped when the complainant pulled back. Spotty employment history, no known address.' Peabody glanced over. 'Can I take the lead on this? I know it has to wait unless she goes after him, but he really is in the wind, so I don't see how she'd nail him down before the cops. But if I could work it – '

'It's yours. Let me know what you need when you need it.'

Eve drove while Peabody reached out to the investigators on the original assault, then the investigators in Queens on the sister's dog, house, car.

Eve might have said something about maintaining objectivity – which is what she didn't hear in Peabody's tone, see on her partner's face. But she knew that kind of involvement, that kind of determination could fuel the drive to re-angle and close a case.

And she had to admit, as she pulled up to the Callahan gates, she didn't feel particularly objective herself at the moment.

She identified herself, got clearance, drove through when the gates opened.

'The asshole has a friend he couch surfed with for a couple months before the assault who claims he hasn't seen or heard from him since. And stated the victim of said assault got hysterical easily, was sort of paranoid and clingy. Claimed the asshole had ended the relationship days before the assault, and how she probably got mugged and decided to point the finger.'

'That's bullshit.'

'That's accessory after the fact.'

'That, too.' Peabody glanced up when the car stopped. 'Okay, I'm putting it away for now, shifting to sympathetic mode.'

They got out. Before Eve could press the buzzer, the female droid opened the door. 'Good afternoon, Lieutenant, Detective. Please come in. May I take your coats?'

'We're good.'

'If you'd wait in the parlor? May I bring you a refreshment?'

'We're good,' Eve repeated. 'We'd like to speak to Ms Pettigrew.'

'Let me check if she's available. Ms Callahan is aware of your arrival and will be down directly. Please sit.'

'Is Ms Pettigrew on the premises?' Eve asked.

'I will check if Ms Pettigrew is available,' she said again, and walked out.

Seconds later, the elevator slid open. Eloise walked out with a tiny black woman in a blue tunic and black baggies.

'Lieutenant, Detective, it's good to see you again. This

is the wonderful, if strict, Donnalou Harris, my nurse and keeper.'

'Oh now, Miss Eloise.' Donnalou gave a hearty laugh as she stepped forward to shake hands. 'I'm pleased to meet you both. As you can see, Miss Eloise is feeling feisty this afternoon. I'm going to be out of a job pretty soon now.'

'Oh now, Donnalou,' Eloise said in a near perfect mimic. 'Let's get comfortable, have some coffee. And don't give me that look,' she told Donnalou. 'I've had enough tea these last few months to last me two lifetimes. And didn't you give me a clean slate this morning?'

'Almost clean,' Donnalou corrected, but gave Eloise an indulgent look. 'One cup, because you could charm the toes off a frog if they had any.'

'Let me just send for Ariel.'

'The droid went to see if your granddaughter's available,' Eve told her.

'Oh, she's out. I convinced her to get out of the house, go to the salon. It took some doing, but she needed to get out and about. She'd only go if Donnalou promised to stay until she got back. And I'm nearly back to fighting weight.'

'Nearly,' Donnalou confirmed.

'I see,' Eve said. 'Do you expect her back soon?'

'I'm not sure.' Eloise picked up the remote to signal the droid. 'Is this about Thaddeus, about your investigation? We heard that another man ... I've tried to keep her occupied so she wouldn't watch the reports, but she's been hoping there would be word. That you'd found who's doing this.'

'It must be hard on her,' Peabody said, sympathy fully in gear. 'I know being able to lean on you, talk to you must help.'

'Nobody's more loving than Miss Eloise,' Donnalou confirmed. 'She pestered Miss Darla – with love – to get her to go out awhile, do something for herself. The girl's selfless. I'm going to miss the pair of you.'

'No, you're not, because you're going to come visit. If Darla's not back by the time we have our coffee, or when you need to leave, I can tell her what you want her to know. Although, I'm trying to keep her mind off all this. Best of all, I've convinced her to take a trip with me in about a week.'

'Two weeks,' Donnalou corrected. 'No flying for two weeks more.'

Eloise rolled her eyes. 'Two weeks. We both need a change of scene, and I think some time basking in the sun on the Côte d'Azur will do the trick. I'm going to book a villa, have the whole family come.' Her face lit up when she spoke. 'I miss my kids! And I've had more than enough of being an invalid.'

'You don't look like one,' Eve observed. 'You seem stronger than you did even a couple days ago.'

'Every day – with this slave driver.' She patted Donnalou's hand. 'And, of course, with my darling Darla. I just … Darla!' Her smile bloomed bright when Darla hurried in. 'I didn't know you were back.'

'I was in the kitchen. I found the most beautiful

strawberries at the market, so I was going to surprise you both with a tea party.'

'No tea!' Eloise said with a laugh. 'Please let it be coffee.'

'Well . . .' When she got a nod from Donnalou, she smiled. 'Coffee it is. Just let me tell Ariel. She found me back there, told me we had guests, so I have her putting it all together.'

'You sit down, Miss Darla. I'll take care of it.' Donnalou got up.

'Thank you.' Darla sat beside Eloise as Donnalou went out. 'She's an absolute treasure. I don't know what we'd have done without her. I hope you haven't been waiting long. I went straight back to the kitchen when I got home, didn't check in with Donnalou or Ariel. I had marketing.'

'We haven't been here long.'

'Grand convinced me to get out.' She looked at her grandmother, wiggled her hand and its pale pink nails. 'And you were right, as always, Grand. I needed to get out, but next week, we're both going for the works. I already booked a day.'

'Heaven.' Eyes closed in anticipatory bliss, Eloise let out a happy sigh. 'Absolute heaven.'

'And I'm sorry, Lieutenant, Detective, I'm stalling a little. Trying to hang on to the good feeling just a bit longer.' Lips trembled, then firmed. 'You have news about Thaddeus?'

As she spoke his name, Darla reached out to take her grandmother's hand.

'We're actively pursuing several lines of investigation. Eloise said you're aware there's been a third murder.'

Darla cast her eyes down, nodded. 'It's why Grand talked me into getting out. It's all so horrible.'

'The three men who were murdered all have connections to women in your support group.'

While Eloise gasped, Darla fluttered a hand to her throat. 'I – I don't understand.'

'McEnroy connected to both Jasmine Quirk and Leah Lester. You connect with Thaddeus Pettigrew. Una Ruzaki's ex-husband, Arlo Kagen, was murdered last night.'

'Dear God, Darla! To think I've been urging you to go back to that group. You can't, you simply can't until this is all settled.'

'I don't understand.' Now Darla pressed a hand to her temple. 'I simply don't understand.'

'It's possible one or more of the women in the group is behind the murders.'

'Oh no, no. That's not at all possible. These women are victims.'

'This must be hard for you.' Peabody spoke gently, kindly. 'A group like this, all of you become close. I've spoken with several of the women myself, and understand what they've been through.'

'But ... how? We only use first names. How could you find them to speak to?'

'It's our job to find them.' Speaking briskly, Eve looked directly in Darla's eyes. 'To interview them, check alibis, opportunities, frame of mind. You knew some of these women, by full names.'

'Yes.' Darla let out a trembling breath, worked up swimming tears. 'But we kept that confidential. It's a matter of trust.'

'Not in a murder investigation.'

'Believe me,' Peabody put in, 'we're treating the women we speak with as compassionately as possible. We don't want to add to their trauma.'

'But it does, you see. Unless you've been through the betrayals, humiliation, the violence, you can't understand. You can't know.'

'Darla, they have to do their job.' Eloise took Darla's hand again, rubbed it between both of hers. 'Someone is killing these men. One of the men was Thaddeus.'

'I know. I know, but ...'

Donnalou came back, wheeling a cart. 'Coffee party,' she said cheerfully, then stopped. 'What is it? Miss Eloise—'

'I'm fine I'm fine. But would you get Darla a soother? I don't think coffee's what she needs.'

'Of course, right away.'

'You don't understand,' Darla murmured when Donnalou hurried out again. 'We share intimate details of our lives in our group. We bare our souls to each other. None of them are capable of doing this.'

'They're your friends.' Peabody leaned forward, all understanding. 'Your sisters. It's sometimes really hard to see inside a friend, a sister, who can hold a very dark secret.'

'I won't believe it. Unless ... someone infiltrated the group somehow. With this terrible purpose.'

'Any suggestions?' Eve asked. 'A name?'

'No, no, I swear!'

'Peabody, read off the list of full names we have, the women we've already interviewed. If you can add to that, Darla, it would be very helpful.'

Eve watched her as Peabody read, saw the flicks of anger quickly masked by downcast eyes. The tightening of the jaw. And if she wasn't mistaken, the tiniest of smirks.

Satisfaction.

'I – I don't know all of those names. Not the full names. I knew a few, yes. Like poor Una, and Rachel. And I haven't been back since Grand took ill. Not since the end of last year. It must be someone new, someone I don't know. Or, I'm sorry, you're just wrong.'

'Here's a nice soother.' Donnalou came back in full caregiver mode. 'You drink that up, Miss Darla. You look a little pale. You drink that up, and I'm going to take you upstairs so you can lie down for a bit.'

'Yes, yes, I think I want to lie down for a while. I'm sorry. I'm sorry, I need to lie down. I feel sick. I don't feel well.'

'You come on with me then.' Donnalou helped her up. 'You can drink this upstairs. I'm going to tuck you in for a nice nap. Haven't I said you need more sleep? Sleep's a healer,' she continued as she led Darla out.

'My poor girl,' Eloise murmured. 'So many shocks,

and after wearing herself out looking after me. Well, I'll be looking after her now. I'm very sorry we couldn't be more help.'

'We appreciate the time,' Eve said as she rose.

'I hope you find who's doing this quickly. Darla won't get over this until you do.'

'Yes, I'm sure you're right. We'll see ourselves out.'

Eve waited until they were back in the car.

'You were right,' Peabody said before she could speak. 'All along. It shocked her we had all those names, that we're looking directly at the group. More, it pissed her off at first. Not the kind of pissed off when you think a friend is getting a raw deal.'

'No, not that kind of pissed. And she's working out how she can change the focus. Either to someone she doesn't care about, or away from the group. She needs a little time to work it out. She's a planner.'

'She wouldn't mind going after one of us, to pay us back for trying to spoil those plans.'

'Saw that, too? Good.' Eve drove out of the gates. 'Watch your back. And take a cab home.' Eve pulled over, dug out the fare.

'No, I've got enough.'

'Take it, and take a cab. Go home, bake a pie or something to clear your head.'

'I might.'

'Then get ready. She's going to want to move tonight. We boxed her in some, and she won't waste time.'

'I'll be ready,' Peabody said as she got out. 'You watch your back, too.'

'Count on it.' As she drove, Eve contacted Baxter. 'Change of schedule. Move up the stakeout.'

'To when?'

'To now.'

19

Eve figured Linus Brinkman might appreciate a heads-up on being a target of a homicidal, sadistic whack job, even if it interrupted his massage.

She intended to start with him, then work her way through the list of potential targets. Talking to each of them face-to-face about their schedules, their habits, and yeah, their asshole behavior might give her a solid lead toward Darla's next target, her planned method.

She leaned toward Brinkman anyway, and the evening's gala.

With parking at a premium and traffic thick, she squeezed into a loading zone, flipped on her On Duty light.

Brinkman lived in an old, well-restored building right on Park, with a doorman, a scattering of terraces, and a pricey view.

The doorman, in steel gray with silver trim, gave her a once-over.

'May I assist you? Are you visiting a resident?'

'Brinkman, Linus.'

'Are you expected?'

'No.' She pulled out her badge. 'Brinkman, Linus,' she repeated.

'Is there a problem, Lieutenant?'

'Yes.' She left it at that, moved around him, and would have pulled open the wide glass door if he hadn't moved nimbly to beat her to it.

'Wynona at the desk will clear you.'

'Okay.'

She crossed a quiet lobby with its white marble tiles, the conversationally arranged chairs in subtle gray, the massive table with its massive floral arrangement.

Wynona — Eve assumed — sat behind a deeply carved counter Eve thought looked as if it had once been a bar. Her hair, scooped back at the temples, fell in burnished brown waves down the back of her simple black suit.

She smiled her practiced smile. 'Good afternoon. How can I assist you?'

Eve badged her. 'Linus Brinkman.'

'Of course. I'll let Mr Brinkman know you're here.'

'No. I'll just go up.'

'I'm afraid I just came on twenty minutes ago. I can't tell you if Mr Brinkman is in residence. If I could call up—'

'No,' Eve said again, and moved to the elevator. 'Clear it.'

'Of course.' Wynona didn't look pleased, but cleared the elevator.

Eve rode up to the third floor in the silent car with the light scent of a spring meadow scenting the air.

In the third-floor hallway, a table held a slim arrangement of flowers. It held as quiet as the elevator as she walked over soft gray carpet, past wide white doors – all with solid security.

She pressed the buzzer on the corner unit, waited.

Mr Brinkman and Ms Gerald are unavailable at this time. You are free to leave a message here or at the desk in the lobby. Enjoy your day.

'NYPSD.' Eve held up her badge. 'Dallas, Lieutenant Eve, on official police business.'

Your identification will be scanned for verification.

'Yeah, yeah,' she muttered, and waited again.

Your identification has been verified, Dallas, Lieutenant Eve. Please wait.

She waited.

A woman in an actual maid's uniform, complete with frilly white apron, opened the door. Eve judged the woman with her short bob of blond hair, stoic blue eyes, in her mid-forties.

'I'm sorry, Lieutenant Dallas, Mr Brinkman and Ms Gerald aren't available. Is there something I can do to help you?'

'You need to make them available.'

'But you see, Ms Gerald is in the master suite with her technicians and consultants.'

'Fine. Where's Brinkman?'

'I'm not sure he's arrived home as yet. His technicians and consultants would be in the adjoining parlor area.'

'Let's go.'

'But—'

'Do I look like I have time to waste?' Eve demanded. 'The pair of them can get fancied up after I talk to Brinkman and leave. Show me where.'

Stoic or not, the maid looked nonplussed – and intimidated. She gestured, began to lead the way through a large living area full of fuss and color, past a bar area with oversize leather chairs, and to double doors, where she knocked.

'Is that Linus?' The impatient demand snapped out as the maid opened the door to a bedroom – lots more fuss and color – where another blonde reclined in a salon chair while a team in flowing red lab coats fiddled with her hair – miles of it – her face – currently covered with some sort of pink goo – and her feet.

'No, Ms Gerald. It's—'

'Did I say I wasn't to be disturbed, Hermine? Did I?'

'Yes, ma'am. But it's the police.'

'I don't care if it's God. I'm fricking meditating.'

Eve stepped forward, scanned the woman tucked under a puffy white blanket. 'Lieutenant Dallas. Tell me where to find Linus Brinkman and you can go back to meditating.'

'Oh, for— I don't know, do I?' She opened one annoyed blue eye while the tech massaged the pink goo into her face. 'Go away.'

To solve the issue, Eve turned to Hermine. 'Adjoining suite?'

'Ah . . .' No longer so stoic, Hermine crossed the room, knocked on another door, cracked it open. 'Mr Brinkman,' she began.

Another tech pulled the door wider. 'He hasn't come in yet. We're on the clock. He's going to miss his massage!'

With alarm bells sounding in her head, Eve strode back to LaDale. 'Have you spoken to him since he landed?'

'No, because he hasn't bothered to answer his 'link. I talked to him when he was on the shuttle, and that's it. Now he's ruining everything.'

'What's his car service?'

'How the hell am I . . . Hermine!'

'Yes, ma'am. Mr Brinkman uses Luxe Rides.'

Eve dragged out her 'link, got the contact.

'Will you get out? How am I supposed to fricking relax? Ulysses! I'm going to get lines in my face from all this stress.'

'Never,' he purred, and began slowly, carefully removing the goo.

Disgusted, Eve walked out of the room, stood by the door.

'Luxe Rides. Abigail speaking.'

'Lieutenant Dallas, NYPSD, regarding Linus Brinkman. Did your company pick him up at the transportation center this afternoon?'

'Could I please have your badge number, as that information is confidential?'

'Christ.' Eve rattled it off. 'Check it. Fast.'

'Just one moment.'

The screen went to holding blue while Eve paced.

'Thanks for waiting. Mr Brinkman canceled that pickup, as his trip was extended. How else can I help?'

'How did he cancel it?'

'Ah, I see we received the cancellation from his office at two-ten this afternoon. Is there a problem?'

'Yeah.'

Eve clicked off. Hermine, who'd hovered, eased closer.

'Lieutenant, Mr Brinkman contacted Ms Gerald, from the shuttle, after that. I know it had to be nearly three, as the stylists and technicians were here, setting up for her. There's been some sort of mix-up.'

'You think?'

Furious, Eve headed out, using her 'link as she went. 'Baxter.'

'We're nearly there.'

'I want to know if you see anyone go in or out. I think she has another one in there already.'

'Can you get a warrant?'

'I'm working on it. Any activity, in and out of the gate, on the grounds, any, tag me.'

She toggled from him to Peabody as she sprinted across the lobby. 'She broke pattern,' Eve said as soon as Peabody answered. 'I'm going to the transpo station to view the security feed, but she had to pick Brinkman up there when he landed.'

'How did—'

'I'll explain later. Tell the cab to turn around. Meet Baxter and Trueheart at the Callahan house. They'll be staked out shortly.'

'I'm getting out, taking the subway. It'll be faster.'

'Fine.' She jumped in the car, tried Roarke.

'Three in one day,' he said, 'and a gala tonight.'

'Forget the gala. She snagged the target. Under my fucking nose.'

His easy smile vanished. 'Where are you?'

'Heading to the transpo center to see how she did it. I need something, some fucking thing to wrangle a warrant because I know she's got him in there.'

'I'll meet you at the station. You may need an EDD man,' he said before she could protest.

'Yeah, yeah, I may. Gotta go.'

And thinking EDD, she tagged McNab. 'Clear it with Feeney. I need you on an op. Clear it and hook up with Baxter, Trueheart, and Peabody at Eloise Callahan's address. Check with them on where they're staked out.'

'On it. Do you want the van?'

She considered; though she hoped not, why risk it? 'Yeah, yeah, bring the van. Move it.'

She hit the sirens, the lights, and moved it herself.

Even with that, a double-parked delivery van, then a jackhammer-wielding road crew cost her valuable time.

She pushed her way through the transpo center to the private shuttle terminal. When she pulled to the curb, jumped out, security blocked her way.

'You can't leave that vehicle there.'

She pulled out her badge. 'I'm a cop. I need—'

'Then you oughta know the law, am I right? No unattended vehicles in this zone. Move it or lose it.'

'I need to see the feed for—'

He expanded his chest. 'You ain't seeing nothing till you move that ride. Parking's through that gate.'

'For Christ's—' She considered arguing, seriously considered kicking his ass. But calculated either would take more time than just parking her damn ride.

She jumped back in, drove through the gate, pulled into a priority, reserved spot, ignored the automated warning telling her she had no authorization. She flipped on her On Duty light, giving the warning a hiccup while it processed the new data.

And sprinted back to the terminal.

'Wasn't so hard, was it?' curb security asked with a smirk.

'Bite me,' she suggested, 'and contact your head of security.'

'Cop or no cop, you can't talk to me like that. I oughta—'

She grabbed his shirtfront in a fist, jerked him to her. 'If you don't get your head of security in the next five fucking seconds, I'm arresting your dumb ass for impeding a police officer in the course of her duties, for obstruction, and if I don't get that feed in time, I'm going to kick in accessory to murder.'

'You oughta get a grip.'

She got a grip, on her restraints, and had him holding up his hands, backing off. 'Throttle back, just throttle back. I'm just doing my job here.'

'Five, four, three—'

'Okay, okay.' He tapped the mic on his lapel. 'I need Darren out here. Some cop's going nutso.'

It took under a minute for six-foot, four-inch Darren to stride out. He had a tough-looking body in a black suit – with just a hint of bulge where his sidearm rested. He had dark skin, hard, dark eyes, a shaved head, and a kick-ass look about him Eve could respect.

'Let's see the badge.'

Eve held it up. 'NYPSD. I'm investigating a series of homicides, and believe one of your passengers was abducted from this center this afternoon. He'd be the next.'

'Abducted? That seems far-fetched.'

'Linus Brinkman. He would have arrived on a Lodestar private shuttle, coming from Las Vegas, at approximately fifteen-thirty this afternoon. Someone not Brinkman can-celed his car service and set up a replacement. I need to see the feed, at the gate, out here at pickup. Check the manifest, for God's sake.'

'There are privacy laws that require a warrant for—'

Fury flashed and poured out of her hot enough to have Darren breaking off.

'Three men, abducted, tortured, castrated. You keep up with current fucking events in New York, Darren?'

His eyes changed. 'Yeah, I heard about it.'

'Check the manifest. If Brinkman got off the shuttle, he's right now hanging naked by the wrists.'

'That sounds like bullshit, Darren. This one's nutso.'

'Quiet, Len. Come on with me, Lieutenant. We'll start with the manifest.'

As they turned to go in, another car pulled up. Roarke got out; the car drove on.

'Sir,' Darren said. 'I didn't know you were scheduled today.'

'I'm not. Lieutenant.'

'Do you own this place?' Eve demanded.

'Not entirely. Darren, I hope you're assisting the lieutenant in every way.'

'Yes, sir. We're just going in to check the manifest. Didn't put it together,' he muttered as he walked them in. 'Saw the vid last year, but didn't put it together.'

'What the hell does that have to do with anything?' Eve snarled out.

'Just saying.' He walked straight to the check-in counter. 'Monika, check for the arrival of Linus Brinkman.'

'Lodestar. Company shuttle,' Eve added.

'I don't have to check. I know Mr Brinkman. He arrived right on time. I even waved to him as he walked through to meet his driver.'

'Security feed. Now.'

'What gate, Monika?'

'One. Gate One.'

382

'Come with me.'

He crossed the terminal lobby, swiped through a door, and kept going at a quick pace. He swiped through another door in what was basically a tunnel, and they entered the security hub.

He brushed aside one of the two men monitoring the various gates and exits, dropped into the chair, got to work himself.

'You said fifteen–thirty?'

'That's right.'

'Monika said on time, so ...' He swiped, tapped, shifted feeds.

Eve watched Brinkman, casual pants, light jacket, rolly bag and briefcase, march through the gate. After a quick wave toward the counter, he kept walking.

'Follow him,' Eve ordered.

'Let me switch cams. You can see he walked out on his own, and ... here we go, that must be his driver.'

'Not his driver. Enhance, zoom. Zoom on the driver – and I want a printout of him, full body, close-up face.' As Darren zoomed in, Eve swore under her breath. 'It's a droid.'

'Doesn't look like a droid.'

'Closer. Go in closer.'

'Fine, but ... son of a bitch, you're right.' Darren let out a low whistle. 'That's one damn top-grade droid.'

'That's how she does it. That's how,' Eve muttered. 'Droids. Brinkman's asking questions. Probably where's my usual guy. This one's programmed to give some reasonable answer. And he's going with the droid. Outside, move outside.'

'They're heading to pickup – at the island. At least that's where a car service would wait. Give me a . . . Yeah, moving out. Droid's opening the back door.'

'Zoom. Get as much of the interior as you can.'

'I'm not going to be able to get you much.'

It was enough for Eve to see a pair of crossed female legs as Brinkman hesitated. Then a hand reach out to shake his as he slid inside.

'That's how she does it. She just dosed him. Closer on the hand, enhance and freeze. See it? In her palm.'

'Mini pressure syringe,' Roarke said. 'I doubt he even felt it.'

'I need the make and model, the year of the car. I need the license plate.'

'It's a Vulcan, a Town Coach, luxury model. Last year's. We make them,' Roarke told her.

'Capture that plate,' she ordered Darren as the car pulled away. 'Echo, Charlie, Zulu, eight, four, three, eight. Print out those close-ups, and get me a copy of the feeds inside and out.' She turned away, pulled out her PPC to run the plates.

'Bogus name and address – had to figure it.'

'Give me two minutes,' Darren told her, 'and I'll have what you need. Still, it's damn near impossible to program a droid to do any harm to a human.'

'Damn near isn't impossible. I've got Baxter and

Trueheart sitting on the house,' she told Roarke. 'And Peabody by this time. McNab's coming in with the van. I've got to use what we got here to fast-talk a warrant. I'm going to need Reo and a really cooperative judge because nothing I've got ties her to it. I've got nothing that wraps her in it.'

She checked her wrist unit. 'She has to wait until the nurse leaves. She has to get her out, then find a way to get her grandmother down for the night. It's too early, but she knows I'm sniffing. She knows, so she's going to want to get started soon.'

She paced as she worked it out. 'She grabbed him early, broke pattern enough for that. I'm looking at tonight, and she beats me to him. Gives me the car, the plate, the fricking droid because I can't tie those to her – yet

'I need a goddamn warrant. I need to get into the garage, into the house, into the basement. Goddamn it, she got him in there right under my nose. The grandmother thought she was still out getting a damn manicure. She got one, too. Covered her ass with that. She'd just gotten him in the fucking house and I'm right there. Right there.'

'You can blame yourself for that,' Roarke suggested, 'if you want to be an eejit.' He clamped a hand on her shoulder, as she looked entirely capable in that moment of punching him. 'Which you're not, as an eejit couldn't have narrowed the target to this one, had her residence already staked out.'

'Doesn't help unless we can get inside.'

'Here you go, Lieutenant.' Darren handed her a

packet. 'Printouts and copy. I sure as hell hope you get to him in time.'

'Yeah, thanks. You drive, okay?' she said when they started out. 'I have to figure out how to box Reo on this one.'

'I've no doubt you will. The name she's used to register the car? Maybe it's somehow connected. To the support group perhaps.'

'Maura Fitzgerald isn't on the list. So far.'

She gestured to where she'd parked the car, saw his smile spread. 'What are you smiling at?'

'It pays to be a bit of a film buff, and a longtime fan of Eloise Callahan. That's how I know she won her first Oscar at the tender age of twenty-two for her portrayal of a young woman named Maura Fitzgerald in the classic *Only by Night*.'

'You're shitting me.'

'Not a bit. I wouldn't be surprised if you find the address she used features in one of her grandmother's vids as well.'

He opened the car door for her. 'Would that help with the warrant?'

'It sure as hell won't hurt.' Elated, she broke her own rule, grabbed him, kissed him hard. 'I'm going to bang you like a drum in Italy.'

'I look forward to it – and perhaps a bit of drum practice beforehand.'

'I take her down tonight, we'll practice.'

While he drove, she did a search on the address.

'Well, for Christ's sake, you nailed it in one. It's the address used in *Apartment 8B*, starring Eloise Callahan. All right, Reo, I'm putting you to work.'

Eve made her pitch; ADA Cher Reo listened, then pushed at her pretty blond hair.

'Dallas, you want me to talk a judge into issuing a search warrant because of a name and address used in old vids, your gut, a women's group? To search a Hollywood legend's New York mansion because you think her granddaughter – with no previous record of bad acts – is a crazy serial killer?'

'Not think, know. It's circumstantial, Reo, but it piles up and it adds up. And I'm telling you there's a man, whose major crime in her eyes is dumping his wife for a younger woman, hanging naked in the basement of that house. He'll be tortured, castrated, and bleed to death if you don't get me in that house. Did you see the crime scene photos?'

'Yeah.' Reo blew out a breath. 'Yeah, I saw them.'

'He'll end up like that, and he'll be on us.'

'Okay, all right, let me start pushing on it.'

Before Eve could speak again, Reo clicked off.

'She'll get it,' Eve stated.

'She knows you,' Roarke said. 'She knows you don't bullshit on something like this. She'll get it, yes.'

'You need to pull up out of range of the gates,' she began. 'There.' She gestured. 'That's Baxter and Trueheart, get behind them.'

He maneuvered, hit vertical to cross the avenue, and dropped down behind the police issue.

Eve leaped out, hustled down to the passenger window Trueheart had already lowered.

'No movement, Lieutenant.'

'Peabody's heading back. McNab's bringing the EDD van. Reo's working on a warrant. We're going to ... Gates are opening. That's the nurse, on foot. Hold on.'

Striding along, chatting on her 'link, Donnalou didn't spot Eve until they were nearly face-to-face. 'Oh, Lieutenant Dallas. I didn't expect to see you. No, Harry, I'm heading home now. I'll pick something up. See you soon. Sorry,' she said to Eve as she slid the 'link away. 'Just letting my husband know I'm on my way home. Are you going back in?'

'What's the status in the house?'

'Status? I'm not sure—'

'Where is Darla?'

'Oh, the soother and a little lie-down helped. She's feeling better so she and Miss Eloise are going to have their little tea party after all.'

She looked from Eve to Roarke to the second car. 'Is something wrong?'

'Where are they having their tea party?'

'I really don't understand, but up in Miss Eloise's parlor.'

'Does the house have a basement?'

'I − not as such. There's a lower level. That's Ms Darla's workshop − off-limits,' she added with a puzzled smile. 'She only spends time down there when I'm looking after Miss Eloise.'

'You haven't been down there?'

'Well, no. I wouldn't have any reason to. Could you please tell me what this is about? You're scaring me a little.'

'I'm going to call for a police car to take you home. You are not to contact anyone in the Callahan residence, or have anyone else contact anyone in the Callahan residence. If you do, I'll have to charge you with obstruction of justice.'

'Well, my God!'

'Look at me. Who and what are your priorities in that house?'

'Miss Eloise and her health and well-being, of course. She's my patient.'

'And what I'm telling you is for her health and well-being. Keep looking at me,' Eve insisted. 'Give me, as a medical professional, your evaluation of Darla Pettigrew.'

'I don't think that's my place. I—'

'I'm making it your place.'

'I— She's devoted to Miss Eloise. I'd say she can be a little secretive, and has periods of excitement, periods of depression. She's had a difficult couple of years, with the divorce, the loss of her business, and now all this. She – she's working on a new project downstairs, she says. It keeps her busy and happy from what I can see.'

'I'm going to call an escort for you.'

'I – I won't call Miss Eloise or Miss Darla. I don't want to get in trouble with the police, and if you're telling me the truth, I don't want to do anything that hurts Miss Eloise. But if she needs me, I need to know she can reach me.'

'If she needs you, I'll contact you myself. My word on it.'

20

Peabody jogged up just as Donnalou got in the cruiser.

'We're waiting on McNab and the EDD van,' Eve told her.

'Got it. Was that the nurse?'

'Yeah, she'll hold. Reo's working on a warrant, and according to the nurse, Darla's feeling better and having a tea party with Eloise.'

'That's when she'll slip her a sedative.'

Eve nodded. 'Yeah. She'll get her grandmother in bed, make sure she's out, then she'll head down to what the nurse calls her workshop in the basement. Off-limits, working on a new project.'

'You handled the nurse quite well,' Roarke commented.

'She's a pro, somebody who has a calling – that's my take of her. Eloise is hers, Darla's not. Can you take a look at the gate security without getting in cam range?'

Roarke merely cocked an eyebrow and strolled toward the gate.

Baxter got out, leaned against the car, and watched.

'I need McNab and the van, and I need that damn

warrant. Trueheart.' She signaled to him to get out. 'McNab will use the EDD magic, get us the locations of people and droids inside the house. We get that, get the warrant, we go in fast and quiet. Roarke's going to bypass gate security.'

'I bet he is,' Baxter commented. 'It's top-of-the-line from what I can see, but I bet he is.'

'When we're in, you, Trueheart, McNab go around to the back – there'll be side exits on a place that size, so spread out, keep connected, and enter on my go. Any droids, shut them down. They're also top-of-the-line, so you may need McNab for that.'

'We take the front?' Peabody asked.

'You, me, Roarke. We'll need him to get us in quiet, and potentially to deal with any droids.'

She paused when Roarke strolled back.

'I can get us in.'

'How much time will you need?'

'It's a very fine system. Ten to fifteen.'

Baxter let out a laugh. 'If only we'd met in my misspent youth.'

Roarke returned the grin. 'If youth isn't misspent now and then, it's not youth. Would you like me to get started, Lieutenant?'

'Yes, but no. Have to wait for the warrant. There's the van.'

It shouldn't have surprised her to see Feeney hop out. Her old partner and current EDD captain wore one of his shit-brown suit jackets with a wrinkled beige shirt and dirt-brown tie. His silver-threaded ginger hair sprang out around a droopy, hangdog face.

'I didn't expect to get the brass.'

'You think I'd miss a chance to get inside Eloise Callahan's? I grew up on her vids, kid. She was – probably still is – my old man's hall pass. He's going to be pretty down if I help arrest her.'

'He's safe. I don't see her in this except as a dupe. McNab, I want people, droids, locations, movement.'

EDD Callendar hopped out of the van. 'You got it, LT.'

'She was right there,' Feeney said. 'We'll get it done faster with the pair of them.'

'Just as well. Once Roarke gets us through the gates, we need to surround the house, EDD man on each team to get through the doors if the master's no good, to deactivate superior droids. Vic and suspect are going to be in the lower level. I haven't been through the house, so I don't know, as yet, how to access.'

With her hands on her hips, Eve looked back at the gates. 'She has to keep an eye on the grandmother. She probably has house monitors.'

Feeney rubbed his chin. 'We can shut them down, but she'll likely notice when her monitors go blank.'

'Can't be helped. Better that than her spotting a bunch of cops swarming the house.' She checked the time, strained against impatience. 'We get in, we find the basement access. The house has elevators. Must have one that goes down. Lock that down, that's what she'd do, right?'

Feeney nodded. 'Wouldn't want an unexpected visitor while she's slicing off some poor bastard's balls.'

'Yeah, well, we unlock. One team goes down that way, another by the steps. If there's outside access, we cover that, too. She'll be armed – she's never used a stunner on a victim, but she'll have an electronic prod. Christ knows she's dangerous. And I hate to say it, I fucking hate to say it, but she's insane. Not just garden-variety. She's going to hit the legal bar there.'

'That's a goddamn shame,' Feeney commented.

'Tell me.'

When her 'link signaled, she had it in her hand in a finger snap. 'Tell me what I want to hear, Reo.'

'Warrant coming through. I need a damn drink – and you owe me a whole bunch of drinks.'

'I'll pay up. You may want to stay on tap. I'm going to be bringing you a serial killer, real soon.'

'I'll hold off on the drink until I hear from you. Take her down, Dallas.'

'Fucking A. Roarke, get started.' She pivoted to Feeney. 'Get me some numbers, locations.'

He jerked a thumb toward the van, where McNab and Callendar started the scan.

'Need a minute, Dallas, to work the angles,' McNab told her. 'Callendar, how about you set up a remote?'

'All over it. They move, we'll know it.'

Eve nudged around Callendar, kept her focus on the van's main monitor.

'Coordinate heat and e-sensors,' Feeney ordered.

'Getting it, Cap.' McNab's forest of rings on his earlobes danced as he ticktocked his head, bopped his shoulders to the e-nerd's internal beat. 'Coming up now. And there we are. Two droids on the main floor, at the rear, north. No readings on the second floor. One e-reading on the third floor, one human type.'

'In bed,' Eve said. 'She's down, lying down. That's the grandmother, with a droid on watch. And that's Pettigrew, lower level, that's east, and that's going to be Brinkman – he's vertical, arms over his head. She's got him hanging from the ceiling. That's center of the area. Is that an e-reading with him?'

'Yeah, one droid down there.'

'Got the remote up – got them on there,' Callendar said.

'Strap it on,' Feeney ordered as he opened a drawer, took out earbuds. 'McNab, you man the van, Callendar can team with Baxter, I'll take Trueheart. You, Peabody, and Roarke take the front. That suit you?' he asked Eve.

'That'll work.'

She took the earbuds Feeney handed her, climbed out of the van. 'Trueheart, you're with Feeney – take the west side, find a hole, get inside. Baxter, you and Callendar peel to the east side. Lock down any exits on the east side, continue to the rear. Two droids on the north side. Take them down if Peabody and I haven't reached that point. I need the elevators shut down.'

'Can do,' Callendar assured her.

'We close off all exits to that basement. We close her in.'

She passed out earbuds as she worked it out. 'Big house. She may have more droids, have them shut down. Could she activate by remote?'

'If they're programmed for it,' Feeney said.

'Clear the house, floor by floor. Main, second, third. Find any more droids, take them out. Roarke?'

'Another minute or two.'

'Roarke goes in the front with me and Peabody, then heads up to the third level. He'll take out the droid there, determine the grandmother's status.'

Impatient, she rolled to her toes, back on her heels. 'Once we're through the gate, we need to shut down any exterior cams. We'll wait until we go through the door to shut down interior.'

'She's moving into the center of the basement level, Dallas,' McNab said in her ear.

'Roarke!'

'And there we are,' he said, cool as ice. 'Two seconds and . . .' The gates quietly slid open. 'I assumed you didn't want everyone to climb over.'

'Good thinking.'

'Slick work,' was Baxter's opinion.

'Move fast,' she said as she passed Roarke the last earbud. 'If she notices the monitors shut down, she could just take the vic out. She may have other weapons. Move fast, deactivate any droids who may be hostile or programmed to alert her. Find the access to the basement. Let's go.'

She took the short drive at a jog, watched her teams peel off. 'Roarke, take the stairs to the third level once we're in. You've got one known droid to take out, and the grandmother to check on.'

'Do you want the MTs if she's in distress?'

'Life-or-death, yeah. Otherwise check the house 'link or Eloise's personal. The nurse is bound to be on there. Donnalou Harris, contact her.'

She stopped at the entrance door. 'Alarms, locks.'

'A moment or two,' he said, and got to work.

'Hold for security system shutdown,' Eve warned the teams. 'Wait for my go.'

The light had changed, softening toward dusk. A fresh spring breeze kicked up, making the bulging tips of ready-to-pop blooms shiver and sway. Eve listened to the teams' chatter in her ear, and thought of the man hanging by his wrists a floor below.

'Very clever,' Roarke muttered, 'but expected. Here we are now, aye, here we are. Time to go to sleep, and . . . done.

'System's down,' he told Eve. 'All exterior locks down.'

'All?'

'Well, we do like to be thorough.'

She only shook her head, shifted the weapon she'd already drawn in her hand. 'Hear that? You're go. Move in, move in!'

She heard Baxter's admiring 'Slick work' as she went in low with Roarke and Peabody going high beside her.

Absolute silence. That struck her first, how silent a

wealthy house could be. She signaled to Roarke to take the grand stairs, pointed Peabody in the opposite direction.

'We need to find the basement access. Callendar, elevators.'

'Got it going now.'

'Movement?'

'Just basement level, both humans still in the center area, but movement from both.'

'She's circling him, Dallas,' McNab added. 'He's jerking. Still upright, jerking and swaying. Fuck.'

Bad for Brinkman, Eve thought, but Darla seemed too busy to notice blank monitors.

'Two droids down,' Feeney said. 'Two damn nice droids.'

'One on the third level,' Roarke reported. 'Medical type. It's down. Ms Callahan seems to be sleeping peacefully.'

'Hold off on medical for now. Clear third level.'

'We're clear,' Baxter reported. 'And I think we've got your access door.'

'Got one here, too,' Feeney said. 'Kind of a fancy pantry deal off the main kitchen.'

'We're heading back. Clear as we go, Peabody.'

'It's so quiet.' Peabody swung, weapon first, into another doorway.

'Serious soundproofing. Clear.'

'I'll say. Clear.'

'Another droid, shut down, now locked down,' Roarke said. 'Closet in what I'd say is Pettigrew's suite of rooms. So we're clear on the third. I'm coming down.'

'Sweep the second on the way.'

'How about Baxter and Trueheart take that,' Feeney said as she and Peabody finally reached the kitchen. 'We could use another e-man on these doors. I've seen fricking vaults with less cover.'

'Baxter, Trueheart, clear second level. Roarke, main level, rear. What's with the door?' she asked Feeney.

'Scanned it,' he told her. 'She's got it locked down, alarmed, and with a couple of fail-safes to kick it off. We gotta take it in layers. If we try a straight bypass, try to take it down, you're going to set off secondary alarms and seal it.'

'It's the same deal with mine.' Both frustration and admiration tinged Callendar's voice. 'Maggest of the mag.'

'Shit, shit. McNab, secure the van and get in here. Work with Callendar. What can we do?'

'Give me room,' Feeney told her.

He ran a scanner over the door, tapped his shit-brown shoe, tapped a few commands. 'Not that way,' he muttered. He glanced over as Roarke walked in.

'We got a trip lock, motion lock, both with internal alarms and panic lockdown.'

'Is that so?' Roarke's smile read challenge accepted. 'I've worked with those.'

'Yeah, me, too, but we've got a fail-safe running between the alarm and lockdown, and another threaded through a secondary seal.'

Feeney narrowed his eyes. 'What do you look so smug about?'

'It's one of my systems. I helped design it. It's really quite good. But if one knows the ins and the outs . . .'

Feeney held out his scanner.

'Thanks, but I have my own.'

'Can you walk my boys through it?'

'We'll see. A bit of room, Lieutenant,' he added as Eve breathed down his neck.

'There's a man being tortured on the other side of that door.'

'I'm aware, but this is going to require some delicacy.'

Eve stepped back. 'Maybe we can lure her out,' she said to Peabody. 'Maybe we turn the third-floor monitors back on and—'

'And quiet,' Roarke snapped.

Eve hissed at him, but signaled Peabody out of the room. 'If we can get her out.'

'We're made if we turn on the main floor, and she could panic, kill Brinkman, like you said.'

'I know. I know.' Eve circled and paced. 'There's got to be a way. She's going to check the monitors at some point, likely soon, and she'll wonder. Maybe that would send her out, but . . . No.'

Frustrated, impatient, Eve raked her fingers through her hair. 'She'd have some way to check, she knows this stuff. She'd cop to them being shut down.'

'Well, son of a bitch.'

She heard Feeney, so edged back closer.

'You got that, McNab?'

'We're right with you – okay, maybe a step or two back, but we're getting it. Super frosted goodness.'

'You don't override now,' Roarke said. 'She's too clever for that. So you back off, and slide around the corner, slow and easy. One click up, two back, one left, two right.'

'Roger that.' Callendar's voice came cheerfully. 'Maggier than the maggest of the mag. It's just melting off.'

'A bit more. She'll raise a shield, so now it's going under. Do you see it?'

'Got her.'

'It's kind of sexy,' Peabody commented. 'The sexy nerds.'

Eve only closed her eyes. 'Any movement below?'

'Same type,' Callendar told her. 'Both are in the central area.'

'And so will you be now.' Roarke flexed his fingers. 'Do you have it, McNab?'

'Just doing the last . . . Whee! There she goes.'

'On my go. Let's keep this guy alive. Baxter, Trueheart, e-team behind. Peabody, with me.'

Peabody stepped beside Eve, took a breath in, let it out. 'Let's take this bitch down.'

'And go!'

She heard the screams the instant Roarke pulled open the door for her. Shrieks high and sharp with shock and pain. And the voice bellowing through them.

'Why aren't we ever good enough! We give and give, but you use us, beat us, rape us, leave us. It's time you paid. You all paid!'

Eve rushed the steps, swung straight into the main area with its wall of monitors, its work counters, its half-built droids. Its painted concrete floors.

Darla stood, the electric prod reared back as she prepared to slash the man whose bruised face contorted with fear. Blood oozed from his wrists where he struggled against the restraints that chained him to the ceiling.

She stood, Eve saw with a surprise she rarely felt with killers, in a skin suit, a breastplate, a luxurious silver-edged black wig that spilled in waves over her shoulders, with a glittering silver cat's-eye mask on her face.

'You've got to be kidding me.'

Now Darla's face contorted, but with rage. 'No! You won't stop me. I'm Lady Justice, and Linus Brinkman has been found guilty and sentenced to death!'

'Step away from him, Darla.'

'Justice! My name is Justice, and that's what he and all like him must face.'

'Drop the weapon and step away from him. That's not a suggestion.'

'Wilford! Defend!'

The droid lunged forward – and so did Roarke. He tapped a command on his handheld. The droid stopped, shut down.

'You bastard! You'll be next to face real justice. Get out, get away, or I'll jam this prod right down his throat. You won't stop me.' She raised the prod high. 'You won't stop—'

Eve stunned her. 'You're stopped,' she said as Darla

jittered. The prod clattered to the floor as Roarke moved quickly to catch her before she fell on the concrete.

'Baxter, Trueheart, get him down. Peabody, call for a bus, and contact the nurse for Eloise.'

She moved over, crouched beside Darla as Roarke laid her on the floor.

'She's quite barking mad, isn't she?'

Eve pulled out her restraints. 'Not my call to make,' she said as she clamped them on the unconscious Darla's wrists. 'But oh yeah. Barking.'

'Please, please, please.' Brinkman wept, shuddered. 'Please don't let her hurt me anymore.'

'You're safe now. You're safe. Okay if I hunt up a blanket for him, Lieutenant?' Trueheart asked. 'He's in shock.'

'Yeah. Then you and Baxter can take her in, book her. I'll be in when we're done here.'

Baxter angled his head as he studied Darla. 'It's like a girl superhero costume. A little classic Wonder Woman, a little Dark Angel.'

'A touch of Rose and Thorn.'

'Yeah.' Baxter nodded at Roarke. 'Yeah, her, too.'

'MTs on the way,' Peabody said. 'The nurse is coming. That's a good call, Dallas. Eloise is going to need her.'

When Darla's eyelids fluttered, Eve crouched down. 'You drugged your own grandmother.'

'Grand? Grand?' She started to struggle. 'No, no, no, I'm not finished!'

'Yeah, you are. You have the right to remain silent.'

402

She didn't take that right as Eve read off the Revised Miranda, but continued to rage, to weep in frustration, to curse.

'Maybe give them a hand with her, McNab.'

He turned from studying the e-toys, actually looked stricken.

'Help them get her in the vehicle. You can come back and play.'

'On it.' He pranced toward the stairs.

Feeney studied the workstations as well, rubbed his hands together. 'Let's get this stuff logged, Callendar, and start having some fun.'

'All over and back, Cap.'

Eve called for sweepers while Peabody helped a blanket-wrapped Brinkman off the floor and to a sofa. 'You got him, Peabody?'

'Yeah. He'll be all right. You'll be all right, Mr Brinkman.'

'She hurt me. She hurt me. I don't understand.'

'I'll go up, wait for the sweepers and the bus.'

'I'm with you, Lieutenant.'

Eve glanced at Roarke as she started upstairs. 'You know you want to play with those e's.'

'I do, and I will. But for now ...'

'How did you take out that droid?'

'Ah. I did a quick analysis of the one upstairs. Brilliant work really. A pity. In any case, I was able to program a shutdown. It would've been a shame for you to destroy it.'

'Wouldn't have hurt my feelings.'

He skimmed a hand over her hair. 'You've a long night ahead.'

'But a better one than the last couple, and no trip to the morgue in the morning.'

McNab all but flew back in, had the grace to stop, send Eve a sheepish smile. 'Um, need any help here, Dallas?'

'Go be a geek.'

'Born one, live one, die one. You in, Roarke?'

'Go be a geek,' she repeated, this time to Roarke when she heard the sirens. 'I'll send the MTs down for Brinkman.'

'If you insist.'

Alone, Eve let in the MTs, directed them. She contacted Reo, then Mira. Yeah, a long night, she thought, as she watched a cab drive through the gates. A long night for everyone.

'Miss Eloise?' Donnalou said as she jumped from the cab.

'Upstairs. She's been sedated.'

'You sedated her!'

'No. Darla did, probably shortly after you left. She's sedated her routinely so Eloise wouldn't know what she was doing in the basement.'

'What was she doing in the basement?'

'Killing men.'

Donnalou took a staggering step back. 'That can't be true.'

'Tell that to the man currently being treated by MTs down there because we were in time to save him. I'm going to need to talk with Eloise.'

'I need to check on her. I need to—' She stopped, seemed

to draw herself together layer by layer. 'Do you know what she was given?'

'No, but I imagine she kept the drugs downstairs. I'll let you know.'

Donnalou went up, Eve went down. And found all the e-geeks huddled around workstations, gadgets, and droids.

'Peabody?' she asked, and Callendar pointed left. Before she headed in that direction, Eve walked over to Brinkman and the MTs.

'Mr Brinkman.'

'He's a little loopy,' one of the MTs told her. 'We had to give him something. We'll take him in, probably they'll keep him tonight, treat these burns, the lacerations. You're gonna get more out of him once he settles down.'

'Okay, it can wait.'

She went toward Peabody's direction just as Peabody started in hers. 'Dallas, you need to see this.'

'Did you find Brinkman's clothes, the rest of his things?'

'Yeah, she's got a damn warehouse. I started flagging what looks like the previous victims' clothes, 'links, wallets, and all that, then I got curious, and looked around more. The place is huge.'

Peabody stopped, pointed. 'Warehouse. Vic stuff organized over there, and her, well, wardrobe over there. It's like a costume department.'

Wigs, about a dozen in various styles, displayed on a counter. The counter with a lighted triple mirror, a chair, dozens of drawers, held, Eve saw, facial enhancements, eye dyes, implants, face putty, temp tats, temp skin coloring. An array of clothes from business suits to evening wear, shoes, bags, hung neatly on rods and posts. Jewelry glittered in clear drawers in a clear stand.

Another full-length triple mirror, a board holding photos showing Darla in various outfits – no, Eve thought, costumes. Another board matched those costumes, those personas with victims – those she'd killed, more already targeted.

'Why don't you go up, get the sweepers in here? I need to find where she kept the drugs.'

'Then you better come through here. I sort of don't want to go in again, but . . .'

Peabody led the way into another area. A comp – more house monitors. A glass friggie holding bottles of medication, clear drawers of syringes.

A ceremonial blade, as Morris had hypothesized, lay waiting on a counter – its hilt carried the same inscription as the breastplate.

LJ

And, above, the reason for Peabody's reluctance.

A shelf held jars of liquid preserving the genitals she'd removed from her victims – all carefully labeled.

'Barking mad,' Eve mumbled.

A long night, she thought yet again as she finally made her way to the third floor. Donnalou sat beside Eloise's bedside.

'It's going to take some time to finish processing the

basement, and any areas Darla might have used. It would be better if Eloise stayed elsewhere for the next few days at least.'

'I don't understand any of this.'

'Can you wake her up?'

'It would be better if she woke naturally. The sedative your partner brought up is mild, but—'

'She's going to need an explanation. I have to leave shortly, and she deserves an explanation. And I think she's going to need you to stay with her.'

'I will stay with her, as long as she needs me. I'll wake her. Please be gentle. This is going to break her heart.'

Donnalou took a little vial out of her nurse's bag, waved it under Eloise's nose.

Her eyes fluttered; she gave a little sigh. When she started to roll over, Donnalou took her hand. 'Miss Eloise? Miss Eloise, it's time to wake up now. It's Donnalou.'

'Oh, did I fall asleep again? Donnalou, I'm getting so old and lazy.' She sighed again, opened her eyes. And saw Eve.

'Lieutenant Dallas?' Eloise pushed herself up to sitting while Donnalou fussed, arranging pillows at her back. 'My goodness, did I have a relapse?'

'No.' Eve pulled a chair to the side of the bed to make it easier for Eloise to see her face.

'Oh God, oh God, something happened to Darla.'

'She's not hurt. She's in custody.'

'I— What?'

'Eloise, I'm going to say something I think you already

know or suspect. Darla is and has been ill, mentally and emotionally. There were probably signs. You took her into your home because you love her, and maybe you thought that would help, would be enough, but there were probably signs.'

Eloise, pale as the sheets around her, reached for Eve's hand. 'What did she do? Please, tell me, what did she do?'

Eve told her.

21

Eloise said very little while Eve laid out the facts and evidence she had. Tears welled up more than once, and Eve realized it took an iron will to pull those tears back rather than let them fall.

'I need . . .' Because her voice came out raw, Eloise took a moment. 'Would you excuse me just a moment? I'd like Donnalou to help me get up, get presentable. If you'd wait for a few minutes in the parlor there?'

Work to do, Eve thought, so much yet to do. But respect for that iron will had her rising. 'I'll wait.'

'I won't keep you long.'

Eve walked into the elegant little sitting area, closed the door behind her. Photos, so many photos. Family, Eve deduced, and others of Eloise through the years, at events, with other luminaries, at marches, on red carpets.

A full life, from what Eve could see, lived to the fullest.

She pulled out her 'link as it signaled, saw Nadine on the readout, nearly ignored it.

Not entirely fair, Eve decided, and answered.

'In the middle of things here, Nadine.'

'Me, too. I thought I should let you know I have two women I've already convinced to go on the record about Cooke. It's going to blow wide open in a matter of days, and I'm lighting the fuse.'

'Justice,' Eve said, 'hopefully the right kind.' Now she considered. 'Something else is about to blow, so save space, time, whatever you save. It'll be big.'

Nadine's cat's eyes glowed. 'You caught Lady Justice.'

'I've got her. I'm not going to give you the details this minute because there are others who are going to take a hit on this who don't deserve it. So I'm going to give you the details as soon as I'm clear because you'd cushion that hit. You'll use your weight on the right side of it.'

'Then I'll stand by.'

'I'll get back to you.'

Eve pocketed the 'link.

Moments later, with Donnalou beside her, Eloise came in. She'd put on what Eve figured was a dressing gown, as it looked too quietly glamorous to be called a robe.

The soft, warm blue draped over her small frame to just above her ankles. She'd brushed her hair back, applied some subtle makeup.

'Thank you for waiting. Donnalou, would you mind getting us all coffee?'

'Of course, you sit down now.' The nurse helped her into a peacock-blue chair, walked over to a serving bar.

'I want to say I'm grateful to you – I want to call you

Eve, and I hope you'll allow it, because there's an intimacy between us now. I respect your rank, your work, but I need to speak to you as a woman as well as a police officer.'

'That's fine.'

'You were correct that I knew Darla was – is suffering from an illness. I believed living here, even tending to me – and she did tend to me so devotedly – when I fell ill helped her cope. I swear to you I had no idea how deep the suffering, how severe the illness. She hid it very well.'

When her voice broke, she paused to fight for composure, then took the coffee Donnalou offered. She sat, sipped, drew herself up again.

'I swear to you, I never saw this in her. Self-destruction, that I feared when the life she so desperately wanted crumbled, but not this. I can't conceive of it. I love her with all my heart, and I never saw this in her. I would have gotten her help. Her father – my son – he would have gotten her help.'

'I believe you,' Eve said without hesitation. 'I saw it when I met you. This is not on you in any way.'

'Oh, but how can it not be? She's the child of my child. You saw it in her, didn't you? How did you see it?'

'It's a different thing. It's training, it's ... I don't love her,' Eve said.

Nodding, Eloise looked down at her cup. 'It's too late to get her the help that would have saved the lives she took, to spare those who loved those men the grief of loss. But she is the child of my child. I'll engage the best attorney available, the best doctors.'

'I have the department psychiatrist coming in to evaluate her. Dr Charlotte Mira. She's the best there is.'

'I know her from the book, the vid, but—'

'You should engage your own. I'm telling you that Dr Mira will evaluate your granddaughter, and that you can trust her. I'm going in to interview Darla, and Dr Mira will observe.'

'Will I be able to see her, speak with her?'

'Yes, later. Is there somewhere you can go for a few days? This isn't where you want to be now.'

'Yes. I have friends. Donnalou will help me pack what I need. You've been very kind and very patient with me. I won't forget it.'

'I'm just doing my job.'

'Kindness isn't a job, Eve, it's a choice. I'm keeping you from doing what you must.' She rose, extended a hand. 'Thank you. I'm going to pack what I need, contact my son. He'll want to come to New York.'

'I'll contact you when you're clear to see her.'

Eve went downstairs where sweepers and uniforms and techs moved through the house. She wished she could spare Eloise the journey through the logjam of cops, but it would be one more point of pain to push through.

In the basement it was more of the same. Much more.

Peabody broke away from a conversation with a couple of white-suited sweepers. 'I'm having them get scrapings from the floor for the match. We've got her cold but more evidence isn't wrong.'

'More the better. Let's go get her in the box.'

As Eve did, Peabody looked toward the e-team still swarming the toys. 'I think they'd like to live here.'

'Hold on.' Eve crossed over. 'The droid there? That's the one she'd have used to drive her to get the targets, and to help her transport them to the dump site. I need his memory banks.'

'We'll get to 'em,' Feeney assured her. He actually had roses in his cheeks. 'We got plenty on here, too. Docs, schedules, photos, backup plans if she missed one the first time out, alternate routes, the works.'

'Kept, like, a diary, too,' McNab put in.

'Yeah, her type would. She's a planner, a grudge holder, a freaking organized soul.'

'She also has the skeleton of a business plan in the works,' Roarke said. 'A solid one even in the early stages. If, well, on the mad side of things.' His gaze stayed on her face. 'Are you heading in then?'

'Yeah, I'm going to get her in Interview, so I'll want copies of whatever you get off the comps and out of the droids.'

'Give us a moment,' he said to no one in particular, then steered Eve away until he found a relatively quiet corner. 'Must it be tonight? She won't be going anywhere, after all.'

'Yeah, I need Mira to observe. I have Reo coming in. And I need to hit her while she's whacked about not getting her kill. She'll be more open.'

'Then eat something first.'

'Oh, for fuck sake.'

He simply snagged her by the chin. 'You're near to pale enough to see through. You'll take a moment with your steady partner there in your office and have a shagging pizza while you work out your interview strategy and look over some of what we send you.'

When he put it that way. 'I didn't know they made shagging pizza.'

'Still have some smart left in your very tired ass. What happened upstairs to make you so sad?'

'I was witness to grace and strength, and for some reason it scraped me raw. I'll eat some shagging pizza.'

'Good. And it'll do you no good to snap at me, because I need this as much as you do.' He pulled her in, just held her, felt her stiffen, then give.

'Well, if you need it.'

'I do.' He brushed a kiss to the top of her head. 'I'll be with my EDD mates till you're done.'

'It's going to be—'

'A long night,' he finished. 'Won't be the first of them for us.'

Or the last, she thought as she started out. 'Peabody, with me.'

She had pizza – but rather than in her office with Peabody, in a conference room with Peabody, Mira, and Reo.

'Eloise Callahan's going to get her a serious lawyer,' Eve began. 'I'm going to take the window before she can get that going to get what I can out of her.'

'You and several other cops caught her in the act of torturing her fourth victim.' Reo bit into a slice, went *mmm*. 'We're going to match the hair from the wig, the scrapings from the floor. We have her journal, her documentation. I don't care if she gets the ghost of Clarence Darrow, she's cooked.'

'Not disputing. Confession's always best, and this one will give us chapter and verse. She's never going in a concrete cage off-planet.'

'Legal insanity isn't your call.'

'I know it when I see it.'

'She's right, Reo.' Peabody nibbled her own slice to make it last.

'That doesn't mean she doesn't go into a high-security prison, but it's going to be the mentally defective wing. Still.' Eve looked at Mira. 'If we're wrong, you'll know it.'

'She planned each murder precisely,' Reo argued. 'With alternatives, escape routes, ways to avoid detection. She knew right from wrong.'

'I'll observe, and I'll have a one-to-one evaluation session with her. Eve, what is this pizza? I've never had better.'

'Shagging, apparently.'

'Sorry?'

'It's one of Roarke's deals. He's started stocking my office AC because he's constantly afraid I'll starve to death.'

'Aw,' Reo and Peabody said in stereo.

'Love sometimes comes with mozzarella,' Mira said with a smile.

'I guess it does. I have to tag somebody, then we're going in. Peabody, we square on approach?'

'Yeah.'

'Have her brought up. I'll meet you there.'

Now Eve went to her office, contacted Nadine.

'Late this afternoon,' Eve began, 'officers attached to Homicide and EDD entered the home of Eloise Callahan—'

'The what!'

'On a duly authorized warrant,' Eve continued. 'At that time they apprehended Darla Pettigrew. Ms Pettigrew is charged with the abduction, torture, and murder of Nigel McEnroy, Thaddeus Pettigrew, and Arlo Kagen, and the abduction and torture of Linus Brinkman. Ms Callahan, grandmother of Ms Pettigrew, had been sedated by her granddaughter and is not a suspect or a person of interest in the investigation.

'Those are the highlights, you could say.'

'Jumping Jesus, Dallas.'

'I want Eloise Callahan protected, Nadine. I want you to give her a damn good cushion. She's a victim in this, too.'

'You're sure she wasn't—'

'One hundred percent. Pettigrew slipped her something before she went out on the hunt and had a goddamn medical droid – of her making – guarding her. She did her dirty work in the basement behind doors locked so tight it took Roarke – who designed the damn system – several precious minutes to get through.'

'Okay, got it. Give me—'

'I'm putting her in the box now. That's all I can give you. You do your job, I'll do mine.'

'And good luck to us both.'

Eve put the 'link back in her pocket, rolled her shoulders to loosen them, and went out to meet Peabody.

'She's in there,' Peabody told her outside the door of Interview B. 'Hasn't asked for legal representation, hasn't asked to make any contact. The uniforms who brought her up said she's anxious to talk to us.'

'Then let's not keep her waiting.'

Eve stepped in.

'Finally.' Darla rattled her restraints as she lifted her hands. She looked calm, composed as she sat at the table in her orange jumpsuit.

'Record on,' Eve began. 'Dallas, Lieutenant Eve, and Peabody, Detective Delia, entering Interview with Pettigrew, Darla, on the matters of case files H-33491, H-33495, H-33498, and H-33500.' Eve set down a file as she and Peabody took their seats. 'Ms Pettigrew—'

'Oh now, it's Darla.'

'Fine. Darla, you've been read your rights. Do you understand those rights and obligations?'

'Of course I do. I understand we have to go through these formalities, deal with these fussy little rules, but I'm here to talk with you, both of you.'

'Great.'

Oh yeah, Eve thought, studying Darla's animated face. About to get chapter and verse.

'You're charged with the abduction, administration of barbiturates without consent, enforced imprisonment, torture, and murder of Niles McEnroy, Thaddeus Pettigrew, Arlo Kagen. You're additionally changed with the abduction, administration of barbiturates without consent, enforced imprisonment, and assault on Linus Brinkman.'

Darla rolled her eyes with the same attitude as a teenager caught breaking curfew. 'That's all nonsense.'

'How can it be nonsense?' Peabody asked, all quiet reason. 'We apprehended you in the act of assaulting Linus Brinkman, we found articles belonging to McEnroy, Pettigrew, and Kagen in your workshop. Denying the charges isn't going to fly, Darla.'

'The charges are nonsense,' she insisted.

'You're actually denying you tortured and killed three men,' Eve put in, 'and were in the process of taking another man's life?'

'Absolutely not. I'm not denying the acts and actions, for goodness' sake. It's the charges that are foolish. I executed justice, justice no one else had been able to execute. The city should throw me a damn parade, and every woman who's ever been harassed, raped, beaten, cheated on would cheer.'

She leaned forward. 'You of all people should understand. You're constrained by those formalities, those rules, but you're women, women who must see nearly every day the pain, the humiliation, the degradation men cause women. I did what you're unable to do – what I realize you must be afraid to do. I stopped them from causing more harm, from benefitting from the pain they'd inflicted. None of them deserved to live.'

'And you figure that's your call?' Eve demanded. 'To determine who lives, who dies?'

'Someone has to decide.' Darla slammed a fist on the table. 'Someone has to act! Do you understand what the women in my group have suffered while those men paid no price? No price! I did what needed to be done. I made them pay. Every one of them chose to turn to me, accept me, ruled by their dicks, every one.'

Her eyes went bright. Bright, bright. 'Do you really believe the men you give yourselves to are *faithful*? Are you so blind to see them as loyal? They're built to cheat, steal, take, strike. It's their nature.'

'Did you plan to kill all men?' Peabody wondered. 'Any age restriction on that?'

Darla sent Peabody an amused look. 'We'd be better off smothering males at birth, but until we find a way to propagate without them?' She shrugged. 'Young boys grow into men, and men have a fatal flaw in their programming. The solution may be in droids, or a human/droid hybrid. I hope to begin work on that solution when this initial phase is complete.'

The business plan Roarke spoke of, Eve realized.

'Sure.' Bat-shit crazy, Eve thought. 'But let's stick with the initial phase for now. Start with McEnroy, walk us through your work there.'

'All right. I'm really quite proud of it. Justifiably.'

She told them everything, every step, and her only emotion was that pride.

419

Licks of anger came through as she spoke of her ex-husband. 'I shouldn't be so upset with him.' She held up a hand, took some breaths, then let out a quick, brittle laugh. 'He actually opened my eyes, gave me my purpose, so I should be grateful. Until his betrayal I was content to be under his thumb, to focus my life, even my work, to suit his needs and pleasures. If he hadn't betrayed me, stolen from me, crushed my heart, my pride, I would still be his wife, still be used by him.'

'That's when you moved in with Eloise,' Eve prompted.

'Yes. My darling Grand opened her home to me, gave me comfort. She's the kindest, most loving creature ever born. But naive. She believes, always has, that the man she loved was faithful, that he never strayed, never harmed another.'

Once again, she slammed a fist on the table. 'He was a man, wasn't he? But I let her hold that illusion, as accepting the truth would only hurt her. I'd never hurt Grand.'

'You drugged her,' Peabody said. 'Again and again.'

'She needed rest, so I gave her rest. Sleep heals. She was very ill. I never left her alone, never! I built a medical droid to look after her when I couldn't be there. She's safe and sleeping now, but I have to get back before she wakes. She needs me.'

'Let's move on to Kagen,' Eve instructed.

'Disgusting man.' Darla waved a hand in front of her face as if she smelled something foul. 'Nothing could have been easier, but being in his presence? A chore.'

Eve listened, didn't interrupt, found no need for questions even when Darla, on her own, slid right into the details of Brinkman.

'Really, I'd barely started with him. I did begin a bit earlier than with the others but, to tell you the truth, I wanted to finish with him and get some sleep. I haven't had much in the last several days, and using stimulants tends to make me jumpy after a long period.'

'I bet. And you had other men to deal with.'

'Of course, but that's for tomorrow. I'm an interior designer meeting a man with a wife, and a mistress, who also found it necessary to exploit yet another woman, take her misplaced love before destroying her career. He has a property he wants redone. I'll be Roweena Carson, and I have a marvelous costume for the scene.'

'You do realize this isn't a vid?' Peabody asked.

With all the masks stripped away, her eyes were crazed. Direct, Eve noted, but crazed.

'Of course, but I play the parts, dress the part these men expect before I reveal who I really am.'

'Lady Justice.'

Darla beamed at Eve. 'Yes, exactly. Now that we've cleared this up, and you understand, I really have to get home and check on Grand.'

'Donnalou's with her.'

'Oh.' Darla frowned. 'That's all right then. But—'

'We're going to need you to stay. You can get some sleep, and tomorrow Dr Mira will talk to you.'

'Oh, I'd love to meet her. I just adored her in the vid. But Grand—'

'Donnalou's going to stay with her,' Peabody said and rose. 'She'll take care of her.'

'She's a wonderful nurse. Still—'

'Grand's sleeping now.' Peabody walked around the table to release the chain, help Darla to her feet. 'She's safe, and sleeping. We could all use some sleep.'

'You're right. I'm just exhausted. I'm glad we straightened this all out. I was angry with you at first,' she said as Peabody led her out of the room. 'But then I realized, we women have to stick together. Women for women.'

Eve let out a long breath as the door closed behind them. 'Peabody, Detective Delia, exiting with Pettigrew, Darla.

'Interview end.'

She sat where she was, continued to sit when Mira and Reo came in, when they sat with her at the table.

Mira spoke first. 'I'll interview and evaluate her formally tomorrow, but from my observations she doesn't meet the threshold of legal sanity, and is unfit mentally and emotionally for trial.'

'I'm forced to agree,' Reo said. 'If that wasn't an act—'

'It's all an act,' Eve interrupted, 'but that was as real as she gets. She thinks we'll let her go, seeing as we're all in this big sisterhood, so she can go out and keep doing what these silly rules prevent us from doing. I guess you could say she found the role of her lifetime in Lady Justice.'

'You stopped her, very likely saved more lives, including

her own. She couldn't have maintained this facade for much longer. You can leave her to me, and to Reo now.'

Reaching across the table, Mira touched Eve's hand. 'You and Peabody should take some time off. Get some rest, soak up a little spring.'

'Yeah. Good idea.' She stood. 'I'm going to write this up, and get the hell out before the brass decides I need to do a media conference.'

Reo let out a little laugh. 'Run, because that'll be coming.'

She didn't run, but she moved fast. By the time she finished her report, signed off, her head pounded. But Roarke came in.

'Done then?'

'Yeah, it's done.'

'We got a rundown, basically, in EDD. A trial's unlikely, it seems.'

'Very. She's not right, Roarke, and that's that. Mira will take it from here.'

'And you're all right with that?'

'It's the way it is,' she began, then shook her head. 'I'm all right with it. It's . . . it's justice, the real kind of justice. Are you still playing in EDD?'

'I'm with you, Lieutenant.'

'Great. Let's get the fuck out of here.'

He pulled out a pill case. 'Take a blocker for that headache.'

'Let's get out of here for five minutes. If I still need one, I'll take it. Deal?'

'Deal.' He took her hand, kissed it. 'You're going to have some soup, some wine, some sleep.'

'I could live with that.' She walked out with him, too tired to object to the crowded elevator. 'I'll need to check on the status off and on. I guess you have lots of toys you want to play with, or maybe you have to make up time in your quest to own the known universe.'

'I can do both. I enjoy multitasking.'

'You're good at it.' She got in the passenger side, kicked the seat back. 'We talked about taking a few days.'

'We did.'

'So I put in for the time.'

'Did you now? Starting when?'

'Starting now.'

He glanced at her as he drove out of the garage. 'Is that so?'

'I gave Peabody tomorrow, the next day if she wants it. I was thinking maybe we could go home, throw some stuff in a bag, and take off for Italy. I could bang you on the shuttle – multitasking, because banging would distract me from being up there.'

'Give me a half hour and I can make that happen.'

'I want to wake up somewhere else. Just somewhere else for a couple days and not think about sick, sad women who think killing men is not only necessary but heroic. You've probably got all sorts of things to do, but—'

'The villa hotel project in Italy's important to me, and could use my attention on-site. And I'd like a few days to pay attention to my wife when she's not working herself into the ground.'

424

'It's no use telling you not to worry about me, but I'm going to take this moment to say I appreciate that you do. Even when it irritates the crap out of me, I appreciate it.'

'Your headache's gone.'

'See? That's irritating and appreciated – the way you just know that. So . . . I love you. I love the crap out of you, and I would never want you replaced by a droid-human hybrid.'

'That's very appreciated as well.'

'I'm not naive,' she murmured. 'I know what I've got, who I've got. Anyway, can we switch the soup for spaghetti and meatballs? Like a jump start to Italy. Wine, spaghetti, banging, sleep. Or banging, then the rest. Or—'

He took her hand again, kissed her hand again as they drove through the gates.

'Let's just play that by ear.'

'Works for me.'

They had it all, in their own order of preference. And she woke to spring sunshine, Italian style, snuggled into him.

And had one particular item on the list again.

EXCLUSIVE EXTRACT

Read an extract from

Golden
in Death

The new J.D. Robb thriller

1

Dr Kent Abner began the day of his death comfortable and content.

Following the habit of his day off, he kissed his husband of thirty-seven years off to work, then settled down in his robe with another cup of coffee, a crossword challenge on his PPC, and Mozart's *The Magic Flute* on his entertainment unit.

His plans for later included a run through Hudson River Park, as April 2061 proved balmy and blooming. After, he could hit the gym and some weights, grab a shower, have a bite in the café.

On the way home, he thought he'd pick up fresh flowers, wander through the market, and get the olives Martin so enjoyed, maybe a nice selection of cheeses. Then he'd meander to the bakery for a baguette and whatever else appealed.

When Martin came home, they'd open a bottle of wine,

sit and talk and have some bread and cheese. He'd leave the choice of eat in or eat out to Martin, with, hopefully, a romantic ending to the day – if Martin wasn't worn out.

They often joked Kent as a pediatrician handled the adorable babies and charming kids, while Martin as headmaster for a K–12 private academy juggled charming kids with hormonal and broody teens.

Still, it worked for them, Kent thought as he filled in 21-Down.

Toxic.

He spent an entertaining hour with the puzzle, tidied up the kitchen while music filled the air of their townhome in the West Village.

Kent changed into his running clothes, added a light hoodie. He packed his gym bag, deciding he'd drop it off in his locker before his run.

As he zipped it, the doorbell rang.

Humming to himself, he carried his bag out to the living room, set it on the coral sofa he and Martin had chosen when they'd redecorated six months before.

Out of habit, he checked the door monitor, saw the delivery girl he recognized with a small package.

He disengaged the locks, opened the door.

'Good morning!'

'Morning, Dr Abner. Got a package for you.'

'So I see. You just caught me.' He took the package, offered her a smile as the Queen of the Night's vengeful second-act aria poured out to Bedford Street. 'Beautiful day!'

'It sure is. You have a good one,' she added before she walked down the steps to the sidewalk.

'You, too.'

Kent closed the door, studying the package as he carried it back to the kitchen. Since it was addressed to him, he opened the drawer for the box cutter. The return label had a Midtown address and a shop name – All That Glitters – he didn't recognize.

A gift? he wondered as he cut the box.

Inside the box, under the packing, another box. Small, simple, he thought, smooth, dark faux wood closed with a small lock, the key attached with a thin chain.

Baffled, he set it down, unlocked the clasp.

Inside the box, nestled in thick black padding, sat a small – undeniably cheap – golden egg, closed tight with a tiny hook.

'All That Glitters,' he muttered, flipped the hook. The lid stuck a bit as he started to lift it. He gave it a harder tug.

He didn't see the vapor, didn't taste it. But he felt the effects instantly as his throat seemed to snap shut, his lungs clog. His eyes burned, and his well-toned muscles began to tremble.

The egg dropped from his fingers as he stumbled blindly toward the window. Air, he needed air. He tripped, fell, tried to crawl away. His system revolted, expelling the light breakfast he'd had with his husband. Fighting through the tearing pain, he tried to drag himself across the floor.

He collapsed, convulsing as Mozart's Queen hit high F.

On a bright spring afternoon, Lieutenant Eve Dallas stood over the body of Dr Kent Abner. That late-afternoon sunlight streamed through the windows he'd failed to open, spilled over the pools of body fluids, the shards of broken plastic.

The victim lay faceup – though the contusions on his forehead, temple indicated to her he'd fallen face-first. His eyes, red, swollen, with the film death had painted over them, stared back at her.

She could see, clearly, the smears feet, hands, knees had swiped through expelled body fluids. Footprints outlined with blood, bile, puke tracked the kitchen floor.

Her crime scene, she thought, had been shot to shit.

'Let's hear it, Officer Ponce,' she said to the first on scene.

'The vic's Kent Abner, a doctor, lives here with his husband. Had the day off. Husband – that's another doctor, but the Ph.D. type, Martin Rufty – comes home from work – headmaster at Theresa A. Gold Academy – at approximately sixteen hundred. Sees the body. He walked right in the body fluids, Lieutenant, turned the body over, actually tried to revive him before he called the MTs.'

The uniform, a burly vet, shook his head at the scene. 'Then they come in, and we've got them all over it before we're called in. Did what we could to secure it at that point. Vic's been gone for hours. MTs said he was cold and stiff. And how it looked like some kind of chemical poisoning.'

'Where's the spouse?'

'We got him upstairs. My partner's with him. He's a mess.'

'Okay. Stand by.' Eve turned to her partner.

'Peabody, I'll take the body. Find the security feed, take a look.'

'Got that.' In her pink cowboy boots, Peabody stepped carefully as Eve opened her field kit, crouched down.

She'd already sealed up, turned on her recorder, and now took out her Identi-pad to verify the victim's ID.

'Victim is identified as Kent Abner of this address, age sixty-seven. Contusions and lacerations on the forehead, left temple, also on left knee. They look consistent with a fall. Got some burns on the thumbs, both hands. The body's in rigor. The eyes are red, swollen.'

Carefully, she opened the victim's mouth. 'So's the tongue. Looks like ... bits of foam and saliva, vomit. Blood and mucus, dried now, from the nose.'

She took out her gauges. 'TOD, nine-forty-three. Peabody! Run the feed back to this morning. Check when the spouse left, if anyone came in after that.'

'I've got a male — tweed jacket — mid-sixties, about six-three, one-eighty, carrying the briefcase on the floor in there, coming in a couple minutes after four. Uses a swipe and code. And he's letting the MTs in at sixteen-ten. Two uniforms arrive at sixteen-sixteen.'

Peabody, her dark hair in a short, bouncy tail, peeked around a door. 'I'll run it back.'

Eve continued with the body. 'No defensive or offensive wounds. Head and knee — possible blow, but more consistent with a fall. He's a well-built man, looks strong. He would've fought back if fighting back was an option. Did he eat something, drink something . . . ?'

'Same male – has to be the spouse – walking out at oh-seven-twenty. No activity prior. And . . . we've got a female in a Global Post and Packages uniform. She's ringing it at oh-nine-thirty-six. Vic answers – friendly, like they know each other. He takes the package in; she leaves.'

Eve rose, walked to the counter. 'Standard delivery box? Say, ten inches square?'

'That's the one. I'm zipping through – nothing after the delivery and before the spouse comes back.'

Peabody stepped out.

'Box cutter's right here. He's dead seven minutes after he takes the package. He brings it in here,' Eve said. 'Opens it. Takes out this other box – cheap fake wood, little lock and key. Opens that. We've got broken bits of colored material and shards – shiny gold color maybe on the outside, white interior – on the floor. Maybe hard plastic. Something in the box. Open that and . . .

'Fuck.' She stepped back. 'Call the hazmat unit.'

'Oh, shit.'

'The spouse isn't dead, or the MTs, or the first on scene. Whatever it was must be dissipated enough, but call them in, let them know we have an unknown toxic substance.'

Eve eased around, read the return address on the box.

'All That Glitters.' She ran it. 'Bogus name and address on the shipping box.'

'They're on their way,' Peabody reported, 'and advise us to evacuate the premises.'

'Too late for that. Seven minutes, Peabody. Subtract the couple minutes to walk back here, get the box cutter, open everything. He was basically dead when he opened the box over seven hours ago.' And still, she thought. 'Get Uniform Carmichael and Officer Shelby over to Global Post and Packages, find out where this package was dropped off for shipping, who signed it in, if there's any security feed. Then contact the morgue team, and tell them we may have a hot one.'

'Dallas, you touched him—'

'I was sealed,' Eve reminded her. 'His spouse, the MTs touched him, too. Whatever killed him, it's done its work. It's finished.'

She stood a moment, a tall, lanky woman with a choppy cap of brown hair, brown cop's eyes, wearing a bronze leather jacket, good brown boots.

Basic precautions, she told herself.

'I'm going to scrub up, just to cover protocol. When I have, we'll talk to the spouse. We're going to want whatever he was wearing when he touched the vic bagged for the hazmat team.'

She grabbed her field kit, started off to find a powder room or bathroom. 'Contact the shipping company first. We need to talk to the delivery person.'

Going to be late, she thought as she used the scrub in her kit in a stylish powder room with maroon walls.

According to the Marriage Rules – self-written and -enforced – she needed to let her own spouse know. Roarke understood the job's screwy hours, but you had to follow the rules.

Peabody stepped up to the door. 'Carmichael and Shelby are on their way to GP&P, and I have the name of the delivery person for this route. Lydia Merchant. She clocked out at her usual time, but I have contact info on her.'

'Let's run her in the meantime. Seems long odds she'd make the delivery if she decided to poison a customer, but people can be stupid.'

Eve waited for the special team, tolerated the scan to make certain she hadn't contracted some toxicity from the body – wanted to balk when the lead tech insisted on drawing some blood to test on the spot. But figured not only better safe than sorry, but quicker to deal with it and move on.

Cleared, she and Peabody headed upstairs to talk to the spouse.

'Lydia Merchant, age twenty-seven,' Peabody began on the walk upstairs. 'Employed by GP&P for six years. Clean employment record, clear on criminal.'

'We talk to her anyway.'

Rufty's clothes had already been bagged and sealed. In gray sweatpants and a navy sweatshirt with TAG in gold across the chest, he sat, shocked and grieving, on a curvy love seat in a sitting area of a bedroom done in rusty reds and old gold.

He had a neat brown goatee streaked with blond to match

a shaggy mop of hair. A tall, gangly man, he had a long, thin face, dark, currently watery brown eyes.

He wore, as the victim did, a white gold band on the third finger of his left hand. And his hands stayed clutched together as if they alone kept him from shattering into pieces.

Eve signaled to the uniform who sat with him.

'Start the canvass with your partner. Anyone who saw anything, I hear about it. If you touched the body or anything in or around the crime scene, the hazmat unit needs to clear you.'

'Yes, sir.' He glanced back at Rufty. 'He wants to call their kids, but I've held him off. He for sure touched the body, sir.'

'We'll get to that. Take the bagged clothes down with you, give them to hazmat. Have one of them come up to scan and clear him.'

She moved to Rufty, sat on the deep red chair facing him. 'Dr Rufty, I'm Lieutenant Dallas. This is Detective Peabody. We're very sorry for your loss.'

'I – I need to talk to the kids. Our children. I need—'

'We'll let you do that very soon. I know this is a difficult time for you, but we need to ask you some questions.'

'I – I came home. I called out: "Jesus, Kent, what a day. Let's have a really big drink."' He covered his long, thin face with his long, thin hands. 'And I walked back to the kitchen, and – Kent. Kent. He was on the floor. He was . . . I tried to . . . I couldn't. He was . . .'

Peabody leaned over, took his hand in hers. 'We're very sorry, Dr Rufty. There was nothing you could do.'

'But ...' He turned to her, and the look, Eve thought, said: Help me. Explain. Make it stop.

'I don't understand. He's so healthy. He's always nagging me to exercise more, eat better. He's so fit and strong. I don't understand. He was going for a run this morning. He always goes for a run on his day off, and on his lunch hour if he can squeeze it in during office hours. He was going to finish the crossword and go for a run.'

'Dr Rufty.' Eve waited until those shattered brown eyes focused on her. 'Were you expecting a package today? A delivery?'

'I – I don't know. I can't think of anything.'

'Have you ever ordered from an outlet called All That Glitters?'

'I don't think so.'

'You get deliveries from Global Post and Packages?'

'Yes. Yes, Lydia delivers. But I ...' He pressed a hand to his temple. 'I don't think we ordered anything. I don't remember.'

'That's all right. Look at me, Dr Rufty. Do you know of anyone who'd wish to harm your husband?'

'What?' He jerked. Fresh shock. 'Hurt Kent? No, no. Everyone loved Kent. Everyone. I don't understand.'

Eve countered the spikes in his voice with absolute calm. 'Someone from his office, from his practice, from the neighborhood.'

'No, no. Kent has such a lovely practice. All those babies and little kids. It's all so happy there. He worked so hard for his children, his patients. You can ask,' he said, his voice spiking again. 'You can ask all of them, all of the people who work there. They love Kent!'

'All right. You've been married a long time. Were there any problems?'

'No. No. We love each other. We have our children. We have grandchildren. I need to call our children.'

When he started to weep, Peabody moved over to sit next to him. 'I know this is hard. Did Kent mention anyone who worried him? Did he say anything about someone or an incident that upset him?'

'No. Nothing I remember. No. I don't understand. What happened? What happened? Did someone hurt Kent?'

'Dr Rufty.' With no choice, Eve gave it straight. 'We believe Dr Abner received a package this morning, and that package contained a toxin, which caused his death.'

Tears fell still, but Rufty's body straightened. 'What? What? Are you saying someone killed Kent? Someone sent something into the house, into our home that killed him?'

Eve rose at the knock on the door, let in the white-suited sweeper. 'We need to take precautions. We need to ask you to submit to a scan, to allow us to test your blood, as you touched Dr Abner. It's possible the package he opened this morning contained a toxic substance.'

'It's not possible.' He dismissed it outright, and with the ring of certainty. 'No one would do that. No one who knew Kent would do that.'

'We need to take precautions.' Eve sat again, looked

directly into Rufty's eyes. 'We're going to do everything we can to find out what happened to your husband.'

'You loved him,' Peabody said gently. 'You want to do whatever needs to be done to find out what happened.'

'Yes. Do whatever you have to do. Then please, God, please, let me call our children. I need to talk to our children.'

Eve waited while Rufty was scanned, tested, cleared. Whatever had killed Kent Abner had dissipated before anyone else had come in contact with the body.

'You can contact your children,' Eve told Rufty. 'Is there somewhere you can go, stay for a few days? It would be best if you didn't stay here.'

'I can stay with our daughter. She's closer. Our son lives in Connecticut, but Tori and her family live just a few blocks away. I can stay with Tori.'

'We'll arrange to take you there, as soon as you're ready.'

Rufty closed his eyes. When he opened them, the tears had burned away to reveal the steel. 'I need to know what happened to my husband. To the father of my children. To the man I loved for forty years. If someone did this, someone hurt him, I need to know who. I need to know why.'

'It's our job to get those answers for you, Dr Rufty. If you think of anything,' Eve added, 'anything at all, you can contact me.'

'He was such a good man. I need you to understand that. Such a good man. A loving man. He never hurt anyone in his life. Everyone loved Kent. They loved him.'

Someone didn't, Eve thought.

'I believe him,' Peabody said as they finally left the crime scene. 'That guy was cut off at the knees, and he honestly didn't know anything or anyone that put Abner in the crosshairs.'

'Agreed, but a spouse doesn't always know everything. We need to dig into Abner, his work, his habits, his hobbies. Any extramarital relationships.'

As she nodded, Peabody glanced back at the pretty brownstone with tulips blooming in its little front garden. 'It'd be worse if, you know, it was just bad luck of the draw. If this was random.'

'A hell of a lot worse. The package was addressed specifically so we'll look specifically. Let's talk to the delivery person asap.'

Peabody programmed the address on the in-dash. 'You feel okay, right?'

'I'm fine. Didn't the vampires draw my blood and clear me?'

'Yeah, but I'll feel better when they ID the toxin.' Peabody frowned out the window of the car. 'He laid there for hours. The good of that is whatever it was dissipated, so we're all not dead. The bad is he laid there for hours.'

'Yeah, and think about that. Have the delivery in the morning, knowing nobody's going to go in there until late afternoon. It makes it look like a specific kill. Just Abner.'

As she pushed through traffic, Eve took a contact from Officer Shelby on her wrist unit. 'What've you got, Shelby?'

'They tracked the package to a drop-off kiosk on West

Houston, sir. It was logged in through the after-hours depository — that's self-serve — at twenty-two hundred hours.'

'Security cam?'

'Yes, sir. And the cam had a glitch at twenty-one-fifty-eight until twenty-three-oh-two.'

'An idiot would call that a coincidence.'

'Yes, sir. Officer Carmichael, who is not an idiot, has requested EDD examine the security camera and feed at this depository. However, if the killer proves to be an idiot, she used her credit account, via her 'link, to pay for the overnight shipping. Said payment was charged to the account of a Brendina A. Coffman, age eighty-one, apartment 1A, 38 Bleecker Street.'

'We'll check her out now. Good work, Shelby.'

Peabody didn't have time to grab the chicken stick before Eve wheeled sharp around a corner to change direction.

'Get a warrant,' Eve ordered Peabody. 'We need to look at Coffman's credit history.'

'Brendina Coffman.' Peabody read off her PPC as Eve fought her way to Bleecker. 'Married to Roscoe Coffman for fifty-eight years, lived at the current address for thirty-one years. A retired bookkeeper who worked for Loames and Gardner for — wow — fifty-nine years. No criminal in the last half century or so, but a couple of dings in her twenties. Disorderly conduct and simple assault. They have three offspring — male, female, male, ages fifty-six, fifty-three, and forty-eight. Six grandchildren from ages twenty-one to ten.'

'Start running the rest of them,' Eve ordered. 'It's not going to be an idiot,' she muttered. 'We don't have that kind of luck. But run them.'

'Okay, well, the oldest offspring is Rabbi Miles Coffman of Shalom Temple, married to Rebekka Greene Coffman for twenty-one years — and she teaches at the Hebrew school attached to the temple. They have three of the kids – twenty, eighteen, and sixteen, female, male, and male, respectively – nothing flagged on the kids, no criminal on the parents.'

With no available parking in sight, Eve double-parked, causing much annoyance on Bleecker. Ignoring it, she flipped up her On Duty light.

'Keep going,' Eve said as she got out, studied the sturdy old residential building. A triple-decker of faded brick, no graffiti, clean windows, some of them open to the cool spring evening.

'Marion Coffman Black, married to Francis Xavior Black, twenty-three years – no, twenty four as of today; happy anniversary – is currently employed, as she has been for twenty years, as bookkeeper in the same firm as her mother was. Couple dings in her twenties for illegal protests, nothing since. Son, twenty-one, a student at Notre Dame, daughter, age nineteen, also at Notre Dame.'

'Hold that thought,' Eve advised as they approached the gray door of the entrance to 1A.

Decent security, she noted, but nothing fancy. She pressed the buzzer.

The woman who answered looked pretty good for

eighty-one. She had a bubble of ink-black hair Eve figured wouldn't move in a hurricane, lips freshly dyed stop-sign red, rosy cheeks, and eyes heavily shadowed and lashed.

She wore a deep blue cocktail dress with a high neck, long sleeves, and gave Eve and Peabody a frowning once-over from nut-brown eyes.

'We're not buying.'

'Not selling,' Eve said, and held up her badge.

Brendina's face went sheet white under the rosy. 'Joshua!'

'No, ma'am.' Peabody spoke quickly. 'It's not about your son. Mrs Coffman's son Joshua's on the job,' Peabody told Eve. 'It's not about Sergeant Coffman, ma'am.'

'Okay. Okay. What is it then?'

'If we could come in for a moment,' Eve began.

'We're leaving – if Roscoe ever finishes primping.'

'We'll try not to take much of your time.'

With a nod, Brendina stepped back to let them straight into a tidy living area. So tidy, Eve thought, dust motes must run in fear. The furniture was old, like owned since their marriage began, and polished to within an inch of its life. A half dozen fancy pillows smothered the sofa.

A small piano against one wall with family photos crowded over it.

The air smelled of lemon.

'Is that your needlepoint, ma'am?' A craftsman to the bone, Peabody admired the pillows. 'It's beautiful work.'

'My daughter-in-law got me into it, and now I can't stop. What is this about?'

'Mrs Coffman, did you overnight a package to a Kent Abner, for delivery this morning?'

'Why would I? I don't know any Kent Abner.'

'Your credit account was charged for the shipment.'

'I don't see how when I didn't send it.'

'Maybe you'd like to check on that, while we're here.'

'Fine, fine. Roscoe, we're going to be late again. Been waiting for that man for decades. He never can get anywhere on time. It's our daughter's twenty-fourth wedding anniversary,' she said as she walked to a   very tidy – little desk and sat down at the mini-comp on it. 'Married a Catholic. I never figured it to last, but Frank's a good man, good father, and he's given her a happy life. So we're— Well, son of a bitch!'

And there you have it, Eve thought as Brendina turned.

'I've been charged for that shipment. That's a mistake   it says my account was charged at ten last night. I was sitting in bed watching *Junkpile* on-screen at ten – or trying, as Roscoe snores like a freight train. I keep good records, so I know what I spend and how I spend it. I was a bookkeeper for more years than either of you have been alive!'

'We don't doubt any of that, Mrs Coffman.'

But Brendina's ire hadn't yet peaked.

'Well, GP&P is going to hear from me, you better believe.' She fisted her hands on her hips, her eyes shooting daggers at Eve as if she'd been responsible. 'And they'd better make this good. I'd like to know how somebody got my information, if that's what happened, or if some careless finger at GP&P hit the wrong key.'

'We believe it's the former, ma'am.'

'I'll be changing my codes asap, you can be sure of that! And I'm going to have my boy look into this. He's a police officer.'

'Yes, ma'am. You can have your son contact me, Lieutenant Dallas at Cop Central. In the meantime, can you tell me who would have access to your account?'

Brendina stabbed a finger in the air, then tapped it between her breasts. 'Me, that's who. And Roscoe, but he has his own, and only has my codes in case something was to happen. Same as I have his. Roscoe!'

'Stop yelling, stop yelling. Heavens to Murgatroyd, Brendi, I'm coming, aren't I?'

When he came out, *dapper* was the word that sprang to Eve's mind. He wore a pale blue suit chalked with white stripes, a white shirt, and a bright red bow tie with a matching pocket square. His hair, candlestick silver, was slicked back and shined like moonlight on water. His silver moustache was perfectly trimmed and groomed.

His eyes matched his suit.

'You didn't say we had company.' He beamed at them.

'Not company, cops.'

'Friends of Joshua's?'

'No, sir,' Eve said. 'We're here about a package that was delivered this morning. The shipment was charged to your wife's account.'

'What did you send, Brendi?'

'Nothing! Somebody got into my account.'

He looked at her with affection, and mild surprise. 'How'd they do that?'

'I don't know, do I?'

'Ms Coffman, do you have your 'link?'

'Of course I have my 'link. I was just changing purses when you buzzed.'

She marched into what Eve assumed was the bedroom, marched back out with a gargantuan shoulder bag in vivid purple and an oversize evening purse in glittery red – to match Roscoe's tie, Eve assumed.

'I was just taking out what I need for tonight,' she said, and dug in.

Her annoyed expression changed to alarm. Now she marched to the coffee table, dumped the contents of the shoulder bag.

Eve decided if the woman ever faced an apocalypse with that bag in tow, she'd survive just fine.

'It's gone! Oh my God, my 'link's not here.'

'Where is it, Brendi?'

'For God's sake, Roscoe!'

'Don't worry now. I'll help you look for it.'

Brendina's expression softened. 'No, honey, it's gone. Somebody must've taken it out of my bag.'

'When's the last time you used it?' Eve asked.

'Just yesterday – we were all out shopping. My girls and I – my daughters-in-law, my daughter. Marion wanted new shoes for tonight, and she needed to pick up the wrist unit she got for Frank – she had it engraved. And— God, we were all over. Had a late lunch. I used it to call my sister, to tell her we were changing our lunch reservation to two-thirty because everything was taking so long. She was meeting us, and she gets cranky if she has to wait.'

'Where did you use it?'

'Ah ...' She pressed a hand to her forehead. 'On Chambers and Broadway – I'm nearly certain. We'd only just left the jewelry store, and it's right there.'

'As far as you remember you didn't use your 'link since that point?'

'No. I know I didn't. We went shopping some more, met my sister for lunch. We had a long lunch, and Marion insisted Rachel – my sister – and I take a car home. She called for one and paid for it – insisted. I came home, took a nap. Long day. Roscoe and I had dinner, watched some screen. I didn't go out today. I needed to clean the house, then get ready for tonight.

'I only keep one account on my 'link: my shopping and household account. But—'

'It's all right, Brendi.' Roscoe put an arm around her. 'I'll help you. And it's time you had a new 'link.'

Sighing, she leaned into him. 'Let me use yours, Roscoe, so I can deal with all this. We really are going to be late.'

'Peabody, why don't you leave the Coffmans our cards? You can have your son contact us.'

'Yes, fine, thank you. I really need to deal with this. You can talk to Joshua. He's a police officer.'

2

Back in the car, Peabody strapped in. 'Maybe the killer's looking for an easy mark. An older woman, distracted with a lot of other women. Maybe follow them awhile. Crowded shopping area, bump and snatch.'

'Most likely,' Eve agreed. 'And with her being older, he might think if she can't put her hands on her 'link at some point, she'll just think she misplaced it. Maybe she doesn't change codes right off. He only needs a few hours. Use it, toss it, move on.'

She muscled her way back across town. 'It's not going to connect to the family. Not that having a cop and a rabbi in there exempts them, but it's sloppy and stupid.'

'Are you going to read Sergeant Coffman in?'

'Might as well. If there is any connection, he can dig into that angle. We'll talk to the delivery girl – who's not going to be connected, either, unless somebody has a grudge there, saw this as getting her in trouble.'

'That would be stupid, too.'

'Exactly, but we'll talk to her. She works that route. Maybe she knows someone in the neighborhood who wasn't a fan of Kent Abner's.'

Lydia Merchant lived five floors up in a post-Urban building over a bodega that smelled like mystery tacos. Nobody had their windows open to the spring evening, and most had riot bars.

Despite the five floors, one glance at the pair of green-doored elevators – one with a sign stating OUT OF ORDER, with a handwritten AGAIN! in angry block letters – had Eve shoving open the stairwell door.

Peabody hissed out, 'Loose pants,' and climbed with her through various scents – somebody's Chinese takeout, someone's very rank body odor, someone's heavy dose of cheap cologne (possibly Mr BO), and, oddly, what might have been fresh roses.

On the fifth floor, Eve scanned the apartment door. Strong security here, in the way of locks: three police locks rather than electronics.

Cheaper, she thought, but pretty effective.

She buzzed.

Moments later, through the static on the intercom, somebody demanded, 'Who is it?'

'NYPSD.'

'Yeah, right.'

'NYPSD,' Eve repeated, and held her badge up to the Judas hole.

'I'm calling in to check that before I open the door.'

'Dallas, Lieutenant Eve; Peabody, Detective Delia, Cop Central.'

'Yeah, right again.'

Eve waited, waited. Actually heard a squeal from inside, then rising female voices before locks began to clunk. She heard the distinct metal slide of a riot bar before the door popped open.

The two women who stood gaping hit about the same age. One was tall, busty, blond, the other just hitting average height with a small build. A mixed-race brunette.

Both had big blue eyes.

'Holy shit,' they said in unison. 'You look just like Marlo Durn did in the vid,' the blonde continued. 'Or Marlo, I guess she looked like you. We saw it twice.'

'Great.' She should get used to it, Eve thought.

She'd never get used to it.

'Did somebody break in and kill somebody?' Lydia, the brunette, demanded. 'Somebody's always breaking into this dump, or trying to.'

'No. It's about a package you delivered this morning, Ms Merchant.'

'Really?' Big blue eyes got bigger. 'Which one?'

'Can we come in?' Peabody added a quick smile.

'Oh, sure. You're prettier than the actress in the vid,' the blonde told her. 'I know she was killed and all that, but it's just true.'

The roses from the stairway scent stood on the skinny bar

that separated the crowded living area from a tiny kitchen. A bottle of wine stood open beside it.

'Have a seat, I guess. We were just going to have some wine. Can you have wine? We're celebrating.'

'No, but thanks.'

'We both got raises.' The blonde, definitely bubbly, perched on the arm of the chair. 'I got mine last week, and Lydia's finally came through today. We're moving out of this hellhole!'

'Congratulations. Ms Merchant—'

'Just Lydia's okay. It's really so weird you're both here, in our hellhole. I deliver a lot of packages. I work for GP&P, but I guess you know.'

'You delivered one to Kent Abner this morning.'

'Dr Abner, sure. I deliver to him and to Dr Rufty. They're really nice – always give me a tip for Christmas. Not everybody does. Was something wrong with the package? I handed it right to Dr Abner at the door.'

'Was there anything unusual in how the package came to you?'

'No. It's mostly droids and automation at my distribution center. They load my van, upload the schedule – overnights with A.M. deliveries or special deliveries first and so on. It was – had to be because it was this morning – an overnight A.M. I don't get what this is about.'

'We believe the package contained an as-yet-unidentified toxic substance.'

Lydia's blue eyes went momentarily blank, then filled

with alarm. 'You mean like poison or something? Like terrorism or something?'

'We have no reason to believe, at this time, we're dealing with any kind of terrorist attack.' Not altogether true, Eve thought.

'How do you know there was toxic stuff? Did Dr Abner get sick?'

'Dr Abner's dead. He died shortly after receiving and opening the package.'

'Dead? He's dead!' Those blue eyes filled. 'But . . . Oh my God. Oh my God, Teela!'